Paula Boer has been passionate about horses all her life and believes that humans are no more important than any other animal. She lives on 500 acres of forest in the Snowy Mountains of Australia. Inspiration for her stories comes from the natural world and she loves travel to wild places, many of which she has experienced on horseback, such as riding in Mongolia.

Paula has been a regular contributor to horse magazines and has had many animal short stories published. Her best-selling *Brumbies* novels for middle grade readers, following the adventures of two teenagers catching and breaking in the wild horses of Australia, are based on her own experiences.

For more information about Paula and her books, visit www.paulaboer.com.

THE STEALTHCAT WAR

THE EQUINORA CHRONICLES: BOOK 2

BY

PAULA BOER

The Stealthcat War

All Rights Reserved

ISBN-13: 978-1-922556-13-4

Copyright ©2021 Paula Boer

V1.0

Printed in Palatino Linotype and Badloc ICG.

IFWG Publishing International
Gold Coast

www.ifwgpublishing.com

For my beloved Pete, without whose support I would never have become a writer.

Acknowledgements

It is impossible to list everyone who has helped and supported in the creation of *The Equinora Chronicles*, but I especially wish to thank Megan Matters and Suzy Butz for their honest and insightful feedback, and Cristina Schaffer for her proof reading. Thanks also to Gerry Huntman, my publisher, for his belief in me; Steve Santiago for the fabulous cover (again); and Noel Osualdini for his thorough editing despite the many horse terms.

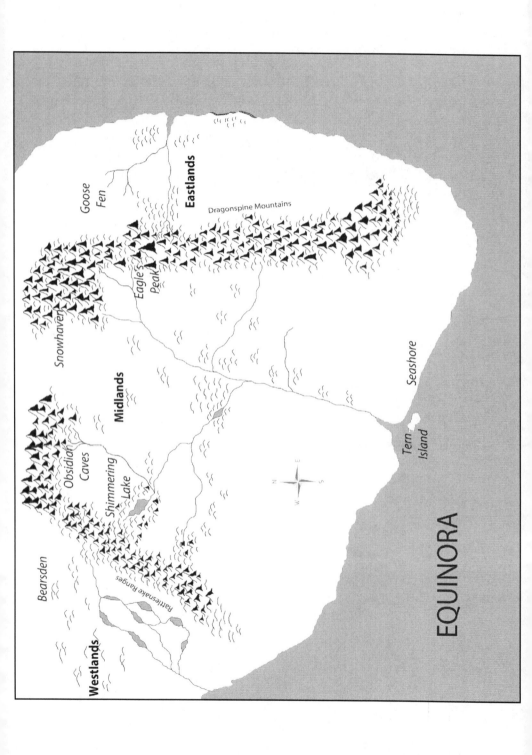

EQUINORA

Westlands

Bearsden

Obsidian
Caves

Shimmering
Lake

Rattlesnake Ranges

Midlands

Snowhaven

Eagle's
Peak

Goose
Fen

Eastlands

Dragonspine Mountains

Tern
Island

Seashore

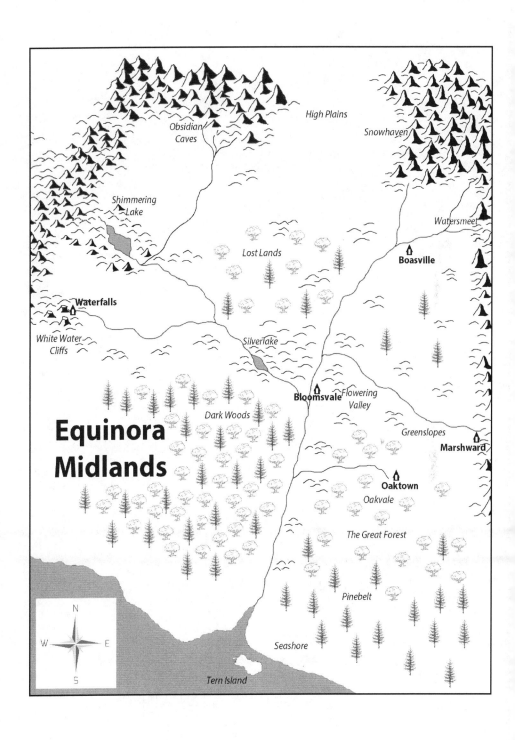

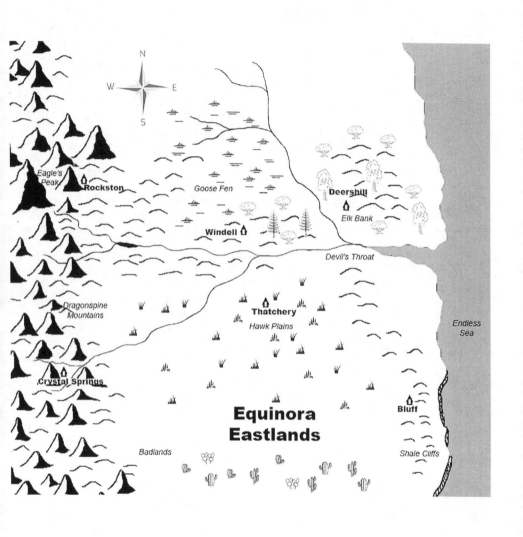

Prologue

A golden unicorn stood tall in front of Shadow, her feathered wings fanned out at her sides. Aureana introduced herself and extended her muzzle to greet him. Her eyes sparkled like stars and her horn glowed like the sun. At this, his moment of creation, power coursed through his veins, energy erupting from his muscles like lava from a volcano, unable to be contained. The urge to run overruled his desire to seek answers for his existence.

He galloped down the hillside, pounding the ground, sparks flying from his obsidian hooves. He stretched out his neck, the weight of the horns around his ears mocking him at every stride, his crimson mane and tail streaming in the wind of his speed. His muscled rump thrust him faster. His strong shoulders absorbed more energy from the land with every footstep. Sweat creamed his black coat, foaming his chest and between his hind legs.

A shrub grew close to his path. He blasted it to splinters with a look, not slowing, pricks from the debris urging him on. A fox streaked across the trail. He blew it to pieces with a snort, fur and flesh sticking to his legs. He had no control over the excess energy that sizzled in his veins. On he raced, desperate to release the tension in every sinew, to drain the power that drove him harder, to eradicate the need to run, faster, further.

The land flattened out, the stony hillside changing to lush pasture ripe with life. A creek meandered through the valley, singing the tale of its origin in the snows far away. Fresh green willows dangled budding branches over the waterway, waving him to slow down.

He galloped on. Wispy clouds drifted overhead against a vast blue backdrop he could never outrun. The tantalising smells of clover and fresh water broke into his manic dash. He steadied to a canter, and then a trot. Finally, he halted. Not even blowing from his exertions, he snatched at the sweet feed and slurped coolness over his tongue. He dug a shallow dip in the bank and rolled in the soft sand, squirming on his back, removing the last itch of power.

He grazed, not wanting to face Aureana, ashamed of his behaviour. Why had she created him from her shadow, her dark side? How was he to be her partner, her equal? He shouldn't exist. He *couldn't* exist like this.

A soft nicker interrupted his self-pity. A dapple-grey mare with snow-white mane and tail, her perfect hooves and slender horn shining as black as his coat, tiptoed nearer. She epitomised beauty, delicate and graceful, tiny and fragile. "I'm Dewdrop."

Shadow held himself erect. "Have you come to gloat?"

Pain filled her soft eyes, black and bottomless. "Of course not. I'm a healer. Are you in pain?"

"Why would I be?" Shadow turned his rump, unable to meet her sympathetic gaze.

She stepped closer. "Jasper has a contorted horn. I ease his pain when he has no ice to temper it."

Shadow resumed grazing, without tasting.

Dewdrop drifted after him, nibbling with tender lips at the fresh shoots. "Aureana is very upset. She wanted to create you with wings so you could fly with her. I fear we unicorns are staid playmates for a goddess. But you're a duocorn, much stronger than us."

The reverence in her voice stole Shadow's heart. He strode over and snuffled her muzzle. "Thank you for your offer, but I'm not in pain. If I were, I'd cure myself. My power oozes from every pore. That's why I ran, to test my strength."

"I'm glad. I hate to see anyone suffering. You'll be able to help us protect Equinora with ease. Come and meet the others."

Shadow averted his eyes. "I have no desire to frolic with unicorns. Tell Aureana I have no need of company."

The unicorns spent their days exploring Equinora and setting themselves challenges to test their powers, their duties needing minimal time. Shadow kept to himself, except when he sought a horse mare to relieve his lust, or to meet Dewdrop. He had no time for the other unicorns, especially Jasper. When their paths crossed, Jasper taunted Shadow about his twin curved horns, even though his own was twisted like an old pine bough. Many a time they sparred, only to have their fights broken up by Aureana, demanding they befriend each other.

That wasn't going to happen—Shadow saw how Jasper looked at Dewdrop.

But the delicate mare had turned down all their advances, declaring she was uninterested in mating. She was the Air Unicorn, the last perfect specimen before he and Jasper came to be. Shadow might not have wings like the goddess, but Aureana had thrown more of her power into his creation than she had into all of the other unicorns together. No wonder he couldn't contain such a force. Yet. But he would, one day.

Whenever he found Dewdrop alone, he bestowed his power upon her, trying to entice her to become his. He demonstrated his love by strengthening every part of her, enlarging her bones and stretching her sinews. He pumped blood through her veins, expanded the air in her lungs, and enhanced her senses.

And with every day, those black eyes looked at him with awe, growing in acceptance as he moulded her. He no longer towered over her, her legs long and lithe, the tips of her ears level with his eyes. Her dapples blossomed like flowers, and her tail swept the grasses in a perfume of musk.

He sidled up to her shoulder and nipped her neck.

She squealed and pranced away, flicking her ears.

He pursued her, snorting and stepping high, his tail thrown over his back.

She matched his stance, dancing with him stride for stride.

A little more taste of his power, that's all that was needed to break her reluctance...

A loud whinny broke Shadow's concentration.

Jasper galloped up, nostrils flared as crimson as his body, his black mane and tail shaking in agitation. "What are you doing, Shadow? Come away, Dewdrop. Moonglow and Diamond are looking for you."

Shadow blocked Jasper's path, his neck arched and tail held high. "Don't interfere. I'm helping Dewdrop develop."

"You? You do nothing but harm. Leave her alone." Jasper trotted circles around the pair, forcing Shadow to spin to remain facing him.

Angry at the interruption, Shadow charged, barging the unicorn with his chest. Jasper lowered his head and tried to pierce Shadow. Instead, his contorted horn slipped off Shadow's shoulder and struck a stone next to Dewdrop. Jasper's power exploded the rock. Shards flew, lacerating the mare's skin. Blood gushed from cuts all over her body. She reared, scarlet streaks pouring from her neck and sides, over her rump, and down her legs.

Shadow bellowed and struck Jasper with his forelegs, gouging hooves into his neck. They locked bodies, thrusting muscle against muscle, drawing on the power of the earth. The grass wilted beneath their hooves and nearby shrubs burst into flames.

Dewdrop staggered around them. "Stop it! Stop it! You're destroying the land!"

Her plea penetrated Shadow's rage. He must end this fight. Sucking energy from the sun and wind, and drawing on his desire for Dewdrop, he released a blast of power.

Jasper reeled, knocked back by the impact. He regained his balance and bolted.

Shadow caught his breath, looking for Dewdrop.

A groan sounded from a few horse lengths away. She lay on her side, flung by his outburst, her legs twisted at awkward angles and her skin in ribbons.

"Don't move! I'm coming! I'll heal you!" He raced over.

She raised her head, pain filling her eyes, and slumped back to the ground.

Shadow skidded to a stop and rested his muzzle against her face, sending streams of power into her prone body, accelerating the enhancements he'd already made.

Her wounds closed, leaving no scars. Her muscles bulged and her bones straightened. Her heart thumped and her lungs gasped.

Shadow continued, not wanting to risk Jasper returning to stop him. On and on he poured energy into Dewdrop's body. She lay at his feet, her body transformed into a supreme being, glowing with residual energy. Her body trembled and her legs twitched. She raised her head and stared with those bottomless black eyes into his heart.

Gold light seared his brain.

Distant screams echoed from the hills.

Jasper galloped back and raced towards him, his horn lowered to charge.

Shadow glanced at Dewdrop. Her dead body shrivelled as his power dissipated.

He fled.

Aureana chased him down, following the trail of destruction he'd left in his sorrow: trees blasted from their roots, boulders smashed against cliffs, and animals ripped to shreds. Swooping over him, she pushed him to Obsidian Caves. There she trapped him in a valley of black rock by building a barrier of power he couldn't break.

Then she left Equinora for ever.

Shadow explored every stone and pebble of his prison, learned every trail and pass, and mapped every creek and cave. A cavern carved by molten lava became his home, dark and hard like his heart. Any creature finding its way into his territory became victim to his vengeance: he practised his power on them, so that one day he'd have enough skill to escape.

Most died. As he had with Dewdrop, he pushed too fast, their cells unable to take the strain. His first success came from an unlikely source, a tiny white spider creeping along the wall of his cave. Every time he enhanced her, she shed her exoskeleton, giving his changes space to develop. She grew and grew, until she was almost as big as he. But Snag remained pale, unable to expose herself to light. She wove a complex web across the entrance to a lava tube, and trapped birds and bats that ventured too close.

Confident from his success, Shadow experimented on a wolf pack foolish enough to seek shelter in his warm cavern, where lava welled and oozed across the floor in a river of molten rock. Inspired by the flakes of obsidian reflecting his power, he transformed the stone into sustenance and fed it to the wolves. They morphed into snarling, blood-thirsty beasts, bent on destruction.

Shadow admired the results. He sent the bloodwolves out to annihilate Aureana's precious horses in revenge for her locking him away.

His intent had merely been to cause havoc in Equinora. Instead, it brought Jasper and his son, Fleet, to his lair. They demanded he call

5

back his beasts and leave Equinora alone. Enraged by their presumption, and furious at his imprisonment, Shadow attacked Jasper.

A man on Fleet's back extracted golden feathers from his quiver. One after the other they flew and struck Shadow, hitting his rump, chest, and neck before clanging to the floor. Not even a scratch marked his black hide.

He and Jasper fought on. Lightning flashed from their horns. Sweat and blood streaked their coats. The smell of sizzling hair and burnt flesh hung in the air. The battle raged. The quest for domination of wills and bodies, the very strength of their determination, added to the tension in the air. Shadow shoved Jasper nearer to the lava to draw from its strength. Jasper did his best to keep away from the seeping rock. Their hooves slipped on the smooth floor as they thrust chest against chest.

Jasper struck the wall of the cavern with his horn. Shards flaked from the ceiling. A shower of stones became a torrent. The roof collapsed.

Shadow carved his way out of the fallen rock, fuelled by the combination of his own anger and the energy of the lava. By the time he caught up with Jasper and Fleet, they had crossed the barrier.

He remained trapped. But he had three of Aureana's feathers.

Seasons passed and Shadow's bloodwolves ceased reporting to him. He scoured the creek for eels and fed them obsidian, sending them out to poison every stream, every river, and every lake. They gnashed their way south until they reached the sea. Shadow gloated the day they devoured Jasper, the other unicorns' screams telling him all he needed to know, the golden light as Jasper died almost as satisfying as Shadow's freedom would be.

And then Fleet returned.

Even with his unicorn ancestry, what could a warmblood horse do? Shadow was in no mood for discussion. He leapt across the lava and bit Fleet deep in the neck. He spun around and broke Fleet's ribs with a kick. He drew energy from the molten rock, the heat flaring and lighting Fleet's tail, singeing his legs, and burning his buttocks.

Fleet fought to survive. He barged Shadow with his chest, pushing and shoving.

Shadow's hooves slipped on the rock, back towards the creeping lava. He reared, his forelegs locked with Fleet's.

Dragged vertical, Fleet neighed, the scream echoing around the cavern.

They tottered on their hind legs, front legs entwined, gnashing at each other's necks. Side-on to where the land's core oozed from the surface, they hovered. Fleet toppled to his side, towards the lava…and fell, taking Shadow with him.

Shadow hit the hot rock, undaunted—now he had even more power. He emitted a blast that radiated around the cavern, shaking the walls.

The earth tremored. The ground split. The lava poured into a crevice.

Shadow swam unharmed through the molten rock to a ledge, exultant and throbbing with energy.

The crevice closed. The earth stilled.

Shadow neighed in triumph, strengthened by the forces from the centre of the earth.

Shadow stole an eagle trapped by Snag's web, and practiced his powers of enhancement. Claw, as he would be known, grew to giant proportions, his body remaining strong. But Claw became fascinated with the golden feathers, always wanting to admire them, sneaking to touch them with his beak.

"Eeerk! Feathers should be mine. Feathers are for birds."

Shadow shielded his treasure with his body. "You have feathers. You can already fly higher than any other eagle, catch anything before it escapes. What do you want with these? They're broken and heavy, no use to you."

"Eeerk! Preen them. Make them whole." Claw hopped from foot to foot, his talons clacking on the stone. "Give to me! Should be mine! Eeerk!"

Shadow braced to fend off the eagle. "What good does it do me if I give them to you? Then I'll have nothing to remind me of my purpose, to get out of here and seek revenge."

Claw penetrated his soul with his stare. "Eeerk! Put in wings and tail. Be strong and carry you. Over the barrier, eeerk!"

Could he? Shadow's heart raced. Could the eagle carry him?

The temptation proved too much. He carried the feathers outside and relinquished the precious objects, trembling with an anticipation laced with doubt.

Claw snatched them with his beak and thrust one into each wing tip. The last one he jammed into the base of his tail. He preened and straightened the barbs. The vanes trilled like birdsong, each golden quill straightening the adjoining feathers until they melded and became gold.

Fully transformed, Claw thrust skywards with greater strength than Shadow had ever believed possible, rising in a spiral until the eagle became a mere dot in the sky, higher than the tallest peak. Only Aureana had ever flown like that.

Shadow reared and screamed, thrashing the air with his hooves. "Come back! I'll curse you for ever if you leave!"

Claw descended like golden lightning, swooping and weaving. He neared the ground, spreading his wings wide to slow, and opened his talons. He grasped Shadow by the back and carried him aloft. The pain of those hooks in Shadow's flesh and the weight of his whole body dragging on his spine were insignificant compared to the glory of being airborne. As Claw laboured above his suspended body, the land receded beneath Shadow's trailing legs. In what seemed like both a lifetime and mere moments, the eagle carried him over the barrier and deposited him with care on the tundra.

Chapter 1

Mystery braced his front legs wide apart, drawing energy from the earth. He drew in a deep breath and placed the tip of his horn against the boulder, power sparking from the copper spiral like sunlight reflecting off the lake. His silver coat shimmered as he strained to cut the rock.

Nothing happened.

Gem nickered in support. "Maybe you have to strike it."

Gauging the weaknesses that veined the stone, Mystery tapped the boulder.

Still nothing happened.

"Try again." Gem fidgeted next to him, glowing emerald, opal, and ruby like the dragons flitting over her head.

Mystery concentrated on carving the stone in two, or even slicing off a chip. He whacked it harder. His skull thudded from the impact. The rock remained intact. "It's no good. I don't know how Jasper did it."

Gem nuzzled his neck. "Maybe you have a different power. Don't forget his element, and yours, is fire, not stone. Just because I'm a healer like Dewdrop doesn't mean your power is the same as your grandsire's."

"At least you had unicorn parents." Mystery stomped away from the boulder to avoid Gem seeing his frustration. He ground his teeth and switched his tail, cross that he couldn't find his power.

The goddess had proclaimed each generation would be stronger than the previous, evidenced by Gem's magnificent colouring. Like her, his horn was spiralled, not smooth like the first-generation unicorns', but his body was silver, more like Diamond's and

Moonglow's white, rather than Tempest's sapphire blue or Echo's rich brown, the deep colours of a stallion. Did that mean he wasn't stronger than them? Gem could not only heal anyone like Dewdrop had, she gave life to Shimmering Lake when she swam, benefitting all who drank the waters, removing the need for them to feed.

She trotted after him. "Wait! Diamond is coming! She sounds really upset."

With the power to translocate, Gem's dam would be here in moments. Mystery cheered up at the distraction; he'd worry about his lack of power another time.

The air shivered. Vibrations ran through Mystery's hooves. Power sizzled in his ears. A mist formed and thickened on the lakeshore. A cloud mirage rose from a heat haze, solidifying into the form of Diamond, her namesake eyes, horn, and hooves twinkling like stars on a moonless night.

He joined Gem to greet her.

Diamond spent little time on niceties. "I've come for help. Something is attacking horses in my territory."

Mystery swapped glances with Gem. "Not bloodwolves again? Have you any idea what the problem is?"

"Let me show you." She touched the tip of her horn to theirs, the three forming a pyramid between them.

Closing his eyes, Mystery emptied his mind to receive the pictures. He and Gem first discovered this technique by accident. The first-generation unicorns had been ignorant of this gift, believing they could only send and receive messages between them. The ability of sharing images had proved to be more entertaining than useful until now, especially as, unlike messages, pictures required physical contact.

Light beamed into Mystery's mind, revealing Diamond cantering across the fens, spray erupting beneath her hooves in a sparkling shower, every drop a prism. Geese honked overhead in V-formation, wings beating in rhythm with her strides. A horse appeared on the horizon dragging a hind leg, his nose almost touching the ground. Tattered flesh hung from the stallion's shoulders and rump. Pus oozed from numerous sores. Pain filled his eyes.

"Help... Lions... Fires... Mares...missing."

The stallion staggered and fell to his knees, crumpling in a heap. His lifeless eyes stared at nothing.

Lions? They lived in the mountains. But Diamond's territory was far to the east, beyond the ranges.

The vision shifted. Tall grasses rippled over the plains, the blue sky vast, the uninterrupted horizon revealing where the herds fattened at this time of year. A dry wind blew from the east, bringing a trail of smoke. Diamond's path followed the trace. The smoke thickened. She skirted a burnt wasteland where charred mounds broke the landscape, one here, one there, more and more. From one, a hoof stuck out on bone, all the skin gone.

With the feed destroyed, the horses would have a hard time this winter. Mystery's heart ached for them—if there were any left. No wonder Diamond was worried. Fires lit by lightning rarely trapped horses, especially where they could outrun the flames. What could have caused this?

He didn't have time to consider the possibilities. Diamond's vision moved beyond the charred bodies. More mounds dotted trampled grasses, this time their corpses unmarred by flame. Instead, stallions' throats had been ripped out, mares' necks twisted in broken contortions, and yearlings lay in tangled heaps, their guts strewn in disarray. The carcass of a foal sprawled torn and chewed, white bones already bleaching where they protruded from parched skin, its spine snapped. Pad marks the size of its skull imprinted the gore-churned mud.

Mystery broke the connection. "This is awful. Have you no idea why this is happening?"

Diamond coughed as if she'd relived the stench in her throat. "There's more. Wait."

A new image appeared of the foothills where aspen copses dotted golden meadows, plants nodded laden seed-heads, and rodents scurried to gather the bounty. Diamond stopped a fox preparing to pounce. "Is everyone here alright?"

The fox skulked. "Must be quick! Cats! No time to chat!" The vixen bounded away, only the tips of her ears and brush visible through the foliage. A huddle of men jogged by in tight formation, spears held outwards in a spiked defence.

This time Diamond broke the connection. "If even the clans run in fright, the situation is extremely serious. I have no power to help. I need a healer. Gem must come."

"No!" Mystery couldn't bear the thought of his lifemate at risk.

"Not even her power can bring back the dead. Take me. I'll find the problem. Then we can work out what to do."

Gem sidled closer to him. "Are you sure? I can't leave Shimmering Lake anyway, but how can you do more than Diamond?"

He arched his neck. "I'm a stallion. If there's fighting to be done, it's not for you mares to do. Of course I'll go. But first we should go to Tern Island and visit Moonglow—a prophecy will guide me."

Near the clifftop, its limbs twisted into a thick canopy by the sea breezes, stood an old pine; sleeping beneath it, Mystery and Diamond found the Spirit Unicorn, asleep. Rainbow dragons the size of fruit bats adorned its branches, settled down for the night with their snouts tucked under their wings. They flapped into the air and squealed in excitement as the unicorns appeared, waking Moonglow.

Diamond strode over to her friend. "What a relief to feel the love here. I was beginning to worry that the whole of Equinora outside of Shimmering Lake might be in trouble."

Moonglow yawned and stretched out each hind leg in turn. "Of course it's lovely to see you, but you didn't call to say you were coming. Or did you? I might have forgotten."

Having the ability to converse by thoughts, even over great distance, the first-generation unicorns rarely ventured into each other's territories unannounced.

"No, sorry, we needed to get here fast."

"Why, whatever is amiss? And this must be Misty. Oh, no, that's not right. Mystery, isn't it?" Moonglow straightened up, concern flooding her sapphire eyes. She welcomed him with a nicker and a nuzzle. "Do you have a problem?"

Mystery returned her greeting. "I'm fine, thank you. But Diamond needs help."

Moonglow shook in a cloud of white hair, sending dragons giggling higher into the tree. Strands of her mane and tail hung from twigs like golden lichen, glowing even in the dim light of dusk. "Are you losing your coat too? Mine is dropping like autumn leaves, an experience I've never known and don't like at all. But you don't look as if you're shedding."

"No, far worse." Diamond shared the horror of the horse deaths, the stallion's mention of missing mares before he died, and the mysterious references to cats. "I couldn't get answers from anyone. We don't know what it means, or what could be behind it."

Moonglow wandered to a small pool where spring water burbled over brightly coloured stones. "Have you contacted Echo? Or Tempest? My island is safe and there are no horses here, but they may want mares in their lands."

Diamond snorted. "You can't think Tempest would send lightning to light fires? Anyway, they mate whenever they want, and they'd never harm horses."

Accepting it was unlikely, Moonglow nibbled at a patch of clover. The sweet flowers fell from her mouth as she chewed. "I suppose you've come for a prophecy."

The vagueness in Moonglow's eyes concerned Mystery. Had the Spirit Unicorn lost the power to see the future? "I have no idea where to start."

"We'll find out tomorrow. It's far too late now."

Diamond stamped a hoof. "No! This can't wait. You must tell us what we need to do," she pleaded, describing the devastation she'd experienced in more detail, including the reek of burnt and rotting corpses and choking smoke. "We can't waste more time."

With reluctance, Moonglow agreed. Her head lowered and her ears flopped. Her eyes glazed over and her tail went limp. The dragons quietened as her golden horn glowed.

> "When birds spy and big cats sneak
> Shadows steal all mares
> Beware he of eagle speak
> No one leave their lairs."

Mystery listened attentively, never having heard a prophecy before. "What does it mean?"

Lifting her head, Moonglow twitched her ears, her eyes refocusing. "It seems the mares are hiding in the shadows somewhere, but from what, I don't know. Do you know a talkative eagle? Or someone who speaks like an eagle?"

Diamond snorted. "Not eagle speak, *Eagle's Peak*. It's the highest point in Dragonspine Mountains. That could be where the cats are coming from. But why?"

Rather than answer, Moonglow dropped her head, her eyes

glazing over again. She trembled, sweat breaking out on her neck and shoulders.

> *"Those warped by stone sink in claws*
> *Run to stay alive*
> *Fires destroy between the shores*
> *Gold-winged one arrives."*

"The gold-winged one? Aureana is coming back?" Diamond pranced on the spot.

Mystery relaxed. It would be wonderful to meet Aureana, Equinora's creator. The goddess would resolve whatever troubled Diamond's territory, and she could show him his power. He sighed with relief.

A full moon rose, engorged in red. An owl hooted a lone siren. Moonglow shuddered. She turned to Mystery, fear blazing from her eyes. "Don't be happy. Before she left, Aureana claimed she would only ever return to destroy her creation."

Diamond gasped. "She never said that to me! Why would she do that?"

Shuffling her hooves, Moonglow avoided Diamond's gaze. "You know after her failures with Dewdrop, Jasper, and Shadow, she believed herself flawed. She claimed if the six of us unicorns couldn't protect Equinora as she intended, then there was nothing more she could do to help."

Diamond strode around Moonglow. "That's nonsense, and you know it. She overtaxed herself creating us, that's all. She still had power to lock Shadow at Obsidian—"

Moonglow reared. "Shadow! What if he still lives? The prophecy might mean him! These cats could be his creation!"

Mystery butted in, tossing his head. "No, he's dead. Fleet, my sire, killed him. You interpreted the reference to shadows as meaning the mares are hiding, remember? Something else is behind their fear."

Moonglow's eyes clouded over, her horn glowing with starlight.

> *"Find power to prevent the end*
> *Youngest cross and fight—"*

Her mouth hung open, her lower lip trembling. A trickle of blood dribbled from her nostrils. Her whole body shook. She collapsed, the thud of her fall loud in the still night.

Diamond rushed over and blew into her friend's face.

Moonglow's ribs rose and fell in shallow breaths. Her skin twitched and ice crystallised on her coat despite the mild night. She gasped, groaned, and scrambled to her feet on wobbly legs. "What ha…happened?"

Diamond circled her, nuzzling and licking like a dam with a newborn foal. "Are you alright?"

Moonglow looked around as if she had no idea where she was. "I…I…" She stood tall and flicked her tail.

"I'm sorry we rushed you. We should have done this in daytime, when you could use the sun's power." Diamond encouraged her to return to the spring and freshen up.

Mystery followed. The Spirit Unicorn was nothing like he'd expected, not strong and exuberant like Diamond.

Still looking vacant, Moonglow drank and wandered back to her resting tree. "The prophecy isn't finished. But no more comes."

Diamond nibbled her friend's withers. "Do you feel better?"

Moonglow shook her mane in a shower of gold. "I'm fine. You woke me and I'm tired. That's all. Now I must rest. Tomorrow I'll try again."

"No, no, there's no need. We'll leave you in peace."

Back home, Mystery revelled in the energy pulsing through his veins as he swam to the shore. Moonlight struck droplets of water as he shook from nose to tail, turning them into falling stars. He pawed at the sand, dropped to his side, and rolled, squirming in luxury. After scrambling to his feet, he hurried back to Gem. "It's glorious in the lake, as always. I needed that. Translocating with Diamond is an unnerving experience."

Gem nuzzled his neck and led him across to their favourite oak, where Diamond waited. "Now tell me what Moonglow said."

Mystery shared the prophecy and the subsequent discussion with her. "The final part states: 'Find power to prevent the end, youngest cross and fight'. That has to mean me. But I haven't found out my power."

Gem nuzzled him. "The goddess will show you, in time."

Diamond agreed. "I believe Aureana will show you on your way to Eastlands. The prophecy must mean for you to cross the mountains on foot, else I would transport you there."

Gem looked from one to the other. "Tell me more about the goddess. What did Moonglow mean?"

Diamond flinched. "I thought Aureana returning would be a good thing. It's generations of horses since she left. But Moonglow is convinced Aureana will only return to destroy Equinora, not aid us."

"Destroy Equinora?" Gem backed in shock, bumping into the tree, and then jumped forward as if stung. "But that would kill us all! Or would she take us to the spirit world first?"

"I don't know. Aureana never said anything like that to me. And Moonglow isn't herself. She may have remembered it wrong."

Gem pointed at the lake with her horn. "I can't feel any evil. If the threat was real, I'm sure we'd sense it." She lipped Mystery's face, flirting. "I don't want you to go."

He wasn't dissuaded; the chance to explore Diamond's territory offered an opportunity for adventure. "The mountains protect us here. We can't take the risk. If the goddess returns, she'll destroy everything, us included."

"Only if you believe what Moonglow says. She might have misinterpreted the prophecy, or been befuddled from the lack of power, due to it being nighttime." Gem threw a glance at Diamond.

Mystery twitched his muzzle in thought. "Diamond and I interpreted her words the same. The mountain lions probably retreat to caves. If I can find their lair, I might be able to work out why they've started attacking horses."

"I still don't see why you should go. Why not Tempest? He's been there and knows the land."

Mystery turned away. "What's the good of Tempest's ability to control the weather? It sounds as if a different power is needed. I welcome the chance to confront whatever is threatening Eastland's horses. I must trust the goddess will guide me. Why else did the prophecy state the youngest must go?"

Gem trotted around him. "I think you should seek counsel from Echo and Tempest. I don't think you're ready. What if Shadow is still alive? How will you fight him without knowing your power, let alone how to use it?"

The reminder did nothing to discourage Mystery. Before he could snap back a retort, a dragon flew into the branches overhead, breaking the tension. The company of dragons, so cheerful and laughing, flitting above the unicorns' heads or pulling their tails in play, always made Mystery happy. It saddened him that normal horses didn't have the ability to see and talk with the magical creatures.

Tatuk, Gem's favourite, grew brighter as Mystery and Gem sent him love, his rainbow scales glowing with health. He flew down and alighted on Gem's crest in giggles. "Welcome back, Diamond!" He hopped across to her. "Are you staying long? We've missed you."

Diamond didn't have a flock of dragons in her territory, claiming she moved around too much to keep them fed with love. She knew Tatuk well from when she had lived at Shimmering Lake to teach Gem how to use unicorn powers before Mystery arrived, but the need to block her thoughts for privacy caused her a great strain. Being second-generation unicorns, Mystery and Gem didn't have the same problem of living in close proximity.

Yet Gem hadn't been able to help him identify his unique power.

Leaving the three of them to enjoy each other's company, Mystery sought a patch of clover to distract him from the question that had plagued him since he came to Shimmering Lake: *Was he really a unicorn?* Neither of his parents had horns, though Fleet, his sire, was seven-eighths hotblood, making him a powerful warmblood.

A bumblebee hovered in front of his nose. "Save some for me."

Like all unicorns, Mystery could talk with any animal, as well as swap messages and images with other unicorns. Despite that meaning he wasn't a coldblood horse, worries about his heritage still lingered like mist over the lake on cool mornings, tendrils of doubt snaking through his thoughts. As much as he loved living at Shimmering Lake with Gem, he needed to prove he was a true unicorn, not a horse with a horn. He needed to prove himself worthy, not only as a second-generation protector, but as Gem's mate. And, the fear he hadn't even shared with her, he needed to prove he wasn't tainted like Shadow, his great-grandsire.

Now it seemed he was destined for a bigger challenge than he had yearned for. He had no idea how he was going to save Equinora.

As the sun rose, Mystery trotted along the lakeshore with a determination he hadn't enjoyed since he was a colt experiencing a new adventure every day. At almost four years old, he was ready to see more of the world. He'd never been east of Dragonspine Mountains, or west of Rattlesnake Ranges, having lived most of his life at Shimmering Lake. Even White Water Cliffs, his birthplace to the south, was still a part of Midlands, with similar plants and animals. Now he had the chance to explore further afield, to the flat grassy plains Diamond called home. But first, he had to cross the mountains.

Diamond had described the way to one of the few passes through the rugged peaks, warning bad weather might make it necessary for him to find a different route. He didn't care. He would head towards the rising sun and find a way. That was the least of his concerns.

"Mystery! Wait!" The cry came from Laila Otter, the healer woman who lived at Shimmering Lake, the only person to do so.

He halted to let her catch up. The excitement of his expedition, and his argument with Gem, had made him forget their early morning ride. "I'm sorry, I should have come and found you. I need to go away."

Laila panted to a stop beside him and ran her fingers through his copper mane. "I know. Meda told me. Tatuk shared the news about what happened on Tern Island."

Meda, a healer dragon, hovered over Laila's head, her wings beating in a flurry, her rainbow scales dull with worry. "There's danger! Don't go!"

Warmed by the dragon's concern, Mystery sent her love to renew her energy and brighten her scales. "Don't worry about me. I'm hoping it'll help me find my power."

Laila fingered his long forelock out of his eyes. "Tatuk says Gem is very upset about you leaving. Isn't there another way to help Diamond?"

"I have to do this. We sought a prophecy from Moonglow, and it confirms this is my task. Gem will be fine." He swished his tail as if swatting at flies, not wanting to reopen the debate about his suitability for the task.

Meda alighted on Laila's shoulder and poked her delicate snout into the woman's ear. "Tell him!"

Laila stroked Mystery's neck and inhaled deeply. "We didn't think we'd be able to prevent you from going, so we're coming with you. Give me time to pack. We don't know what danger Eastlands faces."

His concern about the risks his friends would face on such a journey fought with Mystery's desire for company. "I can't let you come. Moonglow's prophecy said I had to go alone."

The woman shook her head. "That's not the way Tatuk tells it. He agrees that you, of all the unicorns, have to go, but the prophecy didn't say anything about not having help from us."

Mystery stared back towards the lake as if he could find answers there. Laila was right: nothing had been said about not sharing his mission with dragons, or a human. "But it's going to be dangerous. I can't risk you getting hurt."

Laila crossed her arms. "Of course it'll be dangerous. All the more reason for us to come. We're healers. You may need us."

The idea certainly appealed to Mystery. He enjoyed Laila's company, and he had grown up with her. She already lived with Gem when he arrived as a weanling foal. "Gem will miss you, especially with me not here. She won't want you to risk your life either."

Laila stood her ground. "But this is what she's trained me for! What's the point of me learning all her healing skills and remaining at Shimmering Lake? Everything is perfect. If anyone here has an accident or gets sick, Gem cures them. There's nothing for me to do. She's taught me all she can. And Meda has dragon powers. Please don't turn us away."

Mystery needed no further convincing. "Jump on and I'll take you to your cave. You can gather your things while I let Gem and Diamond know you're coming with me."

Laila fingered the amulet hanging on a grass plait around her neck. The jade otter for which she had received her second name remained the only connection she had with people. After leaving her clan during the bloodwolf war, she hadn't ventured outside Shimmering Lake's boundaries. Her medicine bag bulged with salves, potions, and infusions. More hung drying, enough to heal a whole clan or more of almost any ailment or wound, in the jade caves she had made her home. There she had great views over the lake and loved to watch the changing colours as the dragons flitted across the surface, dangling their feet in the energising waters.

But it wasn't enough. Not that she missed people—quite the

opposite. She had no desire to have a partner or children; the animals were her family, giving her great delight as she learned their habits. And from the first day she had met Meda, when the dragon gifted her one of her scales to enable her to see and talk with all dragons, the tiny healer had been her constant companion. Laila had attached the ruby scale to her jade otter so that it always hung against her neck.

Shyer than cheeky Tatuk, Meda escorted her to places where Gem couldn't go, into deep caverns and high onto rock ledges. They explored the cliffs and caves, finding lichen and mosses and feathers. They made up poems about the antics of the animals and the properties of each medication to make it easier for Laila to remember.

Meda plucked at her hair. "Are we going, or sitting here all day? Mystery's waiting."

"Sorry." Brushing leaves from her grass skirt, Laila shrugged into her woven pack. She had long since discarded her hogskin clothes and anything made of hide, preferring not to remind herself of the animals they came from. Another reason she had no desire to return to a village was the clan's love of eating meat. She couldn't bear the idea of consuming flesh after helping Gem heal the animals.

And none of the clans wanted her as a healer. Laila had left home to escape Jolon, her abusive father, as much as it saddened her to leave Macha, her mother, and Delsin, her younger brother. Delicate and dreamy, Delsin always bore the brunt of their father's bad temper. If she could have helped him, she would have returned. But there was no point; once people learned none of the healers would take her as an apprentice, no one in her clan would listen to her or let her apply her skills.

Now she had a chance to use her knowledge to help those who lived in Diamond's territory. It was time for her to see more of the world, as she had always wanted, no longer constricted by the dictates of a clan. She could do as she pleased, even if it meant leaving this paradise and endangering her life.

Chapter 2

Cool water splashed Mystery's belly as he cantered through the foothills of Snowhaven. Having moved to Shimmering Lake so young, he had never experienced winter. The season didn't faze him. At last he was on his way, even if his purpose remained unclear. Gem had remained reluctant for him to go, worried about his safety, tempting him to stay by mating. Finally, Diamond's fretting, and Laila's and Meda's offer to accompany him, overcame her resistance.

The ice-melt brought on by the spring sun chilled his hooves. Laila shivered on his back. He drew energy from the rocks beneath his feet to increase his warmth. "How do people cope without the power to heat themselves?"

Riding with her legs soft against his sides, Laila grasped his mane as he dodged around the deeper puddles. "We light fires, like the ones I use to make tea, though bigger."

Mystery thought back to the clan at White Water Cliffs where he was born. There had only been a few people there, and they had camped in caves. He didn't remember any large fires. "Isn't that dangerous?"

Laila gripped with her knees as he leapt a creek. "We use a hearth of rocks. They never get out of control. The hard part is finding enough fuel to last through the long winter nights."

"I think you might need to light one tonight. It's getting too slippery to keep up this pace in the dark." It was only an excuse; Mystery had no need to drink or graze, but Laila needed to eat and rest, though she never admitted it, presumably not wanting to slow him down. Dropping to a walk, he scanned the hillsides for a sheltered spot. He found a copse that offered dry timber, and came to a halt. Banks of yellow marigolds and blue flax dotted the grass. A brook burbled close by. "How about here?"

As Laila set up her camp, Mystery pawed the ground to clear a space of stones. He slumped to his side and squirmed, revelling in the scratchy earth. He rolled onto his other side, waving his hooves in the air as he twisted and writhed.

"If you wait a moment I'll give you a brush." Laila unlaced her pack, rummaged deep inside, and walked over with a porcupine-quill comb in her hand. "Let me do your mane too, it's all tangled with sweat. You'll get cold now we've stopped."

Mystery rose and welcomed the grooming, enjoying the attention as much as the massage. He searched the nearby trees for Meda. The tiny dragon sometimes rode on his crest, at other times she flew. Now she was nowhere in sight. Like most dragons, she often disappeared for no reason known to him. Not worrying, he snuffled Laila's hair. "You're getting fit. When we started out, a long ride like today would have made you tired and sore. I suspect we'll have to go slower soon, once we get into the mountains."

Laila continued to wisp his coat with long rhythmic strokes. "Do you think there'll be snow higher up? How will we find our way now we've had to detour south of Diamond's suggested route? We're still too far north to take the pass the clans use, not that I know the landmarks. We rarely had visitors from afar. It's an arduous trek."

'Don't worry, the goddess will guide us." The ways of the clans remained strange to Mystery. "Why do people cross the mountains at all?"

"The annual gathering at Oaktown always attracts a few East-landers, either looking for a mate or to trade goods. Their deerskins are highly prized, and we offer hog products in return. People from Waterfalls, the village at your birthplace, bring flints. They're renowned for the best arrow shafts, too."

After thanking Laila for cleaning his coat, Mystery suggested she search for food. "See if you can find Meda. She may not realise we've camped already. I've tried calling her, but she must be out of range. I can't send messages to dragons as far as I can to other unicorns, especially in these hills."

He dropped his head to graze. Tearing up mouthfuls of sweet alfalfa, he luxuriated in the freedom of his adventure. Not that he didn't miss Gem. He'd never been without other equines before. But this trip was his and his alone. Grateful that Diamond had offered to remain with Gem, Mystery considered calling to let her know how far he'd come, and see if they'd received any information from the others.

No, if there were news, they would have called him. If he contacted them, they might think he needed their support. He'd wait until he had something definite to report.

Laila shrieked. "Mystery!"

He leapt into a gallop. The smell of Laila's fear led him through the pines. Drawing on the power of the land, he built his reserves in anticipation of danger. He reached the edge of a clearing and slid to a halt in a spray of mud and stones.

Laila stood in the centre of the glade, her back to him.

A giant bear stood off to one side, its head far above the height of his own, its massive paws slashing the air. Its huge mouth gaped with yellowed ivories. A bellow erupted from its broad chest.

Mystery whickered to Laila in an attempt to reassure her. "Step back towards me. Slowly."

He raised his voice. "Greetings, mighty bear. We're sorry if we've intruded. We mean you no harm."

The bear spun to face him and dropped to all fours. It lumbered past Laila, almost brushing her with its fur. She took the opportunity to scurry to the nearest tree and scramble into the branches.

Mystery braced for an attack. He didn't want to harm the beast, though if those claws raked his sides they would do serious damage. He arched his neck to point his horn against a charge.

When the bear reached within a horse's length, it stopped and reared on its hind legs again. "I don't recall hearing of a silver unicorn stallion."

Surprised at the comment, Mystery tipped his head in a half-bow and introduced himself. A winged rainbow flashed over his head.

Meda alighted on his crest. "I was on my way to get you. This is Kodi."

"The guardian? I've heard about you, mighty Kodi." Mystery couldn't believe their luck. To have stumbled upon the guardian of the goddess' feathers was a stroke of good fortune. Or had the goddess arranged this meeting? The bear was sure to know a way across the mountains.

"But I haven't heard of you." Kodi groaned as he scratched his massive haunches with his long claws. "Are you Jasper's replacement?"

Mystery acknowledged that he was the new Fire Unicorn. "How did you know Jasper had died?"

Kodi pointed his muzzle to the sky and keened. "I felt his passing. We were very close. He lived with me at Snowhaven, not far from here." After a pause, he settled to the ground. "So who were your sire and dam?"

Relaxing his stance, Mystery explained the goddess had granted Fleet and Tress the honour of producing him. "They've had more foals since me who are strong warmbloods, but no other unicorns will be born unless one of us dies."

Kodi nodded. "I understand. There can only ever be six of you. So what brings you to the mountains? And who is the woman? The only other person I've met was Fleet's companion, Yuma."

Laila remained in the tree as still as a rock, her face a grimace.

Mystery recounted their purpose for being there. Laila still didn't move. "You can come down. Kodi won't hurt you."

She scrambled down the rough trunk and sidled towards him. Meda flitted across and alighted on her shoulder.

Kodi's eyes followed the dragon's flight.

Laila stopped midstride. "He can see Meda! I thought only those with hotblood or carrying a scale could see dragons."

Mystery let out a long sigh. "You haven't heard anything he's said, have you? I wish I could do something about that."

Kodi held out a furred arm towards Laila. "You can use your horn on the dragon scale she carries to share your power of speech. As long as Meda allows you to enhance the scale, the woman will be able to talk with all animals."

Meda flew up onto Mystery's head. "Of course I give permission! I didn't know you could do that."

"Neither did I. Gem didn't show me that. I guess it never occurred to her, as we can talk with everyone anyway. How do I do it?" Without expecting an answer, Mystery placed the tip of his horn against Laila's amulet, sending thoughts of speech styles and language. A tingle of power rose up his legs and coursed along his spine.

A flash of light burst from the ruby scale.

Laila grasped the amulet. "What have you done?"

Kodi nodded towards her. "You're a long way from home."

"Mystery! I can understand him! Thank you."

Mystery introduced Kodi to her and explained the bear's role as guardian of the goddess' discarded feathers.

Laila remained close to his left hand side, one hand on his withers. "Greetings, Kodi. Can you understand me now?"

The great bear released a gruff rumble deep in his throat that sounded like a chuckle. "I could always understand you. I'd be a poor guardian if I couldn't talk with those who entered my territory. But what Mystery and Meda have gifted you will be of much use. You'll be able to talk with all animals now."

A rush of excitement raised the hairs on Mystery's neck. "This will make life much easier."

Then he shook away the tingle. "Is this my power?" It didn't seem much. He'd hoped for something far more dramatic.

Kodi blinked and twitched his furry, round ears. "Any unicorn can do that. I gather from your remark that you've yet to know your individual strength."

"I'm hoping I'll discover it on this journey."

Kodi stepped to Mystery's right-hand side and rested a mighty paw on his withers next to Laila's hand. "You will. I can sense a great power in you, and you have two loyal companions. Now, is there anything else I can help you with?"

Mystery waved his horn at the high peaks covered in snow. "Can you tell us a way across those mountains?"

Kodi rose to his full height, his hair bristling. "I'll do better than that. I'll accompany you to Lion Pass."

Laila strolled alongside Mystery, admiring the stunning vistas of snowclad peaks and heavily forested slopes, the fresh greenery of budding deciduous trees, and the tumbling white water of melting rivers. Having to go at Kodi's lumbering pace gave her a chance to stretch her legs and look for alpine herbs such as white marsh marigold, good for inflamed wounds.

Since moving to Shimmering Lake, she had become accustomed to talking with the unicorns and dragons. Her newly-acquired ability to chatter to the voles, owls, and lizards she encountered along the path amazed her. Kodi proved excellent company, sharing tales of the early days of the unicorns. She hadn't appreciated how old they were; the first generation had lived for longer than people could recount. Although mortal, no unicorn had ever died from old age. No wonder tales of them were embedded in the clans' myths and legends.

Kodi was no ordinary bear, either. He ambled alongside her, his nose twitching for the scent of wax-covered balls of nectar buried in the ground. "I know I shouldn't eat so much—the bumblebees need their food more than me—but I can't resist it."

Laila ruffled his fur and leant her arm over his back. It had taken her a few days to become so familiar with the massive creature. Now she couldn't imagine why she had ever feared him. "I guess we all need a weakness. Bumblebee nectar seems like a healthy one to have."

Mystery nudged Laila's shoulder. "The track's opening up. I want to stretch my legs."

Kodi waved for her to mount. "Don't wait for me. I'll catch you up where the trees close in again."

The wind in her hair with Mystery beneath her always gave Laila a thrill. Although she had grown up around horses, people had never thought to ride them until the bloodwolf war. What an amazing experience that previous generations had missed! And nothing compared to riding a unicorn, with their limitless energy.

What lay ahead for them? It was hard to imagine the suffering Diamond described when surrounded by such beauty and power. But Diamond had seen horses slaughtered, grasslands destroyed, and men running in fear. It wouldn't be the first time unicorns had protected horses and people. Whatever could be causing the problem this time? With Shadow dead, the unicorns had no idea what could be behind the troubles. Had the goddess already commenced destroying Equinora? Is that why Moonglow suffered?

Laila had always believed the Mother created the world, but it certainly hadn't occurred to her that the Mother was a winged unicorn. But why not? Laila wanted to learn so much more. Visiting Eastlands, with its wide-open spaces and long, sandy beaches had been a dream since childhood, even if the circumstances were far from what she could have imagined as a young girl stuck with gathering and grinding, weaving and stitching. Now she did those things with pleasure, for herself, not at the expectations of others, but still she'd yearned for adventure, for something apart from the chores she needed to do to keep herself alive.

Mystery halted, his sides streaked with sweat.

Invigorated by the gallop, Laila leapt off and twisted a handful of grass into a wisp. Silver hairs covered her hands and arms as she rubbed down his coat. "You're shedding. I didn't think you needed to change coats. I hope you're not ailing from whatever is affecting Moonglow."

Mystery twitched his lips in pleasure. His head cocked at an angle as Laila scratched the ridge of his neck. "There's nothing wrong with me. I'll need thicker hair in the mountains. It's already much colder here than at Shimmering Lake, but I don't mind. It's wonderful to see such different country."

"Do you ever dream of getting a territory of your own?" Laila picked up each of his hooves in turn and checked them for stones. The hard soles shone like his copper horn.

"I wouldn't want to leave Gem. I can't understand how the other unicorns can bear to live alone all the time. Don't you miss people?" Mystery held his tail aloft for Laila to brush the long strands until they gleamed.

"You're my family, you and Gem and Meda. As much as I want to see the land east of Dragonspine Mountains, I'm not looking forward to meeting any Eastlanders. I doubt they'll accept me any more than my own clan."

After finishing Mystery's grooming, Laila went in search of a meal. Squirrels had missed a few cones still containing last season's nuts. Probably fewer animals lived at these higher elevations. Fresh greens grew in abundance at this time of year, and roots were easy to dig in the moist soil.

She returned to camp to find Kodi had arrived. After sharing the small treat of pine nuts, she lit a small fire using one of her flints and a handful of dry leaves, placed a small pot in the embers, and brewed mint tea. She wrapped tubers in the leaves she had gathered, and roasted them in the coals.

The sun settled behind the peaks. She shivered and pushed together a bed of bark and dry grass. Maybe she should have kept her furs for trips such as this. She collected another armful of logs and built up the fire.

Watching the flickering flames, her eyelids drooped and her head nodded. She lay down, Meda nestling under her chin in her usual place, content to snuggle up with her discarded scale through the night. Dragons rarely shed the precious gems, only dropping one when they had a growth spurt. Rather than shed their whole covering, they shuffled their scales to accommodate their larger size, making room for new ones. It was during this process that sometimes one came adrift. The privilege of Meda gifting the ruby to her, plus the added boon of Mystery's enhancement, warmed Laila as much as the dragon's body. She soon drifted off to sleep.

A twig snapped.

Laila opened her eyes, but the blackness of the night was total. The fire had long since died away, with not even a faint glow from the embers. Attempting to pick out what had woken her, she sat up, clutching Meda to her chest, trying not to rustle her bedding.

A low rumble came from the furred hump of Kodi's sleeping form. His long breaths eased in and out, his chest rising and falling in time to his snores. Mystery was nowhere to be seen, no doubt off grazing on the lusher pasture by the stream. He only ever dozed for brief moments.

The hairs on the back of Laila's neck prickled like caterpillars walking over her skin. Something wasn't right. She stared into the dark, alert for any movement.

As a half-moon shone between scudding clouds, a pair of golden eyes hovered between the trees. They were too low to be those of an owl. She strained to focus. What she had presumed was a large rock covered with lichen took on a different form. There had been no rock there when she'd gone to sleep.

A whiskered face peered above shoulders bunched in readiness to spring.

Laila remained motionless. If she tossed her bedding onto the fire, it might flare up and give her light, maybe even scare the beast away. Was there enough heat left to ignite the dried grass?

But if she moved, the lion was sure to pounce.

Meda struggled in her arms. "Hey cat! We're not for you. Go and find a skunk or something."

Laila clamped the dragon's snout closed. "Shhh. That's no way to—"

The lion sprang. Its powerful hindquarters launched it halfway across the clearing in a single bound. It thrust into another leap.

Laila felt rather than saw a movement to her right.

Kodi swiped a giant paw at the lion as it soared past. Snarling, the cat changed direction mid-air and attacked. Lighter and more agile than the bear, it scrambled to make contact with Kodi. He parried each attack with teeth and claw, drawing blood from the enraged animal.

Hooves thundered.

Mystery arrived in a hail of clods, snorting.

The lion darted into the trees, disappearing as if it had never been there. The metallic smell of blood and the strong scent of cat lingered.

Mystery raised a foreleg. "Laila, where are you? Are you okay?"

She stood, still clutching Meda to her chest. "We're fine. Kodi, are you hurt?"

The massive bear licked his forearm. "No, this blood isn't mine. That was a narrow escape. I guess this place isn't called Lion Pass for nothing."

Meda scratched at Laila's shirt. "The lion wouldn't have been able to hear me. I was only trying to send it the thought of going away."

Laila stroked Meda's scaled back. "I know. I'm sorry I grabbed you. I was frightened."

Mystery nuzzled each of them in turn. "Thank goodness you're alright. In future I'd better stand guard while you sleep."

Adrenalin dissipated through Laila's arms. "I should have built the fire up higher. In future, I'll find a more sheltered spot. Maybe Kodi and I should find a cave each night. We've seen plenty."

Kodi shook his shaggy head. "I need to get back to Snowhaven and the last of the goddess' feathers. This is where I leave you. Take extra care in deep snow. Spring is a dangerous time in the mountains."

Chapter 3

Cold seeped up Mystery's legs as he clambered over the rocks. The frozen ground prevented him from drawing energy from the earth, and his muscles shrieked at the unaccustomed activity. He had never experienced mountains like these, with their cutting stones and loose ledges. As he stumbled and tripped his way along a narrow track, Laila grasped his mane and dug in her knees.

He halted. "I think it might be safer if you walk."

She slid from his back. "I agree. The closer I am to the ground, the better. It might be hard work climbing, but these drop-offs upset my stomach."

Every day the conditions worsened. Mystery missed Kodi's guidance, especially when navigating through treacherous passes, vastly different from the run from Shimmering Lake to the foothills, filled with easy-to-find landmarks. Now the only guide was a mighty spire of rock—Eagle's Peak—jutting high above the other mountains to the north. Was that where the lions came from, as Diamond interpreted from Moonglow's prophecy? He intended to find out, if only he could reach the elusive mountain.

Despite trying to keep moving east, Mystery was forced by the deep gorges to wind his way up and down in whatever direction the path led. The pines still grew thick along the mountainsides, providing shelter at night and fuel for fires, but no matter what he did, he couldn't get nearer to the black pinnacle. Numerous dead ends meant retracing his steps.

Laila paused to snap off a couple of stout branches to use as walking poles. Meda perched on her shoulder, drowsy from the cold. Laila stroked the greying scales of the tiny dragon and drew her down inside her cloak, cuddling her close. "I wish we could fly like you. Could you find a way for us?"

Meda dug deeper, her voice muffled as she refused. "Too high. Too far. Too cold."

Mystery trudged on, worried about them both. "As we can't find a way to Eagle's Peak, we'll go to Eastlands first. If we were meant to reach the spire, the goddess would guide us. We can come back in summer if need be."

Laila had woven grasses and feathers into a soft wrap, having long ago discarded any garments made from animal skins, but the blanket didn't look warm enough. Slowing his pace to accommodate her short stride, he also became chilled. And this was springtime! At least they hadn't arrived at Dragonspine Mountains in winter. Instead of discovering his powers and saving horses from whatever horror assailed them, he slogged each day without knowing where he was heading, or what he was going to do when he reached wherever the goddess meant him to be.

He crested a ridge with a bounce in his step, keen to see a descent to open grasslands, maybe even the distant sea. His heart plummeted as another range of mountains confronted him, the hillsides heavy with snow. He groaned. "So much for the warmer climes of the east. Maybe I should have let Diamond translocate us. I'm not achieving anything other than cold feet from crossing on foot."

Laila reassured him with a pat. "Then we wouldn't have met Kodi, and you wouldn't have enhanced my amulet. This is what we're meant to be doing."

Trudging down into the valley, Mystery lifted his legs high to navigate the wet snow, no longer able to sense the ground beneath his hooves. The further he descended, the deeper the drifts became. Not even the slightest breeze stirred, and clouds smothered the peaks like smoke from a damp campfire. "I need to rest. My strength is draining faster than I can replenish it."

Laila floundered behind him. "You need to eat. You can't rely on Equinora's energy alone. Maybe you can dig down to the grass when we reach the valley."

"I suppose so." Mystery hung his head and blew warm air on Laila's hands. "How are you going?"

"It's hard. I keep sinking up to my thighs and I'm soaked."

Mystery nudged her. "You'd better mount. Let's get to that creek where the snow is patchy so I can graze and drink. You can rest, and construct something for your feet to stop you sinking."

The flow of the stream kept the snow from thickening on its banks. Mystery nibbled at whatever shoots he could find, taking no joy in eating the coarse vegetation, not like savouring the rich clovers and herbs at Shimmering Lake. He thought of Gem and what she might be doing, swimming with the aquadragons, or chatting with Diamond. He'd prefer to be back with them, enjoying the sun and the mutual grooming.

But horses needed him. Somehow, he must find his power and prove he was worthy to be a unicorn. He sucked freezing water over his numb tongue and strengthened his resolve. "Let's go before we get too cold."

They made quicker time climbing out of the valley. Laila traipsed on in her pine-frond snowshoes and hung onto Mystery's tail. The clouds broke up to reveal a blue sky. Though its warmth didn't reach through the trees, Mystery's spirits lifted with the renewed source of energy. He wove through a stand of dense pines on a steep slope and came to a sudden halt. "Meda, can you sense anything? There's a scent I don't know."

The dragon poked her nose out of Laila's shirtfront and blinked. "Wolves. There's a pack close by."

Mystery proceeded with caution, his ears pricked and nostrils flared. Strong whiffs of meat eaters and wet fur wafted in currents without indicating where they lay. "Laila, jump on. We may have to run in a hurry."

Before she had a chance to do so, Meda crawled out of her hidey-hole and perched on Laila's head. "You could try calling them. Let them know who you are."

Mystery's first instinct was to avoid a confrontation, especially with the tales of savage wolves told by his dam when he was a foal. But Meda was right. Better to face an enemy than be stalked like a mouse. "Hello, wolf pack! Show yourselves!"

No one responded. The trees remained silent and still.

Mystery called again, introducing himself and his companions.

A grey nose appeared from behind an enormous tree trunk. "What brings a unicorn to Dragonspine Mountains? We've never seen your like before. In truth I thought you were a legend."

Mystery stepped towards the wolf, arching his neck and holding his tail high. Even in the low light, his copper horn and hooves sparkled like wet crystal. "We need to cross to Eastlands. A great danger is threatening horses and people."

"What do we care about them? They're only meat to us." The large male emerged from hiding, other grey shapes appearing behind him. Three females and two younger males crept closer, lips pulled back over their teeth and eyes glowing like embers.

Mystery stepped back and lowered his head. "Have you seen or heard anything about these great dangers, or experienced anything out of the ordinary? The goddess threatens to return and destroy Equinora. Tell me all you can."

One of the females gave a low growl. "I'd rather eat that skinny beast beside you. We haven't found food for days, and I've pups to feed. Can you use your magic to help? Isn't that what unicorns are supposed to do?"

Laila stepped closer to Mystery and grasped the base of his mane.

He wrapped his neck around her in a sign of protection. "I thought winter was a good time for wolves, when other animals find the going tough. You should be fat and teaching your young to hunt."

The lead male advanced and sat in front of Mystery, his shaggy head as high as Mystery's nose. "Normally that would be true, but something strange is happening. The snows have lingered, deeper and wetter than ever. Anything that dies disappears under its cover. And the valley where we normally make our dens is closed to us."

"What do you mean?" Mystery couldn't imagine a valley closing, unless a rockfall had blocked the pass.

The wolf licked at one front paw. His protruding ribs and matted fur revealed his poor condition. "I don't know what I mean, only that we can no longer access our spring home. I've been there many times, but now I can't find it. The paths no longer lead there. We had to den under a boulder instead of in our usual caves."

The ground shifted, tiredness upsetting Mystery's balance.

The wolves shot to their feet and streaked back into the trees.

A rumble penetrated the forest.

The earth quaked again. The air filled with powdered ice, frozen flakes hovering like fireflies in the gloom.

Meda shrieked. "Avalanche! Run!"

Laila leapt astride.

Mystery was already on the move. Not wanting to go back the way they had come, he galloped uphill, cutting across the steep incline in order to avoid the falling snow, dodging trees as their branches lashed and their trunks toppled. His hooves slipped beneath him as the ground rocked. Snowballs crashed against his legs. He staggered, righted himself, and cantered on as fast as he dared.

He shied. He jumped. He ran.

The roar grew louder. Ice crystals blinded him. Laila hunched low on his neck. Trusting his instincts, he pounded on, drawing on the power released by the wind racing ahead of the snow.

He drew ahead of the devastation. The avalanche rumbled behind him.

He slowed, breathing hard. His muscles twitched as if he still raced over uneven ground. Light returned. He halted, and faced back.

No sign of the path or their tracks remained. Billows of snow settled, and sunlight sparkled on the moisture in the air. The forest had gone; even the tallest trees lay smothered.

Laila quivered on his back. "The wolves! They'll be buried!"

Mystery scanned the slope to identify where they had met the pack. Nothing looked familiar. "They knew the avalanche was coming before I worked out what was happening. They might have escaped on the other side of the fall. It's impossible to see that far."

Meda flapped her wings and hovered. "I'll check. I'll know if they're beneath the snow."

Mystery paced the drifts, creating a hard pack beneath his feet in an attempt to keep warm and access Equinora's energy.

The dragon returned. Her head drooped and her scales lost their colour, drained of vigour by sorrow. "They didn't make it. I could sense where they fell. None are alive."

Laila wrapped her arms around Meda. "They had pups! They'll starve without their parents."

ystery's warmth seeped through Laila's leggings, helping her control her shivering. But it wasn't only from the cold. Concerned about Meda's pallid scales, Laila tried to cheer up to prevent her emotions weakening the dragon, sending love to her as Gem had taught. The ruby on her amulet warmed. "Meda, could you find the pups? I don't think you'll have to fly far or high. Can you distinguish between wolves and other animals likely to live nearby?"

Meda stretched her wings and resettled them on her back before slipping under Laila's clothes. Only her pointed snout protruded. "I don't know. I've never thought about it. Maybe."

Mystery had already recommenced their trek east. "I should be able to smell them if we're near enough. Fly up and look for boulders large enough for a pack to den beneath, and guide me. Between us we might have a chance."

"Alright."

Heartened at the prospect of aiding the pups, though unsure what she would do if they found them, Laila sat up straighter. She eased Meda out from her cloak and held her aloft. The dragon soared and circled in an ever-widening pattern.

Riding in hope, Laila pictured the wolf pack and marvelled at having understood their conversation. When Mystery had enhanced her amulet, she had wondered if she would only be able to hear animals with power, like Kodi. Then she'd come to enjoy the chattering of the little creatures that scuttled through the leaf litter and the gossip of the birds. Hearing the wolves had sent thrills through her blood. How much easier it would be now to help any in need of healing.

She smiled as she thought of the gruff voice of the male wolf and the whine of the old female—exactly like she would have imagined them to sound. Back in the days of running errands for her mother or being bullied by her father, she'd never dreamt she'd be able to converse with wolves. The clans feared the packs, but she loved all animals. Now that they were gone, the pain of their loss was far worse for having comprehended their speech.

Mystery branched from the narrow trail he had been following. "Meda has seen a possible location." Stepping high through deep snow, he angled down towards a dip in the hillside.

Massive rocks had swept a path through the trees that now littered the terrain. Meda hovered over a pile of boulders, the moss and lichen on their surfaces showing they had lain there for years, the wind ahead of the avalanche having blown them clean. Others nearby looked as if they had recently rolled from a raw gash higher up the mountain.

Laila placed a hand on Mystery's neck. "Can you scent anything?"

He flared his nostrils and paced the torn ground.

Meda swooped down to land on his crest. "There's someone alive nearby."

Laila slipped off Mystery's back and ran to each rock in turn. A fluffy grey tail protruded from one. She gasped. Using her back against the boulder and thrusting with her legs, she attempted to shove the rock aside. It wouldn't budge.

"Careful! You might start another landslide or avalanche." Mystery tiptoed over.

Laila pointed to his horn. "Now you can find your power! Break the rock!"

"I've tried. Many times. Nothing happens." Mystery shuffled from foot to foot.

"But then you were in Shimmering Lake. Maybe Gem's influence is too strong in her territory. Try again!"

Acquiescing, Mystery lowered his horn to the surface of the rock, sliding the glinting copper over the bumps and ridges to find a weak spot.

Laila waited, concern and excitement mingling as Mystery sought his power. He exhaled with a shudder.

Nothing happened.

"Try striking it." Laila crouched next to the protruding tail, and stroked the soft fur.

"All that happened last time was I got a headache!" He braced his legs. "Move away!" His eyes blazed and sweat burst from his neck. He rapped the rock hard.

The stone didn't crack or move.

Meda darted towards them. "Not that one. They're all dead. Over here!"

Laila stumbled towards another cluster of rocks. A faint whimper egged her on. She sank to her knees and crawled into a dark opening between the boulders, trying not to think about what she might find or how she'd tackle frightened and possibly injured wolf pups. She squeezed down a gap.

The smell of warm bodies and the feel of hot breath on her face stopped her. She could see nothing. "Where are you, little ones?"

Another whimper, louder this time. A wet nose touched her arm. She flinched and cracked her skull, took a deep breath to steady herself, and reached out with tentative fingers. "Can you walk? Are you trapped?"

A weak voice cried: "I'm hungry."

"Are you hurt?"

"Nooo, I'm cold. I'm hungry. Where's my family?"

Relieved that at least one pup had survived, Laila squirmed out of the den. "Follow me. We won't hurt you. We've come to help."

Laila retreated to the light and brushed dirt from her knees.

A pink nose poked out after her. "Who are you? I'm hungry."

A scrawny pup emerged, her head and paws too big for her lean body, one ear folded over and the other standing up. She sat on her haunches, her enormous paws pressed together, brown like the top of her head and ears in contrast to the rest of her grey body, guard hairs protruding from her ruff in tufts. Her long whiskers twitched as she studied the area around her.

From the cub's blue eyes, Laila guessed she was between one and two moons old, old enough to wean. "Are you alone?"

"I don't know. The adults went hunting. My brothers and sisters were playing outside. We'd been told to stay in the den... They never could resist wrestling in the snow."

Laila rummaged in her pack. She didn't have any meat. Perhaps the pup would eat a vegetable mash. She soaked a pumpkin biscuit in a handful of snow and offered it to her. "Try this."

Meda hovered nearby, the wolf paying no attention, obviously unable to see the dragon as she landed and poked Laila's legs. "The pup's sick. She's full of worms and there's something not right with her heart. She's close to death."

Having found one survivor, Laila couldn't bear to lose the precious life. "Can you help her? I have some wormwood if I can get her to eat it, but it's very bitter."

Getting her to eat didn't prove a problem. The cub devoured anything placed in front of her, including all the dried fruit Laila had been rationing.

Mystery paced around the boulders. "We shouldn't stay here. There's a high chance there'll be another avalanche. I'll be happier when we get out of these ranges."

"We can't leave the pup. I'll have to carry her." Laila stroked the soft fur of the wolf's neck. "What's your name, little one?"

"Runt, coz I'm the littlest." The wolf rolled on her back to be tickled, her rounded belly covered in soft down.

Captivated by the ball of fluff, who seemed nothing like the ferocious wolves of folktales, Laila scooped her up. "I'm not going to call you that. How about *Paws?* You seem to be all paws to me. Now hold still because I want to check you out."

While Laila hugged the tiny body to her, Meda sat on her shoulder, strengthened by her love. The dragon's rainbow scales glowed and changed to green, from the top of her head to the tip of her tail. Once they matched the emerald legs that marked her as a healer, she breathed out a stream of mist, shrouding the pup in vapour.

Paws squirmed as the warmth penetrated her fur.

Laila grasped her tighter. "Steady, little one. This will help you grow big and strong."

Meda finished her healing.

Laila quizzed her with a raised eyebrow.

"Mending a heart isn't the same as healing wounds. Her other organs are weak, too. I've done all I can." The dragon gave what Laila interpreted as a shrug.

Mystery nudged Laila's shoulder. "We must go. The ground is trembling again."

Chapter 4

Ripe grass heads wafted in waves across Hawk Plains, where horses dotted the vast openness, grazing in small groups. Away from the herd, Golden Breeze waited for Wood Lily to nurse her new foal. The filly was strong and healthy, twitching her tail as she guzzled. "We should go."

The roan mare nuzzled the foal at her side and licked the curly mane. "I suppose so. I'd normally want another day, but I know the queen will be anxious for us to return."

Breeze had accompanied Lily to her birthing place to bring herbs to ease the afterbirth from her womb. A mature mare, she had borne many youngsters and hadn't needed any other assistance. Although the flat plains offered little shelter other than belly-high grasses, the filly had been born in the cool of dawn. Now the sun glared above them, warming Breeze's palomino coat, and a light wind rippled the sea of pale green.

A shadow engulfed Breeze, yet no clouds broke the perfect blue to the horizon. A tingle crept up her neck and she shivered from an instinctive anxiety. She raised her head.

A giant eagle swooped low, braking with wings wide and feet stretched out.

"Look out!"

The bird dived. As big as a horse, its hooked beak and glowing eyes pointed straight at them.

Lily reared.

The eagle dropped towards her, wings outstretched. The tips of its feathers flicked, manoeuvring it towards her foal. Golden talons opened wide, swung over the prone filly, and grabbed her.

Lily screamed. She lashed out with her front hooves to beat the bird out of the air.

The eagle ignored her and lifted the foal with ease, sweeping the filly high away, the newborn's legs dangling.

Breeze had never seen an eagle so big, had never heard of one taking a foal. She fidgeted in confusion, helpless, without even words to comfort Lily, the mare's pain evident in her eyes as she continued to rear. Then she raced off, tearing across the flat lands beneath the eagle's flight, neighing with every stride.

Breeze stared after her friend, immobilised by shock.

A giant cat rose from the grasses behind Lily and leapt at her flank.

Lily galloped harder, her hoofbeats drumming on the hard ground.

The lion bounded behind, driving her rather than trying to bring her down.

Chasing after Lily wouldn't help. Breeze fled back to the herd.

Queen Meadowlark saw her coming and trotted over. "Where's Lily?"

In a rush of words between gasps, Breeze described the sudden appearance of the giant eagle and the lion. "There was no scent of the cat, not even when it revealed itself. It didn't make a sound."

"How awful! Poor Lily. We must tell King Socks." The thickset mare lumbered off at a canter.

The old stallion was grazing near Snowflake, a mare who had slipped her foal over winter. She had come in season early, and the pair flirted on the outskirts of the herd. Socks snorted as Breeze and Meadowlark advanced. "What's up?"

Breeze retold the events.

Socks struck out with a foreleg in anger. "Not another one! Still, this is the first time someone has seen what's taking the mares. I'll send a few warriors after the lion. They might be able to save Lily... if it hasn't already killed her."

Breeze shuddered as she relived the attack. "I know this will sound odd, but I think the lion was following the eagle. It's too much of a coincidence it was there when Lily's foal was taken. And I've never seen a bird so big, its wings and tail as golden as the sun. We never saw birds like that at Flowering Valley."

Socks lifted his head and sniffed the air. "I've never seen an eagle carry a foal. These are fearsome times."

Meadowlark arched her neck and pricked her ears. "Why would a lion drive a mare away? Maybe it's taking her to its cubs. At least every day sees us further from Dragonspine Mountains and the lions' haunts."

At least a quarter of the herd had disappeared in the last year. The bachelors sent to seek help from the unicorns hadn't returned. No one knew if they hadn't found one yet, or if they had been slaughtered. With spring underway, the horses had been preparing to migrate to their summer lands nearer the coast.

The king walked around the three mares, quizzing Breeze about her story. He halted and cocked his head to one side. "If nothing else, the warriors may be able to track Lily and find out what's happening. We must know what we're up against if we're to keep everyone safe." He cantered off to organise the bachelors.

Breeze remained where she was, uninterested in grazing, fearing he might send Willow. Her colt had been running with the bachelors for two winters. She also feared for Butterfly, only recently weaned. Her filly wasn't afraid of anything, always off gambolling with her friends despite warnings from Meadowlark and herself. Maybe now she'd listen and stay close.

Breeze escorted Meadowlark to find the youngsters. "Do you think the lions will follow us to Shale Cliffs? I don't want another experience like that, especially being so heavily in foal."

"Who knows? I can't believe they're here. I've only ever heard of them haunting the mountains, which is why we don't shelter there in winter." The queen described how the lions usually ambushed their prey from the protection of rocks or trees rather than stalking animals in the open. "Can you remember how to find the fresh water springs near here? They should be full of snowmelt, and you look as if you need a good drink."

The old queen had been teaching Breeze the lay of the territory in anticipation of her taking over as lead mare one day. Breeze absorbed all the knowledge she could; her ascendancy would take more than the recommendation of the king when Meadowlark died. Breeze's first year had been full of confusion and sorrow, homesick for the meadows and streams of Midlands. Blackfoot, the Head of Warriors from Flowering Valley, had led her over the mountain pass and delivered her to King Socks as agreed with her sire.

In return, the grey stallion had been granted territory to the north at Elk Bank. He had been going to return to Midlands and fight in the bloodwolf war before building a herd. By now, he should have returned and gathered mares. A few small herds ran north of the river. Their diversity, in addition to mare swaps from across Dragonspine Mountains, helped to lower the risks of inbreeding.

King Streak had sent Breeze to his former bachelor friend at Hawk Plains as part of one such swap. Streak and Flash, his brother, had run with Socks as colts before they moved west to establish their own territories. Memories of her birthplace reminded Breeze of Tress, her best friend. Heartbreak filled her as she remembered the leisurely days when she and Tress would wander down to the village to be brushed, swapping gossip and dreaming of the stallions they may go to. Tress was supposed to have come east with her, in fact was intended to be Meadowlark's protégé, not her. But Tress had run away in pursuit of the black stallion, Fleet of Foot.

Sweat crusted Breeze's neck and chest. She needed to shed her winter coat. This herd didn't have a clan of people to groom them, something she'd always enjoyed. Recovering from her fright, she ripped up fresh green shoots, gorging on the rich grass without enjoyment. She could do nothing to help Lily; she had to think of her unborn foal. Having wintered in the warmer but barren Badlands, the better pick helped improve her mood in spite of her lingering anxieties.

She grazed alongside Meadowlark, switching her tail against biting flies. "I'd forgotten how annoying the insects are once we get to moister ground. I don't remember them being this bad at Flowering Valley."

Meadowlark lifted her head, her thick forelock covering her eyes. "They're why we never venture north of the river to Goose Fen. It's either too cold up there or the biting insects drive us mad." The bay mare stood much taller than Breeze and twice as broad, displaying bulky muscles over heavy bones.

A slate-grey mare trotted up to the queen, her powerful hindquarters rippling with muscle. "I've located the springs. They're flowing better than ever. Come and look. There're already tadpoles squirming in the shallows."

Breeze held back. Shale didn't like her. The older mare minded her manners in front of the queen, and then either ignored Breeze or laid her ears back whenever they were alone.

Meadowlark hastened off to enjoy the fresh water.

Let the others drink first, it was too hot to run, and Breeze's swollen belly made shoving uncomfortable. She was in no mood for petty herd squabbles. Images of the eagle attack and the giant lion chasing Lily still played across her vision. The roan mare had been as close to a friend as she'd had since leaving home.

She reached the pool.

Shale pawed the water, spraying her shoulders and back as the other mares wandered off, their thirst slated.

Breeze sipped the churned waters, a fresh loneliness consuming her.

Meadowlark stood with Socks a little way back from the herd. The queen called her over. The stallion's liver chestnut coat glowed slick with water, and mud caked his hips and ribs from where he'd rolled. He peered to the horizon. Having such a vast territory to roam meant the mares often drifted off in small groups to lessen the pressure on grazing. It was hard for the king and queen to know where everyone was at all times.

Socks blew into Breeze's nostrils. "I'm worried about sending more stallions out with the need for them to guard so great here. I still hope the delegation sent for help will return with good news. Can you tell us more about Fleet's search for a unicorn? How long did it take? Where did he go? Did he have any special instructions about how to contact them?"

Not believing unicorns existed, conversations about them always made Breeze squirm. She scratched her nose on her foreleg. "I don't know. He was gone a few moons." Fleet claimed he had met a second-generation unicorn, Gemstone. Breeze had her doubts; not even the legends told of an emerald unicorn with a ruby mane and tail, and an opal horn and hooves. He could easily have made the whole story up. She and Blackfoot had left soon after Fleet's return, and they'd heard nothing since.

Meadowlark nuzzled Socks' neck. "I'll insist mares don't go off to foal anymore. It's too risky. Until we have better protection against these lions, and now the eagle, they must cope with the lack of privacy."

As wise as the instruction may be, Breeze hated the idea of other horses around when her foaling time came. It wasn't unheard of for mares to steal a newborn if they had lost their own. However, she trusted Meadowlark. More placid than Queen Starburst at Flowering Valley, the old mare ruled with a gentle nature and years of wisdom. "Have any of the stallions seen Blackfoot take up his territory? He might know more."

Socks arched his thick crest. "That's a good point. I'll send someone to find him. If I offer him a few mares, he might help, and sending them north to him could be safer." He trotted off towards a pair of bachelors in the distance.

Breeze and Meadowlark settled to graze side by side, drifting around the herd in a leisurely patrol, watching the mares and youngsters without obvious intent. Occasionally, the queen shared the bloodlines of a particular horse, or taught Breeze about a plant that didn't grow in Midlands, widening her education as they roamed.

A loud whinny carried across the plains.

Socks came galloping back, his nostrils flared red and blowing hard. Skidding to a halt next to Meadowlark, he tossed his head in frenzy. "Gather the herd. We must move to the cliffs now. Sandy is back alone and tells of unimaginable horrors. The others who went to get help are dead. And it's not only horses being attacked. Other animals' corpses are everywhere, even humans'. We must flee to the coast before more of us are lost."

Chapter 5

For the first time in many moons, the sun rose higher than Eagle's Peak, blazing warmth across the tussocks. Although sufficient light crept around the lower peaks in spring and autumn to generate a flush of grasses, and the heat sink of the black mountain kept the valley temperate, Shadow was grateful for the lengthening days. For too long he had lived in darkness, in the cold and wet of Obsidian Caves, trapped.

A bird scudded across the sky, growing as it neared, blocking the sun's rays. The giant eagle swooped down with fanned wings, alighting with a delicacy belying his size, as tall as any horse. Claw blinked his pupil-less eyes, the swirling orbs like whirlpools of molten gold. He settled his wings to his sides with a rustle, the golden feathers glimmering against his tawny chest. "You'll be happy, eeerk! I found a good one. She's on her way, eeerk!"

Anticipation sent adrenalin through Shadow's body. "Is she young and strong?"

Claw swivelled his head towards the east as he clacked his hooked beak. "Don't know, eeerk! Much warmblood. She obeyed mind message. Probably doesn't know why, eeerk! Stealthcat have easy chase."

Shadow pranced on the spot, his black coat shining and his thick mane and tail flowing like the crimson waves of lava from his former home. "I'll go and meet her. The other mares will be safe."

How his life had changed since he gave Aureana's feathers to Claw! He had galloped for days, absorbing energy from the land blurring beneath his feet, from the wind blowing through his ears, and from the sun warming his back. Vowing never to be contained again, he had searched every mountain and valley until he had found this special place. Only one pass led in or out. He had locked his new territory with a barrier of power to prevent trespassers, the irony of his actions adding to his thrill of being free.

Cantering across the valley, Shadow sparked with energy, strength pouring into him from the rich earth and every breath increasing his well-being. His dreams of building a herd from mares with unicorn ancestry was becoming a reality. All those with power would be his. His to control and breed with, their offspring's offspring strengthening with each generation from his blood, until they could overpower the pretentious unicorns and eradicate them from Equinora. Without Aureana's presence, he would rule supreme.

Claw continued to serve him well, selecting warmblood mares for his stealthcats to drive here. Now another mare was on her way. He tossed his head with glee, his crimson forelock catching on his curved black horns, shrouding his eyes. It had grown thick over winter and hung over his face like oakmoss in an ancient forest. He rubbed the hair free on his knee before trotting to greet the newcomer.

When he reached the rocky track leading through the towering conifers, he smelled the approach of a horse. A red roan cantered into view, her black mane and tail tangled with sweat and her strawberry body coated in foam.

Shadow admired her colouring, though she was older than he'd hoped. *Welcome.*

The mare halted nearby, trembling, and tossed her head in alarm. "A lion! We must run!"

The feline has gone. Rest easy.

She didn't respond.

Shadow's excitement trickled away, worried that her brown eyes meant she had only a low proportion of hotblood. If they'd been emerald or sapphire, or black, they would indicate more power. Never mind, he was sure she heard him.

Her eyes rolled. "It can't be far. I think I lost it through the trees. Hurry!" The roan tried to dodge around him.

He blocked her way. She was a big, solid type, with a look of intelligence in her eyes, if not power. From her swollen udder, she had recently foaled. That would explain Claw's satisfied look: he had feasted well. "There's no point running. You're safe inside my barrier."

"We must flee! We're in danger! Who are you?" The mare shivered in fear and exhaustion, sweat creaming her neck and dripping down her legs as she wove her head from side to side.

"Relax, I've told you, the lion has gone. It's under my command. I'm Shadow, one and only duocorn, created by the goddess in her likeness. I rule here. Follow me. I'll show you where to drink and refresh yourself." He turned and wove between the trees to the valley floor.

The mare skittered behind, fear emanating from every twitch of her skin and flick of her ears. She kept her neck bent to one side to watch for pursuers.

Shadow attempted to reassure her with a steady look. "The stealthcat will be feasting on his reward. You've no need to fear my catchers while you remain here. And remain here you will."

The mare's fretting didn't worry him. They always took a few days to settle. Then they would display either anger or joy, depending on what they had left behind, those lower in the ranks pleased to have a chance to rise higher, though those were rare; most of the warmblood mares had high standing within their former herds.

The roan sipped at the fresh creek and looked around. Other mares grazed in the distance, some alone and others in small groups. "I've lost my foal, and there are none here. Where am I? Why do lions work for you?"

Shadow ignored her questions, her scent distracting him. Losing her foal would bring her into season soon. "What's your name?"

"Lily. I'm Wood Lily. Of Hawk Plains." She moved away, ignoring the sweetgrass along the bank. "My stallion is King Socks. He'll send warriors."

Shadow curled his upper lip. "I'm sure that's true, which is why I'm satisfied my stealthcats will be well fed. So, Wood Lily of Eagle's Peak, now *I* am your king."

Lily kept her distance, casting furtive glances between him and the other mares. In between mouthfuls, she continued to fight with words. "I've never heard of you. You haven't negotiated for me. King Socks will kill any who oppose him."

Anger flared in his blood. He lashed his neck forward and bit the mare on the neck, drawing blood. "Enough of your cheek. You will obey me, and deliver me strong offspring. I will rid Equinora of all coldbloods, and the clans that attend them."

Lily's swollen udder oozed milk, reminding him of the season. He needed to accelerate the collection of mares if he was to impregnate them, so their foals would arrive next spring. That would give them time to build their strength to survive winter in the mountains.

He bit Lily again, driving her towards the other mares. "You're mine now. Don't expect help, especially from the arrogant unicorns. They will pay for my years of incarceration."

Chapter 6

Mystery's silken mane rippled like the long grasses as he cantered across the plains. With every breath, he inhaled the energy of the warm wind on his face. With every stride, he absorbed the strength of the earth. The sky encompassed the rest of the world around him, an occasional hovering bird of prey the only thing to break the endless blue. Renewed from his struggle over the mountains, he sparkled silver in the sunlight, his copper horn and hooves glinting.

He revelled in the open spaces and the speed they allowed. As much as he loved Shimmering Lake, here he could gallop as far as he desired, the endless horizon beckoning him to go faster and further. Tiny mammals scurried from beneath his pounding hooves as he broke the grasses in a wave, barely leaving a track behind him. The appealing scent of blue grama lingered in the air, his stomach rumbling even though he had no need to feed.

Laila rode with ease, even with the young wolf clutched to her chest; Paws had yet to build the strength necessary to keep up this pace. Mystery had hesitated to carry the tiny predator at first, until Laila insisted the animal couldn't be left behind. The two had formed a close bond, one that almost made Mystery jealous. Almost. He didn't really begrudge Laila or the wolf the comfort of a warm body to curl up to at night.

Paws had soon become adept at pouncing on tiny creatures such as frogs and mice—so good that Laila had to remove her amulet when the wolf was hunting as the pleas of the victims upset her. With plenty of nourishment, Paws' adult coat had come through with a healthy gloss, and her ribs had covered over. Her massive feet still looked incongruous on her spindly legs, but she was definitely growing into them. Already she could spring to Mystery's back rather than be lifted.

A change in wind slowed Mystery down. "I smell something weird. Can you see anything?"

Laila shielded her eyes as she turned in the direction Mystery indicated with a thrust of his muzzle. "No. Do you want to check it out?"

He veered towards the scent. Drawing closer, he dropped to a walk, every hair prickling, alert for danger. A faint whiff of blood mingled with something he couldn't define. He sniffed the ground, treading with care.

Paws leapt from the protection of Laila's arms and pounced on a lizard.

Unsure whether the pup was ignorant of potential danger, or showing she didn't sense any threat, Mystery broke into a trot to keep ahead of her. An area free of grass came into view. He halted in the centre and blew the stench from his nostrils. "Death. Not recent. And, I don't know... It's odd."

Bleached bones lay scattered across the bare earth. Laila slid from his back and knelt by tatters of skin. "These are people. Or rather, were." Her voice tremored, and tears welled in her eyes. "Who could have done this?"

Meda flapped next to her, her scales dull. "Not a single bone is unbroken. Even their skulls are cracked open."

Mystery nuzzled Laila's shoulder. "Go and find Paws. I'll have a look around."

"What if whoever did this is still close?" She cupped her hands either side of her mouth. "Paws! Where are you?"

Mystery pawed the ground. "The scent is old. She'll be safe."

"In that case, I'll stay." Laila wandered the killing ground, her head bent over, crouching down from time to time to touch the remains with respect.

Mystery investigated the whole area before returning to where Laila collected items from the bodies. "There's been a terrible slaughter. Are you sure you're okay? Meda has disappeared."

She stood and showed him the beads and other ornaments. "She'll find us when we leave. We should take these to identify who they were. And their clan needs to know where to come and bury them."

An odd scent lingered in the air. Mystery tracked it down to uneven, cylindrical droppings containing hair and fragments of bone. He dug at the ground with a hoof. "This looks like lion scat, yet it smells of rock. I can't make it out."

Laila squatted next to him. "My nose isn't as good as yours. Paws can smell better than anyone." She called the wolf again.

Paws bounded into the clearing and raced up, the tail and one hind leg of a vole hanging from her jaws. She crunched up the body before swallowing and licking her lips. "Is there more to eat?"

Mystery prodded the pup with his nose. "No, gutsy. Have a sniff of this and tell us what you think."

Circling the object, Paws held her head on one side, her lopsided ears waggling as she studied the scat. "It doesn't smell of any animal. It's more like home. Like the boulder our den was under."

Raising his head to stare across the vast plains, Mystery swivelled his ears to listen for anything unusual. Only the chirrup of crickets and chatter of finches mingled with the wind whispering through the long grasses across the plains. "I think we should find a copse for shelter tonight, rather than you sleeping in the open."

Before they sighted any trees, the scent of horse wafted to Mystery's nostrils. The sun had already sunk below the horizon, the warmth disappearing with it. He peered into the dusk and halted. Paws had long ago resumed her perch on his withers, and Meda had returned. "Perhaps you should dismount until we know who's ahead of us. It'll look too unusual to horses if we approach like this. Stay close, in case you need to get back on in a hurry."

With Laila and Paws on either side of him, Mystery strode on and whickered a greeting to the silhouettes ahead.

Three heads shot up as one and faced him, ears pricked. A tall, grey stallion cantered over and stopped a few horse lengths away, snorting through distended nostrils, and showing the whites of his eyes. "I'm not coming close to that wolf. Who are you?"

Mystery introduced himself and his companions. "Others of your herd sought out Diamond, the Light Unicorn. She showed us the horrors here. Do you have any idea yet what's behind them?"

The grey reared and pawed the air. "Since when did unicorns travel with a human and a wolf? How do I know they're not behind our troubles? We've heard the stories of unnatural wolves in Midlands. Is this one of them?"

Laila crouched down to wrap her arms around Paws. "She's not a bloodwolf! We mean no harm."

"A speaking person?" With a kick of his heels, the stallion bolted back to the other bachelors.

Mystery instructed Laila and Paws to remain where they were, and followed the retreating stallion at a leisurely trot.

Having re-joined his companions, the grey halted. He rolled his eyes and flicked his tail as if barely containing a desire to flee.

Mystery stretched his nose forward in greeting. "Laila, the woman, and Paws, the wolf, are my friends. Tell me all you can so I can help save the herds."

The grey stallion remained taut. "I'm Silverblade. I'll take you, but only you, to King Socks. If you truly have come to help, he'll welcome your arrival, but he won't let a wolf near the mares and foals."

"I can't leave my friends here. The wolf won't harm anyone. As you can see, she's only a pup. And you can understand Laila because of her dragon—"

"Dragon! I thought they only existed in legends. Tell me no more. Get your companions, if you must, and follow me."

With the stallions as escort, Mystery crossed the plains until they reached a large herd scattered in twos and threes in every direction. He had never seen so many horses, his parents' herd at White Water Cliffs insignificant in comparison.

Silverblade pulled up and blocked his way. "Wait here. You can't go near the mares, no matter who you are."

It didn't take long for the stallion to return with a liver chestnut who introduced himself as King Socks. "Thank you for coming. You have no idea how pleased I am to see you. I'd given up expecting help from the unicorns. Can you get my mares back?"

Mystery sensed this mighty horse contained more power than the other stallions who had gathered around. *We need to understand the threat first.*

Socks threw up his head and blinked rapidly. "Your voice is loud in my head!"

A suspicion of Mystery's strengthened. "You're a warmblood."

"A what?"

"A horse with unicorn blood. It enables you to share thoughts." Mystery cast a glance across the horses nearby. None had any outstanding features such as emerald or sapphire eyes.

Socks followed his gaze. "I thought it was only those with a close bond that could read each other's minds, like when I'm mating a mare, or a mare with her foal. But my queen, Meadowlark, and I often know what the other is thinking. I had put that down to our years of ruling the herd."

A pang of homesickness pierced Mystery's heart. He and Gem often knew what the other was about to do, even without swapping messages. "How many of your herd can you share thoughts with?"

"I've never thought about it. Wait! The missing mares! All of them, yet none of those who have been killed."

Breeze wandered over to Meadowlark, where the queen stared after Socks. "Where has he gone in such a hurry?"

Meadowlark continued to watch the king canter away. "Silverblade came for him. Visitors have arrived."

Always keen to meet new horses, Breeze peered across the sea of grass, straining to focus in the dim light. She still held on to the hope that one day Tress would join her. "It looks as if they're accompanying a silver horse with a horn, but it must be a trick of the light."

Meadowlark held her head and tail higher. "Really? Then there's hope for the herd. Thank the goddess." She trotted off to meet the stallions.

Not wanting to miss out—though she had always doubted unicorns existed—Breeze broke the herd rules, using the excuse of being the queen's protégé, and followed.

As she caught up with Meadowlark, Breeze spotted a woman walking alongside the silver horse. Horse? No! No matter how much her brain denied what her eyes saw, the horse definitely had a copper horn. He really was a unicorn! Even without sunlight, his coat twinkled and his copper mane and tail flowed like a rushing stream. Unicorns were real!

As she joined them, she picked up the smell of wolf. In an instant, all her hairs stood on end. What trick was this? Her muscles clenched. She could barely force her legs to keep moving. All her instincts demanded she flee. Fear overcame her manners. "There's a wolf! Run!"

The other horses remained standing, unconcerned. The unicorn walked over to greet her. "Don't be frightened, this is Paws. She's friendly."

"Wh...what? I don't understand." Breeze trembled from nose to tail. Only the relaxed stance of Socks, Silverblade, and Meadowlark kept her from bolting.

The king introduced her to the visitors. "Mystery and his companions have travelled far to come and help us."

The glorious unicorn reached forward his muzzle and blew in Breeze's nostrils. Heat rushed through her body as she reciprocated his greeting. "My friend, Lily, was driven away by a lion after a giant eagle stole her foal."

Mystery nickered in sorrow. "I'll do what I can to help."

Breeze accompanied Meadowlark as Socks led the way back to the herd, giving a full account of what had been happening to Mystery as they walked.

When Socks finished, Mystery told of his journey across the mountains. "We encountered the remains of people on our way here. Their deaths must have been horrible. There was little left except their coverings."

The woman striding beside Mystery placed her hand on his withers to halt him. She spoke to Socks. "I must find your clan. Where is their village?"

A person who talked? This must be a dream—first a unicorn, then a friendly wolf, and now a talking human! She nipped herself. It hurt.

When neither Socks nor Meadowlark answered Mystery, only looking at each other in confusion, Breeze decided to see where this dream would lead. "The people here wander like we do. We rarely see them. The ones I lived with at Flowering Valley groomed us and put out feed in winter. I miss them."

Mystery looked at her with interest. "You're originally from Flowering Valley? Maybe you know my mother. She's now Queen Silken Tresses of White Water Cliffs."

This dream felt so real, but for the unicorn to say her best friend was his dam proved it was false. How could a horse give birth to a unicorn? Her imagination was playing tricks, brought on by her missing Tress and Lily. She galloped away from them all, hoping to jolt herself awake. She gasped for breath. Sweat streamed down her chest. Dream or not, she couldn't keep up this pace. She slowed. And for a dream, her sensations were so vivid. Maybe she had eaten something and was hallucinating instead of being asleep.

Mares huddled in small groups all around. A few stared towards the visitors as they chewed mouthfuls of grass; others cast sideways glances as they shielded their young. Shale strode towards Socks and Meadowlark where they conversed with the unicorn, the woman, and the wolf. Could this be real?

Her curiosity, and the need to prevent Shale intruding, overcame her fear. She cantered back to the group, pinning her ears back as she cut Shale off, making it clear the blue roan wasn't welcome.

She composed herself as she neared the leaders, showing off by trotting with her knees high, maintaining long moments of suspension between strides, and slinging her tail over her back. "Sorry, I think I must have been stung by an insect. Do you really know Tress?"

The unicorn politely carried on as if she hadn't run away. "Yes, as I said, she's my dam. My sire is King Fleet of Foot.

Tress had always believed in unicorns. Now she was a queen and had sired a magnificent colt. "But Tress and Fleet are both black." Perturbed, her heart raced with what this news meant.

Mystery twitched his upper lip and faced away. "And Fleet's dam was chestnut. I suppose the goddess dictated my colouring. Who knows?"

That spoilt any ideas Breeze had of her own palomino colouring being special; Tress had always teased her about her belief she was a descendant of the goddess. "Do you have any siblings? Are they unicorns too?"

Socks broke into their discussion. "There'll be time later for catching up on friends and family. We must decide what to do about my missing mares. I don't want to lose any more."

Mystery agreed. "But I must take Laila to talk with the clan. The more knowledge we can gather, the better chance we'll have of solving this problem. Then I'll return and we can work out what to do. I don't believe the lions are working alone. And the droppings we found didn't smell natural."

Lions! Breeze never wanted to see another one. She sniffed the air as if they might be lurking nearby.

Smoke! She searched for the source.

Meadowlark also looked to the east.

This was no dream. Breeze quivered in fear. "Do you smell it?"

Meadowlark nudged her. "Yes. With this wind, it could be dangerous. We need to get the herd together." She set off at a trot, calling to the grazing mares.

Some of the herd must also have sensed the danger. Shale harried them, panic in their eyes, into a close bunch. Meadowlark rounded up the stragglers.

Breeze went to gather the youngsters still playing or dozing on a knoll. The slight rise gave her a better view of the entire herd. The sight shocked her. She quaked and neighed as loud as she could. "Fire! Coming this way!"

She galloped back to Meadowlark, stumbling in the tangling grass in her haste. "The front is huge! And it's moving fast! We need to run!"

Meadowlark didn't hesitate. With a shrill whinny, she summoned the remaining mares.

Socks did the same with the bachelors. This was no time for keeping the two herds apart.

The crackle of flames grew louder. The air thickened with smoke. Breeze had never known a fire to move so fast. Bolting with the herd, she performed her duty, weaving around those colts and fillies slowing down as they tired, chivvying them on with nips on their rumps.

Shale raced in front of her, cutting off her path. The bigger mare snapped at the youngsters and drove them off at an angle, flinging clods from her hooves into Breeze's face.

Breeze dodged and resumed the chase. It was her job to direct the herd, not Shale's.

Shale blocked her, driving the mares in a different direction.

Breeze stumbled, her strength fading as the load of her unborn foal swung with every stride. She struggled to keep up with the fleeing roan. Her legs didn't obey. She staggered. Radiant heat seared her hind legs. She must keep going! Never mind Shale now! Let her save whoever she could.

The fire raged, racing to catch up with her. Thick smoke choked her with every breath. Flames licked at her heels. Her tail caught alight as she raced on, blind with panic.

ystery's first concern was for Laila and Paws. "Hurry! Mount up and hold tight. I need to see how far the fire stretches."

He leapt into a gallop and raced parallel to the flames to keep out of the smoke as he thundered along the fire front. The end curved around the herd. Not wanting to risk being trapped, he galloped the opposite way.

Horses screamed and bolted in frenzy, some following their leaders and others with no sense of direction.

Mystery shrilled a warning to those heading into the flames. None had ears for his cries. The roar of the flames drowned out all sound, as much as their panic deafened them.

Steam rose from his sweat-drenched body. He galloped back the way he had come, hoping to find an end to the fire. The flames curved towards the fleeing herd in a pincer action. How could that be? Columns of smoke mushroomed into thunderheads. No wind drove the fire. Instead, stark against the black backdrop, orange flames swooped and dived like birds of prey. They dropped to the unlit grass as if pouncing on lizards, setting off spot fires before sizzling into smoke.

This fire wasn't normal. It was going to surround the mares. He needed to get them to the opening before that happened. How? His calls were useless.

Maybe some would be able to hear mind messages. *It's a trap! Follow me!*

He watched the flamehawks to determine where there would still be unburnt ground and spurted off, glad at least to feel Laila holding tight. The warm body of the wolf permeated his neck as the woman hugged Paws to him. His lungs seared as he drew breath through his nose, wishing he could breathe through his mouth like them. He started to flag.

Stupid! The fire released enormous amounts of energy. He should be absorbing that rather than running like a normal horse, desperate for every breath. He was the Fire Unicorn! This was his element! He drew in power from the flames. An image burnt on his eyes of where the fire was thickest. Seeing a gap in his mindmap, he led the way, sending out messages to any who could hear him.

A number of mares gathered to his side, gasping and running blind. They followed.

At the last moment, he understood his mistake. The gap in the encircling flames was deliberate.

A pride of lions waited, crouched in the grass. They had no scent. He tried to turn the mares.

Only two were quick enough. The remainder barged through the gap. The lions pursued them in silent bounds.

He had led them straight into the trap! He trotted in a circle to see how the remainder of the herd had fared. Far to the right, Socks had bunched a mob together on rocky ground, the flames flickering lower there than where the grass grew thick. Using his teeth and heels, the king drove the mares and youngsters hard at the flames, barging at those who resisted, to chase them through the peril.

Mystery stretched his senses to the full. Other weaknesses showed in the wall of fire. He rushed from horse to horse, using the same technique as Socks to bully them through the flames. Once they made the leap he didn't wait, moving back to drive another mob through the next gap he detected. The smell of fear and burning hair lingered wherever he trod.

The fire blazed towards the mountains. The remains of the herd stood in huddled groups, their heads down, burns covering most of their bodies. Some had fared better than others, but all would bear the horror for the rest of their lives. All the summer feed had gone.

Searching for the king and queen, Mystery found Socks hovering over a blackened corpse. He lowered his muzzle and inhaled. The charred remains were long past saving. "It's too late for her, come away."

Socks blew through his nose without looking at Mystery. "This is Meadowlark. What a way to die. I had wished her to retire as an honoured mare and live out her days in lush grasslands near a cool stream."

The king's pain seared Mystery as much as the fire. "How many others are lost?"

Socks didn't look up, his ears lank, and his eyes glazed. "I've no idea. Many, I fear, either to the fire or to the lions. If I'd known mountain cats were behind this, I would have forced the herd through the flames at the very start."

"None of us could have known. We need to regroup and work out a strategy to get back any mares still alive." Mystery nudged Socks to get him to take the lead.

"My warriors are gathering the herd and taking them to the spring. At least the water will be welcome, even if there is no grass." After a farewell whinny to his dead queen, Socks lumbered into a trot and led the way from the devastation.

Less than half the original herd gathered at the water. One or two more limped in, their injuries slowing them down. One stallion collapsed as he reached the spring.

Laila slid down to help him drink. "Meda and I will be busy tonight helping the injured. Can you keep an eye on Paws for me?"

"Of course, though she can help. Her saliva will sterilise the wounds if she licks them." Mystery had never seen such pain and destruction of life. No one had words to say, all too exhausted or hurt to even discuss their plight. His guts churned as if he had swallowed stones from the streambed. How much worse must the horses feel, losing their friends and loved ones? And now they were likely to starve, too.

He'd been no help at all, had possibly made matters worse. He must find his power! Trotting over to a bare area of loose gravel, he thrust his horn into the ground. Traces of nickel, gold and silver veined the bedrock. A thin layer of carbon coated the stones from the fire. Perhaps he could bring sustenance to the horses like Echo did.

Drawing energy from the sun, the breeze, and the rock, he concentrated the power to his horn. Nothing happened. He summoned the taste of sweet clover, succulent alfalfa, and nutritious ryegrass to mind. Nothing changed. The stones remained as stones. Damn his lack of power!

He must do something, needed to give the horses hope, if nothing else. "King Socks, it's urgent I seek the clan. They may have the ability to kill lions, better than we can."

A young chestnut stallion strode forward. "I'll show you the way."

Socks forbade him. "You're too young, Willow. I need Breeze to take over as lead mare, and she won't be able to do that if she's worrying about her only colt. Where is she?"

A blue roan strode up. "She's gone. I'll be your new lead mare."

Socks lowered his head. "Gone? Or dead? In either case, my hopes are as dead as Meadowlark. Gather the herd, Shale, until I know for certain what's happened to Breeze."

Socks called to the other stallions. "Is there a volunteer to guide the unicorn and his companions to find the clan?"

Yes, me, I just volunteered and you turned me down.

With a surprise, Mystery heard Willow's strong response. "You must have strong unicorn ancestry. That means Breeze is a warmblood, too."

Willow stared at Mystery, shock in his blazing eyes. "Is that why she's been taken? I must save her!"

These brave horses impressed Mystery; this youngster was willing to risk his life for his dam, and the old stallion had stiffened his stance, taken a grip of his sorrow, and resumed command. Mystery couldn't imagine he would have such control if it had been Gem who'd burned to death.

He shuddered. He must find who controlled these lions and created the flamehawks. It couldn't possibly be Tempest or Echo. The goddess created unicorns to protect horses, but one of their direct male descendants might desire a herd of strong warmbloods. It was the only answer. Maybe they could sow seeds of ideas in the lions' minds like dragons did to shield Gem's territory. Or did they have dragons of their own? No! Dragons would never harm horses, or any animal. They were as much Equinora's protectors as the unicorns.

He must find the king's missing mares. He must find his power and defeat whoever was behind this terror. He must find a way to prevent the goddess from returning and destroying Equinora.

Chapter 7

Laila peered in the direction Willow indicated and squinted. Triangular hide shelters rippled in the heat mirage, the crossed ends of their pole frames pointing to the blank palette of the sky. Everything appeared grey from the smoke of the wildfire that tainted the air and obscured the sun. "Perhaps I should go on alone."

Mystery nuzzled her foot against his side. "Are you sure? What if you need to flee? You don't know what might be there."

"I can see people moving around. I'll be safe." She slid to the ground and shifted her pack to ease the weight. Coarse vegetation prickled her bare legs.

Paws bounded out of cover, looking pleased with herself and licking her lips.

Willow snorted. "I wish she'd stop doing that."

Laila stroked the young stallion's neck to settle him, and chuckled at the antics of the pup. "Maybe horses should have amulets so they can converse with wolves. Don't worry, she can come with me."

She left the two equines to graze, and strode towards the dwellings. As she neared the encampment, she called out and waved. A few people turned their heads to watch her approach without signalling back.

A scrawny lad hurtled towards her. He pulled up with a shriek as he spotted Paws. "What...? How...? Who are you?"

Laila signalled for Paws to sit, and greeted the boy. "I've come to share news with your elders. Can you take me to them?"

Paws wagged the tip of her tail. Her tongue lolled as she panted in the heat.

The boy pointed to the wolf. "Is it safe?"

Squatting down, Laila wrapped her arms around Paws' neck and gave her a hug. "She's my friend. I rescued her in the mountains. She won't hurt you." In fact, she had no idea how the young wolf would behave among a lot of people. The pup had grown a lot and learnt to fend for herself. She may well steal any food she sniffed out. Perhaps it would be better to visit without a wolf at her side.

Laila ruffled Paws' ears. "Go back to Mystery and Willow. I won't be long."

Paws whined and placed one of her oversized feet on Laila's knees. "I must stay with you. You're my pack leader."

"No, do as you're asked. Sometimes the pack leader has to do things alone." Laila continued to argue with the wolf.

The boy backed away in silence, and then fled.

Laila was puzzled. Of course! He would have found it odd to hear only one side of the conversation. She entreated Paws again: "You'll make it difficult for me. I'll be back before sunset."

Paws slunk away with her tail clamped between her legs and her ears down. She blended in with the dry grasses and disappeared.

Laila's heart thumped. Accustomed to the company of her animal friends, being alone on the vast plains shrank her to insignificance. No, not totally alone: Meda rode on her shoulder. At least other people wouldn't be able to see the dragon and take Laila for a dangerous spirit woman, especially with her unusual woven coverings, laced with feathers.

Meda's sharp claws tightened as her own body stiffened. Entering a village reminded her too much of Bloomsvale and the tension that always hung in the air. She had been an outsider even at her birthplace because of her lack of desire to participate in gossip and care for children, preferring to be alone. There, the trees, hills, and familiarity sheltered her. There was none of that here. But she'd gain nothing by dithering. She straightened up and followed the track the boy had taken.

A strong man blocked her way, his arms folded over a muscled chest. An eagle feather hung from each of his braids. His deerskin leggings and tunic hugged his bronzed body as if they were his own skin. "I'm Chief Dohate Climber. Are you in need of help? Where's your clan?"

Holding her open hands palm upwards, Laila introduced herself with formality. "I've come from Midlands to offer aid. I'm a healer."

"Surely you haven't crossed the ranges on your own? Not even my hunters travel alone these days."

Laila didn't want to lie, but didn't want to tell this man about her unusual companions just yet. "There are no other people with me. I know there are many dangers facing us all, which is why I'm here."

The chief nodded. "What you say is true, though I can't see how one woman will help, even a healer who can travel unescorted in these times. From what Lonan, my son, says, I suspect there is much more to your story. I'll gather the elders and we'll hear your tale." Dohate spun on his heel and marched away.

Laila jogged to keep up. A handful of people clustered around the dwellings, their drawn faces doing little to welcome her. She strode between the silent watchers, avoiding their gaze.

Dohate led the way to the centre of the camp where the ground had been swept clear. A small fire glowed in a ring of stones amid worn and patched shelters. A woman offered Laila a bladderskin of water to wash her hands. She freshened her face, too, and slipped off her pack.

The chief indicated for her to sit next to him and introduced his wife, Amitola Smiles, and their spiritman, Koko Skyreader. The latter didn't speak, studying her with sparkling eyes that suggested mischief rather than mysticism. Three other elders completed the circle: Hacki Storyteller, the Headwoman and Dohate's mother, her eyes glazed with blindness; an old healer woman introduced as Abey Mouse; and Paco Hawk, the pouches of a hunter slung from his belt. The hunter also said nothing, greeting her only with a glare and a sniff. The rest of the clan gathered behind the chief.

After sharing food, as sparse as it was, Dohate swallowed the last of his bread and invited Laila to speak.

She cleared her throat, stumbling over where to start. Meda perched on one of the tepee poles opposite her, encouraging her with nods of her snout. Laila drew in a deep breath. "You're right that I didn't come here alone, though I have no clan. I rode over the mountains on a unicorn."

The roar of laughter that erupted from the hunter pierced Laila like a thorn. This wasn't going to be as easy as she thought. "It's true. He's grazing nearby with a horse."

Amitola handed her a clay cup. "Here, drink some water. The plains can be a harsh place to wander at midday."

Shaking her head, Laila accepted the vessel without drinking. "I'm fine, thank you. Do your clans not know the legends of the unicorns? According to our stories in Midlands, they were the first of the Mother's creations. Surely you've heard the ballads if you've ever visited the annual gathering at Oaktown."

Hacki cleared her throat. "As storyteller, I know the songs. But they're only that, songs to entertain. No one believes them as fact."

Rather than argue, Laila took a different approach. "Have any of your clan seen mountain lions on the plains? They're taking horses and causing panic."

The hunter grunted. "We've seen the big cats, those of us who've survived. They've taken many of the clan. Good, strong men and young boys."

A murmuring rose from the people gathered behind Laila.

Dohate held up his hand. "Give our visitor a chance to speak. It's been a long time since we had news from an outsider. As strange as her story sounds, she is here, and unknown to us. Let us listen before we judge."

Laila rummaged in her pack and extracted the beads and other accoutrements she had rescued from the bleached corpses. She explained where she had found them. "Do you recognise these?"

First Dohate, then the others, ran the ornaments through their hands in silence. Each shook their heads as they passed them on. Even blind Hacki fingered the items. She placed one on her tongue. "These are not from our clan. Perhaps Crystal Springs. More likely Rockston, north of the river."

The chief returned the objects to Laila. "These are totems only carried by elders. If they have been slain, the clan no longer exists. Tell us more of what you found. I would know how you came to travel with a unicorn, if your tale is true."

The sun was well down in the sky by the time Laila had answered all the questions thrown at her. Doubt still clouded the faces of the men she addressed, though the women seemed more inclined to believe her story. Or maybe they didn't want to argue.

Abey Mouse offered Laila a chance to prove her healer skills. "I'm short of herbs. The troubles have left little time for gathering. Always we move, searching for a safe place. Will you go gathering with me tomorrow? There are many plants here that don't grow elsewhere."

Laila hesitated. She didn't know the Eastland plants or their uses. Would her lack of knowledge mean the clan would disbelieve her? "First I'd like to introduce you to Mystery. He can translate for Willow to explain what the herds have experienced. But the horse isn't accustomed to people. It may be better for only one of you to come."

Rising to end the meeting, Dohate nodded. "I'll accompany you now. If this unicorn really exists, you are welcome among us. Tomorrow we'll seek answers to what threatens both people and animals."

Lonan rushed in to stand next to his father. "It's a trick! She's got a wolf! I told you! Don't trust her."

Resting his hand on his son's head, Dohate laughed. "Of course anyone who rides a unicorn would have a wolf. Don't worry, I'll be careful. Why would anyone send a woman to trick me?"

The boy's fear shone from his eyes. "They might want to capture you as ransom for food or something. We don't know that they're dead!"

Koko Skyreader also stood. "It should be me to go. You're too valuable as chief if this is treachery. If it is true, I will interpret the sayings of the animals."

Paco Hawk glared at Koko and took up a stance on Dohate's other side. "If there is treachery, it must be I who goes, the clan's fiercest hunter, not a spiritman. I'm not afraid of mythical beasts."

Dohate waved his companions down. "What is all this talk of treachery? We've never been at odds with other Eastland clans, or those of Midlands. You're becoming afraid of your own shadows."

Even Dohate's wife looked concerned, grasping her husband's arm. "Send someone else. We have no idea what magic is out there, no matter the good intentions of our visitor. She—"

Laila coughed to interrupt. "Wait here." After hours of explaining her situation, she had become frustrated with all the posturing. "I'll bring Mystery to you. That way you can all see I speak the truth."

As the clan discussed this suggestion, Meda flittered down, alighted on Laila's shoulder, and leant close to her ear. "You can't. They've disappeared."

Mystery skidded to a halt behind a giant eagle. The bird held out his golden wings and clacked his beak, hopping from foot to foot as he snatched at something hidden in a crevice. The smooth, barren rock radiated heat as Mystery clattered towards the sounds of snarling. "Stop! What're you doing?"

The eagle refused to back away, his golden eyes swirling like the dust devils that chased each other across the plains. "Eeerk! Getting dinner. Out of my way."

Mystery stabbed at the eagle with his horn. "Paws is my friend. She's not for you. There are plenty of carcasses to feast on. You've no need to kill."

Torn between concern for the wolf, and anger at her sneaking off to hunt without his knowledge, Mystery peered into the crevice to make sure she wasn't hurt. He and Willow had been grazing and sharing news of their homes when he'd noticed she was gone. After tracking her through the long grasses, he had heard yelps. Galloping in pursuit, he had left Willow far behind.

The eagle stretched his wings to their full span, twice as long as Mystery. Each feather gleamed gold, flashing in the sunlight. "Corpses for stealthcats, eeerk! I like fresh, not charred."

"You're not having this wolf." Mystery's heart pounded. Nothing had prepared him for an outsized bird of prey. He reared and lashed out with his hooves. "Who are you?"

Preening his tail as if he had all day to wait, the great eagle refused to leave. "Eeerk! I'm Claw. Who asks my name?"

"I'm Mystery, the Fire Unicorn. I've come east to discover what is endangering the horse herds."

The clacking of Claw's beak almost sounded like laughter. "Eeerk, I tell you. Shadow, gathering noncorn mares. Warmbloods easy to sense overhead, eeerk!"

"Shadow?" Mystery backed up. Was the eagle quoting Moon-glow's prophecy, or could he really mean the duocorn?

Claw ran his beak along the golden feathers of his wings, the vanes trilling in harmony. "Horses make good meat. Strong flavour, eeerk!"

Outrage coursed Mystery's veins. "Don't speak so! Horses are the goddess' favoured creatures. You mustn't feed on them."

Claw sprang into the air and flapped over Mystery's head. His dangling talons lashed at Mystery's neck. "Eeerk! Out of my way! Feed on wolf or horse! Maybe even unicorn!"

Had one of Shadow's offspring taken his name? Mystery must know more. He couldn't let the eagle go. The crackle of flames and the smell of smoke blew over the rocky outcrop. He sensed the sedimentary layers warming and cracking through his hooves. The world spun on its axis beneath him, the power rising up his legs and feeding his anger. He reared at the tormenting eagle, and struck with his horn. He gnashed at the golden tail feathers and grasped one with his teeth. The metal on his tongue tingled and sent a shockwave of energy through his veins. Blinded by the power, and struggling to hold Claw, he released the bird.

The eagle soared away, climbing rapidly on the updraught of the fire, his mournful cry lingering in the air.

Paws slunk from her hiding place. "Has it gone?"

Mystery checked the wolf had no injuries. She was shaken but unhurt. He urged her to leap onto his back. "The fire is closing. We need to get away."

Paws settled along his spine, digging her claws into his sides and grasping a mouthful of mane.

Which direction would be safest? His eyes stung and his lungs burned from thick smoke. No natural fire could travel so fast, and there was little wind. Flames encompassed the rocks. "Get back in the crevice!"

Paws didn't need to be told twice. She leapt to the ground and squeezed into the hideaway as a spiral of embers like Claw's eyes twisted across the rock.

Sparks fell in the dry grasses between the cracks. Mystery leapt from one to the other, stamping them out. Embers alighted on his skin, singeing his silver coat. He reared and screamed. If only he could control the weather like Tempest! He called on the goddess to create a storm to douse the fire.

No clouds appeared. The smoke thickened.

Digging his hooves into the rock, he drew in strength from the wind, summoned power from the carbon in the smoke, and pulled energy from the shifting tectonic plates of the earth.

Nothing happened. The fire blazed all around him.

A flapping sounded above the roar of flames. A suffocating shadow enveloped him, blocking the heat. Had Claw returned to feast? Or was this the shadow of the prophecy? Dread cooled him with the darkening shade.

It wasn't the eagle.

A giant, crimson dragon landed at the edge of the rocks, his scales brightening as flames licked over him. A tongue of fire streamed from the creature's snout, twisting on the hot air currents and coiling around them both. "Enjoy the wondrous energy of fire and sun and heat! Never be cold oh so cold the warmth it makes me glow and gives me strength!"

Mystery only knew dragons like Tatuk and Meda. Like the rest of those at Shimmering Lake, they were tiny in comparison to this monster. He stared in awe at the creature before him. "Who are you? Why are you setting fire to the grasslands?"

The dragon pointed his snout to the sky and cackled like the crackling fire. "Setting fire ablaze to burn and release that wonderful energy from life fed by the sun, ablaze, ablaze, burn! Blaze I am and blaze I will and warm the flesh feed to surge high, high in the sky my paradise!"

Mystery stepped back until he bridged the gap in the rocks where Paws hid. "I don't damage the land to draw on Equinora's energy."

"Blaze, burn, fire, feed, how different is that to what you draw from the water's flow and sap rising and wind blowing? You feed on that which trees tap into the earth and steal their source their lifeblood their energy. How are you so different to me to mine to drawing on fire to thrive survive feast and prosper?" The great dragon continued to fan the fire with his wings, the smoke and heat absorbing into his flesh as he danced through the flames. The scales that coated his body, from his serrated neck to the tip of his thrashing tail, sparkled like giant rubies. Even his eyes glowed with scarlet whirls. He pranced around the border of the rocks.

Mystery spun on his hindquarters in order to keep facing him. Pieces of the puzzle came together. "You help Claw by creating the fires to drive the horses."

Blaze stopped his antics and glared at Mystery. "Fires that drive and burn and feed with mighty power of the goddess my mother my beloved golden flying beauty. Her feathers should have been mine, mine, not that beaked monstrosity who stole them to fly, fly to the sun and carry Shadow over mountains and valleys. Mine! What need does the beaked fury have of more feathers that should belong to dragons? Gold and feathers and golden feathers belong to dragons, lords of the air and flame and fire and power."

The dragon lifted into the air and soared away, scarlet wings beating in slow rhythm, wafting the flames as he departed.

Mystery gaped and choked on the thick smoke. His legs wouldn't move, yet his thoughts raced. The duocorn was alive! He had escaped Obsidian Caves with Claw's help. Shadow had created Claw and Blaze. Did other monstrous animals work for him? Mystery hadn't been prepared for creatures like these. He must find his power!

Paws crept from under his protection. She stared at the speck disappearing through the thinning smoke. "I'm glad Meda isn't like that."

Mystery nuzzled the wolf's ears. "Me too. Dragons are usually loving, kind creatures. I don't think we've seen the last of Blaze, or Claw."

Paws whimpered and slunk to her belly. "I'm sorry I went off. There were these ground squirrels that smelled so yummy."

Mystery snorted. "No doubt. But we must stick together. Hurry up and jump back on. We need to get back to Laila and Willow. That great dragon is heading their way."

Chapter 8

The lion perched in the tree above Breeze, switching its tail from side to side beneath the branch.

Flies had settled in the corner of the mare's eyes, and sweat sheened her body. She lay on her side, heaved, and grunted. Exhausted from her flight over the mountains, she only cared about delivering her foal. She closed her eyes. Her groan slipped into a sigh as a slithering mass emerged from her body. She breathed deeply and craned her neck to peek at her new baby. Alive, thank the goddess.

Breeze heaved herself up onto her front legs and lurched to a shaky stand. She couldn't afford to rest. The tiny new life flicked her ears and scrambled out of the creamy sack that had kept her fed and safe. Breeze encouraged her foal to stand, stimulating the filly with her tongue and muzzle. Proud of the long-legged buckskin, she glowed as the foal found her teats and commenced suckling.

Above them, the lion's amber eyes followed their every move.

Breeze shifted to block her foal from the predator's stare. Why hadn't the lion attacked her? It had driven her along the narrow track through the mountain pass, chasing her with hisses and extended claws. Exhausted, she had collapsed. When her contractions had commenced, the beast had climbed the tree and settled to watch. Maybe it had been waiting for the birth for an easy meal; the filly wouldn't be capable of outrunning the beast.

Breeze shuffled her feet. She would die fighting if necessary. The sun traced across the treetops, dappled light casting warm and cool patterns over her coat. Her drying hair prickled. She wanted to roll, but daren't relax.

The lion remained dormant on its perch.

Her filly alternated between sleeping and suckling, keeping close to Breeze's side as she picked at the little feed beneath the trees. Conifers blocked out most of the view of the slopes, and their needles carpeted the ground around their thick trunks. Squirrels raced along branches and shrews scurried among the tree litter while woodpeckers rat-a-tat-tatted in the dimness.

Still the cat lazed, dozing, or washing its whiskers with enormous paws.

Her filly stopped suckling.

Time to move. Breeze grazed as she wended her way along the path. Hopefully the lion wouldn't notice her leaving. She encountered a clearing and chivvied her filly along, loping across the meadow before re-entering the trees. She cast a quick glance behind. Her heart sank.

The lion padded along their trail, maintaining equidistance behind them.

Her foal trotted alongside, flicking her tufty tail and leaping in the air as insects alighted on her skin. The buckskin filly reflected Breeze's colouring, except with a black mane and tail, and the tiniest snip of black on the tips of her ears. "Your sister, Butterfly, is palomino like me, but far more delicate than you. Even Willow, your brother, wasn't as large and strong at this age. In celebration of the success of your birth, I'll call you *Chase*."

Should she turn back and try to rejoin King Socks' herd? But she had no idea where she was. She had run without thinking, safety her only thought. The fire! The screams of those trapped rang in her head. She could taste the smoke as she remembered those terrifying moments. What had become of the others? From galloping with a group of mares, she had found herself alone. Except for the lion. There had been others of its kind in the melee. Did each of them drive a mare to some distant lair?

Chase squealed.

Breeze jumped, ready to bolt. But the filly was bucking and kicking in excitement as she explored her new world. Never mind what the rest of the herd was doing. Breeze had a different responsibility now; she was no longer second mare, carrying out Meadowlark's wishes. She must find a safe place for her baby, and rest. She broke into a canter down the hillside, and checked to ensure Chase maintained the pace. "Keep up! We'll stop and feed soon."

Over the next few days, Breeze's fear of the lion lessened, though she never fully relaxed. Chase grew bolder and stronger, ignorant of the pending threat that lurked in the shadows. Breeze's attention waned as she recovered from the ordeals of racing over the mountains and giving birth. Finding food and water kept her on the move.

A pool glinted at the base of a waterfall. She trotted over and sipped at the snowmelt, her tongue numbing from the chill. Hoofprints of deer, the shy creatures she had observed through the trees, pockmarked the rim. Their trampling had partly obscured a larger footprint. Was that from a horse? She sniffed the ground. No scent remained. Perhaps she had imagined the shape in her desire for company.

Not wanting to wade through the cold water, Breeze tracked around the edge of the pool to where it overflowed into a tumbling stream. She picked her way among the stones and neighed for Chase to keep up. A narrow track veered away from the water. It might lead to open grazing. She started along it.

The lion leapt in front of her, crouching and hissing.

She stepped back and bumped into Chase. "Stay behind me!"

The lion blocked the path, snarling, growling, and swiping the air with its massive paws. Breeze lowered her head and flattened her ears. There was no point going that way. She hurried back to the pool, pushing Chase in front of her, and headed back the way they had come, up the mountain. At least the lion—

Pounce! The mighty beast leapt clean over her and landed on the track. It curled its lips and hissed, its belly slunk to the ground, its tail lashing.

Chase squealed and ran back into her legs.

Breeze shied and returned to the pool in a hurry. "We can't stay here. We'll have to cross."

Chase hesitated at the water's edge, the freezing water lapping her tiny hooves. Breeze bumped the foal's rump with her nose and drove her with her chest into the pool. The water was only knee deep. They waded across, stumbling over the slippery stones. When Chase dithered, Breeze thrust against her, propelling her on.

The soft sand gave way. Chase screamed before going under.

Breeze barged against her and shoved her along. The filly floundered, but kept moving. When Breeze's hooves hit firm ground, she bounded on in freezing splashes and scrambled out the other side. She shook off the frigid water and licked her trembling foal.

The lion remained on the far bank.

Relieved, Breeze hid among the trees to give Chase a chance to suckle. The new path headed northwest, away from the open plains that she had left far behind. At least the track continued downhill; it might lead to warmth and pasture. With her spirits lightened by having the pool between herself and the lion, and Chase's hunger satisfied, Breeze trotted off through the towering pines.

A flash of amber cut the track behind her, long tail lashing. The cat must have crossed the stream away from the pool to resume its pursuit.

Breeze broke into a canter, again shoving Chase in front. She ran down the steep slope, zigzagging along the track, dodging low branches, and jumping fallen logs. Chase flagged at her side, head low and toes catching on even the smallest twig or stone. Almost stumbling from exhaustion herself, Breeze emerged from the trees. The open space might offer some degree of safety.

The lion exited the tree line and peeled away. It loped off.

Breeze pulled up, blowing hard. Chase crumpled to the ground. Breeze's heart hammered as she sniffed at the fallen filly, ensuring her baby only needed rest. The poor thing wasn't old enough for this. Had the cat really gone? She raised her head to make sure.

An emerald valley spread before her, dotted with grazing mares. Sunlight sparkled from a stream bisecting rich pasture. A familiar red roan feasted on the fresh pick.

"Lily!"

Shadow tossed his crimson mane and held his matching tail over his back as he pranced up to the newcomer. A dark gold palomino, she had trotted over to the roan as soon as she had entered his territory at Eagle's Peak. He introduced himself. "I see you know each other. That's good."

Surprised that the mare had a new foal suckling, he studied the filly. The stealthcats had never let one live before. The buckskin stood tall and strong, her large knees and long cannon bones sure signs that she would grow into a big mare.

The filly finished drinking, and turned her face towards him.

Shadow stepped back and threw up his head in alarm. Only once before had he seen anyone with such eyes, as reflective as the obsidian of his former home, as depthless as the lava tubes that tunnelled the mountains. As black as himself.

Dewdrop.

The memory stabbed his heart. He galloped away, trying to outrun his past. Those early days after his creation, when all the unicorns herded together, had promised so much. When he had lived with Aureana and practised his powers, life had been exciting—until it had all gone wrong. That was Jasper's fault, taunting Shadow about his curved horns, implying he was evil, when Jasper's contorted horn was the abomination. And then Shadow's life had turned upside down.

He shoved away his memories of the days leading to his incarceration at Obsidian Caves. He was free now. Reaching the creek running through Eagle's Peak, he met the stealthcat who had driven the palomino here. It lapped at the water, the end of its tail twitching as it crouched, its ears pinned to its skull, and its shoulders hunched as if ready to pounce.

Shadow slowed and drew strength from the land. He shook his forelock from his eyes and advanced on the stealthcat. "Why didn't you feast on the newborn? It did well to reach here."

The stealthcat purred and licked its paws. "I want morrrre rrrrock. Then I'll savourrrr the flesh."

Shadow had agreed the stealthcats could have any coldblood horses or people as a reward for bringing him warmblood mares. He couldn't let the black-eyed filly die. "Not this one. Now she's here, she's mine. She obviously has strong unicorn ancestry. You should have eaten her before you got here."

"Morrre rrrock. I want morrre rrrock."

"You can have more soon. Claw's gone to fetch some. Until then, you'll have to wait. Go back into the forest and catch yourself a deer." Stamping his hoof, Shadow laid back his ears and snaked his neck at the stealthcat. It wouldn't do for the creature to forget who was master.

Shadow spotted the golden eagle circling overhead. He set off for the cave where the other stealthcats lived. Arriving at the same time as the giant bird of prey, he gruffly greeted several other stealthcats waiting outside the lair, drawn by the approaching eagle. Claw deposited the rocks from his talons onto the growing heap. Shadow transformed the sphalerite into rich nourishment, hot and steaming with power. The felines pounced, licking and gnawing on the altered stones. The metal within the ore enhanced their senses, particularly those of taste and smell, and masked their scent to prevent horses detecting them.

The mouth of the cave darkened, and hot air rushed into the confined space. Shadow left the stealthcats to sate themselves and stepped outside.

Claw perched on a boulder, preening his feathers.

Opposite him, Blaze ranted and raved, his scales grey and his leathery wings dry. He threw his snout to the sky and huffed out a gush of orange flame. "Give me my glorious golden feathers you thieving carrion eater that reeks of death and fumbles in the air like the rocks you carry. What do you know of how to use the goddess' gift of gold designed for fire-breathers so I can fly, fly to the sun and revel in the heat and light and wind and be the magnificent creation that I am meant to be not stuck low to the ground where I can burn, burn, burn all I must." As he hopped from foot to foot and flapped in agitation, the dragon's skin crackled and a few of his scales fell to the ground, bursting against the rock into clouds of dust, leaving raw wounds on his hide. Sores under his wings oozed stinking pus.

Claw ignored the taunts and peered at Shadow. "Eeerk! Stealthcats greedy. Not going again."

Shadow huffed. Why couldn't he create animals with better manners? His powers of enlargement always resulted in something amiss. Blaze could only sustain himself by destroying other life with fire. Claw had been unable to catch enough prey to support his massive size until he'd augmented his powers of flight with the golden feathers.

"Stop it, the pair of you. I'm sick of your whingeing. Blaze, there's a stand of dead trees on the far side of the valley. Go there and burn it if you must. Claw, I need you to keep the stealthcats happy. I want to intensify the search for mares while the season is right. Get ready to search further afield at first light tomorrow. Go as far as the coast if you must. There are bound to be plenty of horses and people there at this time of year. I don't care how many you kill, just make sure the stealthcats round up all the warmblood mares."

Chapter 9

Mystery found Willow and returned to where he had split up from Laila. The wind settled, the occasional breeze shrouding the plains in swirling smoke, obscuring the direction from which the fire burned. He peered into the gloom. "How am I going to find the clan in this? We daren't wait longer. The fire must be close."

Paws crept up. "I can track her. Let me search." The wolf lowered her nose to the ground and trotted back and forth, tail held out straight behind her and one ear pricked. Her other ear still flopped over like a pup's, giving her an unbalanced look.

She gave an excited yelp. "This is where Laila headed off."

Mystery cantered over and suggested Paws lead the way. She surged off, her head raised now she had the trail, surprising him at how fast she could follow the scent. He galloped after her, Willow at his side. The bent grasses they encountered gave him confidence the trail was right.

Paws slowed. Circling, she sniffed closer to the ground and raced off again.

Mystery spotted movement ahead. "Paws, wait! I'll get Laila. You'll spook the people. I'd hate you to get hurt."

He cantered into the camp. People scurried out of his way, uttering cries that could have been surprise or disbelief. Then, with little pause, they returned to their work. Women bundled babies onto their backs and stashed clothing and utensils into sacks. Men dismantled deerskin shelters and packed their belongings onto drags. Children ferried bundles between the two. Everyone had a job to do and went about their tasks with quiet determination and efficient speed.

PAULA BOER

Mystery located Laila assisting a blind woman.

Under the elder's direction, Laila rolled skins and tightened drawstrings. She ceased her labours and ran over to him. "Mystery! Thank goodness you've come. The people are heading to the coast to get away from the fire. Do you know how near it is? Meda won't leave me to check. She said she's scared. I think she must have inhaled the smoke and become frightened of choking."

The elderly woman joined them. "I can smell horse. Is he here, this unicorn?"

"Let me introduce you. Mystery, this is Hacki Storyteller, the clan's Headwoman." Laila grasped the woman's hand and guided it to Mystery's neck. "Run your fingers up to his forehead. You'll be able to feel his horn."

Fighting the urge to flinch from the stranger's intimate touch, Mystery stood rigid. "Greetings, Hacki Storyteller. Your clan is right to pack up, but I can't advise you which way to flee. There are fires in all directions."

The old woman snatched her hand away from his head is if burnt. "It's true! And he speaks!"

"So do you!" Mystery nudged her. "My powers enable us to converse. Does that convince you who I am?"

Resuming her exploration of his face, Hacki thrummed with emotion. "Indeed, great Mystery. You are aptly named. So the fables are true. If I die tonight, I'll go to the Mother happy I've met one of her finest creations." She ran her gnarled hands back up his horn, her fingers gently exploring the spiral ridges.

The copper tingled. Mystery closed his eyes, sensing the woman's strength, and her weaknesses. Her sluggish blood flowed heavy with iron. Phlegm pooled in her lungs, clotted with pollen and smoke. Her breathing laboured with a wheeze he hadn't noticed before. He let his thoughts drift through her body, linked by her touch. The woman's hands fumbled, contorted with arthritis, and her brittle hips and knees shrieked in pain. "You need to eat more calcium for your bones."

"Calcium, what's that? What plant is it in?" Her touch moved from his horn to his neck.

"Leafy greens, perhaps. I don't know what people eat."

Hacki smoothed Mystery's mane. "No matter. I'm old. But to be granted a meeting with a unicorn! This is a miracle. I must create

82

a new story to be passed on through the generations. But not now. First we must flee."

Laila had returned to binding the deer hides. "Where to? There's no point running straight into the fire. We need to know more." She paused and laid a hand on Hacki's shoulder. "Let me get you something to eat. The dried fish you trade is good for bones."

Hacki continued to stroke Mystery. "All the stores burned. Don't worry about me." She lowered her hand, breaking the connection. "Can you do nothing to help against the fires and beasts that plague us?"

Mystery didn't want to explain how Blaze lit the fires in order to feed, or about Claw and his ability to detect horses with unicorn ancestry. He still needed to sort out the implications of their existence. "Your only hope is to get to water or rock where there is nothing to burn. I don't know this territory. Are there such places nearby?"

A strong-looking man joined them, his face glowing from exertion.

Laila introduced Chief Dohate to Mystery. After expressing the same awe at the truth of a unicorn among them, and their need to depart with haste, he confirmed their plan. "We're heading for the sea, even though it's a bit early for sardines. We don't usually go until later. The clan at Bluff don't wander as we do. They won't welcome so many more mouths to feed, but they'll assist us."

Mystery nodded his approval. "What about the forests to the north? Diamond—the Light Unicorn—has often told of the deer that run there."

"Another—" Dohate grimaced. Another unicorn? How many could there be? He shrugged off his surprise at such news, and said: "Those food sources are seasonal. Never mind, we'll survive on something. But what about the mountain lions? How do we fight them?"

Mystery hesitated, unsure what to say. Should he tackle a lion and hope to find his power? But that wouldn't do anything about Claw and Blaze, and he couldn't risk a confrontation with Shadow until he'd identified his power. "Now I've seen what's happening, I'll talk with the other unicorns. I'll catch up with you when I have news."

After explaining to Laila where Willow and Paws waited for her, and promising not to be long, Mystery sought a safe place to communicate with Gem and Diamond. He needed to be away from the threat of fire to concentrate on the message. Drawing on the power of the earth, he galloped without breathing, closing his eyes and nostrils to the blinding and choking smoke, using his hooves to guide him. He didn't slow until he reached King Socks' burnt territory. Here the air had cleared and offered a haven where he could concentrate.

He focused on Shimmering Lake and pictured Gem swimming with the aquadragons, galloping across the meadows, and climbing the surrounding hills. Homesickness snaked through his belly and clogged his throat. He shook the vision away and concentrated on what he needed to say.

Gem, Diamond, can you hear me?

The answering call didn't take long. They were together, anxious to hear from him. He summed up what had happened since his departure, including meeting Kodi, the guardian bear, and the threat of the mountain lions. *It seems Shadow is alive and has escaped.*

Diamond's gasp stabbed his mind. *How can he have survived? He must have grown in power, more than Aureana granted.*

Mystery relayed the gist of the conversations he'd had with Claw and Blaze, answering Gem and Diamond's queries as best he could.

A dragon? Gem sounded horrified. *Surely one of Aureana's special creatures can't be in league with Shadow?*

Diamond groaned. *Jasper would be heartbroken if he knew Shadow had used the golden feathers to escape. No wonder Moonglow believes that Aureana might return and destroy Equinora!*

Mystery did his best to calm them, even though the task of saving the land daunted him. *Let's not worry about the goddess yet. Do you have any idea what I can do against Claw, Blaze, or the lions?*

Gem's voice quivered between indignation and anger. *Shadow's creatures are a long way from Obsidian Caves. Where do you think he's holding the mares?*

Diamond reminded them of Moonglow's prophecy. *She said, "Beware he of Eagle's Peak." That's where Shadow's territory will be.*

Mystery's mind whirled with the notion of his great-grandsire being behind the disappearance of the warmblood mares, the slaughter of horses, and the eradication of whole clans. *Mares* couldn't survive at that spire of rock, especially not through winter. It's steep and inaccessible with no grazing. Lion country, not horse territory.

Diamond agreed. *You're right. That's probably where Shadow created his latest monstrosities. He could have herded the horses anywhere.* She paused. *Strength alone will not be enough to overcome him. Have you discovered your power yet?*

Embarrassed to admit his weakness, Mystery dithered. *I've tried all sorts of things. I can't break rock like Jasper, or control the weather like Tempest.*

Gem sympathised with him. *It'll come when the goddess decides. I expect it'll be different to any other unicorn's power, which is why I couldn't help you find it. Meanwhile, you must stop Shadow's creatures.*

But he had been powerless against the giant eagle and dragon, and had led the mares into the lions' trap. Was he really the chosen one to save Equinora?

Diamond broke into his thoughts. *Horses and people must learn to fight together, as in the bloodwolf war.*

Mystery had his doubts. *Horses and people alike are scared, and their feed is gone. They're all gathering at the coast. I fear they'll be trapped against the sea.*

Diamond refused to hear of horses and people not getting involved in solving the troubles against them. *They can't rely on unicorns alone. I'll find Yuma Squirrel, wherever he is, and bring him to teach the herds and clans how to work together.*

At least Mystery could help Diamond with this. *Yuma is with my parents at White Water Cliffs.*

Good. Meanwhile, I suggest you warn any warmblood bachelors you can find and explain their bloodlines are at stake.

I'll do better than that. Standing tall and determined to prove himself, Mystery sent out a message to all who could hear. *Answer my call, all stallions willing to fight! Together, we'll build an army of warriors to defeat those who threaten us, and rescue the mares!*

His biggest concern remained undiscussed: What if he were no more than a warmblood horse himself, not a true unicorn?

Laila's heart pounded. Mystery's news had her in a spin. Yuma was going to join them. Although she enjoyed the adventurer's company, she didn't relish losing the standing she had gained with the Eastlanders by bringing them aid from a unicorn. They would be bound to defer to Yuma rather than to her, especially as he had fought in the bloodwolf war. Then again, she didn't relish the responsibility of training and guiding these foreigners. She had already discovered their ways were very different to Midlanders.

At least one aspect she preferred was their deference for their women. As Headwoman, Hacki could even overrule the chief, and not just because she was his mother. Maybe they wouldn't ignore her when Yuma arrived. But that would add to the pressure for her to help resolve their problems. She dithered about which was better, deciding in the end it was a good thing for him to come.

After passing on the unicorns' strategy to the clan, she had wandered away with the excuse of gathering herbs, when what she really intended was to talk more with Mystery about Shadow and his beasts. She reached the spot where Willow had been grazing. She was too late. A dust cloud hovered from Mystery and Willow's departure. She caught a glimpse of them in the distance, galloping off like colts, bucking and kicking with the excitement of their mission. She didn't share their enthusiasm for the conflict ahead, and missed them already. It had been a long time since she had been without the company of a unicorn.

Meda must have gone with them. Laila had no idea why the dragon would leave, but her shoulder remained cold without the presence of her dearest friend, even with the summer heat. Hopefully, Mystery would return with the warmblood warriors soon. Already living back with a clan oppressed her, even as a guest, participating in their daily routines and following their rituals.

At least she had Paws. The wolf rested her head against Laila's knee. She ruffled the fluffy ears. With her other hand, she fingered the jade otter that Yuma had given her, hanging from her neck with Meda's ruby scale. It had been years since she'd seen him. He'd left Shimmering Lake soon after he'd escorted Mystery as a weanling to Gem, needing to get back to Waterfalls. He'd wanted her to go with him, but she had known what that would mean to his clan, and had no desire to share his bed and raise his children.

The amulet warmed, a sign Meda was nearby. Relief flooded her veins. Her hair snagged as the dragon fluttered onto her shoulder. "I thought you'd gone with Mystery."

"I wouldn't leave you! I was making sure there weren't any fires ahead while I had his protection." She folded her wings and snuck down to Laila's elbow to be cradled, a position she favoured when she felt threatened.

"What's up? You don't seem happy." Laila had grown to know all the moods of the gentle creature, and shared her pain when they healed injured or sick animals. Meda suffered even more than she did when Paws caught dinner; the dragon didn't have the luxury of removing an amulet to silence the victims' cries of distress.

Meda curled tighter against Laila's chest. "Something's not right. That giant dragon scares me. His thoughts are noisy and confusing. I can't hear him at the moment, though. There's something else."

Laila sent Meda love and felt her tiny body warm. "With many eyes we should see any danger. Stick close to me."

"But I should be protecting you."

"You're a healer, not a warrior. Cheer up, we're almost back at the clan and they'll think I'm mad if they hear me talking to you." Laila tucked the dragon under her tunic and hoped no one would notice the bulge, grateful she wasn't well-endowed like her mother. That was what suckling many children did. Laila vowed again that she wouldn't end up bearing a child every year. If she ever did find a partner, Gem had taught her which herbs prevented conception.

She resumed helping the clan pack up their belongings for the long trek. The way the shelters dismantled impressed her. Eastlanders spent most of the year on the move, only residing in permanent shelters during the worst of the winter. Even the latter option was closed to them now, their lodges at Thatchery destroyed by fire.

Paco Hawk, the hunter, stomped over, pointing to where Paws lay with her head resting on her front legs, her eyes watching Laila's every move. "You can't keep that wolf among the clan as we travel. Send it away or I'll shoot it."

Laila tensed. Meda scratched against her chest. Paws rumbled a deep growl. Clutching her amulet and sending calming signals to her friends, Laila stood as tall as she could. "If Paws isn't welcome, then I won't stay either."

Koko Skyreader, the spiritman, sauntered over, his wry smile and twinkling eyes at odds with the skulls and bones dangling from his waist. Feathers of many colours and sizes hung from a thong at the end of his braids, and streaks of ochre and chalk decorated his face and arms. He confronted Paco. "Who do you think the silver unicorn will help if Laila Otter isn't here? Do you think he'll bother to aid us if she's been chased away?"

The hunter snarled and pointed again to where Paws lay with muscles bunched. "The woman must come with us. The wolf must go. We have children and old people, too many to guard from a predator in our midst."

Anger bubbled in Laila's stomach. It was attitudes like this that had made her reject living with people. Ignorance generated fear. And rather than be educated or show concern, men became bullies. "I've raised Paws from a pup. She doesn't know other wolves. People are her pack. She's more likely to defend you than attack your weak."

Koko crouched and held out his hand to the wolf. Paws sniffed the offered fingers, then licked them. "See? The woman is right. Be glad we have animals on our side."

Kicking at the ground, Paco harrumphed. "Like the mountain lions, you mean? Be it on your head, spiritman. Don't say I didn't warn you."

Not wanting the tension to add to the clan's problems, Laila called after Paco: "Paws and I'll travel away from the rest of you. Just allow us to share your fire at night so we can be safe."

The hunter didn't respond.

Koko stood and shrugged. "The clan's safety is his responsibility as much as the chief's. You can't blame him. You're welcome to share my fire at night. I don't mix with the others."

"Thank you, but I don't want to intrude. You must have your reasons for wanting to be alone. I'll see if Abey Mouse will share her hearth with me. I think we'll have a lot to share."

As if naming her had summoned the old healer, Abey joined them, eyeing Paws with a sideways glance.

The wolf panted, her tongue lolling as if in a big grin. She didn't growl at the woman.

Abey kept her distance. "Are you ready to move to Bluff? Dohate wants us to leave while there's still plenty of light. The big cats stalk at dusk."

Chapter 10

Mystery perked up at the sight of the rolling hills ahead, having missed the varied terrain of Shimmering Lake. At first, after crossing Dragonspine Mountains, he'd been delighted at the openness of the plains. Now the flat country had lost its appeal, despite the freedom it offered to gallop forever. Besides, with Willow at his side, he had to keep his pace down to that of a normal horse. He splashed through the shallows of the river marking the boundary between Goose Fen and Elk Bank, revelling in the spray of fresh water.

Willow floundered in a deep pool behind him. Then the liver chestnut found his footing and bounded onto the bank. He shook off the water streaming from his back. "How do you always know the best place to cross?"

"Sorry, I should have told you there was a hollow off to the left." Mystery couldn't explain the ability of unicorns to feel the world beneath them. At least he had that power.

Willow trotted alongside, his ebullience returned. "Never mind, that should be the last of the rivers. This is the territory King Socks granted Blackfoot, the stallion who escorted Breeze from Flowering Valley. Even if he's not here, there should be plenty of bachelor mobs. Most of the colts head north when Socks chases them off. Only a few of us are permitted to stay as guards."

They had only encountered a few mares stolen by renegade stallions, and none of the horses had been warmbloods. Fortunately, they saw no sign the mountain lions had come this far north. As they cantered towards a copse of aspens, Mystery picked up the scent of horses. He soon spotted a small group watching them and whinnied, introducing himself and Willow. He had learnt not to bother explaining their mission to coldbloods, only sharing the news of fires and warning them to be on the lookout for big cats.

Mystery waited until he was within a few horse lengths of a pair of stallions with broad foreheads and deep blue eyes to send out a mind message. *Can you hear me?*

I can.

So can I.

Mystery's pulse raced at the strong responses. The taller and heavier stallion shone a deep sorrel, the lighter-boned one a blue roan. *I'm glad to find you. What are your names?*

The larger of the two stepped forward. "So unicorns do exist! I'm Whisper. This is my full brother Murmur. Our dam named us for our ability to communicate with her without talking."

Murmur stepped forward as he was introduced. "We heard King Socks had sent emissaries to seek help from the unicorns, but none of us really believed you were real. And in truth, if you were, we expected a mare. The legends tell of a white unicorn who visits bachelors on moonlit nights, shimmering with silver, granting pleasures."

Mystery didn't need reminding his colouring wasn't usual for a unicorn stallion. "That must be Diamond. She protects all the land east of Dragonspine Mountains."

Murmur pranced towards him. "Diamond! I'd like to meet her! I wouldn't mind starting a herd with a white unicorn."

The thought of these bachelors considering Diamond as a mate shocked Mystery. Was that because of his parentage? "She's not there at the moment." But it shouldn't have surprised him that a horse stallion would consider mating with a unicorn mare. The opposite had obviously occurred often enough, and Gem had taken lovers before him. Would she take another while he was away?

He couldn't worry about that now.

At least he had finally located two strong stallions with warm blood. "Diamond sought my help. Have you suffered from fires or giant cats here?" *I have much to share with you, but perhaps it's best if we converse alone.*

Holding his head high, Whisper barged ahead of his brother, flicking his tail over his back as he passed. "We don't have secrets. We'd never survive here like that. What's good for one is good for all."

Mystery appreciated the sentiment. It wouldn't hurt for them all to know about Whisper and Murmur's ancestry, anyway. He followed them back into the shade where the mob waited. The evening breeze carried the scent of summer leaves as he described all that had transpired since he had left Shimmering Lake. A weasel scurried around their feet, and shy deer crept close and lingered on the edge of the copse, their fawn bodies blending in with the tree trunks. Hummingbirds and woodpeckers settled in the branches above their heads to listen, too.

Willow added his side of the story.

Mystery expanded on anything relevant to the other creatures who wouldn't understand horses. The inhabitants of the forest also needed warning: fires here would be far more dangerous than on the plains. He also explained that Whisper's and Murmur's ability to use mind messages evidenced their unicorn ancestry.

The stallion brothers grew in stature. The other horses fidgeted. One mumbled through twitching lips while another pricked his ears and sighed in acknowledgement; the warmbloods would have already proven themselves strong.

Murmur interrupted. "So will we grow horns? Will we be able to fly? What other magic do we have?"

Taken aback by a horse considering he might be able to fly, like the goddess, Mystery coughed. "Nooo. I doubt you'll notice any other powers than sharing thoughts and your obvious strength. Maybe you'll live longer. I really don't know. Even my sire, who's almost pure hotblood, has no other powers."

A pinto at the back snickered. "He must have had some magic to entice your dam!"

Mystery refused to rise to the bait. "Queen Silken Tresses has no warm blood. The goddess chose me as a foal. There must be six unicorns for Equinora to be protected, but no more."

Questions flooded from the stallions amid shock that the goddess might destroy Equinora and excitement at the prospect of mares needing their protection. The more Mystery explained, the more entangled his answers became.

Willow came to his rescue by interrupting with a loud snort. "There'll be another time to share these stories."

Mystery sent him thanks, blocking out the others. "As I've said, we're here to gather all the warmblood stallions to fight."

He dipped his horn at Whisper and Murmur. "Your strength

will help save all horses, warmbloods and coldbloods alike."

Whisper blew a spray from his nostrils. "Why should we join you?" He turned from Mystery and confronted Willow, arching his neck in a show of muscle above his broad chest. "Why have you left your king to defend his mares without your strength?"

A hush fell on the group.

Willow lowered his head. "My dam, Golden Breeze, has been taken."

Mystery glanced between Whisper and Murmur. "Who is your dam? Perhaps I met her?"

"Wood Lily."

At the familiar name, Mystery flinched.

Murmur described her with pride. "She's close to Queen Meadow-lark."

"I'm sorry. She's also been taken, before Breeze even. We've no idea where they are."

Without glancing at his brother, Murmur strode up to Mystery and bowed. "In that case, count me in. I'm honoured to be invited to accompany you, and will help search for my dam."

Whisper pawed the ground. "If the stories are true, we're needed here. There's a chance fleeing mares will come this way. Now's not the time to go gallivanting off on some ridiculous adventure. Anyway, we've no proof Lily, or this other mare, are even alive. And it's years since either of us ran at Lily's side. She's no concern of ours. Let King Socks reclaim her."

The pinto who had spoken before approached Murmur. "Horses without unicorn ancestry are at far more risk than your dam. Being devoured by a lion is much worse than being driven off to some other stallion. Our priority should be to save those mares without unicorn ancestry."

Whisper tossed his head in agitation. "All mares are valuable to us. There are so few available to build new herds and strengthen the bloodlines. I'll protect them all equally, but here; I'll not go chasing off into the unknown."

A thickset bay with muscled shoulders and a powerful rump, who had been quiet until now, shoved his way between the other stallions. "You're not our leader. Don't think to make yourself king with this news of your heritage. If any mares turn up, I'll fight you for them. I was here long before you."

Mystery hadn't expected to argue with warmbloods about their mission, believing they would be keen to rescue the mares and prevent good grazing from burning, or worse, if the goddess returned. It seemed the horses couldn't grasp the severity of their situation.

Whisper and the bay stallion continued to argue.

Mystery listened to the other coldblood stallions as they wandered off to graze or went to the river to drink, discussing whether Whisper should go or not. Most of them agreed they'd fend for themselves well enough without him. Few of them liked the idea of him assuming superiority due to his warm blood.

The horses dispersed into smaller groups to continue their debates. The silhouettes of the trees merged into the night sky, and stars twinkled into view. Crickets chirruped on the bark and bats clicked overhead, swooping on moths fluttering around the glow of Mystery's copper horn.

He had said all he could to Whisper and Murmur. "Willow and I must leave soon. Will you both join us? Can you at least show us where we'll find other bands of bachelors?"

Murmur confirmed he would accompany them. "Most of the stallions wander alone. We can look for their spoor."

His brother turned his rump and lashed out a hind leg. "You're a fool. I'm staying."

Finding stallions, let alone warmbloods, proved harder than Mystery had imagined. By the end of summer, he had only gathered a small band. They had met Blackfoot, who had gathered a herd of mares, some of them warmblood. A noncorn himself, he had insisted on defending his herd rather than accompanying them. Mystery understood, although he would have welcomed the older stallion's company and experience.

Willow and Murmur became firm friends, bound together by the loss of their dams and their siring by King Socks. Mystery missed Gem and the easy companionship of another unicorn. It tired him to forever explain why he was here and what he could and couldn't do. And it never failed to hurt when horses asked him about magic.

He avoided describing the unique power of each of the unicorns. The only thing he mentioned was Moonglow's prophecy that had brought him east. The Spirit Unicorn claimed her prophecies came directly from the goddess. His very existence proved that was so; she had foreseen his creation. But she hadn't seen what his power would be. Or that he had anything special other than the ability all unicorns had—drawing strength from Equinora. Even strong warmbloods like his sire could do that, the same as using mind communication.

Mystery's search for warriors brought him back to the foothills of Dragonspine Mountains, albeit far to the north of where Kodi had directed him across Lion Pass. Clouds hovered over the ranges like hawks waiting to pounce on unsuspecting rodents. A lone eagle soared on the updraughts in hypnotic loops, circling without moving its wings. Eagle's Peak dominated the skyline, pointing to the sun as if accusing the goddess of abandoning her creation.

Why had the prophecy mentioned the spire of rock? Nothing could live there, other than an eagle, certainly not horses. Had Shadow carved out a cavern in its darkness? But that wouldn't suit warmblood mares, and the forested lower slopes offered no feed. Maybe the lions originated from caves near the peak. When he had gathered all the warriors he could, he'd lead them into the hills and investigate.

He halted at the edge of the trees with one forehoof raised, and sniffed the air. Every hair on his body stood erect. Something wasn't right. *Wait here while I check this place out.*

Well-trodden tracks led to and from the forest edge, though their coating of pine needles and cones indicated it had been a while since their last use. Mystery stepped with care and followed the trail into the trees, his ears flicking in all directions and his nostrils distended. A metallic scent lingered in the air.

His eyes adjusted to the dim light. Hairless skull fragments and smashed bones picked clean of every sinew lay scattered around a clearing. What must have once been deerskin dwellings hung from branches, torn and shredded, support poles tangled among the ruins. A central pit contained dead coals, long cold, and ashes lumped from rain. There was no sign of any other fire. Blaze had not been here.

Mystery called to the stallions, sharing that nothing threatened. He paced the perimeter of what must have been a village until they arrived. "Do any of you know this place? I think from Chief Dohate's description this must be the village they call Rockston."

None of the horses had ventured this far west. Murmur sniffed at the corpse of a child. "It must be. The only other settlement north of the river is near the coast."

Willow agreed. "If this is the work of the lions, why would they kill people? Humans can't have unicorn blood."

Mystery described the scene he and Laila had encountered further to the south when they first crossed the grasslands. "The same metallic tang lingered there. I think it's zinc. Do people use it? Or does it have something to do with the attack?"

With no one able to offer a suggestion, Mystery led them back to the open spaces. Searching for warmbloods in the mountains, where grazing was limited to small clearings in the forest, was pointless. Even if horses were able to survive there, he'd never find them.

Finding the human remains increased his worries for Laila, Paws, and Meda. He imagined Laila wandering Shale Cliffs in search of useful plants for her medicines, Paws at her heels sniffing at burrows and chasing off at the slightest hint of a meal, and Meda fluttering around offering advice or helping care for anyone in need. Not hearing from Meda should mean they were safe; the dragon had promised to communicate with him in an emergency. They daren't risk mind messages at other times, so as not to give anything away to Shadow.

He'd better head to the coast and scour the southern lands for any more warmblood stallions before venturing to find Shadow's and the lions' lair. Lost in his thoughts, Mystery ignored the coolness that drifted across his body.

A giant eagle swooped, talons open and beak clacking.

The stallions panicked, screaming and barging into each other in their haste to flee.

Mystery galloped among them. "Get to the trees!"

Willow and Murmur were the first to bolt to safety. The other stallions followed in close pursuit.

The giant eagle rose towards the sun, his feathers glinting gold and reflecting dazzling beams of light to earth.

Mystery blinked against the brilliance. "Claw! Leave my friends alone! They're not for you."

Claw plummeted down in a rush of wind. He folded his wings and alighted on a nearby boulder. "Eeerk! What are you doing, unicorn?"

Mystery pranced around the rock, his heart racing, and anger seething in his guts. "We want the mares back and the killing to stop."

"Eeerk! Hogs might fly!"

Mystery halted and stood proud, his horn pointing at Claw's chest. "These stallions are creatures of the goddess. They're under her protection and that of the unicorns."

"Eeerk, males no good, only cat food! Like people, tasty!" His cackle echoed from the pines.

"Why murder people? They don't have anything to do with horses in this part of Equinora." Why did the magnificent eagle work for Shadow?

He continued to quiz Claw. "With those beautiful feathers you could fly anywhere, do anything. You could be free and using your powers for good. Surely that is what the goddess intended, not this killing and destruction."

Claw ruffled his feathers and hopped from foot to foot. "Ugly dragon, eeerk! Blaze wants feathers! Shadow protects, eeerk!"

"And what about the people?"

"Easy prey, slower than deer or hogs. Tender, too. Clean skin, eeerk!" Claw resumed his preening, lifting one foot to peck between his talons.

The stallions peered from the edge of the forest, regrouping as silently as deer. Mystery tossed his copper mane in an attempt to keep Claw distracted. "How could Blaze steal your feathers? They're part of you now, aren't they? And wonderful they are. They look as if they've always been yours."

Claw bobbed his head before attending to his tail. "Mine, eeerk! Dragon burn me, steal feathers."

Mystery had thought a lot about the need for Blaze to feed from fire. And he couldn't see how a scaled creature could benefit from feathers, though he understood their appeal. Anything that powerful from the goddess would be a great gift.

Was that Mystery's answer to finding his powers, and why the prophecy sent him east? Maybe he needed to touch one of the goddess' feathers to discover his power. "Would you let me stroke your wing or—"

Claw flapped into the air, screeching and snaking his head as he hovered. "Keep away, eeerk! Keep away!"

Mystery backed off, lowered his head, and licked his lips. He thought of a different tactic. "I may have a way to stop the dragon wanting your feathers."

Claw landed back on the boulder. "Eeerk! Stop Blaze? Stop thief?"

"If I can get him to leave you alone, will you stop leading the mountain lions to find warmblood mares?"

"Stealthcats, eeerk! Greedy scentless lions, eeerk!"

Hope rose in Mystery's heart. "I'll keep your feathers safe from the dragon if you'll help return the captured mares to their territories."

Claw launched and flew away without answering, his beating wings raising dust as he gained height. His feathers glinted against the sun until he became a mere speck against the blue, heading towards Eagle's Peak. Was the mountain connected to Shadow? More importantly, had the eagle accepted the deal?

If so, how was Mystery going to protect Claw from Blaze?

Chapter 11

Abey Mouse proved interesting and fun company. Laila had never had a close relationship with a woman other than her mother, and that had been all about getting the chores done. There had never been time for them to enjoy braiding each other's hair or sewing fancy designs on their clothes like other mothers and daughters did. Unlike the healers of Oaktown and Bloomsvale, Abey readily shared her knowledge of the Eastland plants with Laila, interspersed with stories of people from the clan and their ailments, often making the younger woman clutch her sides in laughter. The woman's ability to mimic the aggressive hunter Paco, or the cheeky spiritman Koko, equalled her extensive wisdom of how to treat real or imagined complaints.

The two women established an easy routine, with Laila lighting their cookfire of an evening when they stopped to camp as Abey erected the hide shelter. They remained on the perimeter of the huddled tents, Paws still not accepted by many of the clan. That suited Laila. Sometimes when she had spare time, she swapped stories with Hacki, the blind storyteller, sharing those aspects of Midland's life different to those of Eastlanders. Other times she sought sanctuary away from people to have a chance to talk with Paws and Meda. The dragon had trouble accepting that Laila couldn't converse with her with clan members within hearing distance. Laila had no wish to share the secret of her healer companion, suspecting the clan would be fearful of a magic dragon even though they welcomed the presence of a unicorn.

Superstition ruled Eastlanders as much, if not more, than Midlanders. The clan refused to halt at a potential campsite if a shrub threw a strange shadow or animal tracks criss-crossed the path. The latter she could understand: no one wanted to be trampled in the night. Maybe there was a real reason to be wary of the prickly bushes that smelled of resin, though their dead limbs made excellent kindling. Whatever the reason, if one of the elders didn't like a spot, the whole clan moved on without argument, no matter how low the sun settled in the sky. Today was one of those days, with three sites being bypassed that Laila could find no fault with.

With her eyes scanning the plants underfoot for anything useful, Laila almost bumped into Abey, who had halted and was staring with shielded eyes to the north. A shimmering mirage sparkled and grew in front of them, surrounded by a cloud of dust. Small children ran to their parents as their older brothers hastened to find their fathers.

Amitola, the chief's lifemate, rushed to wave Abey and Laila forward and greeted them in a whisper. "Hurry. We must gather within the circle of warriors. Never mind the wolf. It had better come too."

As the men extracted bows from their packs, the women checked the arrows, straightening out any rumpled flights. A hush fell over the clan, an expectant fear hanging in the air.

Peering into the cloud growing ahead, Laila counted eight legs and three heads, the monstrous beast losing its brilliance as it advanced. Panic rose in her chest as Meda scratched her way to Laila's shoulder.

"She's come!"

"Who?" The dust settled.

Laila let out a sigh of relief as she saw what the dragon meant. "Diamond!" The white unicorn, with her sparkling horn and hooves, stood with a man on either side of her, gripping her mane. She recognised the squirrel-red hair of the older one in an instant. "Yuma!"

Abey grasped her arm. "What trickery is this? There was nothing there a few moments ago."

Laila tore free and raced in front of the warriors, waving her arms. "Don't shoot! It's Diamond!" As she spoke, Yuma and the other man found their feet and staggered towards her, breaking the apparition of a monster.

Yuma ran his hand through his hair and took a deep breath.

"Laila! We made it. I don't ever want to travel like that again. Give me a horse to ride any day rather than translocate with a unicorn."

Forgetting her earlier reluctance at him coming, Laila rushed forward and slung her arms around him. "It's so good you're here. The mountain lions have taken so many people and horses. Fires are destroying the land. There's a giant—"

"Whoa! Let me get my breath. Don't you think we should introduce Diamond?" Yuma straightened his jerkin and strode towards the clan, hands open palms up in greeting.

After the introductions, Diamond insisted on Laila telling her in private all that had transpired, even though the elders argued it was their story to relate. Laila shrugged and strolled alongside the unicorn, recounting all that had happened since she and Mystery had left Shimmering Lake.

By the time she'd finished, the clan had established camp and settled for the night. Her stomach rumbled from the enticing aroma of freshly baked vegetables and bread. Diamond's arrival, with people hoping a resolution to their problems was drawing near, had created a festive atmosphere.

Yuma sat with Dohate and the other elders, sharing details of how Midlanders had won the bloodwolf war. As Laila joined them, he introduced the young man who had accompanied them. "This is Nodin Farshoot."

Laila gaped. "Nodin! You've grown! Last time I saw you, you were playing tag and falling out of trees."

The young man frowned. "That was a long time ago."

Sorry she had embarrassed the son of Yuma's friend Chaytan, Laila sat next to him. "Of course. And with a name like Farshoot you've obviously proven yourself more than capable. It's good to see you. How's your father?"

The youth mumbled under his breath and turned away.

Yuma gave a slight shake of his head. "Chaytan has paired with Winona, my sister, at Waterfalls. They're expecting a child soon. Nodin volunteered to accompany me to help the Eastlanders."

"That's great. Do you think the two of you will be enough to help?"

Yuma's laughter sent tingles through her loins. "No, of course not. But we can start training the men and women who want to ride. We stopped off at the other clans before coming here. Men are crossing the mountains on horseback to come and fight. Diamond couldn't transport more than two of us."

"How can you leave Waterfalls? The lions might start marauding on the west of the mountains, too."

Yuma frowned. "You forget Diamond came for me. I could hardly say no. What would you have me do? Abandon Eastlanders to a similar fate as my family?"

Laila flinched. "But aren't you chief now? Couldn't someone else have come? You must have shared the skills with others."

Instead of responding, Yuma answered a question from Paco, who sat on his other side.

She couldn't say anything right. It had been too long since she had conversed with people, and Yuma's presence unsettled her. It would be better to talk to him alone in the morning.

Laila excused herself and headed to where Abey had set up their lodgings. Diamond had left to find somewhere to roll the sweat off her coat. Laila kicked herself for not offering to groom her. Yuma had distracted her. He was different to what she remembered, more serious, not the cheerful adventurer interested in trilling birdsong on his pipe or mimicking the actions of animals that had always made her laugh.

Maybe travelling with Diamond had also shaken Nodin from his previous cheerful self. She had lived with Gem and Mystery for so long, she'd forgotten that most people still found the presence of unicorns daunting, especially when they used their powers.

She finished her meal, cleaned up her platter, and waited for Abey to return. The healer was bound to have questions before they settled for the night.

Instead of Abey, Yuma materialised out of the dark. He squatted beside her and reached a hand to her shoulder.

Paws gave a low growl from where she lay in the shadow of the tent.

Yuma sprang up, grabbed Laila's shoulder, and dragged her upright with him. He tugged her away. "Get behind me!"

Laila staggered with the force of his pull. "What are you doing?"

Paws crouched, ready to leap, her lips pulled back over her teeth. She snarled, her black nose wrinkled, and her eyes stretched to slits.

Yuma tussled with her arm and snatched at her hand. "Laila, a wolf! What's it doing here?"

Laila waved a hand to prevent Paws from pouncing to save her. "Yuma, stop this! Paws, it's okay! You're both my friends. Let me introduce you." She tugged free of Yuma's grip and knelt next to the wolf, wrapping her arms around Paws' neck and uttering soothing nonsense.

Yuma stepped back, hands on hips. "Are you mad? How can you touch a beast like that? Let me get my arrows and shoot it."

Horrified, Laila leapt up and stood in front of Paws. "How dare you? Paws is family. She won't hurt you."

Yuma's eyes widened in horror. "Hurt me? Have you forgotten? Bloodwolves murdered my family. They destroyed my clan!"

"But Paws isn't a bloodwolf. And they were poisoned into madness." Stroking the wolf's head, Laila eased the stress vibrating through the animal's body like a tensioned bow. "She also lost her family."

"Don't expect me to forgive and forget. How do you know it won't transform into a bloodwolf? Do you know what makes the mountain lions kill people and horses?" Yuma's mouth twisted in revulsion. "Get rid of it now before you get hurt."

Shaking in anger and shock at Yuma's attitude, Laila ran her fingers through Paws' ruff. "Never! I rescued her after an avalanche. She's been with me since a pup. She's ridden Mystery. He'd never allow her on his back if she was any threat."

Yuma calmed but didn't come any closer. "Laila, I only want you to be safe. If Mystery accepts it, then I must. But if I think it's a danger to anyone, I'll kill it.

He stomped back to the central fire.

The cooler nights of the open plains became warmer and more humid the closer the clan came to the coast. Afternoon breezes hinting at the taste of salt dissipated at sunset, leaving the air muggy. Laila and Abey no longer erected their shelter at night, preferring to sleep under the stars. With little fuel to keep the cookfires burning to ward off danger, Dohate posted guards around the camp. Even the older children took turns.

Laila squatted on her heels, chewing the end of a grass stalk. Diamond hadn't stayed long, saying she had to return to Shimmering Lake. No doubt Mystery would be disappointed to have missed her, though perhaps they conversed or would meet up somewhere else.

Life wasn't the same without unicorns around. Not just the thrill of riding them, which Laila certainly missed: the very air seemed filled with magic in their presence. Even when discussing serious issues, or worrying about the threats to horses and people, the proximity of unicorns made Laila's soul swell with wellbeing. Nevertheless, she didn't regret leaving Shimmering Lake. Every day she learned something new, and she had the company of Paws and Meda.

Despite the lack of clouds, no moon shone. Laila peered into the darkness. The hairs on her neck prickled. Yet Paws lay at her side, head on her legs, and Meda huddled inside her tunic, neither of them showing any concern.

But something didn't feel right.

Laila clasped her amulet for comfort. She caught a scent on the air. Cat! But how could that be? Mystery had told Meda in a brief message of warning that stealthcats had no scent. No ordinary lion would stray so far from the mountains. Did other felines stalk the plains? If so, nobody had mentioned them. Her imagination must be playing tricks. She hummed in an attempt to squash the fear bubbling in the pit of her stomach.

A rustle from the tall grasses shushed her. She leapt to her feet but didn't cry out. She hesitated, not wanting to raise a false alarm, yet certain something lurked outside the camp.

She laid one hand on Paws' soft head and whispered for her attention. "Can you sense anything?"

The wolf rose and sniffed. "No."

Woken by the disturbance, Meda popped her head out from underneath Laila's smock. "What's happening?"

"Shhh. Something's out there. I'm sure of it."

The dragon stretched her delicate wings and settled on Laila's head. "I can't see or hear anything."

Laila picked up a stout stick and crept towards the source of the sound. Her heart pounded. She flattened the grasses bordering the camp.

She halted, one foot mid-air as if to avoid treading on a snake. "Look! A pugmark."

Paws dropped her nose to the ground and whimpered. "It's fresh, but no smell. I don't like it."

Meda flapped into the air and hovered far above Laila's head. "Stealthcat!"

Laila shrieked a warning to the clan.

Pandemonium broke out, people grabbing bows and arrows or scooping up infants. Children poked embers back to life, and boys scrambled for stones for their slings.

Enormous cats emerged all around, long curved fangs dripping saliva over lurid red tongues, ears pinned to their chiselled heads, whip-like tails lashing the air as they pounced. Their huge claws slashed at anyone within range, drawing screams from their victims.

Paws dashed at the heels of one stealthcat, stretching to nip its tendons. She ducked to safety as the great beast reeled in the air, an arrow protruding from its neck. People ran in confusion, bows twanged, and men shouted. Rekindled flames threw elongated shadows across the camp, making the stealthcats appear even more grotesque. Some women huddled with their youngest children, others wielded firebrands to protect the archers.

The air filled with cries of pain. The smell of spilled blood and viscera smothered the campsite like fog.

The attack ended as fast as it had begun.

Cries simpered to moans as people bound wounds and looked for loved ones. Laila hurried to help Abey where she tended the wounded lined up next to the central fire. Flickering light showed people's faces twisted in pain. Around the edge of the camp, men thrashed and flattened grass to create a larger haven. Someone stirred a stew and handed out bowls to shaking hands. Laila opened her healer's pouch and extracted bone needles and sinew for sewing wounds. Meda perched on her shoulder, waiting to huff her healing breath in assistance.

Laila shut her eyes to the gore and closed her mouth to cut out the stench. Relaxing her taught muscles, she focused on her job; reliving the horror of the attack would help no one. Only when they'd tended the injuries could she could think about the implications. For now, Meda needed her strength. She filled her mind with the images of the dragon tree at Shimmering Lake where Meda granted her the ruby scale; of Gem swimming in the waters, bringing sustenance to all who drank from it; and of galloping on Mystery along the shore, warm wind in her hair. With joy in her heart, she sent as much love as she could to the dragon.

Dawn had arrived by the time Laila finished tending those in need. She had stitched gashes and swabbed bites. She had administered soothing teas and rubbed in antiseptic tinctures. She had bandaged wounds, in spite of Meda's success, so as not to draw attention to the miraculous healing. Bodies lay under makeshift shelters, most now only needing rest. One man had died, too far gone even for Meda. One child was unaccounted for, presumably taken by the assault.

Meda lay curled between Laila's breasts, fast asleep, her body dull. It would take a while for her power to return and bring back the glow to her scales. What if the stealthcats attacked again?

Too tired to eat, Laila accepted a mug from Amitola and sipped at the hot tea. "How many beasts do you think there were?"

Amitola shook her head, dark shadows under her eyes reflecting how Laila must look. "Dohate says more than he could count. It was only your warning that gave us a chance at all."

Shrugging, Laila couldn't explain the unease she had experienced. "Anyone on guard would have done the same. What I don't understand is why Paws didn't detect the threat before me."

A gruff voice interrupted over her shoulder. "It's probably in league with them. I told you not to trust it."

"She certainly isn't, Yuma." Laila struggled up from her knees. She didn't want to argue. "Come with me, I want to show you something."

Leading the way to her bedroll, Laila surveyed the devastation. Packs lay strewn around people nursing their wounds. Dried blood darkened the earth. Hides lay ripped to shreds by sharp claws. Although one woman had a pot of broth simmering and another sliced vegetables, all the people wore haggard expressions. No one had truly expected the mountain lions to follow them this far east.

Paws bounded up to greet her. The wolf had been tireless in harrying the giant cats, enabling the shooters to do their job. She licked blood from Laila's arm.

Laila soothed her with a stroke. "Don't worry, it's not mine. I want you to talk to Yuma. He still thinks you're a threat despite your hard work in defending the clan."

Paws slunk to her belly and grovelled at Laila's feet. "I don't like him. He doesn't like me."

106

"I'll lend him my amulet so you can talk with him." She unlooped the thong from her neck and handed the precious jade otter and ruby dragon scale to Yuma. "Hold this."

Paws clamped her tail between her hind legs. "I don't want—"

As soon as the amulet left her touch, Laila regretted her decision. Meda winked from view. Paws' comment turned into a whine. Although Laila had become used to temporarily losing sight of the dragon when Paws went hunting, she hadn't expected the sense of loss of being unable to communicate with her while someone else could.

Yuma fingered the amulet. "How does this work?"

Laila nodded to the wolf. "She can understand you now. You'll understand her, like you do Gem, or Mystery, or Diamond, when she speaks."

Yuma clutched the pair of stones tighter. "Listen well, wolf. If you ever harm Laila, I'll come after you with arrows and fire and a wrath you'll never have dreamed of."

The conversation continued. Laila could only guess what Paws was saying.

Gradually Paws crept closer to Yuma until she sat on her haunches and lifted one front leg.

Yuma shook her paw and nodded his head.

Laila laughed, breaking the tension.

Handing back the amulet, Yuma let out a long sigh. "Okay, I'll admit she's not a threat to you, and she did help in the fight. But don't expect me to like having her around."

"You should ask Mystery to enhance your dragon scale when he comes back so you can talk with all animals too. You can already bring birds to you with your music."

"No way! I don't want to turn vegetarian. Talking to animals that have their own magic is enough for me, though it would be handy to talk with horses."

Shocked that Yuma would turn down such a gift, but unwilling to argue with him, Laila shared what had been playing on her mind: "Maybe it was my enhanced amulet that let me detect the stealth-cats."

Yuma paused before replying. "If it was, having such a thing would make it harder for me to kill them. Did you hear what any of them were saying?"

"No. I don't think they spoke. You wear one of Tatuk's scales. Are you sure you won't ask Mystery to enhance it for you?" Laila stroked Paws, pleased the rift with Yuma had been settled.

"I wouldn't want to stop hunting. Anyway, that's not important now. There's a more serious issue to address. The jade arrow tips didn't have any more effect on the stealthcats than flint."

Laila reeled. "How can that be? Surely more people would have been taken without the barrage you and the men set up."

Yuma shrugged. "We could have done that with any arrows. The jade tips made no difference that we could see. If Shadow really created the stealthcats, he's used a different method to his bloodwolves. I have no idea how we can defeat them."

With Laila's ability to detect the stealthcats, and Paws' aggressive defence of the clan, people came to accept both the stranger and the wolf in their midst. Yuma was also welcome with his experience of fighting, though Laila saw little of him. During the march to the coast, he ranged ahead with the other scouts or took his turn guarding. Laila spent even more time with Abey making medicinal preparations; the stealthcat attack had left their supplies low.

Meda regained her vigour within days as Laila sent her love and gratitude. Though their opportunities for conversing were limited, Laila always found time to have a few moments of privacy with her every day. People accepted her talking to Paws despite their inability to hear the wolf's responses. They could see the animal responded to her and rarely left her side since the attack. Some even threw scraps and bones for Paws when Laila joined the clan for the evening meal.

The stealthcats continued to stalk the clan but didn't attack again. Dohate ensured that fighters stood guard throughout the night. Laila took a shift as often as she could, especially on moonless nights.

Last night had been quiet. She'd struggled to stay awake, only Paws' company helping her through until dawn. There had been no time to rest after her shift, with Dohate keen to press on to the coast and the safety of Bluff's cliff homes. Easing her back as she cradled a basket of saskatoon berries in the crook of her arm, Laila inhaled the salt breeze that promised they were nearing their destination.

Abey chattered as they worked. "The caves will be cool, though we may have to share with others. Normally the Bluff clan vacate the smaller caves for us, but they won't expect us this early."

Laila shrugged. She could always camp on the beach. She wouldn't leave Paws outside if the Bluff clan didn't welcome the wolf. Her own cave back at Shimmering Lake was spacious and beautiful, the jade walls reassuring and intriguing. She loved their colours and textures, the grain of the stone shaping her imagination like clouds. She missed the security and peace of that refuge.

But she had done the right thing in coming east. She watched the line of men, women, and children plodding on their journey. The faces of the Thatchery clan were haggard and their shoulders slumped. No one slept well and they were hungry, the pace faster than they were accustomed to. Laila needed no reminding of the skeletons she and Mystery had encountered at the base of the mountains.

Or the goddess' threat to destroy Equinora.

She looked behind her, back to the ranges, not that she could see them so far off. What drove the mountain lions this far east?

If only Mystery would return.

Meda changed position on her shoulder. "I know what you're thinking. He must be alright. I'd know if he was in trouble."

Laila sighed. "Why doesn't he send word? It would help if I knew where he was."

"We agreed to remain silent unless there was trouble. I didn't tell him about the attack. We don't want Shadow to know, remember?"

Laila didn't respond. Abey wandered over, no doubt wondering why she was talking to herself. Paws had gone hunting, her grey coat melding with the drying stands of switchgrass as if she had never been there.

She smiled at Abey, who had a similarly laden basket of saskatoons. "Will this be enough?"

Abey nodded. "For today. We'll need more later. The fruit is good for preserving meat as well as medicines."

Laila enjoyed learning about the different plants in the east. "I see the children found plenty, too." Youngsters ran around with purple-stained mouths as if the terrors of the attack had never happened.

Abey snapped off a small stick from the nearby shrub. "The men harvest the bigger branches for their arrows. Feel this, strong and supple. Look at the straight grain. That young man who came with Yuma Squirrel will be able to craft a bow. The Mother provides, as always."

Sweat dripped from Laila's face. "Nodin has a good teacher in Yuma, like I do with you. Thank you for sharing your knowledge." She shook her hair out of her eyes. "I could do with a break. How about we enjoy this shade and have something to eat?"

With Abey's acquiescence, they settled on the ground. Laila unwrapped the hard cakes the clan ate while travelling.

Paws erupted from the tall grasses. "Run! Stealthcats!"

Laila sprang to her feet, abandoning her pack, and bolted.

"Laila!"

She jammed to a halt and turned.

Abey flailed on the ground, one hand reaching up for help. "My leg! Help me!"

Laila sprinted back to the old healer. Paws snarled and snapped at whatever moved in the grasses. Laila dragged Abey to her feet. She slung one arm over her shoulder to lend her strength. Abey hopped alongside. Paws dodged and darted to keep the stealthcat at bay.

They hurried as best they could towards a stand of hackberry trees visible over the edge of a chasm. Laila slid down the soft sides of the gully and almost fell, unbalanced by Abey's weight. They reached the trees.

Laila leant against the coarse bark and gasped for air. "Can you climb?"

Abey grimaced, sweat beaded on her forehead. "I'll try."

Laila shoved Abey from behind as the old woman scrambled up the tree, choking back her cries of pain.

The tree had a strong, low branch. Laila followed. "Paws! Get Yuma! I won't be able to hold the cat off for long!" She wrenched off a stout limb and snapped off the twigs to make a smooth handle. It was the best weapon she could improvise.

Paws bounded away, leading the giant cat with her, zigzagging through the grasses towards where they had left the clan.

Asking the Mother to keep Paws safe, Laila twisted around to Abey. "Let's hope it doesn't come back before help comes."

Abey closed her eyes, her breathing rapid and shallow. "If it does, I'll go down. While it feeds on me, you can get away."

"No!" Horrified at the idea of Abey sacrificing herself, Laila extracted a flint from the pouch on her waist. "I'll sharpen this stick. I can defend us."

The old woman shook her head. "I'm old and frail. My time is near anyway. Better for you to live."

"Don't be ridiculous. We'll get out of here." Laila whittled the end of her spear with quick slashes of the flint, chips flying in all directions.

"And what then? How can I travel with a broken leg? I'll only be a burden. It'll take weeks for me to heal, and then I'm likely to be a cripple. No, it's better I die here."

Laila refused to listen to such talk. Could she risk retrieving her pack and its medicines?

Meda flapped to a branch above Abey. "I can mend her leg if you help."

Not wanting to answer within Abey's hearing, Laila hesitated. "What then?"

The Eastlander answered instead. "You can take care of the clan."

The thought of being responsible for all the people of Thatchery, tied to their life until she could train another healer, spurred Laila to a decision. "No. We're going to fix you."

Abey shook her head and shifted position in the fork of the tree. "You'll only be extending my suffering. One of those mountain lions will creep up on me and take me anyway. Let me get it over with."

Anger replaced Laila's concern. "Hold still. This'll feel odd but you mustn't move." Grabbing Abey's knee with one hand and her ankle with the other, Laila nodded to Meda. The dragon glowed as Laila sent her love, scales glimmering emerald as power surged through her entire body. When she had totally transformed to solid green, Meda let out a long breath, the gust of air from her snout flowing along Abey's lower leg, where bone protruded from the skin.

Laila never ceased to wonder at the magic of the healing dragon. Her love grew and aided Meda as Abey's leg straightened, the bone clicking back into place and the skin healing over.

The dragon paled grey and slid back beneath Laila's tunic.

Abey's mouth fell open. "How… What… Who are you?"

Laila had known the healing would have a price. "It's not me. It's Meda. She healed you."

"Meda? Is that what you call the Mother in Midlands?" The pain on Abey's face had been replaced with suspicion and wonder, the woman's brows rising and falling like Mystery leaping over logs in the forest.

"No." Laila didn't know how much to say. "Meda is a healer. A dragon."

"Dragon? Where?" Twisting her neck left and right, Abey searched the sky as if Laila was trying to trick her, doubt fighting surprise in her furrowed brow.

Laila hesitated, grasped Abey's trembling hand, and placed it against the amulet lying warm on her chest. "Touch this. You'll see."

The shock on Abey's face confirmed the moment when Meda came into view. After her initial surprise, a smile broke from her thin lips. "Now I understand how you cured everyone after the stealthcat attack. I had been sure many would die from their injuries, yet we lost only one."

Worried that this news might pose a threat to Meda, Laila tucked the amulet out of reach. "Please don't tell anyone else." She hurriedly made up a small lie. "The dragons belong to the unicorns. Mystery and Diamond won't help if they find out you know about Meda."

Abey smirked. "Don't worry. I'll not be sharing this secret with anyone. You can trust me. This magic will ensure we have the best of everything from now on."

Chapter 12

Shadow surveyed his territory with satisfaction; his herd of mares increased with every passing moon, the stealthcats keen to benefit from his provision of sphalerite. Claw had earned his feathers, transporting more and more rocks as the felines became greedier.

Butterflies blinked ochre and charcoal wings as they hovered over the meadow, the buttercups, asters, and columbines offering a feast of nectar under the warm sun. Eagle's Peak surpassed all Shadow's expectations. The flanking mountains offered secrecy as well as protection from the harsh weather. Herbage grew in abundance, making his mares well fed and content. By now, some were sure to be in foal.

And the buckskin filly grew by the day, her powerful body developing fast. Whenever her black eyes caught his gaze, his heart thumped with bittersweet memories of Dewdrop, and of Aureana incarcerating him at Obsidian Caves.

Now he was free he would have his revenge. The time of the unicorns was past.

Chase nudged her dam and ducked beneath her belly. She was a bolshy character, full of spirit.

Shadow watched the palomino as she nursed the foal. What was her name? *Golden Breeze.* It suited her. Her coat glowed like sunlight, blooming from the rich feed. The red roan joined her and they set off at a gallop. Breeze floated like gossamer as she covered the ground, her foal kicking up her heels beside her.

The scent of oestrus wafted to him as the mares stopped at the stream. He doubted it was the red roan; he had mated with her recently and she should be pregnant. If not, it was too early for her to be in season again. It must be the palomino. Aroused, he trotted down to greet the two friends as they finished their drink. "Breeze, let Chase rest with Lily. You come with me."

Breeze stamped a front hoof. "I'm not leaving my foal. She's too young."

"She'll be safe." Shadow snorted his displeasure and nipped Breeze on the neck.

She withdrew. "I know what you want. You want us all dropping foals to feed those stealthcats. They're not having my baby."

Did the mares think he only wanted to breed cat food? "They only take the offspring of other stallions, those without the strength to cross the mountains. Any born of my blood have my protection."

"And what about Chase? She's by King Socks." Breeze's skin quivered as if biting flies were attacking her. "I must protect her."

Shadow nuzzled the buckskin filly. "No harm will come to her. She's part of my herd now. In a few years, she will also bear my offspring. Think how strong they'll be."

Her swishing tail gave away Breeze's instincts, torn between looking after her baby and mating. Her ripeness blossomed with desire, her scent strong. She fidgeted her back legs, dancing side-ways.

Shadow pressed his case. "She's a fine filly, one to be proud of. Your next foal will be even more impressive, sired of my bloodline, full of the power of the goddess. What a beautiful and powerful creature you'll have, maybe even a unicorn."

That power of temptation, combined with the drive of hormones, had proved a successful strategy for enticing reluctant mares. He galloped across the clearing, the thudding hoof falls behind him evidence that Breeze raced in his wake.

He cavorted near a pile of lichen-covered boulders and waited for her, rearing in excitement and pawing the air, his hooves flashing. He flicked his tail over his rump and strutted with arched neck, his mane and forelock rippling crimson as he pranced.

She arrived, exuding warmth from the run, eyes gleaming.

He snaked his head as he paraded around her, sunlight glinting from his twin horns. With flared nostrils, he ran his muzzle over her trembling body and whickered in lust.

She advanced with her head held high and then trotted away, rolling her eyes. She knew this game well.

He followed, energy from the land, the sun, and the wind pulsing through his body with every stride. He flexed his shoulders and danced around Breeze as she pretended to evade him. Sweat gleamed on their necks and lather creamed their chests. She swung her rump toward him, tail held aloft. Wasting no time, he mounted, grabbed her neck with powerful teeth, and thrust his hindquarters.

Make a unicorn—Equinora needed no more of those pompous fools! His mind blanked. Every surge of his loins drove his anger to breaking point, every gasp a desperate attempt to forget Dewdrop's black eyes accusing him as she uttered her final words.

With a wash of heat through every vein, he found release, sighed, and slid off Breeze's back. His memories retreated, birdsong returned to his ears, and the scent of pine tickled his nostrils. He had a new life now, one he would build as he wanted, one where no one directed his actions.

Breeze nibbled at the sweet clovers, their flowers abuzz with bees. Matching him step for step, she grazed alongside as he regained his breath. She wasn't as tall as her friend and was of much lighter build. Where did she get her warmblood from? It didn't matter. He was sure she'd produce powerful offspring from him.

A shiver ran along his spine as a shadow stole the sun's warmth. Claw circled with outspread wings, his golden feathers flashing. Breeze threw up her head and shot him a look before bolting back to her foal. He let her go, confident she'd seek him later in the day, and for the next few days.

Claw's beating wings threw a chill as he clapped them to his sides, landing on the tallest of the boulders. "Eeerk! News for you."

"Your timing leaves a lot to be desired, but I suppose it could have been worse. What news? You're looking flustered." Shadow had little control over the giant eagle, depending on the bird's loyalty and sense of obligation rather than any power to influence his doings.

"Silver unicorn, eeerk! Tried to steal feathers, eeerk! Wants the mares back."

"Is that so? He'll have to find them first. And fight me. I think they're safe." Smug with the afterglow of sex, Shadow browsed the sweet grasses, shrugging off Claw's news.

"He wanted me to join him, eeerk! Promised to keep Blaze away! Don't trust him, eeerk!"

Shadow raised his head. The unicorn might be more of a problem than he had thought.

"Eeerk! Gathering warmblood stallions. Heading this way, eeerk!" Claw ruffled his wings and hovered before descending onto the adjacent rock.

Shadow considered the possibilities. Alone, the young unicorn stood no chance against him, but a band of warmblood warriors might steal a few mares. He couldn't let them get near Eagle's Peak. His instinct had demanded the stealthcats destroy any stallions with even a trace of unicorn blood. Pity they hadn't completed the job. "No horses will defeat me. I'll take the fight to them. They'll regret they ever listened to a unicorn."

Mystery saw no further sign of Claw, or Blaze. He led the warmblood stallions from Rockston back across the plains at a steady pace. Wearing them out needlessly gained nothing, but he fretted at the lack of progress, both in returning to Laila and finding the missing mares. The Thatchery clan should have reached Bluff by now. With autumn bringing shorter days and cooler nights, he was keen to get away from the mountains. Spring would be a better time to investigate Eagle's Peak if he hadn't encountered Shadow by then, which also gave him time to find his power—if he had any.

Worries pounded his brain like his warriors kicked up dust, shrouding everything in a haze. Fire had destroyed much of Hawk Plains and little feed remained for the stallions. Which would be the best way to go?

Murmur, the blue roan stallion, knew the country. "If we follow Devil's River, there may be fresh pick along the banks."

Mystery concurred and led the stallions onwards, debating tactics for dealing with the stealthcats as they trotted over the grassy plains. Was it better to circle the beasts and attack together, or taunt the predators into chasing them individually?

Talk wasn't getting them anywhere. Mystery called a halt. "We need to develop proper plans. We need to strengthen our bodies so we're ready to fight. We need to come up with strategies for any situation."

Willow looked quizzical. "What do you suggest?"

Ideas grew in Mystery's imagination. "We'll drill at dawn and dusk every day. By the time we return to King Socks, we'll be a disciplined group of warriors."

"That sounds good, but how does that help us fight the mountain lions?"

Murmur stood next to Willow, the pair rarely apart. "I'm an experienced fighter—of horses, anyway. As to these cats, the only way to find out what works will be a real encounter."

They reached the river and found plenty of new grass, offering a good place to work. Going further was futile until they were ready to defend the herds, and the clan. If they met the stealthcats before they had trained, many of these horses would die.

Mystery developed games. The horses raced each other from standing starts, spinning around rocks and the few trees growing along the bank. They leapt to outreach each other as they reared, and displayed how high they could kick and leap. They danced on the spot as if they were trampling their enemy, pounding the ground with hard hooves and snorting in feigned anger. The stallions threw themselves into the exercises, the training a chance to compete. A few times Mystery broke up real fights before they became serious, but he let the stallions test themselves. They needed to build their courage, too.

One late afternoon, Mystery sparred with Murmur, enjoying using his muscles, though taking care not to call on Equinora's strength and overwhelm his opponent. He didn't want to discover his power by hurting one of his team.

He sensed a presence overhead.

Claw circled above him, golden wings flashing as they caught the sun.

Did the eagle guide the stealthcats? *Form a circle! Prepare for attack!*

None came.

The stallions raised dust with their fidgeting. They waited. Flies bit deep and drank the moisture around the horses' eyes. Mystery tossed his head to rid himself of the pests, straining to detect any threat on the shimmering horizon. Sniffing the air would achieve nothing. Instead, Mystery watched for the slightest movement and flicked his ears to pick up any sound.

Nothing. No, there *was* something! Vibrations in the ground. Something approached.

Mystery tensed. *Prepare! They're coming!*

Indeed! I do!

Mystery reeled from the powerful mind message. This wasn't one of his warriors. *Who are you?*

A black stallion with a crimson mane and tail appeared like a mirage. Two horns curled around his ears. His eyes flashed red. He slid to a halt and reared, neighing to the sky. Then he strode up to Mystery, his powerful neck arched. "I'm disappointed in you. Don't you recognise the voice of your great-grandsire?"

"Shadow!" Mystery stepped back, the shock overcoming his will to stand. No, he would not give way. He marched forward.

Murmur closed up behind him. The other warriors muttered and shuffled nearer.

Shadow stood proud. "Claw informs me you want the warm-blood mares back. What would a colt like you do with them? You're barely old enough to leave your dam."

Mystery matched the duocorn's stance and waved his copper horn in defiance. "Why do you make the mountain lions kill horses and people? Call them back to the mountains."

"Coldbloods are abominations and should be destroyed! And humans are no more important than the deer they hunt. Why shouldn't my pets feed on them?" Shadow advanced until his nose almost touched Mystery's, snorting hot breath and challenging him with his broad chest.

Mystery ignored the threat. "If you want mares, you should win them like any other stallion, not send lions to fight for you. They don't belong on the plains."

Shadow tossed his head and pranced in a circle, trampling the dried grass to dust. "And who's going to stop them? If I choose to enhance the power of those loyal to me, what is it to you?"

Claw continued to soar overhead.

A noisy flapping accompanied cold downdraughts. Blaze landed next to Shadow and folded his leathery wings with a snap.

The appearance of the giant dragon proved too much for Mystery's stallions. They bolted as one.

The grey dragon thrust his snout towards Mystery. "Never never never the gold for you. I know what you're after stealing my treasures so you can fly like the golden goddess when it is me mine not you that should have her feathers."

Wary of the dragon's breath, Mystery sidled away. "Blaze, why do you burn Equinora? You don't need to destroy life to feed. Dragons live on joy. Join us, and we'll sustain you with love."

Shadow raised his muzzle and whinnied. "What would you know of love? Lust, maybe. I can tell you've mated at least once. What poor mare suffered you? She must have been a weak thing of no consequence."

Mystery choked on the insult to Gem. "She's a second-generation unicorn like me. We're more powerful than you'll ever be."

Shadow shook his forelock out of his eyes and sneered. "Power? I have the power of all unicorns combined and more. What do you know of power?"

The taunt hurt Mystery more than Shadow could have realised. "Go back to Obsidian Caves before the goddess destroys us all."

Shadow reared and screamed. "I am Aureana's equal, created in her likeness, formed from her shadow. I know her like I know myself. She won't destroy Equinora."

Mystery paced and snorted, keeping a wary distance from Shadow. "You're not like the goddess at all. You distort everything that's good. Let the dragon go and join his kind. You abuse him, treating him as a slave, forcing him to murder in your name. It's not natural."

"Natural? Now I see why you've gathered these stallions around you. Gemstone won't have you. And why should she? You're as white as a unicorn mare. Do these bachelors mount you like I mount my herd?"

Mystery choked on the profanity.

Shadow flared his nostrils, their scarlet lining glistening. "You're a throwback, a nothing. You call yourself a second-generation unicorn, but both your parents were horses. Neither of them had power. Your spiral horn means nothing."

Mystery blinked. His heart thumped and his blood ran hot. The stallions who had fled crept back to gather behind him.

Blaze glowed amber, and then red at their approach. Where did he get his power?

The truth came to Mystery with a jolt. The power came from Shadow and Mystery. The poor creature fed on their hatred, maybe even from the stallions' fear, the smell of which lingered like mist on a cold morning.

How could Shadow have so corrupted one of the goddess' beautiful creations? The more Mystery's anger grew, the less he could control it. Blaze sparkled like a riverbed of rubies. He had to stop this. Let Blaze feed on Mystery's love instead. But he couldn't bring Gem to mind. Shadow's words cluttered his head like sticky spider webs.

Flames erupted from Blaze's snout. Fire formed into the shape of hawks and winged towards him. The fiery birds of prey seared his coat and scalded his face. More flamehawks emerged. They attacked the stallions, dive-bombing them.

Sparks flew.

The horses milled in confusion, unable to fight the pain, panic in their eyes.

Mystery neighed above the melee. "Run!"

Mystery led the flight across the burning grasslands. Fires sparked into existence wherever he turned. The stallions followed him like a shoal of fish, matching his every turn. Flames engulfed them, the smell of burnt hair hastening their flight. The warriors tired. He had to do something to save them. What sort of leader was he, to flee at the first sign of danger? Blaze and Claw had risen into the sky and disappeared. He had no perception of Shadow pursuing them.

But still he ran. The stallions raced in a bunch behind him, unstoppable.

Why had Moonglow sent him on this mission and Diamond insisted he tackle this alone? He could do nothing. He must find his power.

Flamehawks chased him, growing in size and number as they fed from the grasses they set alight. Horses stumbled and fell, dragging themselves back to their feet and catching up with heaving lungs and shaking legs. They couldn't maintain this pace any longer.

Mystery drew power from the earth and mapped the lay of the land. He sensed the way the water flowed, both in the river and beneath the ground, running into a lake off to his left. It was too far to reach before the flamehawks consumed them. They needed a different refuge. He searched the underlying terrain for clues. A seam of granite rose towards the fertile plains. Wind and rain had worn away the topsoil to form an exposed platform. Rock wouldn't burn, and the outcrop would be large enough to protect them all. He veered towards the haven.

The stallions blindly followed, trusting him.

And then? If they escaped the fire, would Shadow and Blaze pursue them? If he and his warriors even fled from birds of flame, what chance did they have against Shadow and his beasts?

Was Shadow correct that the goddess would never destroy Equinora? The more time passed, the more Mystery questioned Moonglow's belief in Aureana's return, and the prophecy.

Chapter 13

As expected, the Bluff clan offered hospitality to those from Thatchery, as well as expressing dismay about how the resources of the area could support so many people before the sardine run. In winter, the clan would move down the cliffs and shelter in the caves where they had easy access to the bounty of the sea. For now, they continued to forage and hunt the sparse copses whose windswept branches reached inland as if seeking to escape the harsh salt.

Like many of their customs, the Eastlanders' habit of migrating around the land differed to those Laila had grown up with. To her discomfort, Ahanu Sandskipper, the Bluff chief, invited her to a meeting of elders due to her relationship with the unicorns. So many people looking to her for answers was unnerving. Unable to refuse, she joined Abey where the senior members of both clans gathered.

In deference to the Thatchery elders, unused to the chill ocean winds, a large bonfire of driftwood crackled beneath the starlit sky. Laila kept back from the radiating heat despite the cool that cloaked her back, feeling incapable of advising on the matters discussed. She kept quiet and only offered answers when questioned.

Sitting away from the crackling flames didn't worry her. She had become accustomed to acclimatising to whatever weather she encountered. If she warmed herself too much at the fire, the coldness of the night would be more apparent when she tried to sleep.

One of the guards shouted. Men sprang to their feet.

Laila leapt up, looking for Paws. There had been no sightings of stealthcats since Yuma and a few warriors had killed the one that treed her and Abey. Not even a paw print had been seen once the clan reached the clifftops along the coast. The exposed shale offered more protection than any enclosed spaces, but the hunters of both clans still maintained a nightly vigil, the risk of attack too great to ignore. At least the greater number of people meant the women and children no longer had to be lookouts.

The guards relaxed with the clop of hooves on rock.

Laila's heart surged in the hope that Mystery had returned. Instead, horses carrying riders loomed out of the dark.

Yuma was the first to greet the newcomers. "You've timed your arrival well. We've only reached Bluff today ourselves."

A gruff voice mumbled from the other side of the fire. "… don't need more mouths to feed."

Ahanu waved the man quiet and joined Yuma. "Welcome, men of Midlands. Come and join us. There's food and drink. We're keen to hear of your journey and what you may have seen."

Laila flinched, recognising the leader of the group—her father.

Jolon slid from his mount and dragged on a rope. The horse threw up his head in agitation, the rope lashed behind his ears and around his nose.

Without thinking, Laila rushed forward to help the poor creature and reached to loosen the tangle. A blow to her head rocked her back and left her ears ringing. She staggered away and stifled a cry of pain.

"Leave be. This horse is no concern of yours." Her father growled and stooped down, lashing the horse's front legs together so it could only take short steps.

Yuma shoved in front of Laila to confront Jolon. "What do you think you're doing? Leave her alone. And release that horse."

Jolon turned his back on them. "Mind your own business, Waterfalls man. She's my daughter, and this is my horse. I'll treat them as I wish."

Yuma cast Laila a sympathetic look before stepping forward to place a gentle hand on the stallion's nose. "There's no need to tie the horses. We'll easily find them in the morning."

Jolon dug his elbow into the horse's ribs and bent down to tighten the hobbles. "Not this one. He'll disappear quicker than you can say 'bolt'."

"In that case you shouldn't be riding him. Horses are the Mother's gift, protected by her. Let him go." Yuma slid a knife from his waistband and offered the blade to Jolon.

"Since when were you my chief? You can't even protect your own clan. Go back to Waterfalls where you belong." Jolon yanked on the tethers and smacked the horse on the nose.

Laila was torn between helping the horse and arguing with her father. The stallion decided for her, escaping as fast as he could with his front legs bound, hopping with his hooves together. Blood oozed around his fetlocks from the tight binding.

Yuma grabbed her elbow and grimaced. "I'll sort something out later. You'll get hurt if you approach him now."

Unsure whether Yuma referred to the horse or her father, Laila bit back a retort and allowed Yuma to propel her to where Jolon talked with Ahanu.

The chief didn't appear impressed with him. "The unicorn claims to be our protector. Who's to say he'll continue to help us if you abuse horses? You should let the stallion go."

Jolon stood with his hands on his hips, his legs apart. "I've brought men to help against the mountain lions. If you want our aid, you won't interfere with how we treat our mounts. We can talk about what we want in return later. For now, we'd appreciate that meal you offered."

Ahanu balked but said nothing, turning away and heading back to the fire.

Horrified, Laila struggled to quell her shaking. How could men stand by and allow her father to bully his horse? But she shouldn't be surprised: no one had ever stopped him from hurting his family. To distract herself, she searched the newcomers for familiar faces. None of the others restrained their horses in any way. Some stallions carried packs rather than riders, though already two of the men had unburdened the horses and offered buckets of oats to the weary animals.

Hearing another man ask where they might find water for their mounts, Laila recognised the voice. "Delsin!"

She rushed over to her younger brother and threw her arms around his thin frame. "I never expected you to come."

Although he had muscled up since she had last seen him, he still looked as if a strong wind would blow him away, his bowed legs stunting what would otherwise have been a tall, willowy body. His unusual pale blue eyes sparkled beneath a tangled mess of black hair. "Laila! You look fantastic. Diamond said she'd seen you, but I wasn't sure if you'd be here." As he talked, he rubbed down his skewbald stallion. "This is Rocky. Isn't he magnificent? We paired up at the start of the bloodwolf war, and he's been my friend ever since."

"He's wonderful." Laila burst with questions but refrained from asking them in public. "It's so good to see you. Mystery isn't here at the moment. He's gone to gather warmblood stallions."

She helped him finish grooming Rocky, who then wandered off to graze with the other horses. She slipped her arm into Delsin's. "Come and set up your bedroll at my camp. I'll get you something to eat." Her brother's arrival made up for the unexpected appearance of their father. She led Delsin to where she and Abey had unrolled their beds, and then whistled.

Paws bounced up, her tail wagging.

Delsin snatched a knife from his belt.

Laila placed a restraining hand on his arm. "Don't worry, she's friendly." She reassured the wolf with a stroke. Paws settled on her haunches, her tongue lolling and ears pricked.

Delsin sheathed his knife, crouched down, and offered his hand to the wolf where she sat at Laila's feet. "What's your name?"

Surprised at his reaction, Laila introduced Paws to her brother. "Why aren't you wary like everyone else?"

A slow smile spread across Delsin's narrow face. "I trust you. And since Yuma healed my bloodwolf wounds, I've had a different sense of the world. I see things that others don't, and sometimes I can predict the future. You're right, this wolf is no threat."

Nodding, Laila was pleased. "The Mother has blessed you. I always thought you had a destiny other than slaving for our father."

At the mention of Jolon, Delsin frowned. "He's only accepted my gift because the elders do, and thinks it might be useful to him."

"And what about Bly?"

Paws stood and placed her front feet on Laila's chest. "I like this man. He smells nice. Who's Bly?"

Laila ruffled the wolf's neck. "Bly is my other brother." She eased the wolf to the ground and rested a hand against her stinging cheek. "Is he here too?"

"No. He's one of the lead warriors at home now. He stayed to hunt." Glancing back at the wolf, Delsin pointed to her cocked ears.

"It's as if she's listening. Tell me how you ended up with a wolf. She's beautiful."

Thrilled that at last someone else understood, Laila explained about the avalanche. "Mystery enhanced my amulet so we can talk with each other. She likes you."

"Good! I'd like to be able to talk with her, too."

They continued to catch up with family news as they made their way back to the central fire. Voices buzzed in multiple conversations, the newcomers meeting up with friends they had made from annual gatherings, or sharing their ancestry to see who they might be related to. Although people from either side of Dragonspine Mountains didn't endure the difficult crossing often, enough of them traversed the ranges for trade or to make life partnerships, so a few men from each clan knew each other.

Strips of dried venison were passed around while they waited for a meal, as well as flasks of a strong brew that had already loosened tongues. Laila introduced Delsin to Abey, and squatted next to her on a raised, flat stone. Many people talked about riding horses. The Bluff clan expressed a desire to learn, but no one knew where the bachelor herds were, let alone whether the eastern horses would participate. Laila overheard Jolon arguing with Yuma about his need to use a rope on his stallion.

Her father looked up and saw her listening. "Maybe that's what I should have done with you, tied you up so you couldn't run away. The main reason I've endured this trek is to take you home. Your mother needs you."

No way was she returning to Bloomsvale. There'd be nothing worse, and she certainly didn't intend to be under her father's control again. But she worried for her mother. "How is she?"

"Sick. You should be there helping her, not gallivanting all over the country like some madwoman." Jolon swigged from the flask in his massive hand, passing it to a man behind him rather than offering it to Yuma.

She took a deep breath. "I'm not going back with you. I'm named, and in control of my own life." She gritted her teeth and ignored the rage building in her father's reddening face, his eyebrows furled in a pattern she knew well. "I'm sorry mama is ill, but Bloomsvale has healers, and I was never welcome to join them. They wouldn't want me interfering."

He thumped his fist on his knee. "Ridiculous. As soon as we've dealt with the lions, you're coming home with me, like it or not. Now shut up and bring me something hot to eat."

Fury boiled under Laila's skin. She wouldn't stay and listen to this nonsense. Anger at her father overcame any trepidation of what might lurk in the dark. She beckoned Delsin to join her and called Paws.

Her brother left to grab his bow and quiver from her camp, rolling from side to side on his deformed legs, crippled since a small boy.

Laila watched him. "Meda, could you straighten Delsin's legs like you healed Abey?"

The dragon cocked her head on one side. "I don't think so. That's the way he is. His muscles and tendons, and all his other bones, compensate."

Disappointment washed over Laila. "Do you know what caused his problem?"

Meda hopped to her shoulder. "Lack of vitamins from not enough sunlight."

Their mother had always protected Delsin from the sun due to his pale eyes. She'd be devastated to think she might have caused his disfigurement. "So it would hurt him to be straight after all this time."

"Yes. If he broke a leg, it would heal the same as it is now."

Laila stroked Meda's back. "I understand. It was only a thought. He never complains."

When Delsin joined her, they headed away from the settlement. "Laila, I had no idea father intended to drag you home. I'm sorry. Maybe it's just the drink talking."

Letting the peace of the night soothe her, Laila halted and faced her brother. "Don't worry. I won't let him get to me. I'm not going back. I'm sorry mama is unwell, but I'm no longer part of that family. Paws and Mystery are my family now."

A claw scratched her shoulder. "And me. Don't forget me."

Nodding so that Delsin wouldn't think her mad, Laila acknowledged Meda. Having regretted revealing the dragon's existence to Abey, she wasn't ready to share her presence with anyone else, not even Delsin if they couldn't heal his legs. Not yet. Instead, she stroked Meda as if she was straightening her hair and sent the dragon a flood of love.

Paws bounded around them, wanting to hunt.

Laila removed her amulet and tucked it into her herb pouch. Not only would that prevent her from hearing the cries of anguish from any of the wolf's prey, it would remove the risk of inadvertently responding to Meda. The dragon winked out of view as the ruby scale slipped from contact with Laila's skin. As usual, she experienced a momentary loss as if someone dear had gone away, which in effect was what had happened, even though the dragon would linger nearby.

Accompanying Paws as she scurried around, her nose to the ground, Laila and Delsin meandered in comfortable companionship.

By the time they returned to their bedrolls, Laila had calmed down. It had been wonderful to catch up on Delsin's news. She was particularly thrilled for him that the Bloomsvale elders had finally accepted him as a spiritman.

Their fire had smouldered down to a few coals, the dark blotting out the rest of the camp. Abey rolled over and resumed a light snore as they crawled under their blankets. She and Abey had retained their habit of settling away from other people even with the threat of stealthcats, only partly because of Paws. Once alone, the old healer pestered her for more information about dragons and their magic. Although Laila didn't regret Meda healing Abey's leg, she wished she hadn't revealed the power of her amulet.

With the wolf's warmth stretched along her back, Laila was soon asleep.

Memories of her childhood and the beatings she used to receive filled her dreams. Nothing she did could ever please her father. She had learnt to become a shadow, a wisp of mist, always quiet. Interspersed with her old fears came dreams of Shimmering Lake and riding Mystery, galloping across the grasslands with the wind stinging tears from her eyes. Those tears became drops of pain as the image of Jolon again hovered in her mind.

Laila woke shivering, the coverings strewn from where she had tossed and turned in her sleep. Her back chilled without Paws' warmth. The wolf must have gone hunting, as was her custom at dawn when the night creatures retreated to their dens and the daytime animals emerged.

Seeking Meda's company, Laila reached to her neck to clutch the dragon's scale, expecting to find the warm body snuggled on her chest. The dragon wasn't there. As she felt her cold, bare skin, she remembered she hadn't replaced the thong around her neck after Paws had finished hunting the previous evening, too busy chatting with Delsin to follow her usual routine. Not to worry—Meda would have cuddled up on her scale nearby.

Laila reached into her healer's pouch at the foot of her bed. She rummaged for the reassuring warmth of her amulet and the reappearance of her friend.

The ruby and jade figurine evaded her. Her fingers groped, ever more frantic.

Nothing.

She tore apart the mouth of the bag and searched among the carefully wrapped herbs, the shells of unguent, and the twists of willow bark.

Nothing.

She opened her suede roll of bone instruments and checked every fold.

Still nothing. Her amulet was gone.

Chapter 14

Mystery kept to a steady trot as he led his warmblood warriors east, none chattering as they headed to the coast. The rock platform had provided enough shelter to ensure the fire hadn't injured any of them, but the dragon and flamehawks had sucked out their enthusiasm for adventure.

The faint smell of horses wafted over the lingering ash of the earlier fire where Socks lost so many mares. Was the herd still here? Mystery lowered his nose to search for fresh hoofprints. The burnt grass had been recently trampled, the charred feed churned into the dust. He quickened his pace, tracking the path of dried pellets of dung, the manure lacking the richness and bulk of horses on good pasture. A whinny ahead changed from ringing a warning to one of recognition.

Socks didn't move to meet him. When Mystery came to a halt in front of him, the old king raised his head enough to blow into his nostrils in greeting. "Have you found my mares?"

Mystery hid his horror at the sight of the stallion and his herd. Normally a king would have screamed and demanded the bachelors remain well away. Instead, Socks didn't appear to notice their presence. "I met Shadow. The stealthcats work for him…"

Telling Socks about Claw, Blaze, and the flamehawks would only add to the king's woes. "…but many warmblood stallions have joined me to fight."

Socks gazed to where his mares picked for shoots among the ash. "So you know where to go? You can get Breeze, and Lily, and the others back?"

Mystery dithered about whether to give Socks hope where there might be none, or to be honest and relate how Shadow had chased him away with ease, laughing at his heels. Mystery had no idea if the mares remained alive, let alone whether he could rescue them. "We've got to check on the people first. The fires were raging their way."

A few of the mares wandered up to listen, some with youngsters cowering at their sides. Their ribs and hips protruded, and burns covered the lacklustre coats that draped over their skeletal frames. Their dull eyes looked to him for a solution to their terror.

He turned away, unable to meet their gaze. "Why do you stay here? There must be better feed elsewhere in your territory."

Lowering his head in anguish, Socks sighed. "Mares have aborted their foals. I don't want to stress them more with a long journey."

A blue roan stepped forward. "Please, Mystery, I've tried to tell King Socks that we must move or die. Convince him to let me guide the herd north. We'll be safer by the river."

Would they? Wouldn't Shadow expect them to go there? But Claw could find them anywhere. Maybe the herd was safe now with all the warmbloods gone. He had no experience of running a herd and it wasn't his place to overrule the king. But these mares needed help.

He stepped closer. "What's your name?"

"Shale. I assisted Queen Meadowlark before she...before she—"

"Yes, it's alright." Of course. That's why Socks wouldn't leave. "Your shoulder is burnt. I'm not a healer like my partner, but I'll try to help if you let me."

Shale nodded her acquiescence.

Mystery placed his horn across her withers as he'd seen Gem do with deer. Closing his eyes, he sensed the blood throbbing through her body, strong and pure, rich in sodium, potassium, and magnesium. He drew power from the ground and imagined it coursing into the mare. He sent her love as he would feed a dragon, picturing the scald healing and hair growing.

He opened his eyes and stepped back. Clear fluid continued to weep from the wound. His heart sank. "It's worse than I thought. If you can make your way towards the coast, I'll ask Laila, the healer woman, to help you and all the others in need. I can't go slow enough for the herd, but follow my trail. I'll send her as soon as I can."

Without wanting to acknowledge his failure, he left Socks and Shale arguing over whether to move or not, and called to the warriors waiting a respectful distance away. The urgency of finding the clan drove him into a canter, his lack of power burning his mind like the fires that had tortured these horses.

Gem would gather the herd and heal them all. Diamond would translocate the worst cases to the river for good feed. Tempest would bring rain and freshen up the pasture. Echo would transform stones into nourishment. Even Moonglow might have a prophecy to find a haven for them, or reassure them that the stolen mares were safe.

He could do nothing.

Was Shadow right that Mystery had no power? The taunt of not having unicorn parents hurt more than he believed possible.

But he was the Fire Unicorn. He could draw on the strength of the earth. He had enhanced Meda's dragon scale so Laila could talk with all animals. He must have power. He did have power. He did.

The refrain drummed from his hoofbeats. He did. He did.

He just didn't know what it was. Yet.

Mystery trotted along the clifftop, the weight of his horn as heavy as his heart, stomping the shale into dust.

He threw up his head and flared his nostrils. Smoke!

Then he relaxed. The plume came from a campfire. He had found the clan, not Blaze. He broke into a canter and stretched ahead of his warriors, keen to reunite with Laila, Meda, and Paws.

Laila ran to greet him and flung her arms around his neck. "I was beginning to worry about you. I haven't had Meda to reassure me."

Waves of worry, followed by anger, rippled through Mystery. "Is she hurt? What's happened? Has she returned to Shimmering Lake?"

"No, no. Nothing like that. At least I hope not. Someone has stolen my amulet."

Paws bounded up and licked him on the muzzle.

Laila ruffled the wolf's ears. "I can't talk with Paws, or see Meda. It's awful."

The dragon alighted on Mystery's crest, her colours dull. Her tail hung limply instead of in its usual coil when she perched. He sent love to brighten her, and nudged Laila. "She's safe, she's here. She's clinging to my mane."

"Thank goodness! Please tell her I miss her."

"She knows. She can still understand you."

Laila fingered his mane as if she might encounter the dragon, but without contact with the ruby scale, she couldn't feel her either. "Of course. Life here is just so hard without her at the moment."

"Tell me what's been happening." Mystery walked alongside her as his warriors settled on a patch of sweetgrass to graze.

Her arms drooped at her sides as they strolled high above the beach, the salty breeze teasing her hair into streamers. She recounted the Thatchery and Bluff clans joining up, and the arrival of the Midlanders.

A crowd of people gathered nearby. Yuma strode out ahead of giggling children, excitement bubbling out of them as they trailed in his wake. Unable to prevent himself from showing off, Mystery reared and flashed his copper horn, spinning so that his silver coat sparkled in the morning light. The children dashed out of his way before creeping back to stare.

Yuma brushed past Laila and raised a hand to stroke his neck. "Greetings, my friend. You've grown more magnificent than ever since I saw you last."

Mystery snuffled his head. "And you are still the same Squirrel, this time gathering little people it seems."

Laughter erupted from the ginger-haired man. "They're not mine! At least I don't think so. It's good to see you again. Come and meet everyone. They're desperate to hear from you. I'll send some lads out to your warriors. They brought oats from Flowering Valley. I'm sure your army will relish the treat."

Grateful that the stallions could enjoy a decent feed, Mystery followed Laila and Yuma to where the elders waited to greet him. Paws bounced alongside, begging him to translate for her with Laila. "You'll have to wait. Come and sit near us so you can hear my story."

The sun had traversed the greater portion of the sky by the time Mystery had shared all his news with the elders and answered their questions. Although they were delighted that a band of warmblood warriors had come to help, no one knew any more than before of how to fight the stealthcats or stop the fires.

Laila had been unusually quiet during the discussions. When a lull descended on the conversation, she stood up, a sign she wanted to be heard. "Why don't we ask Eastland horses to help people, not just against the stealthcats but in good times, too? The Midlands herds guard the clans from wolf packs in return for grooming and feeding, and help with the hunts so that people can shoot the hogs that dig up the grazing lands."

Paco, the hunter, brandished his bow. "We'd be better off killing the horses and eating them. They'd provide far more meat than the elusive deer."

"No!" Laila's outrage blossomed on her face. "The Mother declared horses sacrosanct. I can't believe you'd even think such a thing. Surely Eastlanders are the same as Midlanders in that."

The Bluff chief, Ahanu, waved his hands to calm her down. "We would never breach the Mother's rules. The horses are safe. But how could they be of use to us?"

Dohate, the Thatchery chief, agreed. "We wander most of the year, so can't grow feed like you do in Midlands. And they couldn't carry us along with our tents and other belongings."

Paco paced around the hearth stones, pounding his feet into the dust as he thrust his bow in the air, his plait dancing on his back as he bobbed his head in imitation of a stallion wooing a mare. "Can you imagine horses stalking deer? Our source of meat and clothing would vanish further than we could track them."

A muttering arose from the other men, some expressing agreement, others keen to ride horses as the Midlands arrivals did. Etania Shells, Ahanu's lifemate and Headwoman of Bluff, signalled to the women. "All this talk needs feeding. Someone light the fire. We can discuss this while we work."

Without needing further instruction, people rose to undertake various jobs. Some gathered dry grasses to ignite the piles of aged manure that were the main source of fuel in this barren landscape, others opened bags of preserved meat and vegetables and sliced them on stone platters with their flints.

Laila fished in her pouch for herbs to add flavour to the meal. "I still think there's a way for people and horses to work together. The stallions are good guards and can see much further than us. Perhaps they could carry the tepee skins, like they did for bringing the supplies over the mountains."

Mystery agreed that horses and people should work together, as the goddess intended, at least until the threat of the stealthcats had gone. "This horror is shared by us all. We must find a solution."

Meda ran up his neck, flapping her wings. "Don't let them tie the horses up. They hate it. It's not right."

Not wanting to let people hear his concern, Mystery queried her using mind messages.

She told him how one of the men hobbled a stallion at night. "Oakbark hates him."

Can he see you? And talk with you? This might mean another strong warmblood could join his warriors.

"Yes, and Rocky. They're nice. Oakbark's rider kicks him in the ribs. He bucked him off. He wanted to go home. That's when the man roped him."

Mystery blurted out his anger in a spray from his flared nostrils. "Who? Who abuses a horse?"

Movement around the fire ceased. Heads turned to their neighbours. No one answered. Several pairs of eyes turned to a heavy-set man who Mystery hadn't met before. The man glared back at him.

Mystery looked at Laila and Yuma in turn. "Who has tied a horse's legs together?"

Laila nodded towards the man. "Jolon. His stallion arrived with a rope on his head, too."

Jolon leapt to his feet. "Keep your nose out of it. And you, unicorn, or whatever type of beast you are—How do we know you aren't causing the trouble? It's bad enough having a wolf among us. I don't know why you don't protect us by killing it. I'll do what I want with my horse."

Mystery snorted. "I'll not help people if horses are abused in any way. They must not be restrained, and only those willing to carry riders or goods should help."

Yuma placed a restraining hand on Mystery's neck. "Don't worry. I released the horse. He's fine. We need this man. He leads all the others from Midlands."

Meda scurried onto Mystery's poll. She settled between his ears and pointed with her snout. "He's nasty! And he's got my scale."

Only Yuma could also see and hear the dragon, due to the diamond scale gifted by Gem's dragon Tatuk. Not wanting to attract attention to her existence, Mystery hesitated. "And who has stolen

136

Laila's amulet? We came to help you, and yet you treat my friends with disdain."

Dohate came forward and bowed. "We're sorry, great Mystery. We have searched everywhere for Laila's amulet. It's not to be found. Nobody's seen it."

Jolon growled. "The stupid bitch must have lost it. She always was a useless daughter."

Mystery stamped up a cloud of dust and switched his tail. "That's not what I believe."

Yuma again tried to calm him down with a stroke. "I've challenged Laila's father about the amulet. He denies having it. I don't know what else we can do without losing his help."

Laila threw down the broken plait of rope and swept her tangled hair out of her eyes. "This won't work. The grass is too weak to take the weight."

Mystery nuzzled her shoulder. "There must be a way for horses to assist the clan transport their belongings. Maybe we should use leather? It's much stronger."

Horrified that Mystery would suggest using an animal skin to lash the wooden poles, Laila shuddered. "That'd be awful. And even if we could tie a slipknot, the horses would have to use their teeth to undo it. We can't ask them to do that."

"I know you've given up eating flesh, but once the spirit joins the goddess, there's no harm in using what remains. It's the way of the world—predators eat meat." Mystery swished his tail over his back to ward off the flies.

"But horses aren't predators." Laila trembled on the verge of tears. Everything was going wrong. Bereft without her amulet, she missed the company of Meda and being able to converse with Paws. The memory of last night's clan meeting still stung. Mystery had shared Meda's conviction with her that Jolon had her amulet. She daren't confront her father. Instead, she used the excuse of working out a harness to ignore her loss.

Yuma had undertaken to teach Eastlanders to ride. Mystery's warmbloods were happy to participate, keen to aid in anything to overcome the threat to the herds. The stallions had watched with interest when a few of the Midlanders demonstrated shooting arrows from horseback, removing the need for the stallions to attack the stealthcats with hooves and teeth. While the Midlands horses rested after their long journey, Meda went to translate Yuma's instructions for Mystery's warmbloods.

A pang of envy twisted Laila's stomach as she thought of Yuma's diamond dragon scale. The fact that he could see and communicate with Meda was both a relief and a torment. However, he still refused to let Mystery enhance the scale to enable him to talk directly with horses and other animals.

She dragged her thoughts back to the conundrum of how to attach the Eastlanders' portable lodgings to horses. Mystery waited for an answer. "I'll see if anyone has spare lashes we can try. But if the horses object, we'll have to find another solution."

She returned with several long thongs of cured deer hide that normally held the skins together on the frames. After several attempts, she managed to balance the poles along Mystery's sides. "Try walking and see how it feels."

After a few tentative steps, Mystery halted. "The poles rub my legs. What if I tow them, like the women do? Can you make a shoulder harness for me like the one you use to carry your packs?"

Worrying that dragging poles would hinder the horses even more than carrying something on their backs, Laila nevertheless constructed a series of straps to circle Mystery's neck. She joined a band around his girth so that the collar wouldn't strangle him. "See how that feels."

Again Mystery walked forward, one careful step at a time. As his confidence grew he shuffled into a trot, before pulling up. "That's an improvement, but the narrow straps cut into my neck."

It took Laila the rest of the day to fashion a thick collar from which to suspend the tepee poles without rubbing Mystery. After a few different attempts, she discovered the best way to load the poles behind him. He could canter with ease under a full load and release the drag himself should he need to. Then with a flick of his head he could remove the collar, thus ensuring that no horse need ever be reliant on a person to unharness him.

"Let's show the elders." Laila's stomach rumbled as the smell of steamed shellfish drifted their way. The riders had long since returned from their lessons and sat in various groups around the camp, many drinking as they shared their experiences, excitement mingled with jokes of sore legs and teasing those who had fallen off.

Seeing Laila and Mystery approach, Dohate and Yuma called the men together. Even the women stopped their work to come and examine the travois. Children sneaked up to pat Mystery as their parents studied the drag and harness.

Yuma placed a hand on Laila's shoulder. "You've done well. I hope Mystery can talk the horses into using it."

Dohate thanked her profusely. "If we can even have the help of one horse for each family, this will make a great difference to us. But how will we repay their help? We're not farmers. We don't stay in one place long enough to grow oats."

At his words, a muttering came from the crowd. Paco's sharp voice stood out. "I still say we'd be better off eating horsemeat."

No one shared his sentiment, most seeing the benefit of a liaison with the herds, especially those who had ridden. A woman with three young children approached Laila. "I have coney skins you could use to line the collar, and where the poles rest against his sides. It might stop any chafing."

Delighted that the clan liked the results, Laila discussed further improvements to the harness. One man suggested hardening the tips of the poles in the fire to prevent them eroding. Poles were precious items and only available north of the river or far to the west at Dragonspine Mountains. Another suggested a crupper to prevent the harness from slipping forward on downward slopes. For each modification Laila made, Mystery said whether it helped him or not. Finally, everyone was happy with the results.

Amitola handed Laila a bowl of fish stew. "I thought it was getting too late for you to cook. Come and share our meal. Abey is with us already."

Wanting to sit down and rest, and glad of the offer, Laila looked around for Delsin. "Do you know where my brother is? For a skinny bloke, he eats as much as a horse."

The chief's partner took her elbow. "He's dining with Koko, our spiritman. Leave them be. It seems they have a lot in common."

After she enjoyed a full supper, Laila went in search of Mystery and found him conversing with the other stallions. Some had agreed to tow the clan's belongings, others would only carry riders with no harness. "The elders would like to thank you. Can you spare time to come and talk with them?"

He agreed. "There's still much to discuss about what we do next."

Most of the people at the settlement had gathered around the central fire. Mothers cradled children who should have been in bed, and older ones sat quietly at the back of the circle. Mystery explained which horses would carry riders, and which would fight unaided. The allocation of stallions to help Thatchery families would happen after the stealthcats were defeated.

Koko spoke up. "Delsin and I have discussed the farming issue. With the speed that horses can carry riders, we can travel to the best land to sow oats in spring, then again in autumn to harvest. It means we can't guard the corn while it's growing, and are likely to lose much to grazing animals, but perhaps a few men could stay. It may even prove a useful way to hunt deer with the corn bringing them in."

A number of conversations bubbled up to discuss the possibilities. Dohate held up his hand for silence. "Amitola assures me that she and the other women can fashion brushes and combs to groom the horses, too. If the mare herd wishes to share these attentions, perhaps Mystery can convey our offer to the king. That way our children can grow up with his, and form bonds early like horses and people do in Midlands."

Laila could see the sense in that. She had loved grooming and playing with the colts and fillies as a girl, often being reprimanded for spending more time with the horses than tending to her chores.

Mystery conceded it was a good plan. "But King Socks' herd is in poor condition after the fires. They need Laila to help them heal." He gave her a knowing look. "Until they are well, my stallions don't want to leave them on their own. We'll only be able to take the war to the enemy when the coldblood warriors are fit to defend them."

Laila fingered the cold space on her chest. Her skills alone wouldn't be enough to cure the horses before another stealthcat attack. Would Yuma aid Meda to heal them?

Mystery looked at her again while speaking to the elders. "My warriors and I are ready to carry those who will come into battle. There is one further condition. One that if not met will mean I will leave, as will all the horses. You will be alone. No amount of grooming or promises of feed will entice us to stay."

A silence descended on the camp. After what seemed a lifetime, Hacki Storyteller crept forward, stretching out her hand to Mystery. "Tell us this final request, mighty unicorn. If it is in our power, we will grant it. In return, I request your warriors stay close at night that we might sleep. Our own guards are exhausted."

Dohate hastened to his mother's side. "Let's hear what it is before we agree."

"No, son. I invoke my right to overrule. We will do whatever guarantees the help of the unicorns and horses."

Placing his horn in the blind woman's hand, Mystery uttered his thanks and agreed his warriors would guard the clan through the dark hours until they went to war, providing his final condition was met.

The firelight flickered on his glistening coat. He reared and pawed the black night. "Laila's stolen amulet must be returned tonight!"

Gasps ran through the crowd.

Ahanu raised his hand. "But Mystery... We have no idea where it is. We would return it if we could."

Etania joined him. "Please don't abandon us. We'll do anything in our power to help. But we can't return what we don't have."

The other elders entreated him, offering him their finest treasures—magnificent shells, soft pelts, and the sweetest flowers. One even offered her daughter as a servant, to be with him forever.

Nothing would dissuade Mystery. "This is my condition. I know the amulet is here. Without its return, my warriors and I leave in the morning."

Chapter 15

An air of hushed expectation hung over the village as Mystery trotted to where Laila pounded herbs into a paste. Some people looked at him with longing, others with regret. Some people turned away or avoided meeting his gaze. He ignored them all.

Laila ran over and hugged his neck. "My amulet hasn't been found."

Sadness washed through Mystery like a creek eroding its sandy banks. His hopes crumbled and dissipated as the reality of his threat drove home. He must abandon these people to their fate. "Let's talk with the chiefs again. Maybe they know more today."

With Laila walking at his side, Mystery entered the main camp. The elders gathered in front of the fire, forming a line to greet him. Each entreated him to change his mind.

Dohate was the last. "We would return Laila's amulet to her if it was at all possible. She has become a valuable member of our community, and we would do nothing to upset her. We've no idea what has happened to the amulet."

Mystery snorted. "I told you who has it. Her father, Jolon, the man from Midlands."

Ahanu joined Dohate. "I have demanded Jolon tell me if he took the amulet, even if he has since lost it. He denies ever seeing it."

Hacki Storyteller tapped her way over on her cane. She held out a shaking hand and stroked Mystery's nose. "Great unicorn, you must be able to tell truth from lies. Challenge the man who you say has Laila's amulet, and let this trouble between us end. We wouldn't anger you by choice, regardless of our need for your help."

Mystery could see no point in questioning Laila's father again, but he would give the man one last chance. "Call him, and we'll see."

Jolon strode forward from the people gathered behind the elders. "I'm here. And before you ask, yes, I do have the amulet."

Shock ran through the gathered clans like an earthquake.

Hacki stepped towards his voice, hand held out. "I won't ask how you came by it. Return it now and no more will be said."

Fists on hips, Jolon pushed out his chest, legs apart. "I don't take orders from a woman."

A combined intake of breath rippled the air.

Dohate hastened to his mother's side. "Hacki Storyteller is Headwoman. Here in Eastlands we revere women's wisdom. You must do as she says."

A coarse laugh erupted from Jolon. "If you want help from Midlanders, you'll not challenge our customs. The amulet is mine and I intend to keep it."

Mystery struck the earth with a hoof. "It is not. Both parts were gifts to Laila, the jade otter from Yuma, and the—"

Laila grabbed Mystery's nose.

Jolon thrust a fist at her. "I'll return it when you're back home. What belongs to you belongs to me. I've every right to it."

Mystery didn't understand people's laws. It didn't matter. The amulet contained Meda's ruby scale, the one that he had enhanced. He threw off Laila's restraining hand. "You must return what is Laila's. Now. It's no use to you."

"No use? If it gets my daughter back where she belongs, instead of gallivanting alone all over the land, it's of great use. The Bloomsvale chief is getting old, has no sons left alive, and wants to hand over to someone else. How will the clan view me as a potential leader if I can't even keep my family under control?" He wagged a finger at Mystery. "Keep your long nose out of this, unicorn. It's none of your business."

Tremors of anger shook Mystery. "I make it my business. Laila is my friend and the items are hers. Without the amulet's return, I will leave you to fight the stealthcats alone."

The crowd fidgeted. A few Eastlander voices asked, begged, and pleaded with Jolon to return Laila's amulet. One Midlander murmured that Jolon had the right to possess anything belonging to his unpartnered daughter.

144

Hacki struck the ground with her stick. "Enough! The Midlander has Laila's amulet. He refuses to return it. It is for Mystery to decide his course of action."

The camp went silent.

Mystery couldn't retrieve Laila's amulet by force. It wasn't around her father's neck or in his hand. He faced her. "Can you get it back from him?"

Laila shook her head, her trembling conveying more than words, tears trickling down her cheeks.

"There'll be a way. For now, let's heal the horses. Get your medicines." He strode away from the elders without a parting word.

Yuma remained by his side, keeping pace at a jog. "Can you carry me, too? I can help Meda by using Tatuk's scale."

Mystery halted. "Your help will be welcome, but there's no need for me to carry both you and Laila. You can ride one of my warriors." He sent out a call for a volunteer.

Oakbark cantered up. *I will carry Yuma. He freed me. And I know the tales of how he rode your sire, King Fleet of Foot. I'll be proud to help him.*

Thank you. "Yuma, this is Oakbark. He has offered to carry you."

Yuma stroked the stallion's neck. "Please tell him thank you. I'm honoured. I know how difficult he found it to have a rider."

A skewbald stallion who had come with Oakbark stood nearby, next to Laila's brother.

Delsin ceased patting the horse. "We'll come too. I can help Laila."

A shout stopped Mystery's reply.

"Get away from my horse, Waterfalls man!" Jolon stomped over, flailing his arms to shoo Oakbark away.

Mystery barged between the man and the stallion. "He's not your horse. People don't own horses. You've done enough harm."

Jolon grabbed Yuma's arm and swung him round. "First my daughter, now my horse. You're not getting away with this." He bunched his fist to strike.

Ahanu had followed him over and now grabbed him by the arms. "Calm down. This is not how we do things here."

Jolon shrugged free and lashed out at Oakbark. The stallion pivoted on his front feet, kicked out with his hind legs, and caught Jolon in the ribs. He grunted and staggered back.

The ruckus brought the rest of the elders over. Dohate helped

Ahanu restrain Jolon. "Leave the horse. There are more important matters to deal with."

Mystery could stand no more. He instructed Laila, Yuma and Delsin to mount up. "People don't deserve the help of horses."

He galloped away, leaving the clan staring at his dust.

Mystery's anger drove him hard. He galloped across the plains with only Laila's warmth reminding him she rode, her steady seat relaxed and light. Neither of them had spoken since leaving Bluff. Why did the clans protect her father? Their stubbornness would be their undoing; they were on their own now.

His tasks were to help the injured horses, find the stolen warmblood mares, and prevent Shadow's creatures killing or stealing any more. How he would do the latter two he had no idea, but helping King Socks' mares was something he could do. It shouldn't take long to find the herd, even if Shale had convinced Socks to move.

His feet skimmed the dry grasses, leaving little trace. He shortened his stride so as not to leave his warriors too far behind. Oakbark and Rocky, carrying Yuma and Delsin, ran among them. Paws raced off to one side to avoid choking from the dust of many hooves.

Meda glided above him. She thrust her legs forwards and landed on his crest. "You're tiring me out. Don't worry so much. The nasty man can't use my scale. Only gifted ones work."

Concerned that his anger was draining the dragon of her vigour, Mystery struggled to suppress his ire, but Meda's claim didn't reassure him. "What about understanding other animals? Remember, I enhanced the whole thing. Maybe even the jade otter is enough to give him power."

Meda's claws dug into his neck and held out her wings to maintain her balance. "I don't think so. Unicorn magic works like dragons'. He can't use stolen items."

Laila had remained silent through the conversation, only hearing his side. "What does she say? Can my father listen to animals? He'd be bound to use it to help his hunting. The animals would have no chance."

He shared what Meda had said. "And don't forget, power feeds on love. I don't think he has any."

What really worried Mystery was abandoning the clans. Not because he regretted his ultimatum, but because he was supposed to be here to help, horses and people. If he really abandoned the Eastlanders, would the goddess return to destroy Equinora, no matter what else he did?

Rocky caught up with him, dripping in sweat and blowing hard. "Slow down! We can't run like you."

Mystery dropped to a trot. "Sorry. We'll take a break. There's water close by."

He led the way to a small spring hidden in a fold of ground. A halo of greenery surrounded the shallow water. Insects buzzed above the surface, tempting frogs to expose themselves to a pair of herons. As the horses arrived, the waterbirds took to the air with laboured wingbeats, their long legs dangling.

Rocky stayed close to Mystery as they enjoyed a cool drink. The stallion raised his head, his muzzle dripping. "I knew your father in the bloodwolf war."

"Really? I'm surprised." Then again, it wasn't so unusual. Rocky's warm blood would have made him of great use in the war, even though he wouldn't have known he had unicorn ancestry. "Did you carry Delsin then?"

Rocky nibbled at the fresh pick. "Yes. He's not like other people. I've always sensed an aura about him. Do you think the goddess selects some men and women for special powers, as well as horses?"

The thought had never occurred to Mystery. "I don't know. Perhaps. Maybe that's why Laila came to Shimmering Lake. If so, she and her brother must have inherited it from their mother. I can't imagine their father is gifted." The reminder of Jolon's treachery resurfaced. Mystery struggled to fight his disappointment and anger; it served no purpose and he needed Meda strong. She would have a lot to do to heal all the horses. How would she cope? Why couldn't he find his power and do whatever was necessary? There must be a way to fight Shadow and his beasts.

The skewbald interrupted his train of thought. "I've only seen their mother from a distance. The bachelor stallions had little to do with the clan before the war. I don't remember her from when I was a foal, so I've no notion whether there's anything special about her."

Mystery didn't want to consider whether people could have

powers from the goddess. He had enough to resolve. "Let's get going. The spoor here is fresh. Socks can't be far."

As he predicted, they found the herd nearby. Shale kept the mares in a tight group, not letting them wander, especially those with youngsters. The king stood a distance away looking old and haggard, his coat dull, and his head down. At Mystery's approach, he perked up and cantered over. "You've come. I wasn't sure if we'd see you again."

"I told you I'd bring the healer."

Shale joined them.

Mystery stretched out his neck and blew into her nostrils in greeting. "I'm glad you have the herd on the move."

She welcomed him. "Your band looks strong. Have you found good grazing? Is there enough to share?"

"The Midlands people brought oats. What little is left needs to be sown to grow more." He turned to Socks. "Have there been any more fires?"

The old king stood a bit straighter. "No. We haven't seen any fresh burns. But this time of year is dry and there's little feed left. Fleeing our summer grazing grounds has taken a toll. As you know, most of the herd are injured. Their burns don't heal, and gashes from the stealthcats fester."

"There's obviously a lot for us to do. We need to start."

Meda crept up to Mystery's ears. "Can you help me?"

Not with power. He'd proven he couldn't heal like Gem. But at least he could send Meda love. She'd need all she could absorb. "We all will. Gather all the stallions who can see you, and Yuma. We'll take it in turns to support you. But don't hurt yourself. You must rest when you need to."

Meda swooped away to summon those stallions with dragon-sight. Yuma had already dismounted and sought out the horses with the worst injuries. Laila accompanied him, treating those with lesser wounds with her salves, and offering them medicinal herbs.

They all worked hard throughout the day. Healed mares lingered close, still gaunt with protruding ribs and hips, hollow necks, and lolling ears. But new hope sparked in their eyes, revealing a brightening of their spirits.

Mystery took a break to return to the pool for a drink. Sharing power with Meda was taking a toll on them all. Even with the energy from many stallions sending her love, the dragon had faded to grey.

He worried for her health, but she refused to stop. And Laila, Yuma, and Delsin needed to make camp while light remained.

He gazed at the setting sun and spotted a bird of prey. His hair stood on end.

The eagle glided closer, growing in size as it neared. A flash of gold sparked from his wings.

Mystery leapt into flight and galloped back to the herd, whinnying. "Stealthcats!" He had no idea if any accompanied Claw, but he couldn't take the risk.

Panic struck. Horses spun, not knowing where to go. The three people ran for their mounts.

Laila grasped his mane and leapt aboard. "Where's Meda?"

"She's gone aloft to see if she can spot any stealthcats." He had barely finished his sentence when the tiny dragon plummeted down to land on his poll.

"They're everywhere! We're surrounded!"

Socks had already driven the mares into a tight bunch, the warrior stallions encircling them, facing outwards to defend any attack. As the reddening sun touched the horizon, the first stealthcat pounced. Neighs filled the air. The ground shook with thundering hooves. Dust plumed.

Mystery pounded the perimeter of their defences, striking out at stealthcats as he passed. Laila clung to his back, her fingers tangled in his mane, her knees clutching his sides. He lashed out with his hind legs, catching one stealthcat in the head. He broke another's back with his front hooves, stamping the life out of the beast before dashing on to the next.

Despite the cries of those caught by the feline's claws, the horses held their own. Mystery backed off to see where the main threat came from. A stealthcat staggered around him, uncoordinated and clumsy as if drugged. He deflected its assault with a flick of his heels. Another stealthcat tried to pounce on Rocky, falling as it launched, its hindquarters wobbling. The same story repeated on all sides; the stallions defeated the stealthcats with ease.

A roar came from behind Mystery. He spun around. An enormous she-cat leapt for his rump. He side-stepped, avoiding her pounce. The stealthcat fell and squirmed on her side. Mystery thrust his head down, pinning her lean body to the ground with his horn.

The stealthcat spasmed, her enormous paws twitching where

she lay on her side. Froth bubbled from her mouth. Blood streamed from the wound in her side.

The rank odour of zinc that Mystery had experienced at sites of previous attacks assailed his delicate nostrils. He withdrew his horn from the stealthcat's body and stepped back, gagging on the stench. His horn burned as the blood dried and crumbled away.

The mountain lion rolled to her belly and licked her side. The mad look retreated from her eyes, and a deep purr rumbled from her throat. She stretched to her feet. "Rrrrock. Differrrrent rrrrock. Much betterrrr."

Shocked, Mystery stepped forward to sniff the predator. The healthy smell of lion rose from her warm coat. She continued to wash her tawny hide, ignoring his presence.

The noise of battle from other areas of the herd quietened as each stealthcat was either killed or chased off. From what Mystery could tell, no horses had been taken. Meda was already back healing those with new injuries.

He needed answers. "Why are you here? Why have you left your mountains?"

The lion sat up and licked the tear in her flank. "Rrrrock. Made senses morrrre. Drrrove mad. Hungrrry. Don't like. Couldn't stop."

She rose with fluid grace and bounded away into the evening, disappearing among the dried grass as if she had never been there.

What did the stealthcat mean? But she wasn't a stealthcat anymore; he could smell her. Had he found his power? Hope surged in his heart. But he hadn't experienced the tingling that had come when he enhanced Laila's amulet. His horn hadn't sparkled. Whenever Gem used her healing powers, Moonglow spoke her prophecies, or Diamond translocated, a shimmer of sparks left a trail of effervescence like pollen drifting from pine cones.

The stealthcat had been sick. He had detected zinc in her blood, the same metal he scented in the cats' scat. Copper counteracted zinc. *That* was how he had cured her, he realised, not with power. And his warriors had defeated the other stealthcats with ease, even if they didn't cure them. Something had poisoned the lions.

He remained powerless. At least his horn had been good for something. But was he a horned horse or a true unicorn?

A whirlpool of thoughts flooded his mind. He called the stallions together. "I have an idea."

Paws trotted alongside Laila as she made her way back to Bluff. Yuma strode ahead with Delsin, their horses brushed down and left to graze near the creek. For the first time in moons, Mystery was in high spirits, cantering off with the warmblood stallions, chasing and nipping each other in play as they celebrated their defeat of the stealthcats and the healing of the mare herd.

Despite being grateful that the horses were cured, Laila hated that she had been unable to assist Meda. Although she had tended minor wounds, the dragon had done the majority of the work. Laila had been tempted by Yuma's offer to borrow Tatuk's scale, but knew the loss he'd feel without the familiar dragon scale against his chest. She couldn't do that to him. Besides, Meda didn't belong to her any more than Paws or Mystery did. True, they were her friends, but they could work their magic as easily without her.

Her stomach twisted at the thought. Her own clan had never accepted her healing skills, and now she was of no use to horses, either. Abey held the status of healer for Thatchery, and Bluff had two healers—an elder and an apprentice. Without her amulet, Laila wasn't needed.

A wet nose pushed into her hand. She crouched down and wrapped her arms around Paws' neck, burying her face in the thick ruff. With autumn well under way, the wolf had grown a shaggy coat, her dark topcoat covering a pale under-layer. Her body had filled out and her feet no longer looked too big for her body. One ear still bent over at the tip, though even that was straighter than it had been.

Paws licked Laila's face, piercing her heart with eyes transformed by adulthood into a deep golden brown.

"I know. I still have you. At least we understand each other well enough not to need words, but I want to be able to talk like we used to." She rested her cheek on top of Paws' soft head. "Let's go and find a bone for you and some soup for me. Amitola said some of the boys had been successful trapping coneys. At least I didn't have to hear their cries. You might get the heads if you're lucky, though I'll stick to fish and vegetables."

Laila had yet to resolve whether eating the fruits of the sea went against her desire not to harm animals. She hadn't talked with any fish or shellfish when she wore her amulet. Perhaps it didn't work through water. Or maybe the Mother meant for her to eat the rich source of protein. She may as well let her body benefit from the bounty provided by the Bluff clan, although she was already tired of the oily, preserved sardines from last year's run.

Paws' tail thumped the ground as she lifted her front feet onto Laila's knees, her body squirming as she wriggled closer, looking as pathetic as she was able. She snuggled her soft muzzle under Laila's chin.

Unable to help herself, Laila chuckled and stood up. "Alright, I'll cheer up."

At least Mystery had relented about not helping the Eastlanders. He'd said he'd visit tomorrow and explain his idea, refusing to give her any information until he'd talked it through with his warriors. It must have something to do with the she-cat regaining her scent.

After a restless night, Laila rose at dawn and peered into the gloom in the hope of seeing the glint of Mystery's silver coat. Everyone else was as anxious as her for a solution, and frustrated that she couldn't tell them more.

The sun had burned off the morning mist by the time she heard hoofbeats. Mystery and his warriors skidded to a halt outside the camp, squealing and rearing as they showed off their strength. Before they settled, the elders had gathered to hear the news.

Laila stood to one side and listened as Mystery greeted everyone by name, drawing out the meeting with formality. Needles of dread crept up her neck. Why was he acting like this? It didn't augur well.

The Eastland stallions settled behind him, ears pricked and necks arched. Rocky and Oakbark stood off to one side.

Mystery flashed his horn and tossed his tail over his rump. "As you know, mountain lions do not normally venture across the plains, nor do they usually attack horses or people."

A few mutters answered this obvious statement though no one interrupted.

"From talking with a she-cat yesterday, I believe the stealthcats have been poisoned from eating zinc that enhances their sense of taste and smell. This addictive drug drives them mad with hunger and makes them aggressive."

The mutterings increased in volume. This was not what anyone wanted to hear.

"My horn is copper, which counteracts the effects of zinc. When it pierced the lion, it returned her to her natural state. I could smell her." Mystery paused, one foreleg raised.

Laila's thoughts echoed the questions erupting from many of the people gathered. She walked over, placed a hand on his neck, and voiced her fears. "Surely you don't intend to fight them all yourself? You can't be everywhere at once."

Mystery nuzzled her before returning to address the crowd. "There's much chalcocite around here. It's high in copper. Maybe you can make arrowheads out of it. I'll show you where to gather the mineral."

Although the proposed solution sounded easy, Laila suspected the reality would prove quite different. Others must have thought the same, as multiple conversations drowned out Mystery's next words. None of them had ever discovered another stone suitable for knapping.

Ahanu raised his hand for silence.

Kele Whale, one of the Bluff elders, stepped forward and reached for the talking stick, waving it above his head, a signal that he wished to be heard. Facing the crowd rather than Mystery, Kele shook his other fist in the air. "I thought the unicorns and horses promised to protect us in return for care. Now we find we must defend ourselves. We'll all be dead before we can work out how to defeat the lions."

Dohate was the next to speak. "Give Mystery time to explain his plan. He's already helped us more than we could have expected."

One by one, the elders held the speaking stick and either asked questions of Mystery or raised their concerns. The atmosphere remained tense with no easy solution being resolved. Children became bored and ran off to play, and women drifted to their chores. Only the elders and those learning to ride remained.

Laila held out her hand for a turn to talk. With the stick clutched at her side, she addressed Mystery. "Perhaps once we've seen this chalcocite we'll know better how to use it. When can you show us where it is?"

He bowed his head. "Now. Tonight I leave to take the fight to the enemy. We're heading to Dragonspine Mountains to locate the lost mares."

Confused, Laila continued to clutch the talking stick despite Dohate requesting to speak next. "How can we leave so soon? What you've suggested will take time to work out. There's much work to be done to protect the clan."

"The clan hasn't met my demand to return your amulet. I refuse to help them anymore. We're not taking men beyond the site of the chalcocite. I'll point out the rocks, then leave."

Laila couldn't bear the thought of not being able to see Meda on their travels, or talk with Paws. "I don't want to leave here without my amulet. Can't we wait a bit longer?"

Mystery blew warm air on her neck. "When I say 'we', I mean me and the warmblood stallions. Not you. It's time to remain with your own kind."

Despite the gentleness of his words, Laila reeled as if he had kicked her. Not go with him? He was abandoning her to life here? She had never imagined he would leave her. Would he ever come back? Would she never return to Shimmering Lake, the only place she considered home? One thing was certain: she would never go back to Bloomsvale.

Chapter 16

Mystery headed north, his hooves thrumming on the hard ground. Eons of rubbing from glaciers had smoothed the surface, eroding the fine earth that blew away to feed the grasslands. The minerals beneath his feet spoke their history of when they had formed in the centre of the planet, erupted to the surface, and cooled into mountains, to then wear away over millennia. Layer upon layer of sand and gravel had settled when the world had been far wetter, compacting back into stone to form the plateau. Trickling streams and torrential rivers had cut deep into the newly formed land, grain by grain, exposing the layers and depositing silt like dunes in the desert. Crevices and gullies laced the granite outcrops.

Rocky cantered alongside Mystery. The horse was a good companion and Mystery liked his rider, perhaps because he was Laila's brother, both of the people exuding an aura of gentleness and harmony with nature. For once, Laila didn't accompany him, saying she needed to replenish her medicines; an excuse only, he was sure. In an attempt to mollify her, he had promised to take her for a long gallop that night, a chance to be without other people so he could translate for her with Meda and Paws. If only he could retrieve her amulet.

The memory of her father refusing to return it pushed him into a hard gallop. A distant whinny recalled him to his purpose. He skidded to a stop and reared in frustration.

Rocky caught up, lathered in sweat. "What's burning your tail?"

"Sorry. I forgot myself. There's a layer of sedimentary rock deep below. The mineral we need is in its seams." Mystery trotted along the band as it rose to the surface. The soil thinned and the grasses grew sparse, further indicating a rock outcrop nearby. His warriors' hoof-falls changed from muffled thuds to loud clattering as they raced to catch up.

He headed towards the barren horizon. A gorge opened before him, hidden from sight until he was almost upon its edge. Instead of the pale granite that usually dotted the plains, dark grey stones with rough sides piled at the base of the canyon walls, the metallic lustre of chalcocite glinting as the sun shone overhead.

The problem was how to reach it. Mystery surveyed the territory. "There's a narrow track at the far end. We may be able to pick our way down there."

He led the way around the rim and reached the far end of the gully, the valley floor far below. The riders slid off their mounts, a few complaining of dizziness from the height or worried about the steepness of the descent. The treacherous track wound back and forth above vertical drop-offs. Mystery started down without pause. Small stones bounced down into the ravine, their clink and rattle echoing off the cliffs.

"Aarrggg!" A man slipped and fell to his knees.

"Murmur! Give him your tail." Mystery raced back to help the fallen man.

The hunter clutched at the stallion's tail and heaved himself to safety. He leant against the blue roan's rump, gasping and clutching his belly. "I'm okay. Keep going."

Mystery walked among the huddled men, sensing where the ground would hold his weight, the scent of fear tingling in his nostrils. "Use your horses for support. They're strong enough to stop you falling."

He returned to the front of the line, encouraging the horses to tread exactly where he did as he passed each one. They reached the bottom without further incident, the gorge floor dark and cold where the sun failed to reach.

Keeping his head to the ground, Mystery wandered among the scattered rock-falls, sniffing at each pile to find the thickest copper deposits.

He came to a halt. "Here. This is very strong."

The men set about collecting rocks about the size of their fists, large enough to produce arrowheads but small enough to grasp for knapping. One man tried to break off fragments to test its sharpness, without success. He grumbled and threw the stone into his sack with a clunk. Soon all the men had as much as they could carry, the dense rock much heavier than flint.

Delsin came up and stroked Mystery's neck. "Thank you. I'm sure we'll find a way to use this. Do you think, before you leave, you could help us carry a few loads to the surface? That way if we need more, we won't need to risk climbing the steep sides on our own."

Mystery acknowledged the merit of the idea and shared the request with the other stallions. "The men can fill more of the sacks as we take the first load. We can empty them at the top if they use slipknots, so they don't need to come back up with us."

Yuma soon sorted out a method that worked. The horses transported a considerable mountain of stones to the lip of the canyon. By their third trip, many dragged their feet, their heads lowered as exhaustion drew close, still suffering the ill effects of stealthcat attacks and lack of feed.

Mystery worried for their health. "Tow your riders up with you this trip. Then take them home with whatever rocks you can carry. I can finish here."

He approached Rocky. "After you've dropped off Delsin, can you gather the warmblood stallions, such as Oakbark, who didn't come with us? I want us to leave to search for the mares as soon as I've said goodbye to Laila."

Delsin froze. "Is Rocky going too?"

"I need all the warmblood stallions I can muster, and his bloodlines are strong."

Delsin's shoulders slumped. "I understand. Please tell him I'll miss him and hope he stays safe."

Mystery stretched his nose forward and lipped Delsin's arm. "There are many bachelor stallions still without riders who'll be happy to move to a new territory. You won't have to travel back to Midlands on foot."

"I'm in no rush to return. I can learn a lot from Koko Skyreader, Thatchery's spiritman." Delsin gave Rocky another pat and made sure the straps holding Rocky's load wouldn't rub. "Maybe Rocky can return for me after you've rescued the mares."

Mystery stood back. The loss on the man's face belied his brave words, like Laila's after he'd told her she must stay behind. Well, he'd had to leave Gem. They all had to make sacrifices. "Can you and

Yuma get a feed of oats for all the stallions who've helped today?"

They each agreed to their tasks and led the majority of the horses up the narrow trail. Only three men remained with Mystery, Murmur, and Willow, one of whom was Laila's father. None of the horses liked to carry Jolon and they'd hastened away before he could hang on to their tails. But he'd have to ride someone back to Bluff. Mystery couldn't ask his friends to carry the brute. Despite dreading the thought of the man on his back, he accepted he'd have to carry him. At least that might give him an opportunity to get the amulet back.

By the time the last of the sacks were filled, the other horses had crested the ridge and disappeared from sight. Mystery sipped from the tiny creek burbling over the stones, and balked at the cold. The few blades of grass that struggled to grow in the dim valley also had a bitter taste. Lingering gained nothing.

He stood still for Jolon to lash two of the sacks over his back. Murmur and Willow stood similarly laden, their knees trembling from the weight. A sense of unease crept over him, like meat ants converging on a corpse. He called to the men. "Don't overload them. There's plenty at the top already."

None of the men answered him.

His feeling of unrest deepened.

Jolon raised his arm, something dangling from his hand. The other two men did the same.

A rope tightened around Mystery's throat. He gagged. He threw up his head and ran backwards. The noose tightened, strangling him. Panicked, he reared and thrashed his forelegs at Jolon. The man let the rope run through his hands before jerking and releasing it, and jerking and releasing it again.

Mystery had nothing to fight. Whenever he pulled against the constricting rope, he encountered nothing. Before he had a chance to run, the rope tugged again, dragging him off balance. He gasped for air through burning nostrils.

Murmur also struggled. Willow had already fallen to his side, his legs bound with leather straps. Then Murmur toppled over and kicked at the man attempting to tether him.

The distraction proved Mystery's undoing. With a huff, he landed on his side, the air knocked out of his lungs. Jolon flung another lasso around Mystery's legs, pulling them together before applying tight hobbles. Having disabled him, Jolon plonked his weight on Mystery's neck, trapping his head. Mystery's horn scraped in the loose rock, sending sparks flying as he struggled. He thrashed his feet, but only managed to cut his legs. His skin burned where his shoulder, ribs, and hip abraded against the stony ground.

"No good fighting, unicorn. You're not going anywhere." The words came from the Bluff elder, Kele Whale. He laughed, a deep hollow sound full of malice.

Mystery quivered. "What do you think you're doing?"

Paco Hunter, one of the Thatchery clan, strode over from where he had trussed Willow. "You were going to leave us. You're not going anywhere until we defeat the stealthcats and the fires stop."

Mystery gathered his wits, drew energy from beneath him, and squirmed to throw Jolon off his neck. With a burst of power, he thrust himself up. His hatred weakened him as much as the ropes constrained him. He staggered and fell back. "You can't force me to help you. Let us go."

Jolon swung back his leg and kicked Mystery in the head.

Pain shot through his jaw as a tooth broke. "Why are you doing this?"

Kele restrained Jolon from another kick. "You can't leave until we know how to defend ourselves. Help us, and none of the horses will get hurt."

Paco rubbed his belly. "Fight us, and we'll be enjoying horse meat for dinner."

Horrified, Mystery pushed away his anger and pictured Gem. He drew on the earth's power and surged to his feet. This time, prepared for the restrictive hobbles, he remained upright. "What do you intend? How is this helping?"

Paco sneered and swished a blade in front of Mystery's nose. "We'll block the exit from the gorge and trap you here. You won't be able to climb out wearing hobbles. Then if the rocks are no good against the stealthcats, we'll come back and harvest what we know works."

Jolon snickered. "Your horn."

Laila pounded the rock on the flat stone that she normally used for grinding seeds, failing miserably to keep her mind on the task rather than her sorrow. Mystery hadn't returned as promised, the men saying he had left to search for the warmblood mares. As if not being able to see Meda or talk to Paws wasn't bad enough, now Mystery had abandoned her. The tension at Bluff with so many people had also increased since he departed. No one had been able to knap the chalcocite into suitable arrow tips.

Smacking the lump of ore against the granite, Laila flinched as her blisters reopened. The stone was sharp, even if it couldn't be fractured into useful shapes.

Yuma wandered up and offered her a hot drink. "That's no way to make heads. But it's useless trying, anyway. Mystery obviously didn't know what type of stone we need."

Laila accepted the mug with shaking hands. "I'm not knapping it. I thought if I could break the stone, I might find something else."

He crouched next to her and rubbed the dust between his fingertips. "Maybe we could stick it to flint arrowheads with resin."

"Mystery said we needed copper. This doesn't look or feel anything like his horn. I thought that maybe the rocks might have something inside, like quartz contains golden flecks." She wiped away a single tear with the back of her hand as if sweat had streaked her face.

"You miss him, don't you?" Yuma hefted one of the chunks of rock and threw it from hand to hand.

"Of course I do. I can't believe he left without saying goodbye as he promised. Maybe he was worried I'd make a fuss." Laila sniffed, straightened her shoulders, and renewed her pounding of the chalcocite.

Pocketing his own rock, Yuma stood up. "I'm sure there'll be a good reason. There's much the unicorns do that we don't understand. The dragons, too. Tatuk always seemed to disappear when I needed him, yet he never let me down."

The reference to dragons pierced Laila's heart. "I'd feel better if I could talk with Meda and know Mystery was safe. Do you think she's gone with him?"

Yuma gasped. "I forgot about your amulet. No, she's here with you. Here, borrow Tatuk's scale so you can talk with her."

The temptation proved too much. Clutching Tatuk's diamond scale in her hand, Laila beamed as Meda blinked into view. "Meda! Thank you for staying."

The tiny dragon flitted from the pile of rocks to Laila's shoulder. "You need to cheer up. You're making me sick, even if you can't see me."

Remorse flooded Laila. "I'm sorry. It never occurred to me." Sending the dragon love, Laila also perked up as the dragon's scales brightened.

"That's better." Meda stretched her neck and wings, her multi-hued scales glinting in the sun. "Mystery must be okay. I haven't heard from him. Trust him. He'll be back."

The warmth of the dragon and her words comforted Laila. "But he said he wouldn't help people unless they returned my amulet. Why is my father being so stubborn? Surely he doesn't want Eastlanders to suffer?"

Clapping her wings shut, Meda paled and snuggled closer. "We should go home to Shimmering Lake. I have more scales under the tree. I'll give you another one."

Hope rose in Laila's chest, and then she slumped back on her heels. "I never thought of that. But by the time we reach Dragonspine Mountains, it'll be winter. We can't cross in heavy snow."

Although he only heard Laila's side of the conversation, Yuma obviously understood what they were talking about. "You can't go. It's far too dangerous."

Angry at his presumption, Laila returned Yuma's dragon scale. "I'd have Paws with me. I might not be able to talk with her, but we understand each other."

Yuma's face reddened. "And what about the Eastlanders? Would you leave them without your healing skills?"

Laila clenched her fists and grimaced. "They don't need me any more than my own clan." Heedless of the effect it might be having on Meda, she threw down the rock she'd been working with, rose to her feet, and set off to find her father.

Jolon sat with Paco and Kele on the outskirts of the settlement, chewing on last night's leftovers and swilling from a flask of fermented grains. Their guffaws turned to jeers as she stomped over. "Want some meat, Laila? Good for making strong sons. I'll bet Yuma will sow you some oats."

Ignoring the ribald comment, Laila halted, hands on hips. "Father.

There are people who need healing. I need my amulet to help them. Please return it. I won't come back to Bloomsvale with you no matter what you do."

Wiping his whiskers with a brawny hand, Jolon turned to his friends. "She needs her amulet. Poor little healer can't work without her totem." Facing her, he sneered. "If you had any skills, you wouldn't need that piece of junk. Or won't Yuma serve you because you've lost the otter he gave you?"

The taunt had little effect on Laila, having long ago learnt to let such comments wash over her. Struggling to remain polite, she held out her hand. "Please. It has properties you don't know. I'm named, and I left Bloomsvale years ago, even if I haven't partnered. You've no right to my possessions."

"It's worthless. I threw it away when gathering the rocks your unicorn said would save the clans. Look where that got us. All that hard labour for nothing." He accepted the flask from Paco, threw back his head and drank, before completing the joke he had been telling when she arrived.

Thinking of Meda, Laila bit back her ire. She had no idea if the dragon remained with her, but it did no good to get upset. At least Yuma had offered that she could use his scale at any time. Was Jolon telling the truth? If her amulet was in the canyon, would Meda be able to find it?

She sought out Yuma, pursing her lips to stop the excitement showing on her face. "Can you take me to where the stones came from? Meda can let you know where her scale is, so I can get it back."

Yuma hesitated, his head to one side. Then he shook his head. "There's no point. Meda says Jolon is lying. He still has your amulet in his waist pouch."

Although Laila expected as much, having the news confirmed plunged her deeper into despair. She thanked Yuma and, in an attempt to calm down, whistled for Paws. The wolf rarely ventured into the camp during the day, keeping to herself until Laila settled for the night. Then she'd stretch out beside her, resting her muzzle in Laila's hand.

Paws bounded over to greet her, yipping and wagging her tail.

Laila ran her fingers through the wolf's thick fur. "Let's find Abey and go gathering. I've pounded enough stone for today."

Abey happily joined Laila and slung her basket over one arm.

"With stealthcats on the prowl, I miss the freedom to go out on my own whenever it pleases me. You must, too." The smile slipped from her face. "I saw you with your father. Did you get your amulet back?"

Laila furrowed her brow. "No. And I don't even know why he took it. Meda assures me he can't use it, and I've told him I won't return with him no matter what. Apart from the fact that Yuma gave me the jade otter, Jolon has no reason to think my amulet is special."

The old healer changed her basket from one arm to the other as if it were heavy. "I think that was my fault."

"What do you mean?"

"I told him about you healing my broken leg. I was so impressed!"

Laila couldn't believe her friend and mentor had betrayed her. "You promised me you'd keep the secret."

Abey wouldn't meet Laila's eyes. "I assumed he knew about your dragon. He is your father. I thought Meda must have always been with you."

Shocked at the revelation, Laila glared at Abey. "I trusted you."

She squatted and wrapped her arms around Paws' neck. Her face softened. "But you've made my decision easy. Regardless of the stealthcats or winter coming, I'm leaving."

Chapter 17

Laila journeyed north along the shore, heading to the protection of the woods to wait out the winter. It was good to be away from people, living at a pace that suited her, and not having to worry about others when making decisions. Sometimes she missed Abey pointing out and explaining the uses of a new mushroom or berry that Laila hadn't encountered before, but the woman's betrayal poisoned the memory.

The thought of cramming into the caves where the Bluff clan bided out the bad weather gave her the shivers. The dark and enclosed space didn't worry her, although her jade cave at Shimmering Lake always radiated a dim light. It was more the oppressiveness from so many bodies, the inevitable arguments that would flare as the days shortened, and the certain knowledge that her father stirred trouble, smug in possession of her amulet.

Laila trusted that Meda still accompanied her, though she missed seeing and talking with the dragon more than she missed Mystery. At least Paws kept her good company. Like the wolf, Laila could fend for herself through the cold moons when she reached the forest. The mixed deciduous woods north of the river were the home of the Deershill clan—not that she intended staying with them, she didn't need to swap the pressures of one village for another—rich with hazelnuts, cranberries, and blue camas, a good place to replenish her supplies for the long trek to Shimmering Lake in spring.

Meanwhile, she enjoyed exploring the beach, clambering over rocks along the water's edge and peering into pools. Crabs scuttled away from her feet as seaweed wafted in the surf. The rhythmic breaking of waves lulled her as she gathered molluscs. Paws had turned her nose up at the shellfish when Laila first offered to share her meal, but with few rodents along the coast, the wolf had soon adapted to the unusual fare.

Satisfied that she had collected enough for them both, Laila deposited her trove up the beach and wandered back to gather driftwood. When she had a substantial pile, she lit a fire and gathered handfuls of red laver. She wrapped a few of her store of roots in the seaweed, scraped away the glowing coals, and laid the packets in the sand before covering them with hot rocks.

She whistled for Paws.

The wolf bounded up the beach, snapping at the wavelets licking her legs and yipping as her teeth closed on air. She chased the surf across the firm sand and pounced on the foam as the sea retreated, bolting back as the next wave rolled in.

Laila laughed. "Dinner's almost ready. Here, I've fresh water for you."

She placed half a gourd on the ground, the dried shell ideal for holding liquid. She had dried the original contents and ground flour for biscuits to munch as she travelled. Keeping to the beach, away from where stealthcats could hide, meant not being able to browse inland for the purple salal fruits she usually gathered for snacks and for her cookpot. She had also wanted to gather the leaves for her medicine bag. Never mind, she had plenty to eat and felt safe, Paws ever on the lookout for danger.

Days passed as Laila continued her journey. Sometimes she scrambled up the rocky cliffs when the tide left no room for her to walk with ease, or the wind blew salt and sand into her face. Paws stayed close, ears pricked and nose twitching, when they hastened along the clifftop. On the few occasions Laila spent the night high above the waves, she sought a rare tree and climbed into its branches for protection, with Paws curled up at the base.

After one such uncomfortable night in the fork of a crooked branch, Laila descended and stretched her stiff back. She crouched, her knees cracking, and hugged Paws. "I don't think I can stand another night like that. In future, we'll keep going along the beach until we find shelter. I barely slept a wink."

Paws nudged her hand with a wet nose.

"I know, we should get moving, though I feel as if I'm carrying bags of rocks rather than food." She dragged herself up, hefted her pack, and set off down the zig-zag path that descended to the beach. With the tide out, they made good progress along the firm sand.

By noon, the colour of the sea had changed from deep blue to aqua and the waves broke in an uneven pattern, indicating a river mouth. Instead, the coastline turned west. The breeze at Laila's back propelled her along, a firm layer of pebbles underfoot; a welcome relief after the rising tide had forced her to trudge through the softer, dry sand.

By evening, what had been niggling at the back of her mind grew in strength to a major concern. No one had told her about a headland when they'd shared their knowledge of the north. Had she come too far? Maybe one of the gullies she had crossed had been the river.

Still, what did it matter? As long as she found a thick forest to camp in, she'd be alright. As winter eased, she'd be able to head west and home. Home. Would Gem welcome her back? Mystery had said it was time for her to live among people, not unicorns, and had broken his promise to see her before she left. Had he shared his rejection of her with Gem?

Pushing her doubts aside, Laila trekked along the beach. Even if Gem didn't let her stay, Meda could retrieve one of her old discarded scales. Laila need only worry about where to go after that if Gem sent her away.

She gazed into the setting sun, oranges and pinks reflecting off a smear of clouds like a blaze on the horizon, time to make camp. Finding a sheltered spot proved easy: the cliffs here had many overhangs. After organising her things around her, she lit a small fire and prepared a meal.

A glow of red on green caught her eye above the water. She squinted to work out what she saw. Debris? No, it wasn't floating along. A reflection from the cliffs? No. Her eyes adjusted to the dim light. The low sun shone on trees across the water. An island? No. Laila's heart sank. That was why no one had mentioned the coast turning west. That was the far bank of a river, a river so wide that she hadn't been able to see the other side at its mouth. She'd have to follow the bank a long way upstream until the river became narrow enough to cross.

As the days shortened, the rising cliffs stole even more light, often causing Laila to stumble on the rough terrain. Gone were the sandy tracts of beach and the firm pebbles near the river mouth, replaced by jagged rocks tumbled haphazardly from the cliff. Now the river raced through a gorge, its growl echoing from the sheer basalt. Spindly shrubs clung to ledges, their roots twisting over the rock face to reach cracks in the hope of absorbing fresh water. She shivered from the looming presence of the walls more than the late autumn wind. Seabirds circled overhead, round and round, their eerie cries piercing Laila's thoughts. She should go back, climb the cliffs, and look for another way inland. But that would take time, winter approached, and stealthcats stalked the plains.

She scrambled along the riverside, knees grazed and fingernails torn. She removed her pack to climb the larger rocks, dragging the growing weight after her. How long would it take to reach a spot where she could swim across? Tangles of branches, bark, and leaves above her head showed how high the tide rose. How low would it go? Perhaps she should return to Bluff, bite back her pride, and wait out the winter with the Eastlanders. But her father would still be there. She couldn't face him again.

Hunching into her shoulder straps, she slogged on, using a stout piece of driftwood as a walking stick. Paws slunk along at her side, tail dangling, head down. The river gradually narrowed, the trees on the far bank beckoning as if promising food and shelter, taunting in their elusiveness. Laila slid over a massive boulder and heard a constant roar like a storm blowing through a forest. Hurrying forward, she kept one hand on Paws' neck for reassurance.

They came around a bend. Laila stopped in awe. A waterfall higher than any tree plummeted over a black wall. Spray rose in myriad prisms. The river surged over the precipice, flowing well out from the glistening cliff before plummeting to the gorge bed. The water had gouged out a huge pool, its depths dark and sinister. She couldn't climb the slippery cliffs, and neither could Paws. The only path was the way they had come. She choked back a sob.

Disheartened, Laila lit a fire and reheated last night's leftovers. Paws sat and leant against her side, her wet fur strong with odours of wolf, rotting seaweed, and dead fish. Laila didn't care. She wrapped her arms around her friend. "What are we going to do, Paws?"

Paws snuggled closer and licked her chin.

The wolf was right; misery wouldn't overcome the problem. Laila brewed mint tea and stared at the river. This side of the pool was the narrowest place she'd encountered. Away from the turmoil of the falls, the waters appeared calm. She watched the tide recede. Two small rocky islands protruded near the centre of the river. If she could make it to one, she could rest before swimming to the next. From there it was a short distance to the far bank, and at low tide not only would there be less distance to go, but the shallower water wouldn't hinder her as much.

With a plan fixed in her head, Laila lay down to rest. She'd need all the strength she could summon. But sleep eluded her. She tossed and turned, imagining all the dangers. The river was cold and might hide dangerous creatures. The pull of the tide might be too strong for her to swim against. The water might destroy a lot of her food; she'd wrapped only her rare medicines in oiled and waxed coverings.

So be it. She couldn't return to Bluff. And winter would be upon her, if not the stealthcats, if she backtracked and headed inland to cross above the falls. That left the river the only option.

Laila awoke to a star-filled night, shivering. Her fire had gone out. She tidied up her possessions, stripped, and wrapped her clothes in a bundle. She headed to the river's edge and dabbled her fingertips. The cooler air made the water feel warm. It would be alright. Her time with Gem meant she had become a strong swimmer. Memories of aquadragons playing in the magical waters reminded her of Meda and renewed her sense of purpose. She must get back to Shimmering Lake as soon as spring permitted. With fresh enthusiasm, she stepped into the river.

Paws whined, hesitating on the bank, pacing back and forth.

"We can't wait any longer. The tide is at its lowest. Look at the way the little crabs are scurrying over the mud." Without waiting to see if Paws followed, Laila dipped into the water, stroking out with one arm as she used the other to balance her pack on her head.

A huge splash confirmed that Paws had joined her. Comforted,

Laila struck out for the island that had grown with the lowering water. It didn't seem that far. She thrust her legs to propel herself forward, trying to minimise any splashing. Even with the slack tide, the flow of the river dragged her downstream. Fearing she would overshoot the island, she kicked harder. Starlight reflected off the surface, confusing her sense of direction. She trod water for a moment to get her bearings before pushing on again.

She gasped from the effort and spluttered as she swallowed a mouthful of river. At least it was only brackish. The tide must still be on the run out, the fresh water from the falls mingling with the salt of the sea. She continued to struggle, swimming crooked. Her right arm ached from holding her pack. She risked changing hands, treading water while she re-balanced her load. Her teeth chattered and her feet went numb.

Something grabbed her legs. She thrashed free. Had it been an eel or only weed? Another grasp tugged her legs. She pushed herself to greater efforts. To no avail. Shoved around, she spun to face the southern bank.

Suddenly she was facing the island again. Laila's head reeled. No animal or plant grasped her. The tide had changed and rushed in to meet the outflowing river, creating a whirlpool. With the islands breaking the flow, the water circled like the seabirds during the day. The current twirled her like a dried leaf.

She panicked and tossed the pack from her head to free both arms. She threw all her energy into swimming, fighting the river as if she wrestled a stealthcat. The flow was too strong. She sank, blinded by the murky water. She spluttered to the surface. Again, she succumbed to the power of the river and went under. Her mind went blank. She had no idea which way was up. Only instinct forced her to kick and struggle against the pull.

Something warm brushed her side. Teeth grasped her wrist. She went under again. All her fight evaporated. Her lungs burned and dots swam across her eyes. Her limbs refused to obey her befuddled brain. She gave herself to the whirlpool, tumbling round and round.

Laila came to, shivering and wet. A new day dawned as water lapped at her feet. Sharp stones pricked the length of her left side. Scrapes on her skin oozed blood, mingling with the water rising around her.

Barely able to raise her head, Laila scraped sand and salt from her eyes to see where she was. Images of crossing the river flooded back to her, the sensations of being tumbled and choking, helpless against the swirling river. With horror, she realised she lay on the first island. The tide was coming in fast. The water creeping up her legs must have brought her round. She didn't have the energy for another swim, not back to the southern bank, nor to the next island.

She called for Paws.

Only the sound of the lapping river at her feet and the sad cry of the gulls answered. There was no sign of the wolf. No food. No fresh water. No clothes. And no one knew where she was or even that she was in trouble. Crying for her lost friend, Laila's head fell back on the sharp rocks.

She passed out.

Chapter 18

The men's laughter echoed in Mystery's head like the crashing of rocks in the avalanche they'd created. Despite them having long since crested the rim, their taunts continued to torment him.

He had to get free. It wasn't only the threat of having his horn chopped from his head driving his anger; his lack of obvious power continued to frustrate him. He didn't dare call the other unicorns to let them know his predicament. Anyway, what could they do? He had tried all he could to summon power to save himself—driving his horn and hooves into the earth, drinking deep of the bitter creek, even eating the few mushrooms he had found. All that had happened was his belly curdled and his head ached. He had even called on the goddess for aid.

Nothing worked.

If his own plight wasn't enough, Willow and Murmur stood trussed and unable to totter more than a few steps. He'd brought them into this; he needed to get them out.

Pushing aside the taste of once-living animal, Mystery chewed at the leather thongs binding his fetlocks. His teeth were meant for grazing, not slicing. He grasped one of the knots and tugged hard, ignoring the pain as the restraint bit his flesh. Blood seeped over his copper hooves as he wrestled with the strap.

The leather stretched. Encouraged, Mystery curved his neck to its extreme and hooked his horn between the hobbles. Sinews popped in his neck at the awkward angle as he rubbed the spiralled edge of his horn up and down. A cramp in his poll seared his brain.

The leather frayed. He bit back the pain as he worked at his bonds.

The first loop snapped, flinging Mystery's head up. With more freedom to move his forelegs, he savaged the remaining straps. His circulation returned, stinging his hooves like a swarm of wasps. Whinnying to his friends, he trotted a few circles to recover his equanimity before rushing to their aid. Releasing their hobbles proved much quicker than his own had, now that he could move his head freely.

Willow's bonds fell away. He thanked Mystery. "I was worried we'd die here and our mission would be over before we'd started."

Murmur stretched each leg in turn and took tentative steps. "I'm not sure I can walk on level ground yet, let alone find and rescue stolen mares."

Mystery acknowledged his own concerns. "We've still got to get out of this gorge. The track is blocked for good."

Mystery told them to rest while he surveyed the area. Their pain would be greater than his. "There must be another way out. The valley would be a lake if this creek didn't flow out somewhere."

He followed the water. In many places, the trickle disappeared below ground before burbling to the surface again. Letting the structure of the rock dictate his path, Mystery trotted to the end of their prison. A wall of basalt towered over a tumble of boulders. Flaring his nostrils, he searched for a way through. A whiff of iron and magnesium threaded with mould gave him hope. Stepping over the sharp rocks with care, he traced the thread until he discovered a narrow fissure and squeezed his way through the gap into open space. He breathed deeply and explored further. The cliff opened into a labyrinth of tunnels, twisting and winding up and down, left and right, forking and branching in all directions.

He returned to Murmur and Willow in high spirits. "I think there's a way out. Let's go."

The stallions needed no more time. They galloped down the valley side by side, their tails streaming in their wake. When they reached the sheer rockface, Murmur reared in horror. "We can't climb that. We're not unicorns like you."

Mystery reassured them and revealed the narrow entrance to the caves. "Grab my tail. Tread where I tread."

Doing as directed, the trio made slow progress through the hillside, the only sounds their clopping footsteps and dripping water. Around bends and turns, across shale and over boulders, they progressed much slower than Mystery had ventured before. The darkness did nothing to deter his step. Guided by his senses, he tracked the breezes through caverns and pinches, studying how the rocks lay ahead using his inner sight. He scented sea air; the path must lead all the way through the hillside.

Mystery walked on with confidence until he encountered an underground lake. He halted at its edge. "We'll have to swim. I don't think it's far."

Murmur balked. "I don't think I can. I've never been out of my depth."

Willow sighed. "It's a favourite pastime of Mystery's, teaching horses to swim. The first time I travelled with him, he had me floundering in the river. He crossed where it was shallow."

Mystery had forgotten Willow's first plunging. "It's not that bad. You only think it's scary because you can't see. Trust me. It's not cold."

Murmur sniffed the water. "What if we can't get out the other side?"

"We will. I can sense a shallow ledge." Even with Mystery plunging into the water first, the warmblood stallions took a while to leap into the lake blind. Finally convinced, they jumped together, sending a wave across the water that rebounded from the far bank and chopped up the surface. As the three of them swam across, Mystery slowed his pace and talked to his friends the whole time, reassuring them. Although the water was deep, it wasn't far. Once on the other side, they scrambled onto the ledge and emerged with relief, shaking their fear off with the water.

Murmur blew spray from his nose. "I could do without any more of that. How much further do we have to go?"

Mystery didn't answer, and led off at a steady walk. A suspicion picked at him like a crow pecking at beetles; a strong draught whistled between his ears, not his legs. The track stopped. The wind blew from a hole near the ceiling.

"Now what?" Willow's tired voice echoed in the dark.

Mystery struggled for a solution. "We can't reach that opening. We'll have to find a different way."

Murmur shivered. "Not via the lake. One swim was enough."

Mystery stretched his senses. "We passed a crevice, but it's too far for me to sense it from here." He retreated the way they had come, keeping alert for all possibilities.

Willow nudged Mystery's rump. "Maybe we should return to the valley and try to climb out over the rock fall."

Mystery didn't pause to think. "No, not yet. I'll find a path."

A scant breeze guided him to a vertical crack. He followed the scent until he reached the opening and poked his muzzle into the gap. "It widens further on."

He squeezed his body through the fissure and slipped on the slime-coated walls, leaving his hair smeared on sharp protuberances.

A shrill whinny reverberated off the rock. "I'm stuck!"

The scrabble of Willow's legs reminded Mystery of the men blocking the gorge with rocks. His anger bloomed, driving him to want to fight, but he couldn't turn in the narrow space. "Don't fight. You'll hurt yourself."

"Do something!"

"Don't panic. I'll get you out." Having no idea how he could do any such thing, cursing his lack of powers, Mystery sought a different route using the map of rocks in his head. Another gap offered a possibility further back along the trail. "Can you go backwards? There's another way we can try."

Willow heaved and puffed, the iron-rich smell of blood mingling with the stench of fear and sweat. He made a frenzied attempt to free himself.

Mystery sensed the stallion had driven himself deeper into his predicament. "Stop! We'll have to try something else."

He thrust his horn against the rock wall. He bit a rock. He drew energy through his hooves. No matter what he did, he failed to discover his power. If his companions weren't relying on him, he would have let the mountain bury him where no one would find his useless body. What was the point of his existence if he didn't have any power? How could he save Equinora if he couldn't even rescue his friends?

A loud neigh rang from Willow. "Stop it, unicorn! I can hear your thoughts."

Shocked out of self-loathing, Mystery regained his control. In his depressed state, he had forgotten to block his mind. "Sorry. Of course we'll get out."

He studied the tunnel that pinched Willow, looking for a flaw. "Murmur, can you get your head beneath Willow's hind legs? If you can raise him, even a little, he should be able to kick away the rock."

Having a positive plan of action calmed Willow. With Murmur raising Willow's hind end, and Mystery guiding Willow's kicks with his voice, the stallion widened the gap until his ribs were no longer pinned. Stone by stone, rock by rock, he broke down the barrier. He surged out of his trap and gasped. "There'd better not be any more of those. Horses weren't built for caving."

After a brief rest, they continued their trek. Although the track rose and fell, and narrowed and widened, no more lakes to swim or pinches to squeeze through slowed them down. Without the passing of the sun overhead, Mystery had lost all sense of time. How long had they been inside the mountain? He had no idea if it were one day or many.

The stallions were exhausted, but neither Willow nor Murmur complained of hunger or anything else. They had assuaged their thirst at every opportunity from the many rivulets that trickled into pools, the underground water tangy with minerals. Even Mystery had tired, and his neck ached. Too busy concentrating on finding the way, he'd drawn insufficient energy from the earth.

He plodded on, one step at a time, sensing the surety of the footing before progressing. A fresh breeze blew into his face. Were they near the exit? His step quickened.

They broke out into open space, but darkness still enveloped them. Mystery's hopes plunged. They were in a huge cavern, tiny points of light dancing on the floor. Fighting off despair so as not to upset the others, Mystery stole a moment to rest.

Willow snorted and trotted in circles. "I've never been so pleased to see stars."

Mystery studied his surrounds. Relief rolled off his back as if he had dumped sackfuls of rock. He stood at the mouth of a cave, the sea stretching before him, calm and soothing. Surf whispered up the beach, a pearly luminescence on its surface from the last sliver of moon. "We've been in the hill longer than I thought. Let's find grazing."

Finding a route to safely climb to the clifftop took Mystery many attempts. He left Willow and Murmur at the base while he scrambled along narrow ledges and tested the footing. Finally, satisfied he had located a path that the others could follow, he went back down and led them up. At the top, they all tore at the short, tough grass as if it were the sweetest young shoots of alfalfa or rich clover.

Despite his urgency to head west, Mystery allowed them a couple of days to recover before heading back to Bluff to find the other warmblood stallions. They must search for the missing mares before Jolon and his thugs discovered Mystery's escape and thought to recapture him.

The people were on their own now. The ropes tied around Mystery's legs had wrenched from him any remaining desire to help people.

Murmur was the first to spot a chestnut with flaxen mane and tail who had been part of the Elk Bank herd. "There's Springrise. The others will be close."

Stallions trotted over to greet them as Mystery shared their story. "We must head west. Is everyone here?"

Springrise swapped breath with Mystery. "Rocky and Oakbark left with two men. Didn't you see them? We assumed you had other business to attend, which is why we've waited here as you asked."

"Were either Rocky or Oakbark roped?" Mystery couldn't bear the thought of more horses caught or possibly killed.

Quick to reassure, Springrise pricked his ears and raised his head. "They went willingly and galloped off as soon as the men mounted."

Mystery wasn't sure whether that worried him even more. "That must be Yuma and Delsin. Oakbark and Rocky wouldn't let anyone else ride them. We'll have to follow, even though it's almost dark. We need every warmblood we can muster to find the mares and can afford no more delays."

Tracking the spoor was easy, even without the moon. Mystery led the way, cantering in the trails across the cliff tops. At least they were heading away from Bluff, and fast, judging from the length of the strides. The warmblood stallions had rested well and gorged on oats. Racing north, they leapt over shrubs and rocks, necks stretched forward, and hooves throwing up stones and dust.

Before long, the smell of horses ahead drove Mystery faster. He recognised Rocky and called out. Sweat creamed between the skewbald's hind legs. The horses were in a hurry. They slowed as Mystery drew near.

Rocky bobbed his head, breathing hard, as Mystery queried them.

Yuma answered from Oakbark's back. "Laila took off without saying goodbye. We're following her in the hope of catching up before a stealthcat does."

Cross with the woman for endangering herself and others, Mystery suspected he was to blame for her leaving. Guilt squirmed like maggots in his gut even though failing to return as promised wasn't his fault. "You'll have to find her on foot. At least you've made good ground riding this far. But Rocky and Oakbark are coming with me to find the mares. We can't help people anymore."

The strong scent of wolf wafted on the breeze.

Mystery trotted out to see who approached. A bedraggled beast crawled to his feet. "Who are you? What are you doing here?" Then he recognised her and snorted.

Looking nothing like the fit, well-fed wolf he'd last seen, Paws' tongue hung to her knees, her ears flattened against her head. Her tail was clamped between her legs as she peered up at him with pleading eyes. "Laila's dying!"

With Paws on his back, Mystery led the stallions along the clifftop. The exhausted wolf dug her claws into his sides and grasped his mane with her teeth. Although he had no qualms at leaving the clan, Laila alone was at serious risk. He couldn't abandon her, with no people to protect her, after bringing her so far.

Oakbark had at first refused to accompany them. "It's not natural to carry a wolf. I can't bear the stench."

Yuma had agreed. "Even if she can be trusted, she needs to rest."

Paws had refused to stay behind. "You won't find Laila in time without me. It's too far around the shore. I found a way up the cliff."

Carrying Paws didn't worry Mystery; she'd ridden him ever since she was a pup, albeit with Laila to help balance her. He took care not to swerve or jump so as not to dislodge her. Having heard his story of how he, Willow and Murmur had been captured and bound, the stallions were as keen to get away from people as they were to help in the rescue. Making good time, they reached the waterfalls at dawn.

Mystery pulled to a halt and peered over the edge as Paws leapt off. "That's a tricky descent."

Willow stood close. "We call this place Devil's Throat. A wolf

179

may be able to scramble down there, but not a horse."

Mystery regarded the terrain, similar to that he had climbed from the cave by the sea. "I can locate sure footing for myself. Yuma and Delsin had better ride me. The rest of you, stay up here."

A growl rumbled above the noise of the falls. "I'm coming too. If I can climb up, I can get back down."

With Yuma and Delsin mounted, Mystery stepped over the edge and placed one hoof on solid rock. Visualising the cliff face, he avoided any loose stones and advanced another step. The two men on his back gripped so tight he could barely breathe. "Relax. I won't let you fall."

Yuma sat nearest his withers, with Delsin behind him. "I trust you. It's just my belly doesn't like what my eyes can see."

"Shut your eyes then." Mystery focused on the treacherous descent and continued one step at a time. Whenever rocks tumbled from around his feet, the riders tensed, distracting him. He fought to keep his mind on the construction of the rocks, picking out their strengths and weaknesses. Even the tiny plants and insects that made the inhospitable place their home became evident as he studied the terrain.

Paws slithered and scrabbled behind him, waiting for him to call as he found sure footing, before descending each section. The horses on the clifftop became mere specks as they watched his progress.

Daylight reflected off the river surface, glinting as the sun rose and lighting the mighty spectacle of the falls. Dazzled by the glare, Mystery peered at the island. His stomach plunged to the soles of his feet. He was too late. Laila's body lay half submerged, her arms flung out from her sides, her hair wafting like seaweed in the rising tide. A grey form draped over her chest, also motionless. "Meda!"

Mystery had never seen a dead dragon. None had ever died while he was at Shimmering Lake, and none lived where he had grown up at White Water Cliffs. Already her scales had started to shed; grey dust drizzled over Laila's bare skin. He shuddered.

"What's up?" Yuma placed a warm hand on his neck.

"Laila and Meda are dead." A pain he had never experienced before pierced Mystery's heart. This wasn't how their adventure to the east was supposed to pan out. They had come to rescue the warmblood mares and discover his power, to save Equinora and return with glory.

Yuma slid from his back and tumbled down the last of the hillside. "How can you be sure? We can't leave them there. They'll be swept out to sea."

Mystery joined Yuma on the beach. "The tide is rising fast. Get back on and I'll swim across."

Delsin remained astride. "Are you sure that's wise? We could all end up drowned."

Leaping aboard, Yuma sat behind Delsin this time. "She's your sister! How can you think of leaving her?"

"She wouldn't want us to risk our lives. If her spirit has gone, she won't object to her body feeding the fish. It's the cycle of life. There's no point adding to her loss with our deaths."

Confused by the men arguing, Mystery looked for Paws. The wolf had waded chest deep into the water. "What are you doing? You've no strength to swim across there."

Paws whined. "She's alive. I know she is. We must save her!"

Mystery stretched his senses. Until now, he had only observed Laila and Meda with his eyes. Paws was right. A glimmer of life flickered. "Quick! Grab my tail with your teeth, Paws. I can use the energy of the whirlpool to propel us."

Drawing on the enormous strength of the river, the whirlpool, and the rising sun, Mystery leapt into the current. Even with his increased might, he misjudged the force of the rushing water. The river dragged him downstream. He overshot the island. He let the current swing his hindquarters around and struck out, swimming against the flow, thrusting his head high to keep his nostrils clear, ears turned back so that they wouldn't fill with spray.

No amount of strength pulled him towards the island. It shrank to a mound as the river carried him away, too deep to gain purchase with his hooves. He pinched his nostrils closed and plunged his head beneath the surface, immersed his horn, and ordered the tide to stop, demanding the river ease. Gasping, he flung up his head.

The island had disappeared. He was further away than ever. How did Tempest control the river? He didn't have time to call him, doubting he could help anyway. Kicking with all his pent-up frustration, fear, and anger, Mystery thrust across the tow and made for the far bank.

As soon as his hooves touched bottom, he dragged himself from the water. The men clung tight. Paws released his tail and raced upstream beside him, past the island. When he judged he'd made enough distance, Mystery leapt back into the water, this time letting the flow draw him back to the island from the other side. He cut across the current to ensure he didn't sweep by. His feet met gravel.

Paws bounded past.

Yuma and Delsin slid down and ran to where Laila and Meda lay, both of them grey, and fell to their knees.

Mystery emitted a blast of love.

Chapter 19

Laila reeled as a fist slammed into her ear. She gulped back a cry and cringed against the tree, digging her nails into her palms. She watched from hooded eyes as Jolon stomped away, scattering her herbs.

Three days after the autumn equinox. A day to celebrate. Her ninth birthday.

No longer able to hear the birds from the ringing in her head, Laila scooped up her basket and searched for hazelnuts. Those the squirrels had left were damaged or rotten. She dug for lily corms instead; she must take something back.

Her mother glanced at the few shrivelled leaves and bulbs. "That won't make much of a feast."

"Father came—"

"There's witch-hazel in the jar. It'll help the bruise." Her mother scooped up baby Delsin, cooing and rocking her latest. She'd lost the last four.

Laila wished she could be rocked and comforted.

Her grazed skin stung as she rolled over. A man leant over her. Laila shrank into the dirt and blinked. The image didn't make sense. Delsin! Delsin a grown man?

She fought off the fog in her brain. Her head cleared. A damp and stinking wolf-skin squirmed above her shivering body. Flailing in panic, she fought against strong hands. The nightmare worsened. The writhing fur slipped off to reveal her naked body covered with cuts and bruises. Another pelt smothered her. She thrashed to escape its cloying softness.

"Steady, Laila. It's okay. You're safe."

The voice sounded familiar. *Who...? Yuma!* What was Yuma doing here?

The snort of a horse confused her further. She must be dreaming. Something wet stroked her arm. A lick. The nudge of a wet nose.

"Paws!" Laila came around and gasped for air. Her lungs seared. Every breath stung as if she'd been punched in the ribs.

Delsin crouched by her side. "It's alright. Mystery is here. We'll get you off the island. But we must go soon. The tide is rising. Can you stand?"

The island. Now she remembered. She struggled to do as asked. "Help me."

With Yuma on one side and Delsin on the other, they dragged her onto Mystery. Unable to sit up, Laila slumped like a sack of rocks along his back.

Mystery fidgeted. "Tie her hands around my neck. She's not strong enough to hold on."

Limp as an uprooted nettle, Laila let her brother strap her onto the unicorn's back. They plunged into the river. Water rose up her thighs. She kicked out, gagged, and spluttered. "Stop! Stop! I can't hold on!"

Mystery struck out for the bank. "There's no time. I must go back for the others. Paws is on my tail and Meda is on my crest. Think about them."

The idea of her dear friends succumbing to the river drove thoughts of Laila's plight from her mind. Meda was still with her. Paws was alive!

Mystery clambered up the muddy slope. He released her bonds, knelt, and slipped her to the ground. "Send love to Meda. She's trying to heal you and needs your help."

He leapt back into the river.

Shivering, Laila scraped together a nest of leaves. Her head throbbed and her lungs were seared as if she had breathed in hot coals. A tingle ran up and down her limbs. Blood rushed to her face, hands and feet, and her heart pounded. Every hair on her arms and legs stood erect from the dragon-healing.

By the time Mystery returned with Yuma and Delsin, Laila had become fully aware. After they gave her some of their clothes to wear, she thanked them with as much energy as she could muster. "How come you're here?"

Between them, they related how Paws had sought help and guided them. When Laila heard how Mystery had been trapped by Jolon, Paco, and Kele, her anger almost overcame Meda. Only Mystery's intervention prevented the dragon from collapsing.

Yuma held out his diamond scale. "Hold this. If you can see her, perhaps you'll be able to help her better. She needs your love more than any of ours."

Seeing the emerald dragon wink into view did more to lighten Laila's spirits than the heartiest meal. "Meda! I've missed you. Thank you for staying with me."

"I'll always be with you. Stop fussing. You're interfering with my healing."

Laila stared, horrified at Meda's appearance, her wings limp with raw gaps between her scales. "What happened to you? Couldn't you fly across the river?"

"My scales fell off before Mystery arrived. I tried to heal you on my own. It was hard without anyone sending me love."

Mystery blew warm air over Laila's face. "Stop talking and let her work. I thought you were both dead when we found you. We must all help her."

As her health improved, Laila struggled to sit up. "Are all my things gone?"

Delsin held her hand and gave her a sympathetic gaze. "We didn't find anything. I'll have a look downstream later. For now, you must rest."

Yuma left her side and set about gathering wood, saying a fire and a feed would make them all feel better.

The sun sank above the falls. Laila's strength returned. Now she only suffered a shortness of breath.

Meda returned to her multi-hues, albeit duller than normal. "You've got fluid in your lungs. That should be gone soon."

Laila hugged the tiny dragon close before relinquishing Yuma's scale.

"No. Hold onto it, at least until you're well enough to leave here." Yuma handed back the diamond as well as a bowl of steaming broth. "What did you think you were doing, heading off on your own like that? The stealthcats could be anywhere. It's not safe for you to travel alone."

Laila didn't need a lecture. "I wasn't alone. I had Paws, and Meda.

I couldn't stay with the Eastlanders after Abey let my father steal my amulet."

Yuma's red face belied his calm voice. "Instead, you endangered us and the horses by having to chase after you."

Indignation replaced Laila's gratitude. "I didn't ask you to come after me. You would never expect anyone to come after you on your travels."

"Maybe not, but you almost drowned. Would have, if it hadn't been for Paws." Yuma chewed hard on a strip of dried meat.

"She was wonderful." Laila softened. "Thank you for coming to look for me. I'm sorry I've caused so much trouble."

"We couldn't let you risk your life. I'm sorry I shouted at you, but we've been worried sick. Eat up. You need to regain your strength."

Laila sniffed the bowl of broth. "I can't eat this, it has animal in it."

Yuma threw up his arms as he rose to his feet. "It's all we have. You used to eat meat before living at Shimmering Lake. You need to now."

Mystery snuffled in her hair. "The deer has already given its life. Better not to waste its gift."

Laila apologised. She must fill her stomach, no matter how distasteful. She slurped her soup, cautious at first and then with more enthusiasm as the warmth seeped through her aching body. She finished the last drop and slipped her arms around Paws. "You must see that Paws is no threat now."

Yuma nodded. "You and Meda would both be dead without her. But don't think I'll befriend all wolves, or change my mind about Mystery enhancing Tatuk's scale."

He tossed more wood on the fire. "So what are you going to do now?"

Flames licked the fresh fuel and twisted into mesmerising tongues. Nothing had changed Laila's mind. "Head north. I plan to winter in the forest before heading back to Shimmering Lake as soon as I can cross Dragonspine Mountains."

Delsin glanced at Yuma and back at her. "That's what we thought you'd say. So we're coming with you."

Appealing as the idea was, Laila refused to accept that she couldn't cope alone. "I'll be fine. You need to teach people to ride and fight the stealthcats."

Yuma plonked beside her. "We're coming whether you like it or not. The clans will cope without the two of us. There're other Midlanders who can teach archery from horseback."

Delsin crouched and wrapped an arm around her waist. "This is no time to be alone. It'll be like when we made up adventures as kids."

Still weak from her dunking, Laila accepted. "Thank you." She hauled herself to her feet and stroked Mystery's neck. "It'll be good to be travelling with you again. I've missed you."

Mystery arched his crest and flared his nostrils. "I'm not coming north. My warriors are waiting on the other side of the river. We're going to find the stolen warmblood mares. I told you before; you must stay with your own kind."

The three people travelled in comfortable companionship, none of them mentioning how much they missed Mystery and the horses. Laila appreciated the help collecting food and water, setting up camp, and cooking. As the days cooled, they kept watch for a suitable place to spend the winter, eventually settling on a clearing under a giant spruce, close to a fresh stream bubbling with trout.

Laila gathered nuts and fruits to dry for the lean times ahead, Delsin stockpiled firewood, and Yuma trapped or shot small mammals to dry their meat and tan their skins. Grateful for once that she didn't have her amulet, Laila stayed clear of the butchering.

They took turns standing guard each night, but without her amulet providing the ability to detect stealthcats, Laila had little confidence in their safety. Still weakened from her ordeal, she couldn't cope with the discomfort of sleeping in the branches. "Let's build a treehouse. Then none of us need guard."

The men agreed, lugging suitable timbers to the spruce, which offered a sturdy base for their home. Laila shimmied up the trunk and laid each piece of wood as close together as she could. She knotted a rope of twisted bark around the horizontal branch and lashed the platform securely.

She stamped her foot to test the strength of the last piece of flooring. "That should hold it. What about a roof?"

Yuma peered up at her from the base of the tree. "Delsin is cutting fronds from a stand of firs. They'll give us protection from wind and rain. But we obviously can't light a fire up there. It'll be cold at night."

"We can make walls and line them with leaf litter, like a big nest." Laila swung down the ladder they had rigged for access to the treehouse. Paws was nowhere in sight. She must have gone hunting, bored with the construction of their winter shelter.

Footsteps rustled behind Laila. She turned to help her brother. And froze.

Her father stood there, hands on hips. "Well, what do you know? My errant daughter."

Laila stepped back, closer to Yuma. "What are you doing here?"

Jolon advanced. "We were hunting deer, to help feed the extra people at Bluff. Doing our bit, like good citizens. Not running away and avoiding our duties, like you."

A twig snapped. Paco and Kele emerged from the trees like wraiths.

Yuma rested a hand on her shoulder. "This is a big forest. You didn't bump into us by accident. You've tracked us here."

Jolon scowled. "Don't interfere, Waterfalls man. I've come for my daughter. She has to cook and mend for me through winter. I can't expect Eastlanders to see to my needs."

Years of anger bubbled in Laila's stomach, her torments from childhood surfacing like fresh sores. "I'm no longer part of your family. Do your own cooking and mending."

"Why, has this Waterfalls man taken you to bed? He hasn't given me my bride price. I don't release you." Jolon snatched at her arm.

She pulled away. "Leave me alone. You gave up any rights to me long ago. Go back to Bloomsvale if you can't look after yourself. I'm staying here."

At a signal from Jolon, Paco and Kele leapt at Yuma, grabbing his arms and pinning them behind his back. Yuma kicked and struggled, no match on his own against the two hunters.

Jolon wrapped one arm around Laila and grasped one of her hands in his other fist. She bit his forearm and received a blow to her head that sent stars spinning in front of her eyes. He grabbed her other hand and held them tight in one mighty paw while lashing her wrists with a thong.

Paco and Kele fought to restrain Yuma, unable to hold his arms long enough to bind him. Curses filled the air as they slipped on the wet leaves beneath the trees.

A shape materialised from behind a wide trunk. Laila struggled in her father's arms, spinning them both round to prevent him seeing her brother. Jolon lifted her in a bear hug and spun back.

Hope rose in her heart.

Yuma had Paco pinned to the ground and was using the man's rawhide strips to lash his feet and hands. Delsin stood over Kele, a thick branch raised as a club, holding him in place until Yuma could bind him, too.

With that completed, Yuma advanced towards Jolon, fists raised. "Let her go."

Jolon dragged her behind him. "Mind your own business. Do what you like with those men, but this bitch is coming with me." He towed her from her new home by the wrists.

Laila fought and kicked out to snag her legs around a tree.

Delsin yelled.

Yuma dashed back to help him, barging Kele to the ground and rolling on top of him.

Delsin snatched at flailing arms and legs, his own yells adding to the grunts of the other two.

Jolon lugged Laila away, out of sight of the fight.

A blur of grey flashed past her face.

Jolon yelled and released her. She flopped to her knees.

Paws had her father pinned to the ground. The wolf bared her teeth, growling. Her feet gouged into his stomach and chest as she twisted to grasp his neck. He wriggled to evade her, jerking his knees upwards into Paws' belly.

Laila staggered and searched for anything to use as a weapon. A stout branch left over from their building propped against a sapling, but with her hands tied, she couldn't part her fingers enough to grip it.

Paws yelped.

The sound tore through Laila's heart. Abandoning the branch, she launched herself on top of Jolon where he straddled Paws. His arm rose for another blow and belted Laila instead of the wolf. She rocked back onto her backside, winded, close to blacking out. Muffled cries and whimpers permeated her ears.

Jolon swung his fist towards her.

Laila braced for a strike that never came.

Yuma grasped Jolon's arm with both hands and wrenched it behind her father's back. He scrambled to rise. Delsin kicked at his legs, tripping him up. The three men fought in a melee of limbs, their battle taking them away from Laila.

She clutched one arm around her stomach and threw the other over Paws' neck. The wolf lay on her side, motionless. Her blood soaked into the sticky ground. Sharp sticks and rough stones dug into Laila's flesh, but she ignored the added discomfort to her ringing head. Was Paws dead? Grief threatened to overwhelm her. A slight lift of the wolf's chest sent her pulse racing. She sent love to Meda in the hope the dragon was near and could help.

The men tussled on. Grunts and curses accompanied thuds and crashes. The brawl moved through the trees, becoming distant, then louder. Or was that only her consciousness fading in and out? Never mind the men; what about Paws, her faithful friend? She must help her.

Battling her own injuries, she gingerly fingered the wound in Paws' side. The blood had stopped flowing, coagulating in a dark mass. A sharp point indicated that whatever had stabbed the wolf remained within her. Laila struggled to remove the flint, dreading the possibility of tearing Paws' organs. She probed further. The flint was too deep. She daren't remove the weapon alone.

She needed Meda, needed Yuma and his diamond scale, needed to be free of the agony ripping apart her head. She attempted to call for help. Only a croak escaped her lips, her bruised face swelling and puffing her eyes closed.

She clawed for the medicine pouch that always hung from her belt. Thank goodness, Delsin had retrieved it from the river. The bag lay beneath her hip. Moving seared her ribs. Biting her lower lip enough to draw blood, she eased the bag to where she could fumble through the contents. She found the hollow wooden tube containing her precious store of bumblebee nectar, knocked off the wax end, and squeezed the contents around the shaft of Paws' wound.

She had done all she could. She passed out.

Chapter 20

Coarse sand massaged Shadow's soles as he galloped in the surf. Many generations of horses had been born since he had last revelled in the salt spray on his coat and the sea breeze teasing his tail out in a crimson plume. Drawing in the power of the tide, he bucked and kicked with glee, squealing in fun as the splashes surrounded him with rainbows.

Room to run.

He had forgotten what it was like. Even his idyllic territory at Eagle's Peak failed to invigorate him like the endless horizon over the ocean. He had regained a sense of space when crossing the grassy plains, travelling day and night, rarely stopping to drink or graze, in no need of oral sustenance. The sun, the wind, and the spinning earth nurtured him like the touch of the goddess.

The reminder of Aureana soured his mood. What had she known of his needs? She had never understood that he used his power to strengthen animals, not harm them. It wasn't his fault she had created weaklings. Why had she given him the power of enhancement if not to use it?

And that interfering, second-generation unicorn was determined to disrupt Shadow's plans to build a warmblood herd. But there must be many warmblood stallions who would be keen to join him in return for mares of their own. Powerful mares of his bloodline. He hadn't heard of Mystery offering them his own offspring. The youngster probably hadn't sired any anyway, too busy with his grand adventure to bother mating with the mares he encountered.

Shadow had journeyed to the coast first in the hope of gathering stallions as he progressed back to Dragonspine Mountains. There should be plenty with unicorn ancestry this far north. His stealthcats had only hunted for warmblood mares south of Devil's River, leaving the bachelor herds up here unscathed.

He turned inland and climbed the wooded slopes, thinking of the captive mares at Eagle's Peak. Wood Lily, the red roan, showed a lot of promise. Big and bold, she had a sharp mind. Her friend, Golden Breeze, was a gentler type, unlike her filly, Chase. Now *there* was one to make his heart race.

His loins stirred as he imagined her in a few years, grown to maturity. What offspring they would have! Her black eyes pierced his soul whenever he encountered her; he had to avoid meeting her unawares. The memories hurt. Dewdrop's eyes. The unicorns never forgave him for her death, and blamed him for Aureana leaving Equinora. But it wasn't his fault. She left because her own powers had weakened. She couldn't bear to witness his successes after her failures.

The ultimate irony had come when Blaze, a young red-legged dragon lost in a storm, flew into Shadow's realm. Shadow had relished enhancing him to feed on fire, one of Aureana's precious dragons who she had created to be friends of unicorns, the arrogant unicorns who mocked Shadow's existence. Blaze had not only proved useful in Shadow's quest for warmblood mares, he also proved that Shadow's power overrode Aureana's, a sweet revenge.

No more for him the wet and dismal Obsidian Caves with only the creatures that loved the dark and cold for company, a land of sharp rocks and stinking pools, where jagged peaks constricted his view of the stars. That was all behind him now. Never again would such a gloomy place be his home.

He'd build his herd of mares and raise his offspring with full use of their powers. Not for him the trail of unacknowledged fillies and colts left behind in his wake like those of the unicorn stallions. He'd make sure his legacy grew strong, knowing their place in Equinora, working for him.

He would rule supreme. All Equinora would be his.

Mystery swam across the river to guide his warriors upstream of the waterfalls. Back on the north side where grass heads ripened, they feasted and drank in preparation for the mission ahead, leaving what little feed remained after the fires in the south for King Socks'

herd and the coldblood bachelors.

Reinvigorated, they raced across the plains, their drumming hooves churning up clods along the riverbank. Rocky galloped alongside Mystery, with Willow and Murmur close behind. Other friendships had also formed among the warriors as they practised attack and defence tactics. All were muscled and agile, horses in their prime, their warm blood strengthening their vigour.

Mystery flicked his toes out in copper flashes and slowed to a floating trot; the others would need to conserve their energy. A cool breeze foreshadowed the end of autumn, tangling his mane and tail. A pang of remorse for not having Laila to groom him dispersed as he watched the stallions catch up; they were better unencumbered by people. Many of these horses had never had a relationship with men. It had done them no harm. Perhaps the first-generation unicorns had misinterpreted the goddess' directions that humans and horses should live and work together.

Could he trust Moonglow's prophecy? He hadn't discovered his power as she'd promised. Maybe second-generation unicorns were weaker, not stronger, than first-generation unicorns as Diamond believed. Perhaps the dragons sustained life at Shimmering Lake, not Gem. She hadn't originally been aware of her influence on the life-giving waters. What did it mean that his grandsire had been the deformed and bad-tempered Jasper, and his great-grandsire was Shadow, the duocorn? He'd prefer to be powerless than live like them, rampaging in anger, raping mares wherever they went. And neither his sire nor dam was even a unicorn.

Regardless of the prophecy, it was his task to save the warmblood mares. His alone. He must prove his worth, to himself, and to Gem. He picked up speed, his frustration echoing in his hoofbeats.

Rocky broke into his turmoil. "We should stop while there's still warmth in the day. A roll and a graze would be welcome."

Contrite, Mystery agreed. "We've made good time. This looks as good a place as any."

The stallions wasted no time in dropping their heads and tearing at the feed. Yet the land vibrated as if they still galloped at full speed. Mystery stretched his mindmap of the earth to find a fault-line that could be causing a tremor. The rock beneath him didn't move. No volcanic action disturbed the peace. No earthquakes built under the seabed.

The thrumming increased. Now Mystery could hear hoofbeats, too. Horses approached, at a gallop.

His stallions lifted their heads to face the oncoming dust cloud. Bays, greys, chestnuts, and roans pelted towards them like waves crashing on the shoreline, leaping and pounding in a froth of sweat.

Shadow led the charge.

Mystery whinnied the signal to stand abreast. He had never anticipated that his adversary would rally warmblood stallions to his side. All reports had said that the stealthcats murdered any they found, only stealing mares. Why would horses fight for the duocorn? Perhaps he had poisoned them, too.

Shadow skidded to a halt only a few horse lengths away, rearing and striking out with his forelegs. "Are you ready to fight this time, unicorn, or are you going to bolt like a frightened colt again?"

Mystery snorted and tossed his mane. "I wasn't running from you. I was saving us from the fire."

Shadow pranced in a wide circle. "Go back to the coast and play with your human friends, those who are powerless like you. Why are you heading to Dragonspine Mountains?"

Mystery reared and boxed with his hooves. "You don't rule Equinora. The goddess left unicorns as the land's protectors. I'll free the mares you've stolen and return them to their king."

"You and whose army? Not that miserable lot ranged behind you." Shadow trotted between the two lines of stallions, hovering between strides, his legs bunched muscle. His arched neck and rocking rump pulsed with energy.

Not to be outdone, Mystery cantered alongside, performing flying changes every stride. His silver coat gleamed, and his horn flashed like his hooves.

Shadow halted and stood proud, addressing Mystery's stallions. "None of you have the power to defeat me. Join your friends on my side and benefit from all I can offer."

None of the horses behind Mystery moved.

A sorrel with deep blue eyes advanced from Shadow's line. "Murmur! This is your chance. Join us and you'll have mares of your own. Warmblood mares. We can build our bloodlines strong."

Horrified that Whisper had left Elk Bank to join Shadow, Mystery waited to see what Murmur would do.

The younger of Wood Lily's sons held his ground. "At what

cost? The death of other horses? The destruction of good grazing? I think not."

Shadow approached each of Mystery's stallions in turn, offering to grant them his female offspring.

Mystery bit back his temper. Already brother was pitched against brother. He didn't want to fight his own blood, as bad as his ancestor may be. That was no way to bring peace to Equinora. And what if he failed? Convincing Shadow to call back his stealthcats and return the mares was a better strategy. Socks would probably be glad to let mares remain in the mountains until spring—little enough feed existed at Hawk Plains—rather than endure the return journey from wherever Shadow had hidden them. Mystery and his warriors could fetch them after the rains refreshed the land, before they dropped their foals and came into season.

Shadow ceased offering dreams to the stallions. Having received no positive responses, he confronted Mystery again. "Gutless, like your sire. Stand and do nothing. No power. Let me knock that horn from your head and make you the plain horse you are."

The taunts washed over Mystery like the falls at Devil's Throat, chilling him but unable to penetrate his skin. "Where are the mares? Let them decide."

"What makes you think they haven't already chosen me? Many already carry my foals. Even if you did find them, what then? Can you lead a herd? Do you have a territory to raise young? No."

Mystery stepped closer, his heart racing as he fought the urge to attack. "If you want mares, you should negotiate with their king."

"Negotiate? I won't deal with coldbloods. I'm only letting you live so you can see me take Gemstone. She should have been mine all along, and would have been if I hadn't been trapped at Obsidian Caves. She's Dewdrop's replacement, the Air Unicorn, and belongs to me."

"Gem belongs to no one. She'd never go willingly with you." *Would she? What if he couldn't find his power? Shadow was certainly strong. Was it true the warmblood mares stayed with him willingly?*

Ridiculous. This was his chance. Now. While Shadow stood before him. Time to fight and find his power, or lose everything.

Was he strong enough to kill Shadow? Could he murder his great-grandsire? Why hadn't Shadow really attacked? Perhaps because he feared if he killed Mystery, the next Fire Unicorn would be even stronger. But stronger than who—a silver stallion with no power? Maybe this was his destiny, for Shadow to kill him so that another unicorn could be born, one from unicorn parents.

The sky darkened.

Blaze landed with a loud flapping of his grey wings. "Where's that miserable eagle who stole my feathers the gold precious flight that belongs to dragons the blessed creatures of the goddess?"

This time, with Shadow's stallions unperturbed, Mystery's warriors held their place, though he sensed their unease with the risk of flamehawks.

The fire-dragon hopped from one red foot to another, his wings held out, so unlike the dragons at Shimmering Lake. How could Shadow so corrupt such a beautiful being? Dragons were magnificent creatures, normally full of laughter and fun, spending their time playing when not helping others, evidenced by Meda's devotion to Laila, offering her own life in an effort to save the woman.

Not like this monster. But it wasn't Blaze's fault that Shadow had transformed him.

Mystery sent Blaze images of jewelled dragons cavorting at Shimmering Lake. He shared his memories of dragons riding his crest and tail in delight. He recalled the joy of galloping with the wind, dragons flitting and giggling in his slipstream.

Blaze ceased bobbing around and pointed his snout towards Mystery. His grey scales glimmered. One by one, they popped into colour. Emerald, ruby, and diamond. Topaz, sapphire, and amethyst. Gaps that had been oozing pus closed and became jade, turquoise, and opal.

"Stop! Right now." Shadow swung his hindquarters at Mystery and lashed out with his heels.

Mystery sidestepped the onslaught. He wouldn't be distracted. His stallions formed a circle around him and Blaze. He streamed images of love and beauty to the dragon.

Shadow rallied his stallions, reiterating his promises of well-fed mares and good pasture. They leapt forward to break the barrier formed by Mystery's warriors. The ring remained firm. Mystery's stallions blocked their opponents without fighting, keeping their rumps to Mystery as he concentrated on Blaze.

The mighty dragon fanned his wings wide to admire his scales.

Flesh built on his bones, filling out his wrinkles and tightening his sagging skin. He radiated warmth, and light gleamed in his eyes. The last grey scale transformed into crystal. He sprang above Mystery's head and spiralled against the pale blue sky, shining brighter than the sun. "Glory glory who needs feathers? Feathers are for birds cumbersome ugly beaked weaklings not like me me me!" His cries of joy rose and fell as he swooped, rising effortlessly and gliding on outstretched wings before tucking them to his sides and diving again.

"Enough!" Shadow barged through the milling stallions and crashed into Mystery's chest. "This means nothing. I'll kill all who don't join me."

Mystery broke away and summoned his warriors. "Don't be drawn into a fight. We need to locate the mares, not overcome those who were once your friends."

Blaze plummeted with a rush of wind, clawing at Shadow. "You kept the beauty from me no love no glory no magnificence! Mystery gives me jewels memories of dragons my own kind and how we are! I will lead him to Eagle's Peak of mares foals stealthcats emerald fields!"

Mystery had only intended to aid Blaze to become his true self. To hear the dragon offer to lead him to Shadow's hideout was more than he could have asked for. "Blaze, you're magnificent. Let's go now, and outrun these thieves."

As if someone had signalled the start of a race, all the stallions spurted into a gallop towards the west, following the great dragon flying fast and low.

Shadow drove his stallions into a fury with commands and promises. They barged and snapped at Mystery's stallions to block their way.

Mystery egged his warriors into greater effort. They responded with gusto.

Help! Mystery! We need you!

Meda! What had happened? She had never sought his aid before. But how could he go to her on the point of rescuing the mares? He stumbled and grazed his nose on the ground.

Shadow thumped into his rear end. "Flagging already, unicorn? Give up now. You won't win. Gemstone is mine."

Mystery recovered his stride and ignored Shadow. He picked

up speed, chasing after Blaze, leaving his warriors in his dust.

The nasty man is attacking us! Help!

Blaze twisted in the air, changed direction, and headed east. "A dragon in danger one of my kind needs me needs you we must go!"

Mystery faltered. Without Blaze to lead him, he had no choice. He'd never find the hidden territory at Eagle's Peak. And Meda wouldn't call if it weren't serious. Laila was in trouble. He couldn't abandon her. He had to go back and travel fast, which meant going alone.

He galloped back the way he had come. "Rocky! Lead the stallions back to Devil's Throat. Don't fight Shadow's warriors. I'll join you as soon as I can."

He didn't have time to travel overland. He needed to translocate like Diamond. Drawing energy from the land, the wind, and the sun, he pictured Devil's Throat where he had left Laila and the men. At every airborne moment between strides, he poured strength into his horn, expecting to land on the riverbank.

It didn't work. He didn't have the power to translocate. Frustrated that he must gallop the whole way, he redirected the energy into his legs and became a blur. Already Blaze was far in front. Mystery had to catch up, fast. He daren't let the fire-breathing dragon arrive first.

Chapter 21

Mystery galloped after Blaze alone. His breath fluttered his nostrils at every stride, drowning out all other sound. His heart hammered in his chest, pounding in rhythm with his hooves. Worry for his friends gripped his innards in a tangled knot. What would Blaze do when he encountered Meda? He obviously hadn't noticed the healer dragon when they had met before, maybe because he had been empty of love. What a terrible existence he had lived until now, starved of the goddess' nourishment, driven to burn in order to survive.

Pity for the oversized dragon mingled with Mystery's fear for Laila, Yuma, and Delsin. What had happened? It had to be something to do with Jolon. Meda had called him "the nasty man".

Blaze drew ahead until even his jewelled dot disappeared from the sky. Mystery sucked energy from the land, his legs a blur from his speed. Where did Meda call from? Without Blaze to guide him, Mystery ran blind. His best hope was to intersect the path the people had been on when he'd left them on the north bank of the river. They had been heading for the protection of the forests, but Mystery had no idea where.

He stretched his mindmap of the land as far as he could, to seek the high levels of carbon in the trees. He detected the retreating sap of the deciduous aspens and ashes, and the dormant stillness of the firs and spruce, mingled on rolling hills of rich loam ahead. The forest drew him on with hope that the people would be sheltered under its canopy.

Reaching the tree line, he slowed to a trot and wound his way through the copses, jumping fallen logs and ducking under low branches. Birds called warnings and animals scurried into the brush at the haste of his passage. A herd of deer leapt across the path in front of him.

He veered after them. "Wait! Can you help me?"

A large buck dithered as his does and fawns fled.

Mystery halted and called a greeting. "I'm searching for my friends."

The stag kept his distance. "Who are you looking for?"

"Three people and a wolf. Have you seen them?"

"If I had, I wouldn't be here. They'd be no friends of mine." The stag leapt away.

The chattering jays perched high above his head proved more helpful. "Further north. Humans are building a nest. Look for a giant spruce."

Mystery thanked the birds and cantered as fast as the zig-zag trails allowed. The aroma of rotting leaf litter and crushed pine needles mingled around him. And, yes, *wolf*. He lowered his head to follow the scent.

Footprints. Three people and a wolf. At least they were still together. He extended his stride, eager to catch up. Another three sets of footprints joined the path, heavier than the first, and moving faster, judging by the length of the stride. Could these be from the men who had trapped him? If so, no wonder Meda had called for help.

Frequent comings and goings muddled the original tracks, but the upper three trails remained fresh and unmarred. He must be getting close. He pricked his ears. Yells and thuds gave him direction. He spurted ahead, heedless of the twigs whacking his face and stabbing his sides. He raced into a clearing, taking the scene in at a glance. Two men lay trussed like hogs ready for the fire. Yuma and Delsin struggled with another man.

Jolon!

Mystery neighed and plunged, biting the man's flailing arms. Afraid to hurt Yuma or Delsin, he refrained from kicking and danced around the threesome, dodging in to snap whenever an opening presented itself. With his harassment, his friends grappled Jolon to the ground.

Mystery reared, energy pulsing down his legs with the desire to drive his hooves down on Jolon's head, blocked by the other men. "Let me at him."

Yuma lashed Jolon's arms behind his back and squatted to lash his legs. The man kicked and struggled.

Mystery poised, his horn aimed at Jolon's chest. "You wanted my horn, Midlander? How would you like it straight through your heart?"

Delsin grabbed Mystery's mane. "No! Stop! He's my father, no matter what he's done."

"He's evil. Let me kill him." Mystery grew larger with pent up rage.

Yuma threw Jolon to the ground and grabbed his legs. "Not now. We'll deal with him later. Laila needs help."

Reason returned to Mystery. Adrenalin burned his limbs as his passion dissipated. "Where is she?"

Only then did he spot Laila's prone form slumped over Paws' inert body. He dashed across, Delsin close on his heels while Yuma finished tying Jolon. "Where's Meda?"

Delsin crouched by his sister. "I can't see dragons. Isn't she here?"

"No." Mystery called for Yuma to hurry. "Have you seen Meda?"

Yuma rushed over and knelt beside Laila, checking her neck for a pulse with one hand and reaching for his diamond scale with the other. "I can't see her. And Tatuk's scale is cold."

Meda would never leave Laila by choice. "Have you seen Blaze, a giant dragon?"

Yuma shook his head. "The one you say sets fire to everything? I doubt we'd be alive to tell you if we had."

"If Meda heard his screeching gabble, she's probably in hiding."

Laila drifted in a haze of dreams: the blissful days at Shimmering Lake, learning the art of healing from Gem, being gifted a scale by Meda and discovering the wonder of dragons, and the arrival of Mystery and him growing into a fine stallion. *Oh, the first time she rode him—the thrill!* The wind in her hair as they galloped over hills and through valleys. Leaping streams and boulders, sunlight glinting off the lake's rainbow waters. They'd stop to swim, aquadragons giggling as they towed on his tail or surfed on bubbles erupting from his strong leg strokes. Then he'd emerge onto the sandy bank and nibble sweet shoots as she lazed and sunned her skin. He'd come and stand over her, blowing in her face, his soft muzzle tickling her cheek.

She could feel it now, enjoying the intimacy.

"Laila. What happened to Meda?"

Pain wracked her guts. No dream held agony like this. "Meda?"

"Laila. Wake up. Meda's missing. She called me and I raced here on the wind. What happened?"

Laila returned to full consciousness. Her midriff screamed. She forced her eyelids apart. She was in Eastlands, in the forest north of the river. The fight with her father! "Paws! Meda... I can't...I don't have...my amulet. Yuma... Delsin..."

Mystery blew warm breath over her face. "They're alright. They have the men tied up. We must find Meda. I can't help you without her."

Laila didn't care about her own wounds. "Paws. Will she live?"

"I don't know." Mystery snuffled over the wolf's body, grief dulling his eyes.

A flask of water touched Laila's damaged lips. Yuma crouched at her side. "Drink this. I've added yarrow and celandine so it won't taste nice, but it'll help the pain."

Laila gagged on the bitter liquid. "Meda. Use your scale."

Yuma continued to dribble the sour potion into her mouth. "I've tried. We can't find her. Tatuk's scale is cold."

She spluttered through swollen lips and twisted her head away. "Has she gone...home?"

Mystery shook his mane. "After she called for help, she guided me until her messages became too weak. She must be exhausted. I had to follow your trail to find you."

That made sense. Meda would have attempted to heal her and Paws. But if Yuma's scale was cold, Meda was dead. She wept.

Mystery paced around Laila. Damn his lack of powers! Couldn't he do anything? His friends lay helpless, dying. Again. He couldn't even face down Shadow, let alone save the warmblood mares. Instead he had fled at the slightest excuse. But he dreaded to think what Blaze would have done if he'd arrived here alone. Mystery had forgotten him in his worry at Laila's plight.

Branches crashed overhead as if Mystery's thoughts had summoned him. Blaze thrashed and flapped as he descended through the tree, snapped limbs cascading in a shower of sticks. "Where is she my dragonheart my soulmate my jewelled beauty who calls for aid? Where is she of my kind that echoes in my mind and brings back memories of glory days in warmth and heat and fire and love?"

Blaze landed, his wings torn and his scales greying.

Yuma nocked an arrow to his bow and stood ready to shoot. "Mystery! Get out of the way!"

"No! Don't hurt him." He leapt between Yuma and the raging dragon, sidestepping and prancing in order to save the dragon from harm. If only Meda hadn't called out in panic to everyone who could hear. Gem would be distraught if her dragons had also picked up the message. Hopefully they were too far away, and only Blaze's enlargement had enabled him to hear Meda from such a distance. Now Mystery needed to pacify him before he burnt the forest and his friends. "Calm down! We'll find her. She must be near."

Blaze tossed his snout, rolled his crimson eyes, and flew across to where Laila and Paws lay. He raised a taloned claw.

"No! They're my friends." Mystery bounded over, thrusting his horn to block Blaze's path.

Blaze leant back with outstretched wings and trumpeted to the treetops. "Where where where are you my beauty? I heard your call and have come to help to save to be with you! Who is the enemy what have they done?"

Mystery pointed his horn at Jolon. "He's the one who attacked my friends. He's the one who locked me in a valley against my will."

Blaze inhaled, swelling to twice his girth. Scales that had paled from his flight, away from Mystery's love, now shimmered red. With a great leap, he landed opposite Jolon and huffed a stream of fire over the man.

Jolon's screams shook the forest. His coverings flared and sizzled as his skin crisped and blackened. The man crumpled to the ground, the flames miraculously not setting the vegetation alight.

Mystery gagged on the stench of burning hair and flesh. "Stop! That won't help us find Meda."

The distraction proved enough. The mighty dragon bellowed at the sky. "Where are you my lady my dragon companion my saviour?"

Something tweaked in Mystery's mind. He stared towards a dense bramble thicket.

Blaze flapped in the same direction.

Hope rose in Mystery's heart. Blaze would be far more sensitive to Meda's calls. "Yuma! Quick!"

Catching up with Blaze, they followed where he'd trampled the thorny briars. Meda lay tangled in their branches, grey and withered. Mystery blasted love to her, followed by another blast to Blaze. "Have strength. We'll save her."

While blocking Blaze from advancing, Mystery instructed Yuma to extract Meda from the prickly tangle and carry her out. Then he explained to Blaze about the power of love. Before he could send another surge of love to Meda, she twitched. One by one, her scales blinked into glowing rainbows. Never had he seen anyone recover so quickly. Awed at Blaze's power, Mystery thanked him.

"Meda Meda Meda my Meda another dragon the only one I have ever known! I'll send you love so you can grow like me and together we'll rule the treetops the mountains the skies!"

Meda sat up in Yuma's arms, her eyes agog. "Laila! Paws! We must save them!"

Blaze hopped from foot to foot, his outstretched wings banging against trunks and branches, sending a shower of pine cones and needles around them all. "Never mind them my beauty my dragon queen lets fly fly fly high high high!"

"No! Not yet. I must heal them. Help me."

They hurried back to where Laila lay curled around Paws. Meda landed on her shoulder. Blaze perched on a log and folded his wings, his swirling eyes staring at Meda as if she might disappear if he blinked. With his energy feeding her, and Mystery drawing on Equinora's life forces to support them both, Laila and Paws began to heal. Yuma extracted the flint from the wolf's side. Her wound closed over. Laila's ribs set and mended. Her bruises dissipated as her injuries healed, though it would still require days for her to recover her full strength.

She hugged Mystery's neck. "Thank you for coming back. We'd have died without you." She turned to Blaze. "And you, mighty dragon: I have never met anyone so splendid. Thank you for saving us all."

Blaze strutted from tree to tree with Meda fluttering around his head. He pointed his snout to where Jolon lay, still alive, mewing in pain. "I won't heal enemies of my friends of those who showed me the glory of dragons and gave me back my memories of times so good so wonderful to be regained and enjoyed together with my kind!"

Mystery doubted Laila would want her father cured anyway, after all he had done to her. His clothing had burnt away from his arms and legs, only his torso protected by his thick leather jerkin. "What will we do with him?"

A groan escaped Jolon's blistered face.

Laila spun to the sound, raced over to the burnt man, and knelt beside him. "Father?"

Delsin explained what had happened. "It might be kinder to let him die. He won't want to live as a cripple, like me."

Laila grabbed her brother's arm. "We can't do that. I have a duty to help him."

Delsin shrugged. "Can you save him?"

Another groan escaped the man's tattered lips.

Her grimace changed to a small smile. She stared into Jolon's eyes, the only part of him not charred. "Father, I can't help you unless you return my amulet."

Salty tears trickled down Laila's cheeks as she hugged Meda to her chest. "You've worked so hard and I've missed you terribly. How are you feeling?"

The tiny dragon sparkled as she raised her snout to Laila's face. "Don't cry, I'm fine. Mystery came. Blaze saved me. And Yuma. Look at me! You can see how well I am."

"Yes, you're right. You're beautiful, more than ever. I've never seen you so radiant." Only the grumbling presence of her father dampened Laila's thrill. Since returning her amulet he had said little, keeping to himself and spending most of the day sleeping. She watched over him, using the time to remake her clothes and replace other items lost in the river. It would be a while before Jolon was able to travel. As soon as Yuma had released Paco and Kele, they had slipped away into the forest, not caring that they left Jolon behind. Fortunately, he was terrified of stepping out of place with Blaze on watch.

Even she was wary of the mighty dragon. Having been enhanced by Shadow, Blaze could be seen by all, and everyone could talk with him. He adored Mystery for saving him and teaching him about feeding on love. But the one he really worshipped was Meda, and he'd followed her around at every opportunity. Laila had to ask him to stop, as Meda refused to leave her and it had become too daunting having him shadow her every move.

Yuma and Delsin spent most of their days working with the few pieces of chalcocite they had brought with them. Mystery still insisted that the chunks contained what they needed to cure the stealthcats.

Meda clambered onto Laila's shoulder. "I don't know why we had to heal the nasty man. Blaze wants to eat him with fire again."

Laila reassured her. "We're healers. We can't help acting as we do. And Paws is okay now, thanks to you."

The wolf lay at her feet, her head curled round to her stomach. Now fully grown, long pale winter hairs covered her dark grey underfur. Both ears stood erect and swivelled to catch the slightest noise. The tip of her fluffy tail smacked the ground as Laila stroked her ruff. "Jolon is sound asleep, and Yuma and Delsin are nearby. Let's find Mystery and go for a run. Blaze can fly along, too."

Mystery took no convincing. Laila had to admit they made a curious sight, her riding a silver unicorn, a tiny jewelled dragon flitting around her head and a giant one soaring above, with a wolf loping alongside. Once out of the forest, Mystery stretched into a full gallop. Laila's braids streamed behind her and moisture seeped from her eyes. Warmth from Mystery's back soaked through her freshly woven tunic, contrasting with the chill on her arms. Her spirits lifted higher than they had been since leaving Shimmering Lake, yet they still didn't have a way to overcome the stealthcats.

Mystery pulled up from his hard pace, not even puffing. He nuzzled Laila as she slid down. "I should be heading back to find Shadow's territory. The stallions are as keen as I am to rescue the mares and bring them back before spring."

Laila ran her fingers through Mystery's copper mane. Hollowness grew in her stomach. "I'll miss you. I hate it when we're apart."

He nudged her. "That's one of the reasons you need to come with me."

The invitation startled Laila. "But I thought I'd be in your way. Why have you changed your mind?"

Pawing the ground, Mystery avoided her gaze. "Blaze won't guide me without Meda coming along. And Meda won't leave you."

Chapter 22

Excitement thrummed through Laila—back with Mystery on his search! No matter the reason for his change of heart, the prospect filled her with happiness. Then the truth hit home. "We can't go yet. We haven't worked out how to use the copper against the stealthcats. Besides, I don't think I'm strong enough. Even that short ride has worn me out."

Laila didn't want to add that her innards felt as if they'd torn again. A long trek to Dragonspine Mountains might do more damage than Meda could heal.

Mystery hung his head over her shoulder. "You should have said earlier. I'd have slowed down."

Laila straightened his forelock. "I was having too much fun to want you to stop. So what are you going to do? Can Blaze tell you how to find Shadow's hidden territory?"

"No." Mystery dithered. "We can't afford to delay for long. I'll do what I can to help the men extract the copper. But as soon as you are well enough, we must leave."

After refreshing themselves in a creek, they made their way back to camp. Dohate and several other hunters squatted with Yuma and Delsin around the fire. Laila suppressed her surprise and left Mystery to find his warriors to explain that they would be spending more time at Elk Bank.

The Thatchery chief rose and greeted her. "We miss you at Bluff. We would welcome you back and grant you status as chief healer of the east."

Taken aback by the honour, Laila fingered her amulet, unable to forget so easily the lack of trust that had caused her to leave. "I hope you didn't come all this way to find me."

Dohate acknowledged he hadn't. "We've come for deer, so that the Bluff clan won't resent our staying. The women are drying sardines to give to the Deershill clan in return for us hunting their lands."

"Haven't Paco and Kele returned with enough? They left ages ago."

Dohate's eyebrows shot up. "We haven't seen them. I've brought more hunters to help. It's not the right season for deer to be here, but we must get food."

Laila hated the thought of killing the shy, gentle deer, but the clans needed meat and skins. "I appreciate your offer, but I've no desire to return south. You have your own healers. They coped fine before I came."

The chief continued trying to persuade her to return. "The stealthcats pursue us. We're worried they'll even attack us in the caves. You're the only one who can detect them."

Yuma supported her decision to remain where they were. "We're attempting to create a weapon. We've more chance of finding a solution with Laila and Mystery's help."

Laila cast a glance to where the horses grazed. "And Mystery can't go south. There's insufficient feed for the herds down there as it is, especially since so much land was burnt."

Dohate spread his hands to indicate their camp. "At least join us at Deershill while we're there. I'm sure the clan will welcome you and it will be more comfortable. They have permanent homes set high in the trees. It's worth a visit just to see it, though I'm impressed with your shelter."

Yuma and Delsin nodded.

Laila hesitated. She should agree for their sake, but loathed the idea of being among so many people again.

A wind tore through the camp, tossing leaves and bark in a flurry. Blaze landed in a run, sending the visitors fleeing into the trees. "Those with claws pounce vile stink lurking in the grasses creeping near! Fly fly fly out of the forest and into the blue where dragons rule!"

Mystery charged into the clearing. "Take cover!"
He shot back along the narrow track. Paws bounded behind him,

lips curled open to reveal glistening fangs. Mystery summoned his warriors and looked for Blaze.

The dragon soared and swooped over the rippling grasses, his scales transforming into glowing crimson. Before Mystery could prevent him, Blaze toasted the ground.

The scream of a stealthcat confirmed a direct hit.

Mystery raced over and stamped on the crackling grasses, bellowing to Blaze. "Use your claws! Not fire!"

It was hard to send the dragon love at the same time as raging war on the stealthcats. Thinking of Shimmering Lake, Gem, and his friends, Mystery found each hiding cat and pounced with thrashing hooves. His warriors fought all around him, rearing and stamping, kicking and biting. Like the previous pride they had fought, these lions were unwell, their coats patchy and limbs weak. With the sheer numbers of stallions, the battle swayed the horses' way.

Blaze swooped, carrying aloft a squirming form before letting it drop from up high. The cat thudded on the hard earth, its back broken.

Mystery pounced on another lion and stabbed it with his horn. Like the one he had pierced before, its scent returned. It rose and fled. The other stealthcats followed: whether after their leader, chastened by the stallions' defence, or frightened by Blaze didn't matter.

The attack was over.

Mystery gathered his troops and showed them how to stamp out the sparks that threatened the grazing grounds. If the flames took hold and reached the forest, there would be no stopping the devastation. He hastened back to the camp.

Laila was the first to slide down a tree trunk and race across to him. The men sheathed their arrows before they descended.

When they were all gathered, Mystery described how the mountain lions arranged themselves to spring from a wide front. "If Blaze hadn't warned us, you would have been cat food. Shadow must have sent Claw to spot the warmblood stallions. Under these trees we didn't see him. I think you should move somewhere safer."

Laila twisted a handful of bark and lichen into a wisp and rubbed down his sweaty coat. "We'll go to Deershill then. And we must work harder to extract the copper from the rocks."

It didn't take long for everyone to gather their things and follow

Dohate to the foresters' village, carrying Jolon on a makeshift bed slung between two long poles. They had promised to escort him back to Midlands when he had recovered, providing he never returned. No one wanted to lose the protection of the unicorns or their newfound relationship with horses.

Mystery remained with Blaze a short distance away from Elk Bark, while Laila and Yuma went to explain their strange companions. The clan who lived in the Elk Bank territory had never been close to horses, let alone a tame wolf and a unicorn, and certainly never a fire-breathing dragon.

At a prearranged whistle, Mystery trotted into the settlement. Surprised, he studied the people's shelters, never having imagined humans could house in trees like birds. The clan had built homes among the branches like giant nests, tangles of limbs and twigs woven with pine fronds big enough even for Blaze to spread his wings inside. Not that he would likely be invited to do so. Mystery chuckled at the vision of the dragon perching inside the green cocoon, poking his nose out like he would have when he emerged from his egg.

The image brought back Mystery's anger at how Shadow could so transform a fellow creature, especially dragons that the goddess had created to befriend unicorns in her stead. Blaze had needed succouring and reuniting with his kind, not enslaving, needing to burn in order to survive. What right did Shadow have to alter another being's form? And surely, the mountain lions didn't want to range far from their homeland and hunt creatures not their natural prey.

Mystery had to find a cure for their sickness, stop Shadow from meddling in the lives of horses, and save Equinora from destruction. How else could he return to Gem?

Mystery followed his daily routine to help Laila, Yuma, and Delsin where they pounded and chipped the chalcocite, letting them know where the heaviest deposits in the stones would yield the most for their efforts. With Blaze on watch for Claw, no more surprise attacks occurred. On the rare occasion when stealthcats lurked, they were soon dealt with, few risking the combined wrath of Blaze's talons and the stallions' hooves. From those he touched,

Mystery gauged that the extended use of zinc had poisoned their blood, weakening them and making them easier to defeat, their reactions slow and cumbersome. The stallions drove any they could towards men waiting in the trees to shoot arrows. The assaults grew less as the defenders' strategies improved.

Maybe Shadow sent his minions for easier prey—warmblood mares. The less Mystery saw of the stealthcats, the more urgent his need to leave became.

Laila swept a pile of dust into a clay bowl and held it up for him to examine. "Don't you have any idea how we can get enough of this into the beasts to counteract the zinc?"

Mystery swirled the contents with his horn, tapping into the raw elements. "Only a small amount of this is pure copper. Do you know if there's any soapstone nearby?"

Yuma nodded. "I spotted a source by the river. I thought I might use it for carving if I ever get time, rather than pounding these infernal stones."

"If you mix the two stones and water together, the copper should separate from the sulphur."

Laila raised her eyebrows. "How do you know that?"

"Understanding minerals is part of unicorn knowledge, like drawing energy from the sun or the wind."

Yuma soon returned with an armful of smooth pebbles. Grinding the soapstone took much less time than breaking down the chalcocite. He mixed the two dusts together and wet them. Bubbles frothed into a scum, smelling of rotten eggs. He held the mixture at arm's length. "Now what?"

Mystery sniffed at the concoction, then pointed to the cookfire with his nose. "Try warming the foam. That's where the copper is."

After much experimentation, a glob of shining copper emerged. Laila grabbed the nugget and held it next to Mystery's horn. "It's the same!" She whooped in delight. "We've done it!"

That night the clan celebrated with a feast, singing along with Yuma's pipe and dancing to the beat of drums. Paws howled along and thumped her tail. Meda flitted between Mystery's crest and Laila's shoulder, firelight glimmering from her radiant scales. Even Mystery shoved aside his personal worries to prance and snort.

The morning brought sore heads and serious demeanours. Now that they had perfected the process to extract the copper, they needed to produce a much larger quantity. The real work was about to begin.

With many hands applied, a pile of copper nuggets soon rewarded everyone's efforts. Day after day, the pile grew until all the chalcocite had been ground and purified. With such positive results, the mood was ebullient.

Mystery went in search of Laila. She had fully recovered from her injuries. It was time to head to Eagle's Peak. After finding her, he went to say goodbye to the Eastlanders.

Yuma intercepted him. "It's no good. We've tried making arrow tips from the copper. It's too soft."

Mystery's glowing satisfaction dissipated as if he had been drenched with hail. "Are you sure? Have you tried different forms?"

"Of course. We've tried everything, even moulding it around flint. If we use enough to make it stay on the shaft, it's too heavy to fly straight." Yuma showed him a handful of tips, all different shapes and sizes.

Delsin joined them. "Did you say the stealthcats licked the zinc from rocks? Maybe we could get them to lick the copper. They must crave salt after their long trek. Perhaps we could put some out with the nuggets hidden inside."

Mystery doubted that would work. "We'd need to get them to eat a lot. They'd lick around the copper and leave what we want them to consume."

Laila stood next to her brother. "Perhaps when Paws catches coneys or squirrels, she could leave some of her dinner for us to use as baits."

"That should work." Yuma started to plan where they would lay out the antidote.

Paws whimpered at Laila's side. "I don't think I could do that. When I catch something I swallow it quick before it can get away. There'd be nothing left."

A small crowd gathered as the discussion continued. Dohate held up a hand for silence. "We will kill more deer for their livers and hearts, which are the best part, a great delicacy we usually relish. Letting the stealthcats have them is a small sacrifice to pay for our lives. They won't be able to resist."

Laila flinched.

Mystery sympathised. "And what of the sacrifice of the deer? What of their lives?" Did he have to be responsible for more deaths?

Mystery's heart raced as his legs pounded, each beat matched by his stride as he attempted to race off his misery. The trees opened onto rolling hills, the grass sparse and coarse, banking down to the rocky coastline. He picked up speed as the crash of waves energised the air, the tang of salt filling his lungs. Faster and faster, he streaked over crests and down valleys, leaping streams and jumping boulders, his tail drawing patterns in his wake like a firebrand waved at night. The wind blocked all other sound from his ears; his eyes had no sight other than the horizon.

No matter how fast he ran, his thoughts battered his skull like bats stuck in a cave. He had come east to solve the problems caused by Shadow. It was his job to rescue the warmbloods, his task to save the coldbloods from slaughter, and his duty to protect people from the stealthcats. But without power, he was no more use than any other stallion. Now animals would die for baits. He had failed. Gem would no longer want him. He was a horse, not a unicorn, not worthy to be her lifemate. And even that wouldn't matter for long. The goddess would return and destroy Equinora.

Despair slowed him to a canter.

A silhouette stood stark on a far hill. A lone stag stood sentinel, his many-pronged antlers denoting great age. The beast didn't budge as Mystery approached at a trot. He scrambled up the rocks that piled to the summit and introduced himself, amazed by the elk's white coat. The patriarch didn't have a single coloured hair on his body. "What do you watch for?"

Glazed eyes turned towards him. "Watch? The sun set. The wind blow. The grass brown."

"Why so glum? You have a vast territory here. There is food, and water. The sea breeze keeps away the biting midges." Did the stag somehow know of the people's plan to kill more deer?

The magnificent beast gazed around him as if he hadn't seen these things. "For what? I lost my herd to a young buck in spring. He injured my hind leg and now all I have for company is my pain."

Mystery had never witnessed such sorrow. Every sinew of the

215

once-mighty stag shrieked in agony. "I have a friend, a dragon who heals. She can take away your suffering."

The stag bowed his head and crumpled to his knees. "I believe you, mighty unicorn. But your very presence tells me that I have already crossed over. Maybe not fully, yet I am on the path. Help me join the goddess. Isn't that why you're here?"

"No!" Mystery nudged the deer and shoved him back to his feet. "Come with me to the forest. Meda will repair your leg."

"The forest? That's a long way. I can't travel so far."

Mystery wouldn't be beaten. "Accompany me as far as you can. When we're nearer, she can come to you. Meanwhile, tell me your life story. You must have seen a lot and gathered much wisdom. And I need help."

Raising his head, the mighty stag widened his eyes. "You? I doubt I can help your kind."

"Walk with me anyway. Show me where I can drink." Mystery headed down the slope, taking care where he placed his hooves as he slipped on the scree.

"I am Chuchip." The stag followed, no need to look where he trod. The further down the hillside they travelled, the bolder the stag became, stepping out regardless of his lame leg, his thick neck carrying the weight of his rack with ease. They reached a creek. The deer sipped.

Mystery drank deeply. "Have you seen mountain lions this far north?"

"No. Not here. But they have taken many of us further south. Our numbers are depleted. The world is out of balance." Water dribbled from Chuchip's ancient lips as he shared how the deer herds had been forced to leave the good feeding grounds and seek safety in the cold north. "Many does slipped their fawns this year. It's not a good time to be king. My successor is welcome to the worry."

They grazed and talked, chewed and walked.

Wandering as if he had no destination, Mystery led Chuchip south. They chatted about everything from generalities to philosophies. Mystery shared his tale from when horses had sought Diamond for help about mares going missing.

Chuchip perked up, a glint in his eye. "Do you think the same is true for the deer? Is the one you mention, Shadow, taking any with power? That might explain why so many are missing."

216

A cool mist swirled around as they discussed all possibilities. Mystery didn't believe deer could have warm blood like horses. He'd never heard of their equivalent to unicorns. They did have antlers, but Mystery's horn proved that was no guarantee of power. But what would he know? There might be more creatures with power in this realm. Look at Kodi, and Claw, and Blaze.

Mystery drifted back to Elk Bank with Chuchip, enjoying the stag's companionship and respecting his solid wisdom, telling him of the confrontations with Shadow, and sharing his doubts about the prophecy. He regaled stories of finding Paws, how the wolf bonded with Laila, and teaching Blaze to feed on love, not fire. He told of Jolon locking him in the gorge, his escape, and the process of extracting copper from the rocks. He expressed his angst over missing Gem, but that he needed to find the missing mares and save Equinora before he could return home.

Chuchip listened with interest but offered no advice.

They approached the edge of the forest harbouring Deershill. Chuchip halted and refused to go further. "I will wait here. You will bring the men."

Confused, Mystery couldn't persuade the stag to go another step. "Why do you want to see the men? It's Laila and Meda we need. I'll get them, for sure, but you'll be safe if you come with me."

Chuchip dug his toes deep into the earth. "I will stand here where all can see me. The men will shoot me and use my body for these baits you talk of. It is better that I offer myself than young bucks or does with fawns be taken. My time is near and you will do me a favour. Let my death be of use."

Mystery balked, horrified at the thought of murdering his newfound friend. "Let your life be of more use. Meda will cure you. You'll be strong again and raise many more fawns. Start a new herd. Lead them to safety. Repopulate the land."

"No. Let me do this thing. All I ask is that people treat my kind with respect."

Nothing Mystery said dissuaded the stag. With a heavy heart, he accepted Chuchip's wish and entered Deershill with dragging feet. He summoned Laila, Yuma, and Delsin to share his news. "One of you must shoot him in the heart."

"No!" Laila grabbed his mane and sobbed into his neck. "Not a magnificent stag!"

"He is old and crippled. Would you have him suffer?"

"Meda can heal him. You know she can."

Mystery nuzzled her shoulder. "He refuses aid. This is his desire. He wants to help."

Delsin wrapped his arms around her. "You know using only offal from the deer killed for meat won't be enough. Trust the Mother. She's sent this stag to us. I've only ever heard of a white stag in spirit stories. His colouring is a sign."

Yuma agreed. "I'll make sure he doesn't suffer. I have a good jade arrow. The power in the stone will aid his journey."

Mystery nuzzled Laila again. "You know this must be done. I don't like it any more than you. Stay here with Paws. Yuma and I will go alone."

Delsin stepped forward and rested a hand on Mystery's withers. "I'll come too. I'll bless the stag's soul and give thanks for his life."

Meda remained deep inside Laila's tunic as she kept herself busy sorting out her medicines. Paws moped around the camp, whining from Laila's sorrow. Also sensitive to her feelings, the men and women kept their conversations hushed. Even the few children at Deershill seemed to understand the gravity of the day.

Yuma and Delsin returned sooner than Laila had expected, each lugging packs swollen with dripping flesh. Mystery trod with care as he balanced Chuchip's remains on his back. The massive antlers draped either side of his neck. The pure white skin hung down his flanks, cloven hooves flapping against his legs.

With bowed head, Laila lingered behind the crowding people. The smell of blood accentuated her remorse.

Dohate welcomed the trio. "The Mother has smiled on us. Look at his crown, what an ancient. He has more points than I've ever seen."

The men distributed the meat to carve into baits.

Mystery called Laila forward. "Take his coat and make yourself clothing."

Laila refused, cringing at wearing another being's skin. "You know I won't do that."

"You must. If the baits are successful, I want to leave immediately. It'll be cold in Dragonspine Mountains, colder than when we crossed on our way here. Don't waste Chuchip's gift. Every part of him must be used."

Despite seeing the sense in what Mystery said, Laila still hesitated. "I'll need his brain to soften the hide. The leather will be too stiff to wear otherwise."

Delsin wrapped one arm around her waist. "It's intact. I'll extract it for you."

Dohate joined them. "No. This is Yuma's kill. He must do the work. The antlers are his. I'll take the heart and liver for the women to prepare. Delsin, you were Chuchip's spiritman. You may have the hooves and tail."

How could they talk of sharing this once magnificent beast between them as if he were mushrooms gathered after rain? Laila whistled Paws and fled the settlement, heading into the forest, heedless of any threat.

When she returned, Mystery had gone to warn the foxes, wolverines, and other meat-eaters about the baits. Although he didn't think the copper would harm them, no one wanted the zinc antidote to be wasted.

The stag's skin lay rolled next to her sleeping place and a lidded pot held the brain. She lit a small fire and set the pot to warm. Tears rolled down her cheeks as she straightened the pelt, easily large enough to make a cloak and leggings. She ran her fingers through the soft fur; she would leave that on for extra warmth. Biting her lower lip, she carried the bundle to a large, flat stone and cleaned off any tissue residue on the underside. With every stroke she thanked Chuchip for his gift, humming a dirge.

Soon her shoulders ached and her fingers cramped. It didn't matter, it was nothing to the pain in her heart. She welcomed the taxing work, soaking the cleansed skin with the liquidised brain, rubbing it deep to soften the skin. She removed the legs to soak in alder bark. They would need to be tough and waterproof to make boots and mittens.

Yuma and Delsin left her alone, only bringing her food, or sitting in silence by her fire when it became too dark to work.

By the time Chuchip's coat was ready to sew, there had still been no sign of the stealthcats. Laila went in search of Yuma. He had offered her needles from the fragments of horn and bone he was carving. She found him transforming one of the antler points into a handle for a flint knife. "Do you think the baits will have dried up? Maybe the stealthcats won't find them, or won't eat them now."

Yuma laid down his whittling flint. "I've had the same worry. The copper may taint the meat and—"

A screech overhead startled them both.

Blaze crashed into the top of the tallest tree before scrambling through the branches to the ground, his wings snagging on limbs and snapping off twigs.

Meda flew from Laila's shoulder onto the top of her head. "They come! Get ready!"

Laila shouted a warning.

Yuma picked up the call, though with Blaze's arrival the camp had burst into activity. Everyone had a role. The best archers formed a circle around the settlement, nestling in strong branches where they could best see a wide range. Other people gathered foodstuffs and stashed them inside the wooden dwellings. Children ran for shelter.

Paws leapt up. Her muzzle pressed against Laila's face. "You must climb! Quick!"

Laila scooped up her leatherwork and ran, stashed it safely in the communal hut, and raced back outside. Looking for Paws, she darted from tree to tree, whistling for her friend.

Delsin grabbed her arm and shoved her against a broad pine. "Paws has gone with Mystery."

"No! She'll be killed!"

Her brother's answer was to hoist her by the leg into the branches.

Blaze had departed. The birds hushed. Silence settled on the camp. Time passed like water wearing down rock. The warmth of Delsin on the limb next to Laila was the only sign of life. Her legs went numb and something spiked her back. She daren't move.

A streak of grey rushed into the clearing. "Laila! Come! Look!" Paws wagged her tail as if she had caught two coneys at once.

Laila slid down the trunk. On reaching the ground, she stumbled as her circulation returned. Ignoring the rush of heat and pain, she dashed across to the wolf and embraced her. "Are we safe? Did it work?"

Paws wriggled in her arms. "Come! Look!"

Laila called down the people from their houses and led a procession to the edge of the forest. There they stopped and stared, still wary, sheltered by the trees.

Mystery pranced among dormant mountain lions lazing on their sides, the black tips of their long tails flicking in pleasure. The giant cats licked their paws and washed their whiskers.

Mystery halted and lowered his muzzle to a huge male. "Why are you so far from home? Why do you hunt horses and people?"

The lion shook his head and sat up, blinking. "I don't know. We were impelled to come. It's strange here, unusual smells and sounds. I don't like it. But the meat was good."

Mystery trotted from one cat to another, questioning them all. None made any move of aggression, all appearing confused. When he had visited each one, he trotted to a knoll.

He reared, his copper horn and hooves flashing, and let out a shrill whinny. The low afternoon sun reflected from his coat in glowing amber. "Go back to your lairs. Raise your families in the rocky hills and valleys. Do not be drawn into unnatural acts by the golden eagle or his master. Be true mountain lions again, strong and independent, not the slaves of others."

As one, the pride rose and stretched. They bowed to Mystery without a word and leapt westwards. The long grasses consumed them without a ripple, as if the lions had never been there.

Mystery reared again, his horn piercing the sky, his neigh resounding off the trees as if they shouted their joy with him. He pranced with his tail flicked over his rump and called his warriors to him. "Now we go to rescue the mares!"

Chapter 23

A huff of flame slithered over the ice. Fragments crackled as they thawed and water seeped through the ever-growing gaps. Mystery sent love to aid Blaze and pawed at the edge of the stream. Even before the dragon finished, the stallions lowered their muzzles and sipped through numb lips, accustomed to his presence, no longer afraid even when he melted deep snow to reveal coarse grass. As they expressed their thanks, the glimmer in his jewelled scales renewed.

Moonlight clung to the cliffs like the frozen waterfall above. Mystery nudged Laila's leg where she sat astride to suggest she dismount. "There's a cave behind the falls. This would be a good place to spend the night."

Laila slid down and wrapped Chuchip's cloak around her. "I agree. The stallions are exhausted after that climb. And this altitude makes it feel like the middle of winter already."

After ensuring all his warriors had access to grazing, Mystery watched Laila and Delsin set up camp, glad they had come along despite his original misgivings about people accompanying him to find the stolen warmblood mares. The rough terrain meant the horses received many knocks and scratches. With Laila's help, Meda soon had them healed. And the tiny dragon had an overwhelming effect on Blaze. No longer did the massive dragon rant and rave. He tagged after Meda like Paws had followed Laila as a pup, his swirling eyes glowing mauve and violet rather than the bottomless crimson pools they became when he summoned fire.

Delsin was also a great help. The spiritman had a very close bond with Rocky. Between them, they coordinated the herd, ensuring no stragglers were left behind and all were cared for, leaving Mystery free to concentrate on finding a path with Blaze. The dragon had no concept of where a horse could tread. Being able to fly, he saw only a direct line to Eagle's Peak. It had taken Mystery days to get Blaze to understand that they must follow a winding route, keeping to the valleys for food and water, and avoiding scree slopes and sheer cliffs. Even then, they still encountered dead ends or insurmountable barriers that forced them to backtrack, wasting time and energy needed for the fight ahead.

Mystery led the way and used his senses to detect trails beneath the snow. The strong horses behind him packed the snow hard for the weaker horses further back. Sometimes the drifts lay so deep they covered the forest, the tips of pines protruding like bulbs in spring through an icy crust. Other times, the horses floundered up to their chests in soft powder, exhausting them and damaging their tendons in the difficult going. Mystery sought firm footing wherever possible, but the concentration needed to gauge the strength of the top layer strained even him.

The stallions were as happy to rest at night as Laila and Delsin. Mystery wandered among his warriors, sharing a word here and there. From hearing their thoughts, he paid particular attention to those considering returning east, encouraging, thanking, and comforting them, without letting on he knew what they were thinking. It was their choice. But the more of them who reached Eagle's Peak, the more likely they were to succeed. Then all would benefit from the return of strong mares to build new herds.

Mystery doubted that Socks would survive much longer. The death of Queen Meadowlark had badly affected the king. A new leader would rise, though probably not without many challenges. So too for the role of lead mare. The end of the stealthcat threat didn't mean harmony would return to Hawk Plains straight away. And the harm done by Blaze's fires would need seasons to recover. The bare soil would suffer with the elements, the goodness blowing away without the tussocks to hold it in place. Weeds would recover first. The grasslands may never fully return with abundance. Thank the goddess Blaze had stopped before he destroyed Goose Fen, Diamond's territory to the north.

Grateful that Dohate had agreed to grow oats for the herd in the south, Mystery hoped the Bluff clan would be convinced to do the same near the coast. The Thatchery chief had also promised that no horse would ever be restrained again. The Deershill chief agreed likewise, even though his people had yet to build relationships with the northern horses. Yuma had stayed to help create more copper baits and teach the clan to communicate with the coldblood stallions.

Would men keep their vows, not only now, but for generations to come? Mystery could do nothing about that. The goddess would decide, or the Mother, as people called her. Certainly, the story of the great white stag had already become legend; he could hear Delsin singing of Chuchip's glory from behind the curtain of ice.

At first light, Laila vaulted onto Mystery's back. Chuchip's hide blended with his silver coat, making them appear like she felt, as one creature. Glad of the furs, though still saddened at the stag's sacrifice, she hugged the white cloak around her, comfortable with matching mittens and boots, leggings and hat. She sat motionless to prevent draughts and preserve her heat while Mystery called the horses from where they had drifted overnight.

None wandered far, the threat of stealthcats always in their minds. Steam blew from their nostrils in the frigid air as they stamped their hooves to remove the balled snow and warm their legs. All had grown shaggy coats. Their manes and tails had transformed into icicles overnight, and their eyelashes and long muzzle hairs sparkled with frost.

They set off in single file, winding along the trail. Waves of snow rolled up the hillside above them like frozen surf, the ridges casting weird shadows among the folds that shifted and stretched with the growing light, fingers of grey reaching out to snare anything that dared venture the slopes. Laden firs bowed under the weight of whiteness, their broken boughs snapped off at obscene angles.

The track wound on and on, up and down, around switchbacks and across frozen creeks. Laila fell into a daze, the surrounding glare removing her sense of distance, Mystery's steady step lulling her, his warmth a constant comfort.

She jolted as Meda landed on her hat. "Rocky says he's worried about Delsin."

Fully alert, Laila raised her hand to bring the dragon down to her chest. "Why? What's the matter?"

Meda ruffled her wings and snuggled close. "He's cold, and keeps slipping. Rocky's worried he'll fall."

Mystery halted. "Something doesn't feel right here. I don't want to stop everyone. Can you go back without me?"

Laila slid off. "Of course. If Rocky doesn't mind, I'll double up on him for a while. I can warm Delsin and Meda can ensure he's physically alright."

As she headed back along the track, Laila greeted each stallion in turn. They strung out in a long line, bays and greys and chestnuts, roans and sorrels and paints, flogging on with determined steps. The wind whistled and blew crystal spirals into clouds, buffeting the horses and stinging their half-closed eyes. Meda flew overhead, darting from side to side, riding the air currents over the horses' backs. Paws, nose to the snow, tracked a fresh set of pawmarks. She raced off downhill, bounding across the tops of the drifts after a snow hare.

"Paws! Don't go far!" A rumble built to Laila's right, up the hill. She slipped.

Meda soared high. "Look out!"

Time hung suspended. There was nowhere to run. A rush of snow hit Laila with the force of a falling tree. She fell, her arms flailing as cold engulfed her. She tumbled, blinded and deafened, arms and legs whipping, gasping and gagging as snow filled her mouth.

The world stopped moving. A huge weight crushed out the last of her air, emptying her lungs, leaving her numb. Her legs crumpled to her chest, her arms held outwards. She twitched her fingers, clawed the snow, and slowly drew her trapped hands up to her face.

Another shake rocked her. She poked her tongue between frozen lips. Her lungs heaved, her nostrils blocked. She struggled to free her limbs. Her numb body refused to move. Cold crept through her bones. All went still. Silent. Dark.

Images of the wolf pack trapped by the avalanche flitted behind her closed eyelids. She remembered finding Paws, alive. She smiled at the memories of teaching the pup to hunt. The sensation of riding Mystery and galloping with the wind warmed her. She floated on a cloud of bliss, love wrapping her as if she swam in the silky waters of Shimmering Lake, cloaking her with health and vitality. She was content. Her breathing eased.

A deep voice whispered in her ear. *Friend of wolves, fear not. Friend of unicorns, take strength from me. Friend of dragons, help arrives.*

Laila drifted, comforted by the voice, warm and snug in her cocoon. Yuma's bird melodies and Delsin's songs of their travels kept her company. The taste of fresh greens and ripe berries refreshed her mouth.

The snow shifted. A breeze ruffled past her face. She gasped and dragged the air deep, searing her lungs with cold. Her mind cleared. Her hands and feet tingled. She heard scuffling overhead. Paws' bark deafened her as the wolf scrabbled with her front feet, flinging snow behind her in a shower. Light streaked into Laila's eyes and flashed copper as Mystery huffed over her face. A dazzle of colour brought a smile to her lips as Meda squeezed next to Paws' head to see her.

Laila's voice cracked. She coughed. "I'm alright." She clambered to her feet with Delsin's help.

He hugged her and then brushed her down, tears sliding down his cheeks. "I thought we'd lost you."

Mystery nuzzled her shoulder. "I heard Chuchip. He told us where to look. I would never have believed you could have fallen so far. He saved your life."

Words failed her. She hugged each of them in turn, fighting back tears of joy. "Is everyone else okay?"

Mystery shook his mane. "No. There are stallions missing, too. We need to find them."

With a glance at Meda and Paws, Laila flung herself back up the hill, hanging on to Mystery's tail. Together, the five of them set about locating the fallen horses.

"Here!" Meda's squeal brought Blaze diving from the sky, transforming to crimson as he plummeted.

Mystery neighed. "Don't burn them!"

Paws, Laila, and Delsin dug as hard as they could where Meda indicated the stallion lay. Once they had cleared his head, they left Mystery to dig him out and searched for the next one trapped.

They rescued three. Two lay dead, one from a broken neck, the other from suffocation.

Mystery grieved. "Shadow will pay for this. That avalanche wasn't natural. I knew something was wrong, I just didn't know what. That snow shouldn't have been able to balance like that. It was a trap, waiting for us to pass and release it with our noise."

Laila's heart ached as she clambered onto Mystery, his grief palpable. Was Shadow responsible, or had she caused the avalanche by calling Paws? She didn't know. What she did know was that without Chuchip's gift of his skin, and the help of her friends, she would never have survived.

Mystery trudged uphill, his footsteps heavy from all those lost, not only the stallions, but Chuchip, and the mares, and all the creatures caught in Blaze's fires. He peered ahead, squinting against the reflection from the snow. The huge dragon circled high above, glinting in a dazzling array of colours against a tiny patch of blue in an otherwise overcast sky. Piercing the horizon to Blaze's left, a black pinnacle rose through a shroud of low clouds like the tip of a tall pine through snow drifts. Nothing grew on its sheer rock.

Eagle's Peak. Maybe Moonglow's prophecy was right about where the mares were. But how could anything live in that bleak place? A shiver ran down Mystery's spine. Cold and disheartened, he focused back on Blaze. The dragon increased his aerobatics, swooping with wings tucked to his sides before soaring again, his long tail streaming as if a rainbow chased him.

Laila buried her hands under Mystery's mane. "Is he trying to tell us something?"

Meda poked her snout out of Laila's cloak. "He says he's above Shadow's hidden territory!"

A big difference yawned between seeing Blaze mark the location and getting there. Mystery called the stallions into a huddle. "We're getting close. Watch out for more traps."

The warriors remained bunched up. Rocky took the rear, with Willow and Murmur directly behind Mystery, and Oakbark chivvying those who dawdled in the middle. The horses lifted their knees high, placing their hooves with precision. They lowered their heads, nostrils distended, and ears swivelling in all directions. At the slightest sound, they shied across the track, barging into each other.

A waterfall loomed ahead, towering higher than the one they had camped behind the previous night. Frozen silent in majesty, layer upon layer of opaque crystal blocked the path. Either side of the falls, sheer basalt cliffs towered. At their base, a rivulet seeped from the rockface and wove over glossy stones to feed a small lake, its surface frozen smooth.

The horses crowded together on the bank. Willow pawed the ground. "Even if we can cross the ice, we can't climb that sheer wall. There must be a way around."

Oakbark snorted. "It's a long way back to any other pass."

The other horses muttered, some turning around and walking back the way they had come.

Even Rocky looked despondent, his ears lolling and tail clamped between his buttocks. "This is it, then. The end. We'll have to go home."

Mystery understood the despair that had descended on his friends. He shook his mane and trotted circles around them, rounding them up. "Don't let Shadow deceive you. He's filling your minds with negativity."

Laila's shoulders slumped and Meda paled on her arm. "No matter what he's doing, we can't get past that. Maybe we should wait out the winter somewhere warm and come back in spring."

"The mares will have foaled by then, and they'll mate with Shadow. Who knows what monsters will result?" Mystery nipped at the stallions who tried to retreat. "There must be a way through. I'll find it."

If he went on alone, would the others desert him? He had to take the risk. "Laila, wait here with Paws. Delsin, don't let the stallions past Rocky."

Closing his eyes to better use his senses, Mystery stepped onto the ice. Crack! Frigid water washed around his feet. He took another step forward. Crack! Crack! The ice crazed into slabs. Chunks tumbled and submerged.

Mystery continued. Step by step he advanced across the lake, smooth pebbles under his soles. At no time did the water reach his knees.

Willow paced at the water's edge. "Careful! It might be a whirlpool like Devil's Throat."

Mystery's senses belied the picture of the waterfall he'd retained. With his eyes still closed, he couldn't detect the cliff, yet he should have reached the wall by now. He opened his eyes. The cliffs rose a short distance away. Placing his hooves with care, he splashed to the base of the towering icefall. The wall blocked his path. He prodded the ice with his horn. Cold slithered along its length like a snake.

He closed his eyes and prodded again to gauge its thickness. His horn met no resistance, no coldness.

With eyes opened, he repeated the process—hard wall, cold.

Eyes shut—no wall, no cold. He advanced. Water swirled around his legs. Then the bank rose. He strode out of the pool and turned to face his friends.

"Mystery! Where are you?" Laila's cry carried her anguish.

"Here! I can see you. I'm fine." He splashed back and joined his friends. "It's an illusion. All you need to do is close your eyes and walk across."

The stallions didn't move.

Mystery paced back and forth. "Trust me."

Oakbark was the first to volunteer. "Let me try."

He waded into the water, eyes tight shut. Halfway across the pool, he faltered. He opened his eyes and panicked, spinning on his hindquarters and fleeing back to the bank. "I'm sorry. I thought I smelled a lion."

Mystery tested the air. "There's nothing there. It's another illusion. Walk beside me with your shoulder touching mine. I'll guide you."

This time Oakbark made it across. Mystery left him on the far bank to return to the others. "He's safe. Follow me."

None of the stallions moved. "Where is he?" "We can't see him." "What trick is this?"

Mystery understood their concerns. He whickered and nuzzled them. "Shadow is messing with your minds. Oakbark is safe. You will be, too."

Most of the horses refused to enter the water. Some tried, only to run backwards, throwing their heads in the air. "We can't do it!" "I don't know where to put my feet!" "It's bottomless, we'll drown!"

Mystery sighed. He would have to lead them over one by one. First, he carried Laila across. Again, he had no trouble. "Wait here."

Laila slid off. "What about Paws?"

A soggy wolf leapt at his side, tongue lolling. Paws shook an icy spray over them all.

"It looks as if she managed on her own."

Laila crouched down and hugged the wolf. "You're so clever."

Mystery returned to the stallions. Guiding Willow across, he told him where to place his hooves. "I promise I won't make you swim this time."

The stallion didn't reply. He kept his eyes shut as instructed and followed, his shoulder rubbing Mystery's, not losing contact for a moment.

One by one, Mystery led everyone over. Rocky and Delsin came last to ensure none tried to turn back.

With them all safely past the illusion, Mystery encouraged the stallions into a trot to warm them up. "It can't be far now."

He broke into a canter between an avenue of trees, leading them ever faster as the track widened and the snow lessened. Blaze had disappeared, yet Mystery no longer needed guiding. The herd thundered behind him, the scent of mares pulling them on. Their excitement built.

Mystery broke into a flat-out gallop. The trees opened up and revealed a green valley, a refuge among the frozen mountains. A free-flowing stream bisected lush pasture and shady trees dotted in copses along the foothills.

Paws yipped and shot off after a fat coney, sending a pair of jays squawking skywards.

Laila gripped Mystery's sides and leant along his neck. "This must be Paws' ancestral home. Shadow created a barrier to everyone, even the wolves."

Mystery's heart swelled. "There's no doubt we're in the right place. Blaze has led us well. Now I can rescue the mares and take them home."

Chapter 24

Shadow ceased grazing mid-chew. He raised his head and pricked his ears towards the entrance to the valley. The green slopes leading to the forest lay in shadow, the snow-clad peaks stark against the late autumn sky. A light breeze teased the orange and red maple leaves, and rustled through the pines. A lull hung over his territory as if every creature paused, one paw or hoof in the air.

The barrier had been breached, not by warmblood mares, nor the return of stealthcats. A ripple of energy pierced his shield. Unicorn!

That conniving two-timing dragon had led that upstart, second-generation, copper-horned colt here. After all Shadow had done for Blaze: saving him when he was a hatchling lost in a storm, enhancing his body and his powers, and teaching him to create flamehawks in order to burn and feed. And Mystery—Who did he think he was to come here, the son of mere horses, pretending to be a pure hotblood? He'd sort them both out.

Cantering around his mares, he bellowed orders. "Get to the other side of the creek and stay there. Keep together. Watch out for fires. Get in the water if necessary."

The mares obeyed. Twos and threes bunched together and splashed across the shallows. All were in foal and their well-nourished bodies gleamed with health. Once on the far side, they turned to stare back at him. Some must have heard the mental queries of Shadow's stallions. Could any hear Mystery's summons from the forest trail? Already, the intruder attempted to undermine Shadow's authority, informing the mares he had come to save them.

Neighing for his warriors to follow, Shadow cantered to a knoll in the centre of his territory. The ground trembled with the approach of many hooves.

Mystery appeared in the lead. He skidded to a halt and reared. A mob of warmblood stallions milled behind him, snorting and prancing, and then settled into a line abreast. Two people and a wolf left the horses and melded into the tree cover.

Anticipation heated Shadow's veins. He'd waited long for the day to assert his authority. He'd show the unicorns who ruled Equinora now. He'd send that pathetic colt running with his flashy tail clamped between his silver buttocks. Shadow stood proud, his black coat glistening, his muscles rippling, and his crimson mane and tail streaming in the breeze. He screamed a challenge. The cry reverberated from the hillsides and echoed off the empty caves; caves devoid of stealthcats, vacant through the interfering of the unicorn trotting towards him.

The intruder wouldn't do any more harm. Shadow would make sure of it. "Come to meet your death, unicorn? You others, go back to the coast. If not, I'll kill you too."

The warmblood stallions behind Shadow blew loudly through their nostrils, champed their teeth, and tossed their heads. Lust and glory swelled their countenance.

Mystery cantered to a smaller rise a few horse lengths away, his stallions remaining abreast behind him. "Let the mares go. You have no right to them. You haven't traded or fought for them, as a king should. They must return to their lands."

"Ridiculous. If you're scared, run back to Shimmering Lake and play with the dragons. That's all you're good for. You can't even get Gem in foal. I'll bring her here and show you how it's done."

Mystery arched his neck and flicked his tail. "You know there can only ever be six unicorns. We still enjoy pleasures. But what would you know about that? All you can do is steal mares, abort their kings' foals, and force your seed into their bellies." He neighed at the distant mares, urging them to bolt behind the protection of his warriors.

Shadow snorted in disdain. "They won't follow you. What have you to offer? You don't even have your own territory. Why would they leave Eagle's Peak, even if they could?"

"They don't belong here. They don't belong to you. Let them return to their homes. Let them choose where they live. If you don't release them, the goddess will return from the spirit world and destroy Equinora. She will eliminate you, me, and every other creature. She will eradicate the land into nothing, as it was before she came, a wasteland."

Shadow stamped his off fore. "What do you know of the past? Nothing. You've never even met Aureana. Trust me; she'd never destroy her creation."

Mystery pranced back and forth, flicking his hooves and tossing his forelock. "Moonglow foresaw the end. Beware her prophecy. You must relinquish your hold. Return to the dark mountains from where you came."

"Enough! Do you think I'll bow down before you?" Shadow plunged down the slope.

Mystery stood fast.

Shadow barged into him, his broad chest thudding into bone. He snaked his head and clashed his twin horns against Mystery's neck. The resultant mental shriek of pain encouraged him to drive harder. Rearing, he slashed with his fore-hooves before snatching a bite of the unicorn's withers.

Mystery retaliated with teeth, hooves, and horn. Locked together, they shoved and struck, parried and kicked.

Shadow caught glimpses of his and Mystery's stallions in battle. One on one, and in mobs, they supported their leaders. The fight raged back and forth across the valley, neither side holding the advantage for long. Blood-scent added to the smell of pain and anger.

Two shadows mimicked the struggle on the ground. He glanced up. Claw and Blaze circled and swooped, talons and claws lashing in flight at their lifelong enemy. The eagle's screech and the dragon's ranting drifted over the horses like mist, drowning out all other sounds as they clashed above. Then the squawks and bellows receded as the adversaries climbed high over the treetops, disappearing from sight as they rose to the spire of Eagle's Peak.

Mystery's horn pierced Shadow's flank. The duocorn flinched. He'd let down his guard. He wouldn't make that mistake again. This colt was stronger than he looked. Drawing on Equinora's energy, Shadow locked neck and shoulder with Mystery, forcing him to stagger back on his haunches. Taking advantage of his opponent's unsteady footing, Shadow smashed his head on the side of Mystery's.

Bone cracked. Rather than weaken, Mystery breathed deep and barged back.

Shadow's source of power drained as the unicorn also drew on Equinora's energy. He drew on all his skills, gathered over generations of roaming the land and developed over years of imprisonment at Obsidian Caves, pulling energy from the wind, the sun, and the spinning earth. His body swelled with power.

But it wasn't enough. A different strategy was needed, something more than physical strength. He summoned every foul and angry thought he'd ever had and thrust them into Mystery's mind. He threw images of raping Queen Opal, of fighting Jasper, of battling Fleet of Foot—all of them Mystery's ancestors. He triggered memories of Blaze destroying grazing lands, of stealthcats devouring coldbloods, of humans ripped to shreds.

The barrage only seemed to strengthen his great-grandson. Almost proud of his descendant, Shadow paused to reassess the situation.

Whack! His head swam as copper hooves connected with his horns. Dazed, he backed up a step and blinked.

Mystery ceased his attack.

Did the colt think he'd won? Shadow was only just beginning. He readied for another assault.

Then the reason for Mystery's hesitation became apparent. Two mares approached at a jog, defying Shadow's orders—Wood Lily and Golden Breeze. How dare they disobey him? Were they about to change sides? About to scream at them to do as they had been told, he caught sight of Chase. The buckskin had started to lose her foal hair, changing to grey, dapples blossoming over her rump. She had become a magnificent filly, strong and tall, a queen in the making.

Chase poked her head round her dam's chest and stared right at him.

Those eyes! She was his. Damn this interfering upstart. Shadow threw himself at the unicorn.

Mystery reeled as Shadow attacked with renewed vigour, rearing and pummelling. Nothing outside the two of them existed. His clouded mind pulled on Equinora's forces, dragging in energy in frenzy. Power flowed through him like the whirlpool at Devil's Throat, swirling his guts before it surged through his limbs. He fought with teeth and hooves, darting over the rolling hillsides, dodging and kicking. Allowing Equinora's power to pump through his arteries, he imagined growing in stature, muscles expanding, and bones stretching. But if he truly enlarged like Shadow's beasts, Shadow did the same, remaining a strong adversary.

Mystery sent messages to the giant dragon and golden eagle, demanding they cease their fight and join his side. They ignored him. He couldn't maintain his fight with Shadow and send them love. Feathers and scales rained down across the valley.

He willed, with all his strength of mind, clouds to form and crash together, to send lightning and strike Shadow down. But the sky remained blue, the sun only blocked by Blaze and Claw struggling above. He had no control over the weather. Where was his power? What was his power? So far, all he drew on was a hotblood's bond with the world. Shadow did the same, the pair of them tugging the forces between them in a war of wills as well as strength.

Back and forth they struggled. Whenever Mystery gained the advantage, Shadow burst forward. As Shadow drove him back, Mystery sought more resources and thrust against him. It was like ramming his body into a granite bluff. He stepped back to recover his breath.

Gold fragments of feathers continued to snow down amidst a hail of jewels. The battle in the air intensified. Screeches and shrieks drowned out all other sound. Blaze dived on Claw, slashing his claws through the eagle's golden feathers. Claw recovered and soared high before diving with beak extended and wings pinned to his sides.

Shadow charged.

Mystery had no time to watch what happened overhead. He lashed out before leading a chase to the tree-line. He was nimble; being bulkier, Shadow would be slower through the thick trunks. Dodging and weaving, jumping over fallen timber, Mystery raced to get ahead. He needed time to recuperate. He needed fresh reserves. As he galloped, he sucked in the energy of the trees, the birdsong, even that of the fungus spreading beneath the surface of the earth.

He broke out into open grassland. Warrior stallions from both sides suffered. Some lay on their sides, defeated. Others limped away. Through his swollen right eye, Mystery saw Laila and Delsin kneeling by a chestnut stallion. Why had they left the safety of the forest?

Shadow attacked.

Their earlier sparring was insignificant compared to the duocorn's renewed efforts. Shadow must also have gained strength from the trees. It was time to end this, one way or another. Drawing on every reserve in his body, on every remaining scrap of energy left in the land, Mystery used the map of the terrain in his head to find a fissure in the bedrock. Between the continental plates, molten lava oozed through the crack. Mystery extended his senses and sucked up strength from the very heart of the land.

Shadow smashed his head into Mystery's, the pain blinding him. He realised his mistake. Shadow also used the lava, the source of his power when he had lived at Obsidian Caves. Mystery ceased exploring the rock beneath him and staggered, unbalanced both physically and mentally, as the energy stopped flowing into him. What more could he try?

Shadow renewed his attack, revitalised by the fresh power. With Mystery's strength also bolstered, he retaliated. They fought their way back to where two mares and a filly fretted, sweat on their coats despite the cold day, fear in their eyes.

Mystery recognised the palomino as Breeze, Willow's dam. "Get out of the way! You'll be hurt!"

Breeze ignored him. Instead, she stepped in between him and Shadow. "Stop! Please!"

Shadow ducked behind the other mare.

Mystery leapt sideways. "Out of my way. I've come to save you. Let me at him."

"No!" Both mares reacted as one. Breeze snaked her head to bite him as if he were a recalcitrant foal. "Stop it! Stop it! You're destroying the land!"

Breeze's words struck Shadow harder than all Mystery's strength. Dewdrop's words. The last she'd spoken.

Mystery hesitated. "What do you mean?"

Shadow remained standing out of reach, blowing hard, his mind a whirl, staring back at the forest where they had raced. All the trees were black, their leafless branches like burnt skeletons. Dead birds lay on the ground, their contorted bodies withered among discarded feathers. Dust blew in eddies where once there had been rich loam, with not a hint of green left.

Mystery searched the sky. "What has Blaze done? I thought he'd stopped burning."

Shadow stepped forward, his head low and ears hanging limp. "It wasn't Blaze. It was us."

Mystery shook his head and pawed the ground. "I don't understand."

Eagle's Peak had become a wasteland. Trees that had bristled with needles pointed accusing tips where they had fallen, desiccated from having their energy drawn out. Shrubs smouldered and disintegrated into piles of ash. Rocks protruded from bare earth where once there had been mossy mounds. The rank scent of death and decay hung in the air.

Visions of Obsidian Caves, his former prison, flashed before Shadow's eyes; the cold, the wet, the darkness. He couldn't bear to live like that again. This upstart unicorn wasn't worth the cost of destroying the land. Let him have the mares, and his warriors, as long as they all left him in peace. He had no desire for Aureana to lock him up again, as would certainly happen if they continued destroying this refuge. Her return wouldn't signal Equinora's pending destruction, rather, that it was in great peril. From them— the hotbloods.

He spat blood at Mystery's feet. "Breeze is right. We've drawn the power from everything, even the soil. Is this what you came here to do? To kill all life? To destroy a valley offering good food and security?"

Shadow darted his neck towards Mystery, his teeth bared, and ears flat. "Leave. Now. You've done enough harm."

Eagle's Peak was his territory. It must be restored and protected. All the horses could leave. Except Chase. The black-eyed filly was his. She was old enough to wean and would be of age within a couple of years.

He could wait.

Stunned into silence, Mystery assessed the damage. It was true. Wherever he and Shadow had fought now lay charred. In some places, nothing remained but ash. Yet there had been no smoke, no heat, no flames. They had sucked the essence out of everything they had touched.

Mystery raced to where Murmur and Whisper clashed with fury, brother against brother. "Stop! Enough!"

The pair broke away, bleeding and exhausted. Standing apart, they gasped for air, their jugulars throbbing.

A rumble grew and Mystery's legs tremored. Heat seared deep beneath him, great fissures splitting the bedrock from where he'd drawn power. Nausea swamped him as a force greater than he had ever known rushed through the land, greater than the whirlpool, greater than the avalanche. The ground shook. Horses staggered all around him, some falling over. Dead trees toppled. The water in the creek boiled and then disappeared as if drained down a mighty crack.

Was the goddess here? Was Equinora being destroyed?

Eagle's Peak erupted in a spray of rock. Billows of debris mushroomed, blocking out the sun. Lava flowed like a giant caterpillar down the mountainside. Ash rained down like grey snow. Mystery gaped as the mountain disintegrated, its former point flattened. His ears rang, blocking out all sound, even the thoughts of the warmbloods. He hadn't imagined the end like this. He hadn't known how the goddess would destroy her creation, but he'd never imagined the land itself breaking apart.

All he could do was gape. He had caused this. Instead of finding his power and saving the mares, he'd brought about the end of Equinora. The sight transfixed him with horror.

Gradually the sky cleared.

Shadow stomped over. "It's been a while since I've experienced an eruption that big. The peak's gone. That'll let more light into the valley."

Mystery couldn't shake the feeling that somehow they had upset the balance of the mountains. "You mean it's not bad? It's not the goddess' doing?"

"It's as natural as water running downhill. They happen all the time at Obsidian Caves." Without further explanation, he trotted away to his warriors.

Still trying to understand the strange explosion, Mystery

cantered to where Laila and Delsin crouched by the fallen chestnut. "Are you alright? Willow! What's happened?"

Their countenance said it all. Even Meda had paled. The stallion lay dead.

"Nooo!" The scream came from Breeze. "My firstborn!"

Her anguish was more than Mystery could bear. Even if he hadn't brought on the goddess' wrath, he had killed Willow as if he'd stabbed the stallion himself. Leaving the palomino to her grief, he fought the urge to flee and checked on his other warriors.

Shadow left him alone.

Breeze's friend joined Murmur and Whisper, nuzzling their necks and licking their wounds. She must be Wood Lily. Plump and in foal, she looked well cared for.

Doubts swamped Mystery. What had he done? Maybe it was he, not Shadow, who was the problem. But no, he hadn't created stealthcats or stolen warmblood mares, killing any in his way.

He sought out Shadow where he protected a handsome filly, the only youngster Mystery had seen in the valley. "You must let the mares go. Let me escort them home. Stay here if you will, but gather mares like an honourable stallion."

Shadow shouldered the filly behind him. "If you care so much about Equinora, leave them here. Why return them to lands devoid of grazing? Who are you to say where they should live?"

Did Shadow have a right to these mares? Horse kings traded their offspring for new blood or lands, though bachelors would fight and steal to build a herd. Unicorns didn't live that way. Look at Gem: she had chosen him, not the other way around. And Gem ruled Shimmering Lake, not him. He had no territory, no herd.

He hadn't come all this way and witnessed all the suffering to walk away now. It was time for change. "The days of bartering for mares like people do for fish and skins are over. Let them choose where they live. Let them select their king. Will you honour their choice if they want to go?"

"This filly stays with me. There's no point her returning to her sire. He'd have to trade her anyway." Shadow neighed for his mares. "Who wants to leave Eagle's Peak? Who wants to traipse across the snowed mountains?"

Breeze arrived first, nudging Chase to get behind the safety of her rump.

Shadow cocked one ear at Breeze. "Leave if you must, but your filly stays."

Breeze stepped across to Shadow's side. "I'm not leaving. And not because you threaten to keep Chase. This is where I want to be."

Her response threw Mystery. "You want to stay with this monster?"

"Monster? I see a strong sire who provides and protects. Since coming to Eagle's Peak, I have enjoyed plenty of food, fresh water, and friendship. Why would I return to Hawk Plains to fight for my right to be queen, a position I don't even want? Let Shale take over from Meadowlark. I don't want to lead."

It had never occurred to Mystery that the mares might prefer life with Shadow. His thoughts buzzed like a swarm of angry wasps. All the horror, all the dead, had been in vain. Why had he come east?

Lily led Murmur and Willow over. Other horses also came close. Stallions mingled from both sides. Mares crossed the creek and came to contribute their wishes. Some, like Breeze and Lily, wanted to remain. Others wanted to return to their homelands or find fresh territories.

Mystery struggled to come to terms with this revelation. Two specks still battled high above. He called for Blaze and Claw to come down. *Stop! The war is over!*

The eagle and dragon continued to fight. A fresh rain of gold and jewels showered down.

Shadow joined Mystery in trying to end their battle. *Claw! Enough! The unicorn has given in!*

I have not! But the fight is pointless. Blaze, stop! Let us all talk.

The greying dragon grew large as he plummeted from the sky. Gaping sores oozed where his scales had shed. His wings crackled like brittle leaves.

Far above, Claw shrank to a dot before blinking out as he flew away, consumed by the ash billowing westwards.

Blaze landed in a heap. Laila, Meda, and Delsin rushed to his aid. Too numb to help, Mystery had no love left. He had betrayed his friends. He had killed those he had tried to save. His heart hurt more than any wound of his flesh.

Laila rose, strode over to Mystery, and rested a hand on his neck. "Meda tells me your thoughts. You're too tired to shield them. Please stop. You're doing more harm. We need you more than ever. We believe in you. Send out your love. Repair what has been done."

To Laila's surprise, Shadow agreed. "We'll work together to heal the sick and the land. I have no desire to live surrounded by darkness again."

Mystery slumped. "You're right. We can't bring back the dead. But how can we renew what you and I destroyed?"

Laila stroked his mane, untangling the copper masses from sweaty clumps. "We must help Meda cure those who are hurt."

Mystery acquiesced and followed her to where the tiny dragon worked on Blaze. When the fire-dragon recovered sufficient strength, they moved on to each of the injured horses.

Meda detected which were the worst cases. With Delsin's help, Laila straightened broken limbs for the dragon to mend, sewed gashes, and drew out bruises. Her medical supplies were soon gone. All she could offer was her love to aid Meda heal. Meda worked until dusk, her scales becoming duller with each horse.

When they had tended all the emergency victims, Laila called a break and slumped against a rock. A bright yellow flower sprouted from the ashen ground, growing even as she watched. "Look!"

Mystery sniffed at the goldenrod and let out a long sigh. "It's the work of the goddess."

Laila searched for more signs of recovery. "There're new plants everywhere. Do you think the ash from the volcano is responsible?"

Mystery shot off and galloped across the valley before returning with a sparkle in his eye. "Quick! Everyone! It's the broken pieces of scales and feathers. We must gather them before they meld with the ground. We'll sow them where they're needed most."

Once Laila knew what to look for, she acknowledged that Mystery was right. Wherever a remnant of Claw's feathers or one of Blaze's scales had fallen, new life thrust forth. She cut reeds from the creek, quickly wove a couple of baskets, and handed one to Delsin.

All the horses scoured the ground for the life-giving jewels, though with the dusting of ash the stones were hard to see. Whenever they found one, Laila or Delsin rushed over and picked it up. Mystery became so good at locating the gems that Laila rode from place to place, sliding off to pick up each one. Paws helped by sniffing out the new growth and wagging her tail. Then before Laila could settle on Mystery's back, he raced off with her to the next fragment.

None of the others had anywhere near as much luck, with Delsin waiting to be called from one horse to the other. He had remounted Rocky in order to cover as much ground as possible. Now he halted next to Laila. "I think you and Mystery should do this alone. The horses are exhausted from fighting. Can you cope?"

"Of course. Here, take my amulet and help Meda with those who still need help."

"I don't need that. Blaze has gifted me one of his emeralds. He rescued it for me before it was absorbed by the earth." Delsin showed her the scale filling his palm.

"You'll be able to see all dragons!" Laila beamed. "Some good has come of today after all. Maybe Mystery will enhance it so you can talk with other animals, too."

Mystery agreed at once and placed his horn on the jewel. A sparkle of copper erupted from the tip. They left Delsin braiding a neckband to hold the dragon scale and continued the search.

With Laila's basket filled, Mystery retraced the path to where he and Shadow had fought. "Throw out a piece of gold or jewel every few strides as I track the worst areas."

A trail of colour burst in their wake, grasses shooting and shrubs blooming. Dust transformed into lush pasture. Trees revived as if it were spring. Pools bubbled and creeks flowed. Soon the air filled with the trill of warblers, flycatchers swooped for insects, and wrens grubbed for snails.

Laila's faith in the Mother returned. Overawed by the might of Shadow and Mystery, she had been devastated to see the destruction of the land on top of all the killings. Now her soul warmed with hope. Blaze huddled with Meda, no longer grey. Although he still had gaping holes from the loss of his scales, his sores had healed.

Claw had not returned.

By moonrise, all the damage done by Mystery and Shadow had been rectified. Horses grazed by the creek, stallions and mares mingling. Many new bonds were being formed, some pairing off, some electing to follow one or other of the hotbloods. After agreeing he wouldn't prevent those mares who wished to leave, Shadow retreated to the far end of the valley with Chase. Mystery drifted among his warriors, ensuring all were well. Murmur and Whisper had made up, though Whisper refused to accompany them back to Elk Bank; he intended to remain as Shadow's Head of Warriors.

Laila found Breeze and Lily standing by a pile of ash. A tear trickled down her cheek. This was where Willow had fallen. Blaze had been able to summon enough power to cremate the stallion. Not a hair of him remained. "It's good you still have Chase. She's wonderful."

The palomino turned to greet her. "At least she can grow into a world where her offspring can choose their own lives. Tress would like that, and be proud of Mystery. I can't be sorry he came."

Offering the horses a handful of grains from her supply, Laila chatted with the mares. "I wish he could do the same for people."

Breeze savoured the rich corn. "Don't you have control of your life? It seems to me you go where you please."

Laila shrugged. "I do. Now. But it hasn't always been so, and other women don't have the same luxury, at least not in Midlands."

Breeze acknowledged that despite living with a clan in her early years, she didn't understand human culture. "What will you do now?"

Mystery answered from behind Laila. "We must go back to Tern Island and talk with Moonglow again. I haven't found my power. I fear the goddess will still return and destroy everything."

Chapter 25

Spray fountained from Mystery's hooves. For the first time since leaving Eagle's Peak, he revelled in Equinora's energy pulsing through every cell. When he had called Diamond to translocate him to Tern Island, she had refused, saying he must journey on his own. Surprised at her reticence, though understanding it took a great deal of effort to move someone other than herself, he had wondered how he would cross the water.

He needn't have feared. Tempest summoned the aquadragons to build a bridge from kelp, twisting the strands with their snouts as he smoothed the ocean. The tang of salt tasted fresh on his tongue and the wind sang like music in his ears as he galloped along the springy platform floating beneath his feet. Laila and Paws clung to his back, with Laila's cries of glee whipping behind them like her braids as they raced the waves. Meda and Blaze swooped and dived overhead in a dazzling array of colours. The giant dragon kept his pace slow to stay with them, never letting Meda out of his sight.

The ocean swell rose and fell in rhythm with the dragons, and dolphins leapt through the crests of the waves, the combined hypnotic movements mesmerising. Mystery concentrated on renewing his energy from the warm sea. After fighting Shadow, the winter crossing of Dragonspine Mountains had drawn all his reserves. Only when he'd reached Midlands and its rolling lower slopes had he started to recover, keeping his use of Equinora's energy to a minimum, still horrified at the damage he had done at Eagle's Peak.

Rocky and Delsin had left them at Greenslopes to head home to Flowering Valley and Bloomsvale. Mystery missed the skewbald's company. The stallion had always been able to cheer him up. Now he travelled in silence, hesitating to share his adventures with Tempest until they reached Tern Island. He didn't want to regale his story too often, especially as he wasn't proud of what he must say. Having confirmed to Gem and Diamond that he planned to return to Shimmering Lake soon, he had only told them the warmblood mares were safe. He would give them more details after seeking advice about what to do next from Moonglow.

The number of mares who had opted to stay at Eagle's Peak surprised him, many volunteering to pair with Shadow's warriors. In return, the stallions had promised to raise any unborn foals as their own. Shadow had agreed that all the horses could stay at Eagle's Peak until spring; crossing the snowclad passes was not something any of them wanted to do. Unlike the warmbloods, Shadow seemed uninterested in the size of his herd, spending his time with Chase, the filly with the unusual eyes. She would certainly make a fine mare.

Mystery, too, had been smitten with Breeze's filly. With her long legs and fine head, her high tail carriage and broad chest, she was a fine looking horse. The youngster had spirit too, racing after butterflies or teasing her elders, clambering high among the pines or streaking across the valley. No wonder her dam was ready to wean her, especially as Breeze would have one of Shadow's foals in a few moons.

Would Shadow's progeny become a new threat? Is that why Mystery had been sent to defeat Shadow? In that case, he'd failed. Worries swirled like a whirlpool as he ran alongside Tempest. Why hadn't he found his power? Maybe he wasn't meant to return to Shimmering Lake. Perhaps he should find a territory and gather a herd of his own. He missed Gem, but it didn't seem right to live at Shimmering Lake with no ability to raise offspring. Gem had said little when he had contacted her, and she had told him often enough in the past that she had no desire to foal a warmblood.

How did Tempest control the oceans, river, and weather? How had he learned to use his power? But the first-generation unicorns had lived with the goddess until she had departed for the spirit world. Mystery and Gem had been born without her guidance. Gem had been older than he was now when she had discovered her power, though she had been using it inadvertently for years. She could not only heal others like Dewdrop had been able to do, but also provided wellbeing to all who drank or swam in Shimmering Lake, streaming Equinora's strength through her body into the water. But all he did was draw disaster to him like magnetite attracted iron.

The splashing of his hooves changed to drumming as the island approached. Reaching firm ground, he slowed and waded ashore. Otters and seals frolicked in the surf. Behind him, the kelp disentangled and wafted away, a few of the long fronds snagging on rocks before washing out to sea. He halted for Paws to leap from his back. The wolf preferred to run. Crossing the sea must have been daunting for her.

She gave a yip of pleasure as her paws sunk into the gravel beach, and bounded alongside Mystery as he followed Tempest up the zigzag path to the top of the cliffs.

Blaze circled overhead, his scales flashing as his tail whipped in pursuit of his aerial antics. His outstretched wings sparkled in their jewelled glory, dwarfing the tiny creatures flitting around his head in greeting. "Dragons dragons dragons! I never knew there were so many so fine so different so beautiful!"

He landed and hopped from one crimson foot to another, his long tail sweeping the ground as the dragons of Tern Island introduced themselves. "Meda my healer my love my friend don't leave me! I want to be with you my rescuer my saviour my Meda!"

Paws retreated from Blaze's antics, her tail tucked between her legs, slinking behind Mystery.

He gave her a quizzical look. "What's the matter?"

Paws quivered. "Why is he acting like that? He's scaring me."

Realisation dawned—being without power, the wolf couldn't see the tiny dragons. She wouldn't have been able to see or talk with Meda, either. "Paws! I'm so sorry. I don't know how to help you with what I take for granted. Laila, Yuma, and Delsin all have dragon scales. Perhaps we can fashion one for you to wear."

Laila slid off to comfort her. Paws whimpered and sought her hand. "I know Meda is there, because Laila tells me, but she's gentle and kind. I don't want to see more dragons. One's enough."

Ruffling the wolf's fur, Laila laughed. "You might change your mind when we get to Shimmering Lake. There are more dragons there than wolves."

Mystery flinched. Would Moonglow advise him to return east until he found his power? What if Gem refused to let him return? How would Laila get there? He'd been wrong to think Laila should remain with her own kind—she'd been living with Gem before he had arrived. They'd come so far together, he couldn't abandon her now.

Mystery picked at the abundant feed on the clifftop without tasting a single mouthful. Tempest went in search of Moonglow. Although they had sent a message of their coming, the Spirit Unicorn didn't stand on ceremony and wasn't waiting for them, though she was unlikely to be far from her dragons. Perhaps she was swimming with the aquadragons.

The thrumming of hooves alerted Mystery to Tempest's return, his white mane and tail rippling over his sapphire body looking like the ocean he controlled. Alongside him, the sunbeams of Moonglow's golden mane and tail radiated over the glistening frost of her coat, but her eyes appeared dull and her movement listless.

Mystery quaked with what she might tell him. "Moonglow, you look dazzling."

"And you look strong, healthy after your trip west—no, east. Tell me everything. Don't miss out a single point."

While Mystery recounted his tale, Laila and Paws walked the clifftops. Meda went along to introduce Laila to specimens that grew only on the island. Blaze, of course, flew along too.

With only Tempest and Moonglow for an audience, Mystery left out being captured and trapped in the gorge, embarrassed at being powerless. He also omitted telling them of the way that he and Shadow had drained Equinora's power.

As Moonglow quizzed him for more details, Laila returned and set up camp. The coals of her fire glimmered in the dark. No moon shone. He remembered the blood moon when he'd visited Tern Island before, reminding him of the sky after the eruption of Eagle's Peak. A shiver flickered over his skin.

He needed answers from Moonglow. "I haven't found my power. Will the goddess return? Will we be destroyed?"

Moonglow paced in a circle. "Let me recall the prophecy.

"When birds spy and big cats sneak
Shadows steal all mares
Beware he of eagle speak
No one leave their lairs

"Obviously the bird and big cats are Claw and stealthcats, yes. And Shadow. Still alive! I was certain Fleet had killed him. Now what about the second part? Mmm, Diamond was right about Eagle's Peak. But did no one leave because they were dead, or did it mean the cats mustn't leave, or that humans were at risk outside their caves?"

Mystery relaxed. "It could be any or all of what you say. So, the prophecy has been met. We're safe."

Stopping as if listening to something far away, Moonglow flared her nostrils. "I've not finished. You youngsters, always so impatient. Now where was I?

> *"Those warped by stone sink in claws*
> *Run to stay alive*
> *Fires destroy between the shores*
> *Gold-winged one arrive*

"Well, Shadow warped the cats with the sustenance he made from stone, and everyone had to run. That's true, certainly. And you say there were many fires."

Mystery stiffened. This is what he feared. The fires had destroyed much of Eastlands, from the river to the sea. Had he been too late? "Is the goddess going to come, even though the mares are saved?"

"Wait. You know there is more." Moonglow paced, her horn glowing and eyes glazed. Sparks rose above her head like fireflies.

> *"Find power to prevent the end*
> *Youngest cross and fight"*

Mystery quaked. He had crossed, and he had fought, but he hadn't found his power.

Moonglow halted. "This is the key. But no more prophecy comes. No more comes! The second part eludes me. It isn't complete!"

Tempest had said nothing the whole time Mystery told his story. "Are you sure you've told us all that transpired?"

Moonglow stepped so close to him he could smell her panic. She stretched forward her nose and blew into his nostrils. "I must know everything. Everything!"

Mystery hadn't described his role in detecting the problem of the zinc and using copper as an antidote, claiming that Laila, Yuma, and Delsin had made the discovery. They deserved credit for all their hard work. He took a deep breath and filled in all the details he'd omitted. Moonglow teased every nuance out of him, one sentence at a time, until he had shared every step he had taken. He told of bolting back east after Shadow had confronted him the first time. He told of Blaze and Claw's battle, despite believing he had taught the mighty dragon to love. He told of the devastation he had created by drawing too much energy from Equinora.

Embarrassed by his ineptness and lack of control, he couldn't meet Tempest's and Moonglow's eyes. He told of forgetting to guide Willow to shallow waters when crossing the river. He told of Jolon capturing him, and leading Willow and Murmur through the caverns. He told of every failure to find his power. When he finished, he stole a glimpse at their faces.

Instead of sneers of contempt or frowns of disappointment, all he saw was delight.

Moonglow arched her neck and flicked her tail over her rump. "To be able to do that! Indeed, you were the right one to go."

Mystery was more confused than ever. "What do you mean? I haven't found my power. Surely drawing on the life of the animals and plants was terrible."

Tempest answered first. "You did what you must to prevent Shadow overcoming you."

"So you would have done the same?" Mystery swayed from hoof to hoof, snatching surreptitious glances at them.

Tempest snorted. "If only I could! To be able to see sickness in another's body and know what will heal, to be able to see the lay of the land beneath earth or water, and to be able to understand the elements of rock and how they work. I've never heard of anything like it."

Mystery shook his mane. "It's no different to drawing on Equinora's energy, and look what a mess I made of that. It's like sharing images between us, and granting the ability to talk with all animals. Kodi said all unicorns can do that."

Tempest nudged him in the shoulder. "Yes, we can, but we can't see what is invisible."

Mystery paced. "So is this my power? Surely not. I've always been able to do that. I thought I was supposed to find something extra when my horn emerged."

The older unicorns pranced in excitement.

Tempest halted in front of Mystery. "If you've been able to see the invisible even before growing your horn, and understand how the elements of the world interact, then that is proof of how strong you are. You and Gem are second-generation, much stronger than us first ones. Believe me, without your power, Shadow's creatures would have destroyed all of Eastlands. And what then? Crossed the mountains and come here?"

The reminder did nothing to improve Mystery's mood. "So you think I've prevented the end of Equinora?"

Moonglow quietened and joined them. A new vacancy appeared in her eyes. "I don't know. You didn't discover your power as such, because you say you've always known how to do these things. I'm confused. Always before, a fulfilled prophecy has been very clear, not ambiguous like this. I'm sure there should have been more that would explain all. Let me think overnight. Go to your friends and rest."

Her words did little to reassure Mystery. She slipped off into the dark before he could question her further. Tempest left to go for a swim.

Mystery sought out Laila and shared a brief account of the discussion.

She pulled a teasel from her bag. "Let me brush away your worries."

He tried to relax as Laila groomed him. It didn't work. "It's late. Get some rest. I need to think on this."

He wandered the island. Dragons roosted in the trees, their snouts tucked under their wings. Bats swooped by his ears, catching insects in the pitch black. Under his feet, the moss lay dormant on a thin layer of moist soil, beneath which basalt held fast to the sea floor. Even deeper, he could feel the shift of the earth's plates, slowly grinding their way one over the other.

Rock. He had inherited Jasper's power over stone, but in a very different way. Reading the geology of the land and understanding minerals was something he'd taken for granted since the day he was foaled. He had never questioned it, never realised the other unicorns didn't experience the same sensations. Having never been without it, it seemed an insignificant power. Was it enough to prove he was a unicorn, not a horned horse? Would Gem still want him? Or worse still, was the prophecy unfulfilled, meaning the goddess would return?

ystery met the dawn with a heavy heart, dreading Moonglow's conclusion. What more did he have to do to prevent the destruction of Equinora? He didn't want to go on another adventure. He wanted to return to Shimmering Lake. To see Gem. To shuck off the burdens of the world, for at least a while.

Moonglow didn't keep him waiting. As the sky pinked in the east, she called him and Tempest to the highest point of the island overlooking the bay. Standing on a rocky outcrop on the edge of the cliff, she stared out to sea.

They stood in silence.

Waves crashed against the cliffs, sending mist pluming through a blowhole. Dragons flitted above Moonglow, their rainbow scales flashing in harmony with the prisms of sea spray. Aquadragons bubbled in the waters below.

Still facing the ocean rather than them, Moonglow released a long sigh. "You wouldn't be here if you had failed. If the goddess was to return, she would be here by now."

Relief swamped Mystery. His racing heart slowed.

Moonglow continued. "But something is not resolved. I don't know what. I am old and tired. My foresight fails. The prophecy wasn't complete, and I don't believe it has been fulfilled."

Tempest nuzzled her neck. "Don't stress yourself. The goddess will explain all in her own time."

"No. I am no longer of use. My powers have drained away as surely as the rivers flow from the mountains. It is time for me to make way for the next generation. A stronger generation."

Mystery had no idea what she meant. "Does this mean that there can be more than six unicorns now? Or do you have to give up your power of prophecy?"

Tempest crept closer to her. "The prophecy might be fulfilled, or it might not. We will know when Aureana shows us. This is not for you to worry about. You still have all your power."

"No. I see no clarity. I have no certainty. I must leave." Without any further hesitation, Moonglow leapt from the clifftop.

A gold flash pierced Mystery's brain, blinding him. He screamed. Dots of gold swam behind his eyelids. His sight cleared but his head still spun. He raced to the edge of the cliff and peered over. "Moonglow!"

The world tremored. Was the goddess returning?

Tempest shook beside him, his mane and tail quivering with grief, his coat dulled to a brooding storm rather than a summer sky. "She should have talked to me. I would never have let her do this. I left her alone for too long."

Mystery searched for Moonglow's broken body in the surf. The aquadragons had disappeared. "Where is she? I can't see her."

Tempest stepped back. "She's gone. She's returned to the spirit world."

"Will she come back?"

Tempest hung his head. "Neither Dewdrop nor Jasper returned. May she find peace with Aureana."

Mystery had never experienced the death of a unicorn and never thought he would. If anyone was to die, it should have been him. Or Shadow. Not Moonglow. Not the Spirit Unicorn, the one who guided them. Intense sorrow drowned him, immersing him in waves of grief. Was Moonglow's death the true price of saving warmblood mares from Shadow? Mares who now chose to stay with him! It was too high a price. Many horses and other animals had perished. But that was Shadow's doing.

Copper had cured the stealthcats. Blaze no longer created flamehawks to burn and feed. People were safe and the horse herds would recover. And Mystery still had no way of knowing how to fulfil the prophecy and prevent the destruction of Equinora.

Had the prophecy ended with Moonglow's death? Is that why she did it, to ensure the goddess wouldn't return? She had said the goddess would have already come back if she was going to, and Shadow didn't believe the goddess would destroy her creation. But what if Moonglow was right, that her power of perception had failed, and Shadow lied?

Only one thing was certain to Mystery. He must hasten to Shimmering Lake and face Gem.

Chapter 26

With a bounce he hadn't experienced for a long time, Mystery trotted along, Laila riding and Paws loping alongside. The nearer he came to Shimmering Lake, the more hope returned that all would be well. Alongside the path, lilies thrust green shoots between flowering snowdrops. In the forest on either side, oaks and maples unfurled new leaves. Hummingbirds dashed with nesting material to their cups in the pines, and woodpeckers excavated fresh holes. Honeysuckle fragranced the air.

The burble of the creek sang Mystery home. Larks warbled and chipmunks chittered. His spirits rose with the temperature. Meda was not with them, staying away for him to prepare the resident dragons for the appearance of Blaze. They were likely to create a commotion at such a giant and worry Gem.

Mystery would soon be with her. He didn't need to inform her of his approach. She would have picked up his arrival as he crossed the veil into her territory. He slowed to a walk, hesitating to use Equinora's energy to aid his speed now that he knew what he drew denied others strength. These days he grazed and drank when he could.

His exertions had raised a sweat down his neck and chest. "Laila, will you give me a groom? I want to look my best."

"Of course." Laila waited for him to halt before sliding to the ground. "I could do with a clean-up myself."

Paws lapped as she paddled in the shallows, while Mystery and Laila splashed in a deeper pool. Refreshed, they emerged, and Paws flopped down under a shady oak. Laila brushed Mystery's silver coat to a sparkle, and teased out his mane and tail into glossy copper ripples. His hooves were trim from all the travel and glistened with each step.

Laila braided her hair, shrugged into her pack, and hung a basket over one arm. "Paws and I will wait for Meda and Blaze. There're plants here I haven't seen for ages that I'd like to gather. That'll give you a chance to greet Gem on your own."

Grateful for her understanding, Mystery floated into a canter. Now was not the time to preserve energy.

As he'd anticipated, Gem rested under her favourite tree. Diamond stood nose to tail in front of her. He whinnied hello.

Gem stepped out from behind her dam, ears pricked, and nickered a welcome. "You're here just in time."

Mystery didn't need telling in time for what. As he sighted Gem's swollen belly, he also noticed her waxed-over teats. Shock halted him before he reached her. He stood rigid in silence.

She waddled towards him. "Don't worry, it's yours. I must have forgotten to eat my herbs before you left. I'm due to foal very soon."

Mystery had dreamed of this day, had imagined nurturing Gem through her pregnancy, expectation growing with her girth. The reality was hard to absorb. "There were still six unicorns when I left. Does that mean it will be a warmblood?"

Diamond sniffed his face and looked him over. "We grieve for the loss of Moonglow, of course, but her death may mean that Aureana will grant Gem's foal the honour of being a unicorn."

Gem nibbled his withers. "I'll love it whatever it is. Don't worry about that. Tell us about your adventures. What's your power?"

Mystery stumbled for words. "There's so much to tell. I don't want to distress you in your condition."

Gem's sapphire eyes held his gaze. "You're here, and safe. That's what's important. You won't hurt me with words. When we felt a hotblood die, we worried it was you. Then Tempest reassured us that Moonglow chose her destiny, but he wouldn't tell us more, saying it was for you to share."

Diamond stepped away from her daughter and remarked how well Mystery looked. "Now you know why I couldn't help you in the east, or go to Tern Island. I couldn't leave Gem, and she refused to let me tell you in case it affected your mission. Anyway, I'll go and meet Laila and Meda. The dragons tell me they're back and are very excited. Have a few moments together before we hear your story."

Appreciating the opportunity, Mystery admired Gem. Pregnancy made her emerald coat even glossier, her ruby mane and tail soft and long, and her opal hooves and horn sparkle. "You're so beautiful. There were times I thought I'd never see you again."

"And I you. Almost a year has passed." Gem nuzzled Mystery's neck.

"Do you still want me here? You'll have a foal to look after." *And,* he didn't say, *you haven't heard my story.*

"I need you more than ever. This is your territory too. I'm sorry I didn't treat it like that before. I've been selfish in governing Shimmering Lake alone. Do you want a swim?"

Nothing could lighten his spirits more. He followed Gem into the lake and soaked up the effervescence, floating on the bubbles before diving down to where the aquadragons played. Buoyed by the water, he plunged and kicked, sending fountains spuming. Time lost all meaning as they cavorted.

Reunited and invigorated, they left the sustaining waters and wandered up the bank to roll in the sand. Laila groomed Diamond under Gem's tree. Paws lay nearby as if she had lived here all her life. A cacophony drowned out Mystery's greeting.

Blaze arrived in a flash of colour. A flock of dragons accompanied him, Meda in the fore. All Moonglow's dragons from Tern Island had come, too. Gem's dragons skimmed the lake, wheeled, and flew towards them. The mix of the two groups flashed in a kaleidoscopic dazzle.

Blaze's trumpet reverberated from the hills. "Dragons dragons dragons I have found my true home the home of my true love where I have always meant to be! This is where I was heading when a mere hatchling a storm tossed eggling a wayward lost soul! I'm home home home!"

Delighted that Blaze had found joy, Mystery cast a glance at Gem. Taken aback by the massive dragon, she shied as he swooped in front of her nose. Diamond held her ground, though she seemed equally astounded.

Mystery sought to reassure them. "Sorry, I meant to explain before he arrived. Blaze was enlarged by Shadow. It was he who set the fires in Eastlands."

Gem stared at him in horror. "What's he doing here?"

Mystery reassured her and explained about Blaze having to feed on fire. "There was no one to send him love. He's fine now. Meda wouldn't have befriended him if she didn't trust him."

Gem rolled her eyes. "Are you sure he's safe?"

Laila supported Mystery. "Blaze worships Meda. If she told him to fly around the moon and live on the other side, he would."

The bizarre notion released the sudden tension. As Mystery was about to tell more of how they had met the mighty dragon, Gem flinched. He nuzzled her with concern. "What is it? Are you alright?"

Walking away, Gem grimaced. "My time has come. Stay here."

Mystery started to follow, anxiety rippling through his veins, worried that Blaze's arrival had triggered the birth too soon.

Diamond nipped him on the neck. "Do as she asks. This is no time for a stallion to hover."

Mystery paced the shoreline, not comforted by Laila's reassurances. Paws trotted alongside, whimpering from the concern she detected. The day dragged as if he towed a fallen tree behind him. He couldn't stand the suspense any longer. "I have to go and see her."

He tracked Gem's scent up the hill, fighting a desire to burst into a gallop. Walking as fast as he could stretch his legs, he placed his hooves with care so as not to disturb a single stone. The scent of blood and sweat wafted to him on the afternoon breeze, tensing his muscles yet heightening his anticipation. He reached a grassy clearing and paused at the edge.

Gem lay on her side in the centre. Diamond shielded her from view. What was wrong? He couldn't bear not knowing. "Can I come closer?"

Diamond snorted and invited him over. "Typical male, can't do as asked. Come and meet your new filly."

Gem scrambled to her feet and licked her baby.

For some reason, Mystery had envisioned Gem's foal as a colt, imagining it would be like him. His surprise at the newborn's gender was nothing compared to when he saw her. The foal's coat resembled a posy of flowers. Like dragons, the filly's colouring gleamed with all the colours of the rainbow. Dapples of purple, green, and red shimmered among yellow, white, and blue. Her fluffy mane and tail stuck up in spikes of gold. "She's beautiful."

The filly placed her forelegs wide apart and heaved to her feet. After tottering a few steps, she found Gem's teats and commenced suckling.

Gem glowed. "So this is what a third-generation hotblood looks like. Imagine how strong she'll be."

"What will we call her?" Mystery's mind went blank with excitement.

Gem didn't hesitate. "Prism."

Stepping closer, Mystery stretched forward his muzzle. "Welcome to Equinora, Prism." Absorbing her scent, he daren't touch the fragile new life. She switched her tail as she drank, deep guzzles of milk pulsing down her throat.

Mystery beamed with pride. Until he reached the filly's shoulder. Lumps grew on either side of Prism's withers. "What's the matter with her?"

Diamond peered at the swellings. "That's odd."

Gem shoved them away. "Leave her alone. She's fine."

Mystery watched, first in horror, then in realisation. He neighed in excitement. "She's growing wings."

"What do you mean?" Gem twirled to face her foal.

Diamond pushed forward, barging past Mystery. The three adults stared. Incongruous lumps sprouted from the filly's shoulders. Tiny golden feathers fluffed out as her wings grew and spread.

Stunned, Mystery couldn't contain himself. It didn't matter whether Prism grew a horn or not. All was well. Equinora was safe. Gem wouldn't send him away.

Their daughter fulfilled the prophecy.

He galloped around the clearing, sending out messages to all those who could hear. *Prism, the gold-winged one, has arrived!*